"Natalie Gellar is truly a delightful woman to read about."
—*Harlequin Junkie* on *Seduce Me*

"At its heart, *Ms. Match* is a 'what's on the inside counts' and Leigh skillfully maneuvers through this theme without bludgeoning it to death."
—*Smart Bitches, Trashy Books*

"*Lying in Bed* by Jo Leigh was a great love story about hidden romance and unimaginable possibilities!"
—*Harlequin Junkie*

Praise for *USA TODAY* bestselling author Nancy Warren

"The genuine bond between this well-matched pair makes this return to The Last Bachelor Standing series feel fresh."
—*RT Book Reviews* on *Breakaway*

"Genuinely suspenseful, this tale delivers all the way to the end."
—*RT Book Reviews* on *Game On*

"This is a well-written story, complete with great characters, a plot that twists and turns in all the right places, and an ending that will definitely leave a smile on your face. Thanks to this series, I am always on the lookout for the next gem from Ms. Warren."
—*Harlequin Junkie* on *Final Score*

Praise for Jina Bacarr

"Fun and kinky short story that is totally engaging and entertaining."
—*Harlequin Junkie* on *Naked Sushi*

"This memoir-style novel is a witty and wonderful story, full of strongly defined characters. It's as much about emotion as it is about sensuality and abandon."
—*RT Book Reviews* on *The Blonde Geisha* (4½ stars)

"This story has plenty going for it—exotic locales, unique characters, humor and lots of deliciously hot sex. It's interesting and fun…not a bad combination."
—*RT Book Reviews* on *Cleopatra's Perfume*

Jo Leigh is from Los Angeles and always thought she'd end up living in Manhattan like any good *Cosmo* girl should. So how did she end up in Utah, in a tiny town with a terrible internet connection, being bossed around by a house full of rescued cats and dogs? What the heck, she says, predictability is boring. Jo has written more than forty-five novels for Harlequin. Visit her website at joleigh.com or contact her at joleigh@joleigh.com.

Jo Leigh,

USA TODAY Bestselling Author

Nancy Warren
and
Jina Bacarr
TANTALIZE

HARLEQUIN® COSMOPOLITAN RED-HOT READS

ISBN-13: 978-0-373-60971-0

Tantalize

Copyright © 2014 by Harlequin Books S.A.

The publisher acknowledges the copyright holders of the individual works as follows:

Definitely Naughty
Copyright © 2013 by Jolie Kramer

Her Valentine Fantasy
Copyright © 2014 by Nancy Warren

Naked Sushi
Copyright © 2013 by Jina Bacarr

Recycling programs
for this product may
not exist in your area.

For questions and comments about the quality of this book, please contact us at CustomerService@Harlequin.com.

® and TM are trademarks of the publisher. Trademarks indicated with ® are registered in the United States Patent and Trademark Office, the Canadian Intellectual Property Office and in other countries.

HARLEQUIN®
™ www.Harlequin.com

Printed in U.S.A.

CONTENTS

DEFINITELY NAUGHTY
Jo Leigh

To the fabulous Breetel,
Yael and Debbi—you guys rock!

And to my editor, Birgit Davis-Todd, for always
being in my corner.

CHAPTER ONE

EVEN FLORENCE KILLING "Shake It Out" couldn't pull Aubrey Hayes out of her funk. She balled up her latest sketch and tossed it atop the pile of previously crumpled drawings that cascaded out of her trash can like a river of failure. She should have brought in the Dumpster from outside just to handle the night's work. A glance at her watch told her the store had been closed for twenty minutes and that the inspiration she'd sought at the old drafting table her boss, Yvonne, had shoved in the corner of the stockroom had deserted her like a rat on a sinking ship. She might as well give it up before she imploded into a puddle of dark curls and red lipstick.

She grabbed her bag, slapped her fedora on her head, wrapped a stripy scarf around her neck and kicked her way out of the mess she'd made. At least the one on the floor. The mess she'd made of her life would take a bit more work. She'd heard about a monastery in upstate New York. Were there female monks? Was the vow of silence a deal breaker?

Aubrey slipped on her coat and made her way into the store proper, where the girl-on-girl manne-quin display she'd set up last week caught her eye. The lingerie was part of the Deco collection. Two styles, both see-through bra and panty sets with detailing to die for. She'd been pleased that Yvonne had approved of her decision to position the two girls a hairsbreadth away from a steamy kiss. Equally pleased that a complementary duo had been installed in the men's department, but with dudes, of course.

That was her boss all over. Groundbreaking, savvy and always standing at the very edge of a cliff, whether she was mounting risqué displays or building a whole new empire of lingerie stores to rival La Perla and Agent Provocateur. Yvonne's risk-taking had gotten Aubrey her job. A quirky window display at a Brooklyn boutique had caught Yvonne's attention last August. The fall window design for Le Muse—daring and different enough to catch the eye of anyone walking down Broadway—had been her triumphant debut.

Yvonne's voice scared the bejesus out of her as she reached the front door. "Aubrey, my love, I meant to come see you. How are things coming along?"

Panic blossomed like a mushroom cloud. "Great," she lied, hoping against hope that her high voice didn't give her away. Although next to Yvonne's elegant French accent, Aubrey always sounded like the hick she was.

"Of course it is. I know it will be fantastic, but the suspense is driving me mad."

"Me, too," Aubrey whispered, then called out, "Have a great night."

"You, as well."

It took longer to lock up because of her shaky fingers, but finally she was outside, the sounds of Manhattan soothing her more than a hot bath. She might have been raised in a flyspeck town in Utah, but the minute she'd walked off the plane at JFK, wow, four years ago, she'd found home.

God, she needed a drink or seven. It wasn't even nine yet, so she had a good chance of getting the roomies together for cocktails. She could always count on Sanjula and Caro for support when her own life went up in flames.

Although this crisis was particularly difficult because there was a secret she had to keep from her friends. The night of the Christmas window extravaganza, the one that was giving Aubrey fits, Yvonne was hosting a celebrity cocktail party in the store. So many models and designers and movie stars would be passing through, her roommates would go insane. But Aubrey couldn't mention a word of it to anyone until Yvonne gave her the go-ahead.

As she pulled her cell out of her bag, her gaze returned to Le Muse. The display window itself was one of the largest in the city. Yvonne had made sure it was equipped with everything a designer could hope for, including enough depth to stage a play if she wanted to. The only limitation Aubrey faced was her own creativity. Or lack thereof.

She had to admit her fall design had been a stroke of genius. A fluke, but a brilliant one. The window display had launched the store's soft opening in October and everyone loved her flashers. Three mannequins wearing opaque plastic raincoats held wide open, their feet planted far apart, arms spread. Really flashing the hell out of the city. Though not at first glimpse.

From the front of Le Muse you could only see the girls' backs. Luckily, a columnist from the *Huffington Post* had been the first to discover that the whole window was a puzzle. Using mirrors, monitors and cameras set up from different angles, there were all kinds of ways to see that the mannequins wore to-die-for sexy lingerie. A bustier and thigh-high stockings on the redhead, a nearly nude—and barely-there—push-up bra on the brunette, and the blonde dressed in a strapless bodysuit. At least, that's what they were wearing now. Aubrey changed things up from time to time, from the outfits to the film clips playing on the monitors. It had been the talk of the town, and in a remarkably short time they'd built a solid base of repeat customers.

If only it hadn't been the very last good idea Aubrey would ever have.

She turned, unable to look at the display for one more second. That drink was calling her very loudly. A gust of wind hit her out of the blue, almost carrying away her hat. Quick reflexes saved the day, and as she reached up to grab for her fedora, she noticed something drifting down from the darkish sky. At first she thought it was a piece of paper, then a floating leaf. She couldn't imagine where in the world it had come from, or why it dropped straight into her up-stretched hand.

Aubrey blinked at her prize. It was a picture. Of a man. A very gorgeous man. She didn't recognize him, and she was familiar with most of the current models working in the fashion world, but from the size of the card, she thought he might be a sports star. Although, didn't they wear uniforms? Mr. Blue Eyes was in a leather jacket, with a white Oxford shirt underneath.

He had dark, thick hair cut with a knowing hand, a bone structure that made her wish she sculpted and lips…well, damn.

Turning the card over led to another surprise. It *was* a trading card, like for a baseball star or something, but she'd never seen a baseball card with so much information up front and center. His name, the very Irish sounding Liam Flynn, was accompanied by his phone number. A Manhattan area code. Huh. Submitted by Mary Whittaker.

Submitted by? That was odd.

His profession was listed as Detective. Interesting. Private? Police? Other?

Then came the jaw-dropping words…Marry, Date or One-Night Stand. He wanted to Date. It said so, right there in black and white.

"Oh," she whispered. This must be one of the cards from that Hot Guy thingy. The one she'd read about months ago. Actually, she'd only read the first paragraph, but if she recalled correctly, there were groups all over New York that were dedicated to women setting up their girlfriends with guys they knew.

Sanjula would know all about it. Her roomie was a sponge when it came to stuff like this. She was up-to-date on every piece of celebrity gossip, and could explain the ins and outs of Manhattan nightlife in excruciating detail.

Aubrey squinted at her phone, then hit speed dial two and waited, her freezing cold nose and earlobes reminding her that if she had any sense at all, she'd go inside.

"Are you still working?" Sanjula asked when she picked up.

"No. I'm done. But I need you to tell me everything about that Hot Guys thing. The cards."

Not missing a beat, Sanjula said, "Hot Guys Trading Cards were all over the news a while back. Someone who owns a printing company came up with the idea for her weekly lunch group. To belong you have to submit at least one guy you can vouch for, a friend, relative or someone you dated. If you choose a card, you have to check in with the person who submitted him, then you call your hot guy and make a date. I personally haven't seen a card so I don't know what kind of stats—"

"Fear not," Aubrey said with a grin. "I happen to have that information at my fingertips."

"Huh?"

"Name and phone, Submitted by, Marry, Date or One-Night Stand—"

"If you knew, why did you ask me?"

'I didn't know. I saw a card. A trading card from Hot Guys etcetera. It came out of nowhere. Literally. It floated into my hand."

"Huh? What do you mean floated?"

Aubrey sang the first bar from "It's Raining Men." "Like that."

"Is he hot?"

"Hold on." She turned her phone, snapped a pic and sent it directly to Sanjula's cell.

"Holy shit!"

"I know, right?"

Sanjula sighed. "Read me the rest of the card while I try not to hate your guts for being the luckiest woman on earth."

"Okay. He's a detective."

"Ooh, how Sherlock of him."

"He wants to date. Not marry, not have a one-night stand."

"Well, that's good, isn't it?" Sanjula said. "You'd want to have second helpings of that dish."

"Maybe. The thing is, he's awfully good-looking."

"And that's bad because…?"

Aubrey sighed. "The being-beautiful baggage," she said. "Ego. Competition. Ego."

"All right. I'll give you that. But it'd be worth it for those blue eyes. Anyway, continue."

"His fave restaurant is Parlor Steakhouse. His secret passion is the Mets. Ugh."

"Hey, it could be worse."

"I know, but come on. Baseball? I was expecting more from you, Liam."

"No editorials please," Sanjula said. "What else?"

"His Bottom Line is 'To find a woman who shares my goals and values.'" Aubrey turned to face the store as another gust of wind hit. "He needs a one-night stand. He just doesn't know it yet."

Sanjula snorted. "Yeah. Or two or three—one for each of us."

Aubrey laughed as she looked up. There, above the doors, was the perfectly lit logo for the store. Her gaze snapped back to the card, then up again at the two bold words. Le Muse.

Sanjula was still talking, but Aubrey couldn't focus on what she was saying.

"Yeah, right," she mumbled. "Love you." Aubrey hung up, and stared at his picture some more.

"Oh, my God," she whispered, letting the breeze carry away the words. She had to admit the whole thing was a bit heavy-handed, but the Fates weren't known for gentle nudges.

Liam Flynn had clearly been sent, special delivery, to be her own, personal muse.

A BEER SOUNDED great. Liam hung up his suit jacket, then turned on his computer terminal as he sat at his desk in the squad's bull pen. He straightened his desk plaque, which someone had knocked sideways. Detective Liam Flynn. He'd never felt more deserving of the title than he did tonight.

"Well done, Flynn." Detective Lieutenant Posner, the woman in charge of the detectives at the Midtown North precinct, stopped in front of his desk. "The bastards were right where you said they'd be. All of them and their computers brought in with no surprises."

"I had some good intel," he said. "My CI really came through."

"I'd heard you'd made an impression on the locals when you were a beat cop. I've always believed that the best safety net is a community that has your back."

"Yeah, well, I made my share of enemies, too."

"I'd have been suspicious if you hadn't." She leaned in, lowered her voice. "Don't think I'm not aware of your impact here. Most of these bums would rather chew off their own arms than do thorough reports, but in the end, seventy-five percent of convictions come from dotting the *i*'s and crossing the *t*'s. Keep it up."

"Yes, ma'am."

Detective Lieutenant Posner smiled and went over to join the huddle of "bums."

Liam heard them laughing from the other side of the bull pen, although he hadn't caught the joke. He rarely did. But he knew that the vice team would be planning which bar they'd go to after shift. They'd choose between the White House, which had the prettier waitresses, or the closer O'Malley's, where the drinks were less expensive.

Maybe, this time, he'd say yes when Harry came around to invite him. The bust on the money-laundering operation had gone like clockwork. It warranted a hoisted glass or two. *If* they decided to go to O'Malley's. The White House was off-limits for him. The one time he'd gone, a waitress had tried to convince him to go home with her. He'd declined, but that hadn't been enough to satisfy Detective Tony Ricci, who'd been trying to score a date with her for months. Tony still hadn't forgiven him.

"Yo, Ridiculous."

Liam's jaw flexed at the nickname he hated. Especially coming from Ernie Rogers, one of the most decorated detectives in the NYPD. Rogers was nearing his twenty, and Liam had wanted to get to know him before he retired, but it had been seven months since he'd joined the team, and so far, they'd talked

nothing but ongoing cases. "The name's Flynn," he
called out, knowing it wouldn't make a difference.

"You comin' with? We owe you a drink for today's
bust. And then you get to tell the class how you figured out that Stevens and Isaacs were both going to
be at that apartment."

"Where?"

"The nation's capital."

"I'll pass."

Harry Bigalow, another old-timer, clapped Rogers
on the shoulder as he shook his head at Liam. "Screw
Ricci. You can't help it if the ladies are all over you."

"You know what? I'm beat. I'm gonna go on
home. I've been up since three this morning."

"You change your mind, you know where we'll
be," Rogers said.

Liam nodded, then pulled up the first of several
forms he'd need to fill out. He stopped listening to
the chatter, the laughter. Fuck them and their juvenile humor. And fuck the complete stranger who'd
taken his picture at last year's Macy's Thanksgiving Day Parade back when he was still in uniform.

He'd found out that she'd put it on the internet
a couple days later. By then it was too late to do a
damn thing about it.

She'd dubbed him *Ridiculously Good-Looking
Cop,* and posted it to the massive social media site
Reddit. It had already gone viral by the time one of
the cops at his old precinct had sent the picture and
the caption to everyone in the department. Maybe
not the chief of police, but he couldn't be sure.

He'd been Ridiculous ever since. By all rights it

should have died down by now, but no. He had no idea why he'd imagined setting up today's bust would change anything. Normally he wasn't that optimistic. Now he was pretty damn certain the nickname would end up on his tombstone.

Most of the time, he didn't give a rat's ass. He did the job to the best of his ability. The more he was promoted, the more the idiots would hate him. Tough. He'd have a career he could be proud of. It had never been a popularity contest.

"DETECTIVE FLYNN." The caller ID gave no name or number. He'd just finished for the night after two hours of paperwork, and he was starving and tired.

"So, are you a police detective, a private detective or a consulting detective?"

Her voice was sultry, and if he'd been at a bar he'd have known exactly what she wanted. But as a cold call? "Do I know you?"

"Not yet."

Huh. "Maybe we should start with why you're calling me. If this isn't a wrong number."

"Definitely not a wrong number. I'm Aubrey, and I'm the lucky girl who got your Hot Guys Trading Card."

"My Hot Guys…" That couldn't be right. Mary had sworn that only one other person had seen the card, and that person was the printer. Even if somehow something had gone wrong, and his cousin hadn't destroyed it as he'd asked, she would have told him. Warned him. "Aubrey…?" He clicked on his pen and turned to a fresh page in his notebook.

"I'm not going to tell you my last name. That would be silly."

"Why?"

She huffed at him. "Some detective you are. Because then you could look me up online and find out everything about me before we met, and not only would that be no fun at all, it could be dangerous. For all I know, you could have a secret identity as a deadly villain."

"You have my full name. And more, if you're holding the trading card."

"True, but I'm harmless. Mostly harmless. Occasionally harmless."

"You're not instilling me with a lot of confidence," he said, only slightly surprised that he was grinning. "Besides, I thought I was supposed to get a call from Mary before we began this little adventure."

"I guess it must have slipped her mind. Happens to me all the time. But as a show of good faith I'll give you some details. I'm twenty-four. I'm a design graduate from Pratt. Well, not an official graduate. I didn't finish three classes, but in my defense they were completely boring and who has time for that kind of nonsense, right? Anyway, I've had a lousy day at work. I was thinking you and I could get to know each other over a drink at the Session House bar. Do you know it?"

She was certainly confident for a woman who was lying her ass off. He wondered if the smidgen of information she'd given him was even in the ballpark of the truth. Although why would a liar try to justify not getting a degree? What could possibly be her game? "Yep, although I've never been there."

"Well, it's a very public bar, although surprisingly quiet for Manhattan. You can actually have a conversation there. Without shouting."

"I don't believe you. Bars in the city are required to reach a minimum of eighty-five decibels or we yank their liquor licenses."

"Ah, a sense of humor. Excellent. You should've put that on the card. Wait, *we* yank their licenses? You're a policeman. That must be exciting."

"It can be."

"I'd love to hear all about it."

Nothing was kosher about this call, or her invitation. Mary had convinced him to try the dating club, sure he'd meet someone nice and steady, but that had been right before the Macy's parade and the last thing he needed after that fiasco was to be on a Hot Guys Trading Card. Mary had taken care of things. She wouldn't have lied to him. She was his favorite cousin.

The only thing to do was meet Aubrey at the bar. If Ms. No-Last-Name was half as enticing as she sounded, it might make for a hell of an interesting night. Mostly, though, he needed to get his hands on that card.

"Well, Detective Flynn?"

"I'll be there in half an hour. How will I know you?"

"I'll find you, Detective. Trust me."

Liam smirked. Trust her? Not a chance.

CHAPTER TWO

AFTER THE BILLIONTH time, Aubrey swore to herself she wouldn't look at the door again. She managed to keep that promise for a whole thirty seconds. And this time it paid off. Liam Flynn in the flesh, wearing a long coat, black, stylish yet designed for real weather. Not that it mattered. He could have been wearing a bunny suit because there was nowhere to look but his face. And—plot twist—turned out he wasn't photogenic. It was as if the picture on the trading card was of the smart twin.

All her clever opening lines were swept away on a wave of lust. Just looking at him made her nipples tighten and her tummy flutter, and there was definitely something going on lower down that she refused to think about. This wasn't good. Not good at all. She was pretty sure a muse wasn't supposed to make her feel this way. If anything she should have been immune to that kind of instant want. When she'd first arrived in New York, she'd worked part-time at a modeling agency and been around tons of celebs. Looks alone were definitely not enough to capture her interest. But there was something about Liam. He was *hers*. Or he would be if she could get her act together.

Maybe this was a test. It shouldn't matter that he

was an eleven while she was a seven. No reason to chicken out now. The truth was she was the kind of person whose looks improved up close and personal. In conversation, she was usually fearless.

She could use some of that bravura right now. A couple of deep breaths did squat so she threw back the rest of her vodka. The burn woke something up. This man was the answer to her problems and she wasn't about to let the opportunity slip through her fingers.

Womaning up, she slipped out of the booth, squared her shoulders and began the long walk across the small bar. Three steps in, he looked at her. Just a glance at first, but his gaze returned a second later.

He couldn't possibly know who she was. And still, the stare continued. As omens went, that seemed excellent.

"Aubrey," he said, the moment she was in hearing range. It wasn't even a question.

"Very good, Detective," she said, stunned that her voice wasn't three octaves higher because at this distance he was *stupidly* handsome. "How did you know?"

"The way you were looking at me, you were either Aubrey or dangerous as hell."

"Who says I can't be both?"

He opened his mouth to speak but seemed to change his mind. Instead, he grinned.

"So, what are you drinking?" she asked.

"Shouldn't we find a seat?" He nodded at one of the waitresses. "I might want something to eat."

"I've got us a booth, but they're short-handed tonight, so I'll get our drinks. It'll give you a chance to look at the menu. I can personally recommend the sliders. And by the way, this is my treat."

His smile had gone a bit crooked. "I'll have a Blue Moon in the bottle, thanks. And I'll open it at the table."

She mirrored his expression, glad that he hadn't objected to her buying the round. And impressed he was being careful about his drink. She'd never gone out with a policeman before, and she'd assumed he'd want to be all macho. "We're the fourth booth down, the one with the hat and purse on the seat."

"You walked over here without your purse?"

"It's underneath the hat." Turning away, she kept her shoulders straight, her head high. She waited until she was leaning against the bar to exhale a half dozen breaths at once. Paulo, her favorite bartender, showed up and she had him put Liam's beer and her double vodka rocks on her tab. Drinks in almost-steady hands, she started back to the booth, but didn't get far.

Lily, a friend from Pratt, body blocked her. "Who is that?"

Aubrey smirked, but in a nice way. "He's kinda cute, isn't he?"

"Please. I'd stab my own brother to have a night with him."

"I happen to know you dislike your brother intensely."

"What's your point?"

Aubrey stepped to the left. "Too bad he's taken," she said, and yeah, that sounded bitchy.

No one else interrupted, thankfully, so she slid into the booth across from the heart-stopping cop.

"Thanks," he said as she handed him his drink, but before she'd settled in, he hit her with a very different kind of stare. "Where'd you really get the card?"

She wasn't shocked. Well, maybe at the timing, but not the question. "Did you call Mary?"

"I left a message, but it didn't matter. I knew you were lying."

"I kind of figured, but hey, it worked because you're here and I'm here…. Besides, this isn't what it looks like."

"It looks like you somehow got hold of something that doesn't belong to you and lied to me about it." He unscrewed the cap on his beer and took a sip.

"Okay, it is what it looks like, but there's more to it."

He took another drink, but his wryly cocked left eyebrow signaled some serious doubt.

"Let me explain."

"I'm looking forward to it," he said, his voice dipping into a register that made her toes curl. Sadly, his earlier amusement had left the building. She had a feeling his grip was already on his handcuffs.

Hmm. Handcuffs.

Not the point. She sipped her vodka and faced him with all the innocent earnestness she could muster. "It fell out of the sky."

His expression changed again, this time to confusion peppered liberally with suspicion.

"The card," she said. "It actually drifted out of the sky."

He finally nodded. Took another drink, then said, "Um, are you off your meds, Aubrey?"

SHE LAUGHED. WHICH didn't illuminate the situation at all. As a cop he'd had plenty of strange encounters, everything from getting spit on by a guy in a Sponge Bob costume to talking down a hysterical woman who was about to step in front of the M train. But Aubrey, with her dark mass of unruly curls, too-wide mouth and cherubic cheeks, was something new.

Maybe it was her confidence that had drawn him in, or her smile, or the way she gleefully challenged him with her gaze. But he'd felt the pull the moment their eyes met. Weird how he'd known she was the one who had his card. Even weirder that he'd actually hoped it was her despite how obvious it was that she was nuts. But then he'd watched her walk to the bar in those towering red heels and tight black dress that was inches away from becoming a public indecency violation. He'd swallowed hard at her very womanly hips and a pair of shapely legs that he could all too easily imagine wrapped around his waist.

Admittedly, it had been a while for him, but he'd had more opportunities than most to take care of business if he'd just wanted to get laid. Sex had never been a problem. He was grateful for that, absolutely. But now that he was approaching thirty, he was trying to avoid letting his dick call the shots.

It wasn't only his dick that found Aubrey intriguing, however.

"Look, I was at work," she said, leaning toward him, her deep purple fingernails clicking on her shot glass. "I'm doing this Christmas window display for a lingerie store. It's a major deal because I'm a nobody and you know what happens with Christmas windows in this city. For God's sake, did you know that the window at Lord & Taylor is on a hydraulic lift so the whole thing can be moved to the basement? That the big players like Macy's and Barney's can spend over a million dollars on their displays?

"Anyway, my boss is kind of the Tina Brown of lingerie and the store was supposed to have opened ages ago, but there were all sorts of delays, so it didn't open until October, but she needs the store to kill at Christmas, so I'm supposed to debut the window live on Christmas Eve Eve in front of reporters and bloggers from the *New York Times* to PopSugar…pretty much everyone who's anyone, so you can imagine the pressure, right?"

Her hand slid across the table to land on his, which gave him a jolt that went straight to his cock. He nodded, although he'd barely understood half of what she'd said.

"I've done a hundred or more sketches and I've got *nothing*. Seriously, nothing. Nada. Zippo. And it's almost three weeks until Christmas! There aren't words to describe how freaked out I am."

She paused, but only to knock back more of her drink. After squishing her face up into an award-winning wince, she took a deep breath and dove back in, her hand still on his.

"So tonight I walk outside, and this freaky wind almost blows my hat across the street. That's when I see it. I had no idea what it was or where it came from until it fell, I bullshit you not, *into my hand*. No exaggeration. Literally into my hand."

She held up said hand as a visual aid. He let out a surprisingly big breath as he pulled his own to his lap. "My trading card," he said.

Pointing her finger at him as if she'd unequivocally made her case, she said, "Exactly. That doesn't just happen." She leaned back against the booth, her deep scarlet lips set in a firm line while her eyes danced.

Danced? He'd never had a thought like that before in his life. He grabbed his beer, somehow knowing things were only going to get worse.

"Okay, so, what I haven't told you is the name of the store where I work."

That was evidently his cue. "No. No you haven't."

She grinned, and leaned in again. "Le Muse," she said, going full French accent on him. The way her eyebrows rose and her sly grin indicated that the name was significant. He had no idea why. "Uh-huh."

"Le Muse, Liam. *Le Muse.*"

"Sorry, I don't follow."

Her clear frustration made him feel as if he should apologize.

"You. It's you. You came down from God knows where and landed in my lap. *Detective Flynn, you're meant to be my personal muse.*"

It took a minute to digest her completely insane idea. Then he had to go through it again, just to make sure he wasn't hearing things. But no. She thought he was a mythical Greek goddess.

Definitely off her meds.

"Maybe I should take a look at the card," he said. "Just to, you know, get a grasp on this."

"Oh, sweetie. No can do. Not yet."

"No? Why the hell—"

The waitress's timing could not have been worse.

"Sorry for the delay, but we're short-staffed tonight."
She had her pen poised at the ready. "What can I get
you guys?"

Liam had been starving when he'd gotten there,
but Aubrey'd knocked the hunger straight out of him.
All he could do was stare.

"I thought you wanted to eat," she said.

He opened his mouth, but before he could respond, Aubrey said, "I'll have the fried chicken sliders and another round, please." She smiled his way
and said, "You're welcome to share."

"What about you, gorgeous?" the waitress asked.

Huh. The way she looked at him, as if he were on
the menu, made him realize he'd expected the same
from Aubrey. But his looks didn't seem to matter
to her bewildering scheme. "That mac and cheese
sounds good."

"You got it. Aubrey, on your tab?"

"Yeah, thanks."

"Uh," he said, but it was too late. They were alone
again. "You don't have to pay for my food. Or another beer."

"Yes, I do. I asked you here because—"

He held up a hand, not willing to be sidetracked
again. "I believe you were going to tell me why you
don't want me to see the card?"

"Oh, yeah," she said, shaking her head as if the
explanation wouldn't have been necessary if only
he'd been paying attention. "I'm assuming you know
what a muse is."

"Yes. How they relate to me in any way isn't clear,
however."

"From the sky, Liam. Dropped from nowhere. Anyway, what a muse does is inspire creativity. That's exactly what my problem's been. Why I can't come up with a great idea for the window. You fall into my hand like a gift, and in seconds I can feel my juices getting all stirred up."

His reaction to that last comment wasn't good. Not good at all.

"I knew it was destiny. The Fates, you know? There's no law that says a muse has to be a woman. I mean, come on. That would be crazy."

"Yeah. That part would be crazy."

She didn't actually say, "Obviously," but she managed to get the point across.

"Not to put a damper on things, but I don't think this whole muse business is up my alley. And you still haven't answered my question."

It was as if he'd taken away her favorite kitten. "You do realize my entire future is at stake. If I blow this window, I'll never get another chance like it. My boss is one of the most connected people in the world. She could literally ruin me. Forever."

"I don't think—"

"Listen, you don't understand. I can't have you distracted by other dates, at least not for now. But don't worry, this isn't a long-term proposal. It's just until Christmas Eve Eve. And it's not even that hard. I mean, all I really need from you is lots and lots of sex."

His next words vanished from his mind. As did most of his working brain cells. "What's that you say?"

CHAPTER THREE

SHE HADN'T PLANNED out exactly how she would ask Liam for a one-night stand, but telling him she wanted "lots and lots of sex" might have been taking it a step too far. Although his rapid blinking and open mouth could also suggest a nail hit directly on the head. Or an imminent solicitation charge.

Instead of answering his question, she moved her right foot until it bumped against his shoe. Slipping off her heel, she shimmied up his pant leg until she found skin. One quick rub with her big toe made him blush. And stammer. But he didn't move away. That took getting arrested off the table.

"Look, Aubrey…"

Feeling much more in control of the situation, she relaxed against the backrest and waited. She liked him flustered. She'd put that right at the top of her list of Fun Things to Do with Muses.

His jaw moved as if he was getting ready to speak, but it took a while for the words to form. "This is all very…weird," he said finally. "You don't really expect me to just jump on board with this, do you?"

"Why not? The offer's legit. We can even go back to your place if it'll make you feel better."

His foot lifted, dislodging her toes. "This something you do often?"

"What, find a trading card floating from the night sky? No."

"Asking men you've just met for lots of sex."

"Not often. Only when it feels right. Haven't you ever had a one-night stand?"

He cleared his throat, looked up and to the left. Ha, she knew what that meant, even if she wasn't a detective. He was making up an answer right this second. "No. Okay, yes, but not usually—"

"Before snacks?" she said, interrupting. "No problem. I'll wait until we've eaten to ask again."

"That's not— You do realize I'm with the police."

"It's okay. I don't mind."

"You don't—" He sighed. "I should have ordered something stronger."

Aubrey contained her grin. While this part of the evening was turning out better than she'd hoped, she couldn't wait to see how entertaining he would be once they were alone. She'd bet that blush of his went all the way down his chest. She'd also wager that he was right this second coming up with justifications for saying yes. Would it be better to help him out now, or wait a bit?

Their drinks were coming, so she'd wait. Give him time to get creative. It was clear he was hooked, even if he insisted on fighting with the lure.

"Why'd you become a policeman?"

"What?"

"Being a police detective isn't the same as being a CPA or a math teacher. The decision can't be a

simple one. There's a lot of political and social sig-
nificance to the job, pro and con. Maybe you come
from a family of cops? Or maybe a police officer had
an impact on your early life?"

He closed his mouth. For a moment, he didn't do
anything but gawp at her. Then he drank from his
beer, but there didn't appear to be any left. When he
put it down, it was very decisive. "Now you want
small talk?"

"Small talk? I didn't ask about the weather. A
career is a big deal. The biggest, except for love."

He sighed, and his very gorgeous jaw clenched.
"Fine, now you want a deep discussion?"

She nodded. "The food's going to take a few minutes. And I'm interested."

Before he could respond, fresh drinks replaced
the empties, and just as the waitress turned away,
Liam jolted, stopping her with an urgent plea. "Wait."

Tracy, whose nametag had somehow moved closer
to her boob since her last visit, looked at him with a
practiced pout. "Can I help you?"

"Whiskey. Double. Please."

"We've got Bushmills, Concannon, Knappogue
Castle, Clontarf, Jameson and Paddy. Any of those
turn you on?"

He looked up at her, blinking again.

Aubrey reduced her tip by five percent.

"Bushmills. Thanks."

"Welcome, honey," Tracy said with a wink. She
turned back to face the bar without giving Aubrey
so much as a glance.

Ten percent.

"Sorry," he said, his attention back where it belonged. "Why don't you tell me about this big window display that's got you so upset?"

"Well, all right, although you've already got the salient points. It's a Christmas theme, naturally. And that makes it harder because, my God, everything's already been done. The whole reason Yvonne hired me is because she saw what I did at this little boutique in Park Slope. That one cost virtually nothing. Just a few colored lights, and some borrowed hay."

"You borrowed hay?"

She shrugged. "Not much. It worked, though. Because the pieces I chose for the display were all elegant as hell, a crystal chandelier, a silver tea set, clothes from the '30s and '40s. But good stuff, expensive stuff. I even had a legit Louis Quatorze commode that went to Christie's afterward."

"And the hay?"

"Oh, the backdrop was a barnyard. With real chickens and a goat. At least for a couple of days. Then it got too smelly."

"*That* got you hired?"

"It worked. Completely. It was written up in the *Post.* I know, the *Post,* but still. My friends who own the boutique got a lot of business from that display."

"Huh." He drank some beer, stared at the salt-shaker.

Holy crap, but his cheekbones were spectacular. Built to highlight his eyes, but also as a foundation for his amazing dimples and square jaw. His face could be an exhibit at MOMA and they'd sell all the tickets they could print.

Liam wiped his mouth with the back of his hand and sighed again. Didn't meet her gaze. Her cue to dial it back a few notches. He was a muse, not a toy.

Tracy arrived with his double and the food, but to Aubrey's delight, Liam didn't give her the time of day.

Aubrey smiled at Tracy before she left, but the gesture wasn't returned.

"I don't know a lot about window displays," he said. "But I'll take your word for it."

"That's okay. We'll talk more about the design as we go along."

He exhaled heavily, his fork hanging loosely over the mac and cheese. Then he finally met her gaze with what she imagined was his getting-the-perp-to-confess-now look. "Did someone hire you to do this?"

"No."

"Because if the idiots I work with paid you, just tell me. I'll make sure you get your money. I swear. Then you can just give me the card back, and I'll let the whole issue drop. Okay?"

"No one hired me," she said, her happy mood cut off at the knees. "I've been completely honest with you."

The music got louder, the room felt colder and time stretched as he looked through her. "Chickens and a goat?"

Everything tilted back to normal, at least on her side of the table. His half smile helped.

"Yes. It was all about contrasts and anachronisms."

He ate for a bit, and she downed a slider. It was very good.

After he finished his appetizer, he shoved the plate to the center of the table and picked up his whiskey. "Lots and lots of sex?"

The last of her worries fled. "Yes."

"How much is lots and lots?"

"Until I get the design right. I don't know how long that's going to take, although it can't be that long because I'm on a deadline."

He sipped his drink. Narrowed his eyes. "You said one-night stand."

"Oh, well, it could just be one night. If you're as inspirational as I hope. But I didn't want to pressure you or anything."

"I don't have a creative bone in my body. Can't draw, can't carry a tune. I do my best writing on reports. I don't even have a favorite movie. How can you possibly think I'll be in any way inspirational?"

Aubrey leaned forward, put her hand over his. "You fell from the sky, Liam Flynn. Into my hand."

"That doesn't mean anything."

"Maybe not, but answer me this. Did you know that the placebo effect has been proven as effective as medication in many cases? That when sports figures find a ritual or good luck charm their stats improve compared to players who don't believe in omens? That the concept of the muse as inspiration is as old as human history? Frankly, it doesn't matter whether you buy it or not. I do."

"Do you actually expect me to answer any of those questions?"

"No." She lowered her lashes and looked up at him. "There's only one question that matters tonight. Will you say yes?"

SHIT. HE WAS going to say yes.

Aubrey was completely nuts. Which wasn't the turnoff it should have been. In fact, he hadn't been this intrigued by a date in a hell of a long time. He was confused, absolutely, but at least Aubrey wasn't boring.

She also wasn't what he was looking for. He'd made a decision about this kind of thing after the Macy's parade debacle. No more one-night stands. He'd had more than his share, especially in college, but that part of his life was over. Now he wanted someone of substance. Date first, take it slow, explore the important things like values and dreams.

He hadn't realized at the time that he would fail to make it to the sex part with any of the women he'd meet. Of course, there'd been only two in the past year.

Hell, almost a full year since—he took a bigger sip of the Bushmills.

"I don't mean to beat the point into the ground, but you do realize I'm not asking you to marry me. This offer has no strings attached. I promise I'm not scary. I have references if you want."

"From one-night stands?"

She leaned back, taking her hand away. "Two, in fact. We're friends now. William lives in London but we can text him if you like, and Gabe is now married with a baby, so we'd have to text him, too. I wouldn't want to wake anyone. I've also got friends who haven't been sex partners who'll vouch for my sanity. Or relative sanity, at least. I'm not certifiable, and I don't take meds. Sanjula and Caro are absolutely up right now if you want to call them. I was going to invite them out for a drink, but then the wind blew, and, well, here we are."

That wasn't the answer he'd been expecting.

"You come here a lot. What about the bartender? Can he vouch for you?"

"Paulo? I haven't slept with him, but if that's not a requirement, you bet. I'll go get him."

"Wait here," he said, then watched for microexpressions. She didn't seem upset that he was actually calling her out on her offer. In fact, she seemed completely okay with it.

"Just watch out for Tracy. She can be tricky."

"I think I can handle it." Still no nervous ticks or touches to the mouth or hair. He was pretty sure he knew what he'd find out at the bar, but he needed a few minutes away from Aubrey. Even when he wasn't looking directly at her he was acutely aware of her presence. Not the best circumstances for making an important decision. He'd made a commitment to himself, and he never took those lightly.

The music seemed a lot louder in the middle of the crowded room, some song he didn't recognize with a heavy bass and one phrase repeated over and over. He could see coming back here. There was a good mix of customers. Some people wore jeans, some work clothes. Several women were decked out in what must pass for high fashion, but he didn't run across a single face that was more interesting than Aubrey's.

She was...unexpected. He could see that she might be too much for some, but damn if he didn't want to say yes simply to be around her longer.

He liked her voice, her mercurial mind. He liked the look of her. Especially the way her hips were so generous and her waist so small. He could practically feel his hands on her already, pulling her tight against him.

After he'd been at the bar for a couple of minutes, the bartender finally came his way. "What can I do you for?"

It was an effort not to flash his badge. Habit. "You know Aubrey?" he asked, turning his head so the bartender could see their booth through the crowd.

"Sure do. Tips well. Doesn't get sloppy drunk. She's good people."

"Not a stalker, not a danger to herself or others?"

The guy rolled his eyes. "Not that I know of, but I can't swear to it."

"Okay. Thank you."

"You a cop?"

That caught Liam by surprise, although it probably shouldn't have. "Yeah, but she's not in trouble. At least, not that I know of."

"Have fun. Need a drink?"

Liam put a five on the counter. "I'm good. Thanks again."

Before he turned around, he knew what his answer would be. It was breaking his commitment, but an offer like hers didn't come around every day. She might not be the woman for his future, but his present could use some shaking up. Besides, he wanted to see her without that dress on. The heels could stay, though.

No use getting all worked up. Time and a place. Right now his biggest decision was whether to tease her or just come straight out with it. Damn.

As the space between them cleared, she looked up at him and her smile made him grin right back. There was no time for teasing, not here. He wanted her at his apartment, he wanted her there soon and he wanted her naked.

Slipping into the booth, he grabbed his whiskey and shot it down. He almost choked on the burn but somehow he managed not to make too big an ass of himself.

She laughed at him, anyway. "Where to next? Assuming Paulo's recommendation met with your approval, that is. My place has roommates. What about yours?"

"I have no business saying yes. I've been up since before dawn, which makes this the most inconvenient timing for a one-night stand in the history of the world."

"No, that would be if we were both on the run, had no place to go and a bad guy was getting too close for comfort." She paused. "Actually, that sounds kind of exciting. Are you chasing any dangerous criminals?"

"Not at the moment."

"Well, I guess there's nothing we can do about it now."

"You finished?" he asked, nodding at her half-full shot glass.

"I don't want any more."

"My place has no roommates. It's New York–size, but at least there's a bedroom."

"Wow, fancy." She stood up and took his hand. "You're a brave man, Detective Flynn."

He thought about that damn card again, and how in hell it had led to this moment. "We'll see about that."

She leaned in close and he met her halfway. It was a slow and easy kiss, more promise than scandal, the touch of her tongue on his lower lip all the incentive he needed to whip out his wallet.

She stopped him with a warm hand on his wrist. "This is on me. Why don't you go down and get us a cab? I'll meet you in a moment."

He nipped at the corner of her mouth, but he liked her idea enough not to argue the point. "I'm going to be a wreck at work tomorrow, aren't I?"

"I should hope so," she said, and he just watched her as she walked away. Okay, now he could start getting all worked up.

CHAPTER FOUR

HIS APARTMENT WAS between Hell's Kitchen and the theater district, just a couple of blocks from Port Authority. Not a long cab ride, not at this time of night. Which didn't mean the streets weren't busy. Despite the cold, the sidewalk vendors were out in full force, as were the folks getting out of movies and plays, the late diners and bar denizens. The city pulsed around them, and Aubrey felt as if she'd won. Now that the game she knew how to play was over, the rest of the night was a giant question mark.

He was a perfect gentleman in the backseat of the taxi. Not plastered against his door, but not touching her, either. His hands were on his thighs, and while she tried not to stare, his fingers had jerked twice now, which was what she did when she was nervous. As they passed the Flatiron, she knew she had to do something to take his mind off *later*. She wanted him to be thinking about *right now*.

She didn't have much to work with in the back of the taxi and she refused to be obvious. He probably wouldn't object to her hand on his thigh, but that wasn't the point.

After inviting Liam to the bar, she'd gone back into Le Muse and done some judicious borrowing.

JO LEIGH 43

Of course, she'd buy the underthings. She wasn't that tacky. But she would put back the shoes she'd taken from one of the in-store mannequins and the bag that held her hat and her overnight supplies. The cost of the bra, panties and thigh-high stockings would put her over her monthly budget, but hell, that was more of a suggestion than a rule. Besides, it was worth it.

She wasn't about to flash him the whole package, not in a car, but she could give him a sneak preview.

The first act was a dramatic sigh. It was breathy and loud enough for him to notice. She angled her face so he'd only see her in profile, but would still be able to catch the slow swipe of her tongue across her lips. Thanks to the reflective glass, she could see his head turn and his eyebrows lift. With her coat pushed open, she swung her right leg over her left, baring a swath of thigh. Her thong was still out of sight, but she'd been sure to uncover a sliver of skin above her stocking.

His sharp intake of breath made her want to grin, as did the way he hadn't lifted his head an inch since she started her little routine. Although she couldn't see them, she'd bet her only pair of Cavalli platforms that those big hands of his were fisted tight, aching to reach over and touch. Aubrey—1, twitchy fingers—0.

The backseat got distinctly hotter and his breathing kicked up a couple of notches. Tension sizzled during what had to be one of Aubrey's favorite things in the world: the anticipation stage. Especially when it happened at an inconvenient place or time, when to act was impossible but to stop thinking about it was worse. As long as the phase didn't go on too long—she wasn't exactly a delayed gratification kind of person.

Too quickly, they turned on 42nd. Her pulse sped as the cab slowed to a stop in front of his building on West 45th. She reached for her bag as he whipped out his wallet. He tipped well, always a good sign.

As Liam opened his door, it occurred to her that this wasn't theoretical anymore. Once they got inside, the lots and lots of sex would commence. God, she hoped they were compatible. If not, this whole project could theoretically go down in flames, which would break her heart. She needed inspiration, and she was pretty sure that if the ancient Greeks had had the foresight to realize that window designers would need help, muses would look exactly like Liam. And, of course, they'd be men.

She waited while he walked around the taxi to open her door. Unsurprisingly, he took a quick glance at her lower regions as he took her hand.

Very surprisingly, he didn't let her go until they'd reached his second-floor apartment.

"After you," he said, pushing his door open.

"I'm glad that we came here," she said, stepping inside as she shrugged off her big coat. She meant to catch it in a striking and well-practiced move, but it slipped past her grip. Wincing hard, she didn't let her shoulders sag as she pasted on her most convincing grin before she turned to get it.

He beat her to it.

Her smile became very real. "Thank you," she said, before turning away from the door. Now was her chance to scope out the room, and learn some things about the detective.

It was a box, like most Manhattan apartments. Small living room, kitchenette and a joke of a dining room were all on view. There was a door, though, at the far end, through which she spied a hint of a bed.

"Would you like something to drink?"

"Among other things," she said, giving the decor a once-over. Leather couch in good shape, midsize flat screen on the wall, two build-it-yourself book-cases that held pictures as well as hard- and paper-back books. Walking by his coffee table she saw a few magazines. *Time, Runner's World, Men's Health.* She'd already determined he was fit under his dull suit, but now she couldn't wait to see.

Unfortunately, there was very little personality on display. The bookcases were her only hope. Not only would she discover his taste in reading, but there were several framed pictures she couldn't make out from where she stood.

"What would those other things be?" He'd come up close behind her, making her jump. She spun around as fast as she could, but he didn't seem startled at all. Pity. She wanted to keep the upper hand, at least for now.

She touched the edge of his shirt collar, letting her knuckles brush against his collarbone. "You never did tell me why you became a detective."

"It's a long story," he said, his voice half an octave lower than a second before. He covered her hand with his own, and the contact made her shiver. The kiss in the bar had been nothing more than an amuse-bouche, and she was hungry for more.

"I've got all night," she said, leaning closer, trailing her other hand down his chest toward the row of buttons on his Oxford shirt.

His warm breath washed over her cheek, ruffling her curls. "No one in my family has ever been a cop," he said, so close she felt each word on her earlobe. "No significant policeman in my life."

He brushed his palms down her arms, then moved one to the small of her back while the other headed north to her nape.

"That's fascinating," she whispered, "but it doesn't answer my question."

Now she could feel the rest of him, the muscled thigh, the solidity of his chest. He shifted just enough to signal his intentions by pressing his hard cock against her hip. As his body warmed her, he tilted her head back with both fingers and nudged her with his nose until their lips almost touched. They breathed each other in, exhaled heat and want. It felt like standing at the edge of a cliff.

Then he kissed her and she let herself fall. Couldn't help it. The second his tongue plunged into her mouth a surge of heat flowed from her chest to her pussy. He started slow, then built to a powerful rhythm that was shockingly possessive.

The wonderful throaty sounds he made as he took his sweet time made her moan with pleasure. She loved kissing, but just making out didn't seem very popular among the men she dated. And frankly, it wouldn't be enough for her tonight.

When she snapped out of her reverie she got busy, showing him she could give as good as she got. What with being dazzled by this delightful new side of Liam, all she managed to do was squeeze his ass. It was a damn good ass, but she couldn't concentrate on that now.

He grunted, moved his thigh between her knees, broke the kiss only to reclaim her mouth from a different, better angle.

Seriously. What the hell? It was as if he'd read the manual. Maybe he really was her muse. His leg moved up beneath her dress, pressing against her crotch. She arched against him shamelessly.

Liam's lips traced a moist line down her throat, and when he reached the tender flesh behind her ear he whispered, "Please," but it was more of a growl than a word.

"Please what?" she asked, one hand moving to his hair, holding him against her so he'd never stop. "What do you want? Tell me."

Pulling back, he met her gaze. He was flushed, those incredible blue irises overwhelmed by dark pupils. Everywhere he touched her seemed to burn. "I want you naked."

"Well?" she said, letting go of her grip above and below.

She would never have guessed he had a smile so wicked her toes tried to curl in her shoes.

His hands swept down her body, only stopping when he reached the fullest part of her buttocks. After a very decent double-handed squeeze, he moved on and, while she knew where he was going, the journey was a lot more interesting because he was staring at her so hard, unwavering and intense. She couldn't tell if it was a dare or a promise.

It didn't matter, not when he had slowed to an aching pace, as if each touch told him something. It was flattering and scary. Scary worked for her. Big-time.

When his hands got to the top of her stockings his lids fluttered and his moan made her insides clench. Using only his fingertips, he brushed across her bare skin. Damn him for his patience. If she hadn't given him carte blanche, she'd have made a fuss. Instead, she stood, mesmerized by his mad skills.

He opened his eyes again as he leaned in closer. Touches that felt light as a feather swirled against the backs of her legs, and she shuddered as he stroked the edge of her inner thigh.

"I knew I wanted to be a cop by the time I'd turned twelve," he said, as if they were having a casual chat.

Her mind tilted, trying to make sense of what he was saying when his touch had taken over virtually every part of her brain.

"It was…the 87th Precinct," he whispered.

He moved his fingers forward, but not up.

"What?"

One finger from each hand dipped inside her stocking tops.

"You asked," he mumbled, busy kissing her collarbone, the bottom of her jaw.

His thumbs brushed the very edge of her pussy.

"Why I became…"

"I no longer give a damn," she said, moving her

hips in an attempt to stop the teasing, "you bastard." But her voice was as wobbly as her legs. Another almost-there touch with his thumbs, and she had to grab him or melt into a puddle. Holding on to the front of his shirt, she shook him. Tried to, at least, but he didn't budge.

"It's not nice to swear at your muse," he said. How could he joke at a time like this?

After a hard swallow, she gathered the paltry remains of her functioning mind.

"You're thinking of old-timey muses," she said, amazed that she wasn't just quietly weeping. "Nowadays it's expected. Especially when the muse is all tease and no—"

He slid both thumbs underneath the damp silk and tugged down. Her thong dropped between her shoes as she gasped. "Oh, fuck me," she said.

"I intend to." He kissed her again, this time not half so possessive, but infinitely more sinful. His tongue swirled over, under, around and he nipped at her bottom lip before he sucked her tongue straight into his mouth.

Leaving her begging for more, he moved down again, taking her slinky black dress with him. Liam found the hollow of her throat irresistible as he continued removing her dress. He nestled his nose at the crook of her shoulder and inhaled her like perfume. He didn't even stop when he bared her breasts.

But he did moan as if he might die any second.

She helped him along with her hands in his dark hair, all soft and silky and willing to go where she suggested. A quick lick across her already-hard nip and then a full breath of air across the damp flesh, and shit, she was going to have to insist they get horizontal soon, or there'd be trouble.

While he paid the same attention to nipple number two, he went back to the job he'd started between her thighs. She expected one of his fingers to slide inside her, but nope. He seemed to like playing with her thigh-highs with his fingers and tormenting her very damp lips with his thumbs. But then he…started…*doing things*. Rubbing her *this close* to where she wanted him to rub, then *right there perfect,* but only for a second. Her knees dipped and her hands clenched his hair. It must have hurt, although from the sound of his low hum as he sucked her tit, he didn't mind.

She gasped as the pressure on her clit increased just enough, and holy shit, the man must text like a demon, because he knew exactly where her buttons were and precisely how to press them.

"Liam," she said, although she could barely breathe, so she doubted he heard her. "Liam, God, stop. I can't—"

He lifted his head away from her breast. "Sure you can."

Shaking her head, tugging at him, she somehow managed to press her legs together, trapping him before he could push her over the edge.

One soft kiss on her right nip and another on her left, and he looked up to meet her gaze. "I take it you want to move this to the bedroom."

She nodded, noticing that despite his calm tone, he looked wild. Almost dangerous. And he'd looked so harmless at the bar. "Anywhere flat will do."

"I was going to go all caveman and carry you once I'd got you quivering."

"I can walk just fine. At least I think so. But points for creativity."

"You'll have to let me go."

She took a deep breath, steadied herself and took one step to part her legs.

He helped her dress puddle on top of her thong, and then he stood up straight. "One second. Okay? Just one second."

"What for?"

The next two steps were his, backing away so he could look at her. Naked all the way down to her stockings, still standing in her very high, very red heels.

It wasn't easy to let him stare like that. At first. But the lack of blinking and the way his breathing quickened transformed her shyness into something brand-new. He liked what he saw. So much, he actually had to press his palm against his very distinct erection.

"Wow," she said. "Thanks."

He squinted for a second, and the look on his face suggested he'd done something bad. "Would you mind turning around?" he asked, his voice more uncertain than he'd been all night.

That made her blush. Well, blush more. It was one thing to be prancing around nude from the front, but to turn around? She'd always been self-conscious about her butt and her hips. The thong had been a risk. But he'd been so sweet and so amazing...

She stepped over her clothes, then closed her eyes

and held her breath as she turned around. It was worse than trying on bathing suits. She counted the seconds, figuring ten was all she could handle.

"My God," he whispered, moving toward her. "You're stunning."

She exhaled when he put his hands on her shoulders and she leaned back against his hard chest. Among other things.

CHAPTER FIVE

THE ELBOW IN his back woke Liam with a start. The room smelled like sex. Better than that. It smelled like Aubrey. The grit in his eyes wasn't enough to dampen his smile as he turned in his bed. Memories of the night flooded his system, making his morning wood even stiffer.

God, she was all dark curls and pale skin in the dim light from the closed curtains. He wanted to kiss her shoulder. Then make a new trail all the way down her back. But he really needed to go to the bathroom. Life was definitely not fair.

Instead of waking her, he did his best to slip out of bed silently. As he stood, he caught sight of his alarm clock. "Fuck!" He should have been at the precinct an hour ago. What the hell happened to the alarm?

"What's wrong?"

"Late," he said, wishing the sound of her sleepy voice didn't go right to his cock. "We've got to hurry."

"I don't have to be anywhere," she said, then buried her face in her pillow.

"I do." With real regret, he yanked the covers down. Last night had been the best thing that had happened to him in a long time, and he'd love nothing more than to join her for the rest of the day.

"Mean," she said.

"If you want to pee, do it now, because I have to shower."

"What about my shower?" she asked, pouting as she lifted up to lean on her elbows.

He would have asked her to join him, but there was no way that would end in anything but sex. He'd never been late, not once, not even when he'd been in the academy. "Of course, you go first, but please be quick as you can. This is a horrible way to end a fantastic night, but we've got to hustle. So…" He jerked his head toward the bathroom door.

"Fine," she said, although it was clear she wasn't happy. "I'll shower at home. But next time, you need to take the day off."

The idea of a next time didn't bother him at all. Neither did watching her scoot off the bed, her small breasts jiggling as she bounced. Her nipples were hard, and he knew exactly how they tasted. Jesus, this was not the time.

She swerved when she got to his side of the bed, kissed his shoulder and ran a finger up the length of his straining dick, making him tense so sharply he bit his tongue.

"Pity we can't take care of that," she said, still looking at his erection. "But you're late and we've got to hustle."

After she closed the bathroom door, he managed to walk the short distance to the kitchen. The phone charger next to the coffeemaker was empty, and he cursed, wondering what else he'd forgotten to do in the madness of last night. Jesus, she'd been so responsive. As if they'd been together dozens of times, but with all the perks of a first time. Unreal.

He looked at his bedroom door, wondering if she was putting on her clothes. It might not be too late to call in sick. He'd only taken one day in all these years, so nobody could complain, and then he'd have the whole day to find out exactly how compatible they were.

His hand was on his cock, hard against his stomach again. What the hell had she done to him? Calling in sick when he'd just been responsible for a major bust? Had he lost his mind?

He turned on the coffee, brought out two to-go cups and willed his erection to go down before she joined him. It didn't.

He was on the steps of the precinct when he remembered that he hadn't gotten the trading card back. Damn it.

AUBREY FLOATED ALL the way home, and it had nothing at all to do with the strong scent of ganja in her cab. Her high was all Liam's fault. Liam. She wasn't sure what he'd do for her designs, but he inspired the hell out of her libido.

When she walked in the door, she found Caro on the Ugliest Couch in Five Boroughs, still in her sleep shirt and tiger slippers. "So he wasn't just a pretty face?"

Aubrey lost the shoes on her way to join her friend. "No, he was not. In fact, he proved unequivocally that I was a hundred percent right."

"About?"

"Him being my muse. Sent from the gods themselves."

Caro clicked off the TV, which Aubrey hadn't even registered. "Tell me."

"We should wait for Sanjula."

"She won't be here until God-knows o'clock, and we both have to go to work, so give me something. For pity's sake, we ended up making s'mores in the microwave and watching *Love, Actually* for the billionth time last night. I need hope in a hopeless world."

Aubrey put a comforting hand on Caro's arm. "Trust me. Magical nights still exist."

"You gonna see him again?" Caro pushed her hand through her platinum-blond pixie cut.

"Well, yeah. He's a babe and he's smart and he's a police detective for real."

"And...?"

Aubrey hesitated, felt a blush bloom and a reticence she'd never had with her friend. "He stole my breath away."

Caro's eyes widened. "That's...wow."

"I know," she said, shaking her head as if to banish her foolishness. The sex had been the best ever, but it was just sex. Anything else was her making up stories because she was still on a high. "Poor everyone else I've ever slept with. Alas, there's a new title holder. Now, I must take a shower and have more caffeine because I don't think we slept for more than two hours."

"I've got to meet this dude."

Aubrey stood up. "Meet, yes. Share, no."

"You're so selfish. And after I gave you my last yogurt the day before yesterday."

Aubrey didn't take the bait. "He's a temp, and I'm going to get maximum bang for my buck. I still have nothing for the window. And Yvonne's getting impatient."

"Be that way," Caro said, getting up, too. "Even though you're a lousy friend, I'm going to make coffee for you. Because I'm just that nice."

"Oh, you're a goddess."

"Well, no. I was planning on having coffee, anyway. Still, do me a favor and ask your muse if he has any single friends."

"I'll do my best." Aubrey made her way through the postage-stamp-size living room/kitchen to the closet that was her bedroom. It was so teeny, her double bed barely fit. But they were in the East Village, close to everything that mattered, so what was a little inconvenience when it came to washing? Or cooking? Or heating?

Nothing was going to bother her today. Because she was going to make sure she and Liam got together again *toot sweet*.

HE'D FINISHED HIS interview with Bart Norris, the man behind the money-laundering scheme. It was the first of many, and since Norris had his lawyer with him, there'd been more questions than answers. It shouldn't matter in the end. The physical evidence and the paper trail were solid. That didn't guarantee a conviction, but it was something.

Liam had stepped outside, taking a rare lunch break away from his desk. He needed the walk in the bracing cold, partly to wake him up, but more to help him stop thinking about Aubrey and last night.

At the door of Ray's Pizza, he found his cell in his hands, his thumbs already fast at work.

Are you inspired?

Before he could think it through, he'd hit Send.
Then he put his phone away, feeling a little stupid and a little hopeful, and ordered a slice of pepperoni from the street window. Three office workers were standing nearby, wolfing down slices from their paper plates. His slice arrived in under a minute and his phone sounded shortly after.

Not yet. Evidently, we need to build critical mass.

He'd just gotten to the crust, and now he shoved too much of it into his mouth and tossed the paper plate in a nearby trash can.

Where? When?

This time, he didn't put the phone in his pocket. Or start walking, or go back and order another piece of pizza, which he'd planned on doing. Instead, he stood there, staring at his smartphone in the middle of 7th Avenue, waiting for her text like an eager teenager. He tried out the idea that he was only interested in getting the trading card back, but even in his state of exhaustion, it didn't fly for a second.

The ding preceded a map. The address Broad-

way and West 80th. Underneath that, she'd written,
Le Muse, 9:00?

Yes.

He hit Send and started a quick march back to the
precinct, wishing he could hurry the clock.

"AUBREY, CUT IT OUT. There are people right outside."

"And there's a lock on the door between them and
us, so…" She went back to unbuttoning Liam's shirt.

He put his hand over hers. "Let's go. We can catch
a cab and be at my place in no time."

She sighed as she looked into his gorgeous eyes.
"You're not thinking this through. I have all my art
supplies right here. If it bothers you so much, we
don't have to do anything. You being naked should
be enough to get my creative juices flowing."

He looked at her with both eyebrows raised and
his lips parted. He added a small exasperated huff,
which made her more determined than ever. The
only things missing from his nonverbal statement
were fisted hands on his hips. God, he was adorable.

"I'm an NYPD detective. I'm not stripping naked
in a storeroom on Broadway. Anyone could come in."

"Not anyone. Only four of us have keys."

"That's three too many."

She moved closer to him. Pressed into him. Felt
his thickening cock through her skirt. "What if I
told you that the other three people weren't on the
premises?"

"It would have been a lot simpler if you'd told me

your plans. We could have met after hours. Not that I'd have taken off my clothes, but I'd have helped you carry your supplies to the privacy of my apartment."

Pulsing against him with a steadily increasing beat, she licked her lips while staring at him through her lashes. "I understand you've never been a muse before, but one of your responsibilities is to honor my process. My process involves drawing your extraordinary body, which will not only give me a dopamine high, it'll put me in a relaxed state, and distract me enough to spark my creativity and let the ideas flow."

"My process is not to get arrested for indecent exposure. And excuse me," he said, although his voice lowered every time she thrust against his cock, "but you've never had a muse before. No one has, because they're mythological."

She shook her head, finally sneaking her hands from his grip. "First of all, physiological responses are science, Liam. You can look it up. Also, you hadn't planned on taking me home last night. Look how well that turned out."

"Yes, you're right. It was off-the-charts great. Except that every man and woman in my department, including my boss, was all over my ass about being late. We had a major bust yesterday, and I was the lead detective. Then I came to work after, what, two hours of sleep? I was unprofessional and irresponsible. I can't do that again. I won't."

That stopped her for a moment. His demeanor had changed during that impassioned speech. She'd already guessed he took his job seriously, but she hadn't considered the implications of their arrangement on his career. Still, she wasn't the only one who needed a change in her routine. Liam may have a cool facade, but for the half hour since he'd arrived at Le Muse he'd been flexing his jaw, furrowing his brow. Even his kisses had been different. Distant somehow.

"Oh, my lovely muse, now I see my instincts were completely on target. You need to be distracted just as badly as I do." Both of her hands went to his delicious ass. She gripped it and pulled him toward her, closing the space between them. "There's so much I want to do to you," she said, lowering her voice. "One decent idea on paper and then we'll take full advantage of your state of undress."

Liam's eyes closed and he rolled his head back with a moan that sounded like giving in. At least she hoped so.

After two shakes of his head, he met her gaze again. "You're impossible. I want you, but I can't do it here."

She wasn't going to give up yet. She still had a few surprises up her sleeve. Or thereabouts. Letting him go, she stepped far enough away that they weren't touching at all.

His hiss of disapproval made her want to smile, but she held it together. "First of all, it's only nine-thirty."

One of his hands moved toward his cock, but he stopped himself. "So?"

"The three other people who have keys aren't here anymore. In fact, we're the only people left in the building."

"You can't know that."

"I work here most nights, specifically because I know I'll be alone. If you want, we can take a quick walk around to double check, but the only person who ever stays this late is Yvonne, and she's at a party in Long Island."

"She could come back."

"In theory, yes. But she won't. She's wooing connections for the Christmas sale."

Again, he huffed, but she made her second point before he could speak. A visual point. One she could hardly believe she was willing to make, but she hadn't been kidding about needing inspiration. Turning so her back was to him, she began to lift her skirt up. It was a hunter-green, knee-length pencil, and it took a while to inch up.

Behind her, his breath got louder.

She hadn't planned to use this maneuver to manipulate him, but he'd left her no choice. She'd selected her wardrobe carefully based on the wild hope he'd be in touch. Her heart hadn't stopped pounding since she got his text.

When her skirt was midthigh, she paused. He made a sound. A half gasp, half choke? It was tempting to make him wait, but she didn't want to. She just kept scrunching up the thick material until he could see the tops of her black stockings, held up by the metal clips of her garter belt.

This time, she was absolutely sure what his moan was about.

THE DAMN PINK ruffles on her garter belt had done him in. His own fault. He'd showed his hand last night when he'd asked her to turn around. She was a dangerous woman, and he'd better get his act together because now he was on the floor of the storeroom, his back sticking to sheets of drawing paper while Aubrey rode him like a mechanical bull.

He was loving every second of it.

She'd kept the stockings and the garter belt, ditched the blouse and her shoes. He shouldn't have been surprised to find she hadn't bothered with the more traditional panties and bra.

The minute he'd seen those frills over her ass, he'd stripped so fast he'd crashed into a shelf full of boxes. He'd been naked, condom in place on his very hard cock, before the bottom of her skirt had reached her waist.

He pushed his hips up to meet her, but she stopped her bucking. He lifted his head, stared at her flushed face, her messy curls and her wild eyes. "God, don't stop. Why are you stopping?"

She didn't answer him. Instead, she leaned to her right and came off her knee, putting her left foot flat on the floor. Then she leaned the other way, and repeated the process.

He was going to hyperventilate. Maybe have a stroke. That'd look good in the papers. At least he'd be known for something besides that Ridiculous meme.

Her left hand went to his chest and the other to her pussy. Then she moved. Up and down and…oh, *fuck,* she squeezed her muscles the whole time.

His eyes rolled back in his head, and he couldn't stop the noises that were coming out of his mouth.

She'd better be right about no one being there, because he was loud.

He held on as long as he could, but he wasn't superhuman. His hips lifted her until she lost contact with his chest and he came until he got dizzy. Before he could catch his breath, she was trembling, her neck arched, her moist lips parted. Now it was her that was loud. The way she groaned and trembled through her climax was so erotic he wished like hell he could get hard again. But when she slipped her fingers from between them and lowered herself to lie on top of him, it was enough.

Too wasted to try to talk, he used the only strength he had left to rub his hand down her back. She kissed the side of his jaw, messy and wet, then she gave it up and let her head rest on his shoulder. With each breath her still-hard nipples poked him and the ruffles on her garter belt scratched his pelvis. It was incredible.

She was incredible.

Thankfully, they still had almost three weeks until Christmas Eve.

CHAPTER SIX

HALFWAY UP THE washed-out concrete steps of the 18th Precinct, Aubrey slowed as she looked at the green doors. She'd been on a tear since she'd gotten Liam's text to meet him for lunch. Sanjula had been with her at Le Muse, and she'd been the one who put the idea into Aubrey's head.

"Don't meet him at the restaurant. Surprise him at the station," she'd said. "It'll be fun," she'd said. "He'll think you're so hot, he'll probably take you into a broom closet and do you right there!"

Aubrey had enthusiastically agreed. Still, now that she was seconds away from walking inside the Midtown North police station, she wasn't quite so certain that this was such a brilliant idea. Then again, Liam had told her she could come by.

She'd been asking to see where he worked for the past ten days. The fact that she kept asking—mostly during incredibly inventive sex—was a testament to her determination, and might have had something to do with him finally giving in.

She looked down at her outfit. It was amazing, if she did say so herself. A black Burberry trench coat, knee length and self-belted with a popped collar that made her feel like a million bucks. The fact that it was borrowed from Sanjula's friend Wendy added to the allure. Wendy was an actual model. The knee-high boots with the five-inch heels were Aubrey's, a great knockoff of a knockoff of Jimmy Choos. Not made of real leather, although they could pass. When it was overcast.

None of which was a problem. What she wore under the coat might be. She wasn't wearing much, but what she did have on was fantastic. She'd borrowed a black Mercy corset that was heavily boned and had panels of stretchy embroidery. It even laced up the back, so he could have fun freeing her, and she'd bought a black Mercy thong to go with. So what if she wouldn't be able to take a deep breath for the next however long? It would be worth it.

Not that anyone at the station would know. It wasn't as if she planned on flashing the bull pen. She wasn't *insane*. But, come on, the danger of walking into the NYPD in almost nothing but a coat and boots was off-the-charts exciting. She'd been all worked up just sitting in the cab.

Regardless, Liam was very serious about his job. He should be. He was a very important detective who'd been responsible for a major bust. While he'd told her a little bit about what he did, he was very modest. She'd read several articles in the *New York Times* that talked about the money-laundering cartel, and they'd mentioned his name in all of them. One day, he'd probably be Commissioner Gordon, uh, Flynn. She, for one, felt infinitely safer living in Manhattan with Liam on the job.

But sometimes a guy needed a little jalapeño to go with his by-the-book sandwich.

Taking a deep breath, she decided to be the chili pepper for her muse. There was no law against her inspiring him. So far, he'd inspired her so much she had too many ideas to choose from. Yvonne wasn't completely freaking out anymore. In fact, her boss was enthusiastic about several of Aubrey's concepts, even though Aubrey herself knew she hadn't hit the mark. Yet. The clock was ticking, though, so she needed every bit of muse action possible. Hence, the outfit.

Best-case scenario? She and Liam would skip lunch and find a place for a quickie. Second best? She'd meet him at his apartment the minute he was off work.

A wolf whistle from a passing bike messenger hurried her step and soon she was inside the building.

Worst case? She wouldn't tell him she was almost naked under the coat.

THE ASSISTANT DISTRICT attorney's call was already forty minutes late, but it wasn't Shawna Vance on the line when Liam answered his phone. It was the desk sergeant. Aubrey Hayes was asking to see Liam. He nearly dropped the receiver but he saw line two blinking so instead he quickly told the sergeant to send Aubrey down and answered the other line. Naturally it was the ADA, who was still holding him hostage on the phone as Aubrey stepped out of the elevator into the bull pen.

He motioned for her to come to his desk while

trying to keep track of the conversation with Vance. Not easy, especially because, well, Aubrey. Finally they hung up. "You're here."

"I know," she said, her smile dimming. "I hope it's okay."

"Oh," he said. "It's fine. It's great. I thought we were meeting at the restaurant, that's all."

"I should leave," she said, turning back toward the elevator. "I'm sorry I bothered you."

He took hold of her arm. "No, no. It really is fine that you're here. That call was almost an hour late and…anyway, I'm starving, so this is great timing. Hold on a minute, I'll get my coat and we can get out of here."

"Sure, okay. I was hoping to get a little tour, but if you're hungry, we should go," she said, looking around. The station could have passed for a paper company in Scranton if not for the Wanted posters on the back wall.

Well, hell. He was being a dick when all she'd wanted was to see where he worked. "I told you there wasn't anything interesting to see."

"There are lots of men in suits."

"That's true. But the boss is a woman and so are three of our detectives."

"Out of how many?"

He narrowed his gaze at her. "Why are you trying to distract me with feminism? You already know I'm an advocate. I'd ask what you have up your sleeve but," he said, lowering his voice, "I'm guessing the answer is nothing."

She looked impressed. For a second. Then she narrowed her gaze right back. "You don't know that."

"Yes, I do."

"You don't. But I'll let it go this time because it's pretty clear that some of your coworkers are intrigued by my presence."

He didn't need to turn around to know that she'd caused some stares. Of course she had. She looked hot enough to melt all the slush in the city. And damn, he was positive she was naked under that coat. Whether it made him an ass or not, he was getting her out of here. Now.

"Do you want me to pretend to be a witness? Or an informant?" she whispered, leaning close to him, which only made things worse. "I can do that. I'd be a really good informant. I've seen every episode of *The Wire*."

"No, no need. We're leaving. Besides, everyone here knows how to mind their own business. All I need to do is turn off my computer, and then we're going to lunch," he said, rounding his desk.

Before they could make a clean getaway, Tony Ricci had crossed the room and stopped right in front of Aubrey. "So you're friends with Ridiculous, huh?"

Goddamn son of a bitch, this was why he'd said no all those times. She didn't know about the meme. Didn't pay that much attention to social media. It was one of the best parts of this thing between them.

"Ridiculous?" she asked, looking at Liam, then back to Tony.

"It's nothing," Liam said, purposefully moving between her and Ricci.

"What, you never heard about the Ridiculously Good-Looking Cop? I thought everybody in New York had seen him on the internet."

"Ignore him." Liam took her arm again, started walking. "He's a jerk. Come on, let's go."

"Oh, yeah," Ricci said, as if Liam wasn't even there. "Everyone knows about Ridiculous. He's the poster boy for the whole department. We use him to distract the ladies when we're doing real detective work."

Aubrey tugged at Liam's grip, turning her head to look at Ricci. "What did you say?"

Ricci folded his arms across his pumped-up chest. "While we're out there talking to addicts and bums, he's surrounded by females. Ain't that right, Ridiculous?"

"Hey." Aubrey pulled out of Liam's hold and faced Ricci. "From what I've read and seen on the news, Detective Flynn was responsible for taking down a major money-laundering scheme with no loss of life. And he's only been a detective less than a year. How do *you* not know this?"

Ricci looked stunned and just laughed.

"Come on, Aubrey." Liam rubbed her arm. Man, was she angry. He could see the fire in her eyes. "Let's go."

She wouldn't back down. "I also happen to know he distinguished himself during his tenure at the 44th Precinct, according to his commendations. So what, precisely, makes him anything less than a *real* detective?"

Ricci's hands went up, and so did his overgrown

eyebrows. "Hey, whoa. I was just joking around. Ridiculous is a great guy, come on."

"That joke's getting pretty old, Detective," Liam said. "Maybe you could give it a rest, huh?" He put his hand on the small of her back, and this time he was more firm about getting her to move, when all he really wanted to do was pull her into his arms. Jesus, the way she'd defended him…she was amazing.

She opened her mouth, but didn't speak. He watched her gather herself, calmly and perfectly. Her eyes were still full of fire, but she was every inch a class act. She turned a smile on Liam. "I'm famished, what say we go get our lunch."

"There's a great Italian place near here."

With a toss of her dark curls, she took his arm. They made their way out of the bull pen and the precinct without another word.

He stopped when he felt a tug on his sleeve, but the spitfire who'd stood up to a man twice her age had vanished. Now she stared up at Liam with so much concern in her eyes, in her whole demeanor, he felt completely at a loss.

"I'm sorry," she said.

"For what? You were awesome in there. I told you. Ricci's an ass."

She shook her head. "I'm not sorry about him. He's a complete putz. I'm sorry for coming here wearing…well, not wearing very much. I can't believe how reckless it was. Anything could have happened. I could have humiliated you."

"Nothing bad happened."

"I didn't know about the meme. The last thing I'd

ever want to do is give those idiots more reason to treat you like a joke."

"The only thing you did was make them jealous as hell," he said, guiding her away from the crowded sidewalk and closer to the building.

"Oh, yeah, they're jealous, all right," she said. "You're hot, smart, good at your job, probably the best detective in the whole borough, maybe the whole city. They should be jealous."

He looked into her earnest dark eyes and felt a tightening somewhere in his gut. "What am I going to do with you?" he murmured.

"I know," she said, looking miserable. "I'm a disaster. I've embarrassed good friends before. People I really care about. By not *thinking*. I get a crazy idea stuck in my head, and I'm like a bull in a china shop."

"That's not what I meant." He brushed her cheek with the back of his hand. "As usual, you've got me all hot and bothered. I can't stop thinking about what's under that coat."

"Don't be nice about this, Liam. It was clear you didn't want me to come to the precinct, and I've proven you right." She opened her purse and pulled out his trading card. "Here's what you've been after. You deserve someone who'll listen to you."

But she had listened. And her fierce defense of him had knocked some sense into his hard head. He took the card, dropped it back into her purse, then kissed her, right in front of the precinct and anyone who cared to watch.

CHAPTER SEVEN

AUBREY HOPED LIAM didn't mind her borrowing his shirt. It was a white Oxford, one of several he had in his neat closet. Poking around in his bedroom without him being home was...weird

Instead of the quickie she'd hoped for, he'd given her his apartment key.

Not for keeps. He only had the one. They'd almost finished their shared penne arrabiata when he'd asked if she thought she could work at his place until he got home. Before she had a chance to answer, he took the key off the fob as if it was no big deal, even though she'd made such a mess of things at the station. Amazing. Wonderful. Unprecedented.

Naturally, she hadn't worked at all. Mostly because she'd gone straight from the restaurant to her apartment, picked up some very important items, debated changing into something sensible, but decided that would make her feel even more idiotic for showing up at the precinct like a hired stripper. Then she'd taxied to his place, where she opened his door with a flourish. Sadly, no one had been there to see.

Now she'd taken off the boots and the coat, but still wore her undies and corset with his white dress shirt covering the ensemble. It wasn't a complete indulgence. She'd had to put on something. His radiator wasn't quite up to the cold, although her nervous excitement was keeping her warm enough.

She took the pre–Christmas Eve Eve/thank-you-for-being-my-muse surprise she'd brought for him out of a large Pottery Barn bag and put it onto his coffee table.

There were magazines in the way, so she put them on top of his bookcase. She looked at the small Christmas tree she'd made with Styrofoam, cupcake liners and novelty tape, all on a sturdy wooden stand.

It worked. It made this place feel festive. She should have gotten tiny little lights, but time hadn't been her friend. Getting the tape for the garland had been a miracle this close to the holiday.

Her grin faded as she wondered if he'd think her surprise was as nifty as she did. They hadn't talked about the holidays except in reference to the window display. She had no idea if he celebrated. Or maybe he took Christmas really seriously, and then he'd try to act sweet but she'd see right through him and end up feeling terrible.

She'd seen Dumpsters in the alley. It wasn't too late to chuck the stupid thing out. Although, there was no indication that he belonged to another religion. And she had no reason to think he was anti-Christmas.

She turned around, looked at the bed where they'd done so many interesting things to each other. Liam was cool. He'd like the idea even if he didn't like the gift itself. After all, he liked her. He trusted her enough to give her his key. Hell, he hadn't even taken back his trading card.

Catching sight of herself in his full-length mirror, she slouched provocatively against his bedroom door frame, one hand raised, the other near her mouth, where she touched her bottom lip with one finger. Something wasn't quite—ah, the right knee had to bend so her hip stuck out and the shirt parted just enough to show a tantalizing hint of corset.

To take a selfie or not. That was the question. Not posing, no, but maybe one with the tree? She could have it printed, put it in a frame for him. A memento of their time together.

She'd take one of him, too. With or without the tree. Several, in fact. Although she doubted she'd ever forget her one and only muse. Despite the on-coming storm of her deadline and increasing pressure to live up to Yvonne's expectations, she wanted to remember him. How he made her feel. This—

Her phone rang. She grabbed it so fast it didn't ring twice. Seeing his name on her caller ID made her giddy. "Hi."

"I'm on my way. Three minutes."

"You left early."

"Damn straight," he said. "I could barely think."

"I know what you mean."

"No new ideas?"

"Not about the window design."

He moaned, and she wondered if the cabdriver heard him. "Two minutes."

"Do you want anything when you get here? A drink?"

"You. I want to see under that damn coat."

She sighed. "I guess that means I should put it back on."

"Good," he said. "Wait, what?"

"Nothing."

"What are you wearing, Aubrey?"

"I'll show you. After."

"You're trying to kill me."

"That would spoil all my plans." She walked over to the couch, crossing her fingers that he'd like what she'd brought him. Both the tree and the corset.

"We're turning onto my street."

"You have your money ready?"

"Everything about me is ready."

"Can't wait."

She heard him talk to the cabbie, then the door slam. Laughing and excited, she hung up, then draped his stern Oxford shirt, complete with rolled-up cuffs, over the edge of the couch. Then she shoved her feet into her boots, donned the trench coat and heard the doorknob turn as she buckled the belt.

He almost knocked her over in his rush to come inside, but she was saved at the last second by a kiss that made falling redundant. When Liam finally moved far enough away for her to undo the coat, she was determined to make it so sexy he'd come in his pants. But somewhere between the bump and the grind, he looked at her as if she was so much more than lingerie and chutzpah.

For a second, maybe two, she hated their bargain. How could she ever have thought of him as something temporary? He wasn't like that. He was meant for a real woman, not a flighty, impulsive girl. Then he bit his lower lip and she dropped the coat.

By the time he'd looked up at her face again, she'd forgotten about the bargain. Let this be what it was.

HE'D NEVER CATCH his breath again. Panting forever would be inconvenient, but he'd deal with it if it meant more mind-boggling sex. They hadn't made it past the couch. In the end, it was her thong, not the corset, that had done him in. Well, what was under the thong.

Since he'd last seen her naked, she'd made a change. Aubrey had been neatly trimmed all over, which he liked. Especially the fact that it made her pubic hair look like an arrow. It still did, but her labia were now as smooth as her inner thigh. Only softer.

When he'd gotten her on the couch, he'd discovered a little wet spot on her panties. To say it got him hot didn't cover half of it. He'd licked her until the silk had been wet, clinging. By the time he'd finally pushed the cloth to the side and entered her, they'd both been gasping— "Oh, shit."

He looked down at her, nestled against his chest, her head resting in the nook of his shoulder. Still strapped in her corset. "Let me—" he said, holding her shoulders until he could wriggle to his feet.

Her face was too flushed and she was practically wheezing. He helped her turn and fumbled with the laces as he freed her.

"Thank God." She inhaled hugely. "Next time," she said between deep breaths, "we take the corset off first."

The marks down her back made him wince and feel guilty for getting carried away…and for finding the sight arousing. She would look incredible tied to a four-poster. His cock twitched, which was remarkable considering how hard he'd just come. Kissing the pink indentions made him feel a little less pervy. As if Aubrey would mind. They'd already had sex in her office, on virtually every surface in his apartment, and then there'd been the hand job in the cab that time. Nope, she wouldn't blink if he brought out, say, four silk scarves. Of course, he'd have to buy a four-poster bed first. Or find the right hotel.

A shiver ran down his back, but it was as much to do with the cold as his thoughts. "Come on," he said, taking her hands. "Let's get you out of those boots and into my bed."

She smiled. Moved her gaze pointedly to the coffee table.

"Oh. That's a Christmas tree."

"Yes, it is."

"Is that garland…?" He bent down to look at it more carefully. "Crime scene tape?"

"Blue and white, for the NYPD."

Liam looked at her, then at the most unusual, yet most extraordinary tree he'd ever seen. "How did I not see this? It's great. I love it."

She stood, kissed him on the cheek. "You're welcome."

Wrapping his arms around her very naked and rapidly cooling body, he pulled her close. "To be honest, there could have been an elephant riding a bicycle in here, and I wouldn't have noticed. That corset. Wow. And what's under the corset, even better."

"Very well put. Now let's get into bed before the chill works its way past my knees."

Once under the covers, they slid into the warm familiarity of how they fit together. His arm under her neck, her leg across his thigh, her curls patted down so they tickled the underside of his chin instead of his mouth. They sighed in unison, as if it had been rehearsed.

"Liam?"

"Hmm?"

"What's the story with that 'ridiculous' stuff?"

The high he'd been floating on since he'd walked in the door sunk like a stone. "Nothing."

"Oh. Okay," she said, tensing against him. "Forget I mentioned it."

"No, I'm sorry. That was a knee-jerk reaction." Part of him wanted to keep the humiliation as private as possible, but on the other hand, it was Aubrey. "I want to tell you."

"I'm pretty sure you don't, which is fine," she said, her warm palm moving over his chest to rest above his heart.

"Last year someone took a picture of me while I was in uniform at the Macy's Thanksgiving Day parade and the woman called me a ridiculously good-looking cop. It hit the internet. Ricci was right, it became a meme, a very viral meme. Most people have forgotten about it by now."

"But not your fellow officers?"

"Nope."

She leaned her head back to look at him. She didn't look happy. "That sucks. I want to punch every one of them."

He grinned, especially at her ferocious frown. If she had the chance, she'd follow through, he was sure of it. "Then I'd have to arrest you."

"Hmm. I have wondered where you keep your handcuffs."

Laughing, he ran his fingers through her hair, the urge to kiss her hitting him hard. But he also wanted her to rest up. They normally didn't spend a lot of time just lying together. Most nights, he watched her work at the lingerie store, then they'd come back to his place and wear each other out. The morning alarm would blare too soon and send them into a frenzy until they went off to work.

Lately, she'd tried syncing their hours, but she still worked nights, too. Since he'd been her muse, she hadn't taken any days off. The window consumed her. Until today. Today she'd come to see him, and while the visit to the bull pen had ended badly, he'd liked seeing her there. Despite Ricci's big mouth.

But the quiet now, her drawing lazy circles on his chest, him rubbing her incredibly soft arm, made him feel more relaxed than he'd been in a long time.

It occurred to him that, seconds ago, he'd been wound up about the meme bullshit. In a sentence, she'd shrunk the perpetual thorn in his side to the size of a hangnail. He loved her for that, if nothing else.

Not *love*. That was stretching things, but... Discounting the sex, which was not an easy thing to do, he really enjoyed being with her. Even when she was laser focused on her sketches. He liked watching her hands as she made magic with nothing more than a blank paper and a pencil.

Did she realize that when she was adding shade to a draft she stuck out her tongue? Not far, just the tip. The side it peeked from depended on which side of the paper she was working on. That she began every new drawing with her eyebrows way up, her cheeks flushed and her lips parted? If it turned sour, her expression became either furious or disgusted, and she cussed so descriptively she could give lessons to his whole division. Only, she did it softly.

It was no use. He had to kiss her. What did she expect, lying there so beautiful and tempting? "Sorry," he said, repositioning himself until they shared the bottom half of the only pillow left on the bed.

"Sorry for what?"

"Never mind. I'm not sorry at all."

She had her eyebrows raised. Her cheeks grew pink as he watched. In fact, she looked just like she did when a new idea hit her.

He kissed her, slipping between her already-parted lips. She moaned and undulated against him as they tasted and licked and nibbled. Somehow, she was both languid and eager at the same time. All her movements slow except for her impatient tongue.

Pulling away, he brushed the curls from her face. "You still surprise me," he said, his voice low and rough.

"That's a good thing, right?"

"Very good."

Caressing the side of his cheek, she said, "I don't know if anyone's told you this before, but, Detective Flynn, you're dreamy."

He couldn't help but laugh. "Dreamy?"

"Huh. Surprised you again, didn't I?"

Liam nodded as he kissed her.

HIS HAND MOVED up her back. Slowly. His kiss deepened as he moved it to her nape where he stayed for a moment. His touch made her feel safe, even though she was in such a vulnerable position. When he moved again, it was to sneak under her curls, his fingers spreading as they massaged her scalp.

She moaned, the sound swallowed. Shared.

A week ago she'd told him that if she won the lottery she never bought tickets for, she'd hire a full-time masseuse based solely on how well he gave head rubs. This wasn't the first time he'd indulged her, but it was the most intimate, and she wasn't sure why.

Maybe it was the slow-like-honey kisses that never quite stopped even when they had to breathe. Or his broken noises that sounded mostly like her name but sometimes like *please*.

It wasn't that long ago they'd been at each other like rabid wolverines, and this was…not what they did. He'd been tender before, and teasing, and silly, and cavemanlike, and rugged, and fast, and hard. This was new. Like sinking into the warmest, most comforting bath in the world, only with a lot more touching and tingling.

She wanted to drown in his scent. His arms. Their

bodies were pressed so tightly together she could feel his cock harden against the curve of her hip bone.

Her own touch was careful as she moved down his body with her lips. She lingered over the dimple above his ass, wanting to fill it with champagne and lick it out. But they had no champagne, and anyway, she wouldn't have stopped these kisses. Not when they lit up all her good parts from the inside out.

Drowning didn't seem to be optional.

One last functioning brain cell warned her that drowning might not be the best thing to do. But it was only the one cell and it was far too quiet. All she could hear was her own pulse. Their shared breaths.

She couldn't even pretend to mind that he abandoned the scalp massage for parts down south. He'd let her know how much he liked her new coif. Now, as his gentle fingers brushed those naked lips, she had to admire her own cleverness. So much more sensation. It was as if she'd taken off a blanket.

His hips started moving faster. She reached for him, and, oh, God, he was hard. He pulled back to hiss as her hand tightened on his flesh. She almost stopped but he shifted to give her more room.

He surprised her by not thrusting again. Instead, he looked at her. Lips in a gentle upward curl, eyes soft even though they were dark and half-lidded with want. She tried to build a rhythm with her hand, but his stare, the tenderness in it, threw her off. He didn't complain. Just moved easily into her grip.

It wasn't what they did.

"What are you doing?" she asked, her voice sounding weird in the quiet of the room.

"Enjoying you."

"Do you need a nap?"

Liam shook his head, although his gaze stayed steady.

She blinked. She blinked and she started pumping him. Just the way he liked it. In a minute, she'd go down on him.

His moan was low, and his eyes rolled back, finally breaking the spell, but he didn't stay lost for long. Gently teasing fingertips slipped inside her pussy.

She grinned. "Okay, Copper. It's on."

His smile didn't change but his head dipped for a kiss. Not like before. A brush of lips, a caress of breath. Although she was doing her job well enough for him to grunt and his hips couldn't stay still, he found her earlobe. First it was panting, hot and wet, but then—

"You are amazing, Ms. Hayes. Talented. Beautiful. Smart. Captivating."

She closed her eyes and stopped her hand. There was nothing she could do but be as still as possible as she tried with all her might not to believe him.

He couldn't possibly know how those words were going to hurt her when this all ended. Which it would. The ending had been the important bit. It was what had convinced him to be her muse at all.

So she'd force herself to forget what he'd said. The look in his eyes. How his touch made her heart ache.

It was time to take a big step back. All she'd asked him for was sex. Not this. Never this. Because the memory of *this* would kill her.

CHAPTER EIGHT

"No, YOU GO on ahead," Aubrey said. "I'm too…" She smiled a little and shrugged.

"Lazy?"

She nodded and snuggled down under the blanket.

Liam hoped that was all it was. After a quick kiss he hurried to the bathroom. As he jumped in the shower, the memories of Aubrey telling off Ricci hit him again. He'd been so worried she'd do something crazy, but she'd been great. Really great. The fact that she'd spent so much time with him when she could have been working was a hell of a thing.

He couldn't wait until she finished the damn window. It wasn't that he minded being at her service, but with his hours and her deadline, they spent most of their time together fucking. Not that he was complaining, but he looked forward to getting to know her better, which would only happen after Christmas Eve Eve.

Funny how the thing that had convinced him to get involved with Aubrey in the first place felt superfluous now. A gimmick that had about run its course. For him, at least. He wasn't going to change anything, not when the clock was still ticking, but that didn't mean he couldn't look forward to later.

He threw his damp towel into the hamper just as his stomach grumbled loud enough to wake the neighbors. It had been hours since lunch and he was starving.

Instead of finding Aubrey curled up in bed, she was standing by his dresser wearing red panties and boots, her corset pressed up against her chest, but not tied.

"Oh," he said, disappointed but trying to hide it. He'd had the feeling something was off. He shouldn't have kept her from work.

When she turned, she smiled. Kind of. At best, she seemed distracted. "I need to go back to the store. I haven't done any work today, and my meeting with Yvonne is coming up fast. I've got to hit the drawing table."

Her decision to leave shouldn't have mattered, but it did. In truth, he hadn't asked her to spend the night or have dinner with him, so there was no reason for him to be bothered. But it felt awkward being naked now. He crossed the room and she scooted to the right when he opened his top drawer to grab a pair of boxers.

"Don't get dressed on my account," she said. "It's snowing out, and I'm probably going to work for hours. You should sleep."

"I don't mind."

She cupped his cheek with her free hand. "You need rest. It's been a long day, and you have to talk to the mean district attorney first thing in the morning."

Turning his head, he kissed her palm. "I don't want you to leave."

"I know. But I don't think I'll have a true minute's rest until I nail down the design."

"You know how much I like the sleepover one. And the subway thing. They're both genius."

"Thanks," she said, lowering her hand and her gaze. "I can't get past the feeling that there's something better. I know there's no time, but I have to keep trying. Just for a couple more days until the meeting." Looking up at him again, she said, "I shouldn't have come to see you when you were working. It was fun, and great, but it was foolish when I'm this tight on a deadline."

"So I didn't inspire you at all?"

The warm smile, one of his favorites, lightened her whole face. "Of course you did. You always do. Unfortunately, I'm on my own for the execution part. Trust me, I wouldn't be good company tonight. But I got to tell off a detective, saw where you worked, had lunch with you and then there was all the canoodling. That's a great day, right?"

"You're absolutely correct. Which doesn't mean I can't want more."

Her eyes got serious for a few seconds as she scanned him from forehead to chin. Then she kissed his cheek right before she turned around. "Do me up, please? Just lightly, though, enough to keep it legal. I need to untie it when I get to the store."

He had to. No choice there, but it seemed a damn shame to lace her up only to send her away. "I don't like you going out at night wearing so little. Anything could happen."

"Then do me a favor, call a taxi? You can walk me down, and if you don't like the looks of the cabbie, we'll send him on his way and call another."

His sigh sounded exactly as disgruntled as he felt. "Fine. I suppose you don't have time for me to make you coffee before you leave?" He skipped every other stay on the corset, leaving the lacing long so she'd have no trouble.

She turned to him again. "No, thanks, I've got coffee at the store. You really are too good to me."

She wasn't joking. He could tell. "Are you all right?"

"Yeah, why?"

"You're awfully serious, considering you owned Tony Ricci, the most obnoxious detective in the 18th Precinct."

"I did, didn't I?" she said, smiling, and there she was again…for at least a moment. The window design must really be getting to her.

"I love my tree. You're amazing." He squeezed her shoulders as he bent to kiss her. Only this one wasn't a quickie. Tasting her again brought back the ache in his chest, the twitch in his cock. Before he went nuts, he pulled away. "I'll go make that call."

"I CAN'T BELIEVE you guys." Aubrey took another bite of the falafel Sanjula and Caro had brought to Le Muse even though her appetite wasn't happening. She'd spoken maybe five words to Caro in the cab ride from Liam's, but her two friends had still shown up, dinner and strong shoulders at the ready.

"You're such an idiot," Sanjula said in her most sympathetic voice. "Seriously. Aubrey, I love you, but you're a moron."

That brought a smile. Unfortunately, Sanjula was right about her being a dope, but not for the right reason. "I should have known the minute I met him. I mean, you've seen his trading card."

"Yes, we have," Caro said. "And being gorgeous doesn't automatically make him the wrong guy."

Caro didn't get it, either. "It's not the pretty that's wrong." Aubrey stood up, walked away from the blank sketch pad on her desk. She hadn't put one mark on it, and she'd had thirty-five minutes to work before the troops arrived. "He's a detective for the NYPD. It's what he lives for. He wants to be the chief of police someday. I mean, come on. I know us both, and *I* can't even imagine us together."

"You've only known him a couple of weeks. No one said you have to marry the guy," Caro said. "But you also don't have to throw him to the curb because you guys made love."

Aubrey shook her head, wishing they'd brought a bottle of vodka instead of a venti latte. "I didn't kick him to the curb. We agreed that this thing between us was only until the window was done. Christmas Eve Eve comes, and he's gone." Damn it, even she could hear the catch in her voice. She stared at a box instead of at her friends. "That's the only reason he's with me in the first place. Remember 'lots and lots of sex with a time limit'? The part that's screwed up is that it was only supposed to be sex. Not…not what happened tonight."

She sighed as she turned back. Who was she kidding? Her friends had seen her drunk off her ass, sick as a dog, crushed by jobs, by unrequited lust, by her own weaknesses. There was no use trying to pretend she wasn't exactly as crazy as she was.

"Let me get this straight," Sanjula said, putting down a too-cute-for-words baby-doll nightie that was supposed to be on a mannequin. "You had an amazingly hot quickie, then he changed things up and took his time, and now you're convinced that the whole thing is the worst mistake since denim shorts with black tights."

"He didn't just take his time." Tears threatened, but Aubrey didn't care. "The way he looked at me was…I mean, he was probably just looking at me all normal and stuff, but I took that look and ran with it all the way to church. I mean it. Whatever the switch is that flips from a simple hookup to a major mistake? That's what happened. I know, because I've been there before. Do I need to remind you both of Phillip? I was practically picking out wedding dresses before I overheard him talking about his 'freshman piece.'"

The girls groaned in stereo.

"Well, this is Phillip times ten."

"Oh," Caro said. "Wow."

"Yeah, wow." Drinking the last of her cold coffee, Aubrey ran her hand over her sketch pad, knowing she wasn't going to be inspired tonight. "Somehow, I have to turn that switch off. Right now. Before I see him again. Or else, I can't see him again."

Sanjula jumped down from the shelf where she'd roosted. "Wait just a sec. Before we go flipping switches all over the place, let's think this through. So, you got more invested in Liam than you'd meant to. Why is that such a bad thing?"

"Detective for the NYPD, Sanjula. Serious detective with upward mobility plans."

"So? Why is that a deal breaker?"

Aubrey blinked at the woman she used to think knew her better than almost anyone. "Because I'm me."

Her friend crossed her arms and gave her a withering look. "The only one who doesn't believe any man, including the bloody president of the United States, if he wasn't married, would be lucky to have you is you."

Aubrey spun toward Caro. "Would you please tell her why that is a ridiculous—oh."

"What?" Caro was clearly confused.

"I didn't tell you. You guys are on the internet a lot. Do you remember a meme from last year about a ridiculously good-looking cop?"

"Yeah," they said in tandem. They should really go on the road.

"That was Liam. Before he made detective."

"No way." Sanjula pulled out her cell. "I knew I recognized him. That is awesome," she murmured, already searching. She wouldn't come up for air for a while.

"Not for him, it's not. The other detectives won't let him forget it. They're horrible. They bully him. And he's so good at his job. He busted a whole money-laundering operation basically by himself. And they all diss him like he's a rookie. He takes it so hard. I can tell. He's a tough guy, he really is, but this has been going on for over a year. I wish I could do something, but I don't know what."

"Aubrey, sweetie?" Caro said in her "I'm going to tell you something you won't like" voice.

Aubrey's chin dropped to her chest.

"I'm pretty sure that switch got flipped before you guys made love tonight. I'm not sure you can flip it back."

That one hurt. Deep down, straight to the heart. "Don't say that. Please."

Caro pulled her into a hug. "But we can do damage control."

"What does that mean?"

"It's your ball game. You call the shots. No more nights at his place. Whether you guys do it here or even at our tiny hovel, quickies only. Keep it light. No lingering. Tell him you have to work. It's not even lying."

"Got it," Sanjula said, looking up from her phone. "But we can look at his picture later. Caro's right. You set the pace and the tone. Girl, you just need to be on top for the rest of your run."

"Won't that get a bit repetitious?"

Sanjula rolled her eyes. "My God, you do have it bad. Metaphorically on top. Idiot."

"Okay," Aubrey said. "As much as it pains me to say it, you're right. I'm taking this too far. I can pull it back as long as I'm in charge. I'll miss Caveman Liam, but it's worth it. Frankly, the idea of giving up the next two weeks was depressing the shit out of me."

"Good girl." Sanjula lifted her cell. "Come check out what a damn hottie he is in his uniform. And, Aubrey? Please, please, please, just leave yourself open. Don't make any permanent decisions when you're so wound up by a deadline, okay? Just let it end when it's supposed to."

Aubrey let her head drop onto Sanjula's shoulder. "I'll do my best. God, he still has that uniform in his closet. Why didn't he wear it tonight?"

"See," Caro said. "There's still a little time left to get in a few rounds. As long as you don't freak out."

"Don't freak out," Aubrey said. "Check."

CHAPTER NINE

"THE FIRST ROUND'S on me," Harry Bigalow announced from the center of the bull pen. "As long as it's what's on tap."

"Cheap bastard." Stan Whitset, who'd been a detective for a couple of years, turned to Liam and Ernie Rogers. "You guys comin'?"

Rogers nodded. "Free mediocre beer? Who could pass that up?"

Liam thought about staying to make some calls, but the White House was on the way to his apartment, and he'd have to stop there before he met up with Aubrey. Besides, he could use a beer, mediocre or not. "Yeah, sure."

Rogers lifted his eyebrows. "Glad you're joining us."

"What?" Liam shrugged. "Oh, yeah, I have time for one."

"Want a ride?"

"Sure."

They talked about one of their current cases on the drive over. Liam had never felt this relaxed with Rogers before. Maybe it was because while Liam was paying attention to the conversation as they'd inched along through traffic, Aubrey lingered in the back of his mind. Scattered thoughts about tonight. About how he'd picked up a coconut cake at the market this morning because he'd finally been invited to her apartment. He wasn't sure why she'd asked him over, especially this close to Christmas. Her roommates would be there, she'd told him that much, but she'd seemed nervous. It was a step up the dating ladder, if he could call what they did dating. Hell, the personalized Christmas tree, now meeting her friends. Maybe he should think about inviting her to his folks' holiday brunch.

He definitely needed a drink.

"So," Rogers said after they parked and were walking to the bar, "you decided to lift your ban on this hole in the wall, huh?"

Liam slowed at the question. He hadn't realized anyone had noticed his reluctance to go to the White House. Rogers probably wasn't the only one, either. Shit, no wonder Tony Ricci was so smug. "Yeah," Liam said, keeping it casual. "Tonight's for Bigalow. Besides, I have plans so I won't be staying long."

"Good for you. Life shouldn't be all about the job."

Funny that Rogers should say that. Just this morning Liam had been thinking the same thing. Although he'd also wondered if his feelings for Aubrey had more to do with the thrill of their agreement than anything else. He had no idea how he would feel if they'd met under normal circumstances.

He definitely would have been attracted to her no matter what, but he doubted he would have considered getting into a serious relationship with her. Thank goodness for that mysteriously appearing trading card. He'd have hated to miss this.

Once inside, he spotted a couple of detectives from the 18th already at the old mahogany bar. He recognized a number of other cops and support personnel from their precinct. A few badge bunnies were circulating, looking hopeful.

He even saw the waitress Tony'd been so infatuated with, but he couldn't bring himself to care. Everybody needed to just get over it already.

Bigalow entered the building to a smattering of shouts, and the crowd waiting for drinks cleared a path for him. He'd announced his retirement today, hence the round. The official party would take place after his last day. Liam didn't know Bigalow well, but his record was good and even though he'd called Liam Ridiculous, he'd never belittled the work.

Rogers handed Liam a glass and they headed for their precinct's section of the bar. It was an informal setup, several tables, a booth, a bunch of chairs. Nothing special, but it was far away from the jukebox so at least it wasn't too noisy.

Ricci was already sitting in the booth, and while he didn't break into song when he caught sight of Liam, he didn't look as if he was itching for trouble, either. Stan waved Liam and Rogers over to a couple of empty chairs. Even before they sat down Stan looked up at Liam. "I gotta know, Flynn. Was that your girlfriend?"

Flynn. That was a surprise. "Kind of," he said.

"How do you kind of have a girlfriend?"

"Long story. She's...not easy to pin down."

"She sure as hell tore Ricci a new one. That seems pretty pinned down to me."

A quick look at the booth told Liam that Ricci did not appreciate the topic. "Yeah, she's something, all right."

"Whatever she is," Rogers said, "if she's the reason that big stick has come out of your ass, you hold on to her."

Liam put his beer down. Rogers was just full of illuminating information tonight. Stick up his ass? For trying to get a modicum of respect from his co-workers? As if he was the one at fault for their juvenile bullying—he stopped that thought right there. "No," he said as casually as he could. "I just finally realized I had to accept the fact that I work with a bunch of immature pricks."

The group around him laughed. He relaxed again and picked up his drink, feeling as if he'd made some headway. He wondered if it would make any difference back on the job. Whatever. He wasn't about to lose sleep over it.

Thankfully, Bigalow sat down, and all the attention went to him. Fifteen minutes later, Liam almost wished he didn't have to leave. He liked hearing the old man's stories. He'd been a detective long before the internet or cell phones, and it was a different job back then.

But nothing outside of a case would keep Liam from spending time with Aubrey. He made a quiet exit. The minute he was settled in the taxi he couldn't help thinking about what Rogers had said, and how easily Liam had taken it in stride. Aubrey just kept on surprising him, but tonight, he'd also surprised himself.

"THIS IS SANJULA," Aubrey said, shocked she could breathe, let alone speak. It was probably too late to turn him around and just leave. She'd had the whole evening planned out. A quick pizza with her friends, which would end with the girls tactfully leaving for an hour and a half. By the time they returned, she and Liam would both be dressed. She'd go to the shop and work, he'd go home. No messy feelings or thinking.

Instead, she was more nervous than Sheldon Cooper giving a speech.

"Nice to meet you," Liam said as he held out a cake box like he was offering a handshake. "I brought this."

His awkwardness made Aubrey's chest ease a little. God, he was so adorable when he had no clue what to do.

"Thank you," Sanjula said, taking the cake from him. "Caro's gonna be here any minute. She had to work late. But since the pizza isn't here yet, that's not a problem. Can I get you a drink?"

Aubrey made him jump when she went to take off his coat. When he looked at her, though, he smiled and let go of a big breath. "Thanks." Before she could turn to the coatrack, he leaned in and kissed her. It was a lip-kiss. Not even a hint of tongue.

Behind them, the door swung open so hard it knocked against the wall. Caro grinned at Liam, then Aubrey. "What did I miss?"

Aubrey laughed. "Well, you're in time for the ritual Hanging of the Coat, but alas, you're too late for the traditional Giving of the Cake."

"Cake?"

"He gave," Aubrey said, nodding at Liam. "We received."

Caro stuck out her hand. "I'm Caro, and my boss is an asshole, but it's really nice to meet you."

"Thanks. Aubrey talks about you guys a lot."

"Yeah, us, too. I mean, she talks about you. To us."

Even Liam smiled, although it was kind of crooked. "I don't want to know," he said. "Do I?"

"Probably not." Sanjula joined the threesome. "It's all been good, though."

"Glad to hear it." Liam looked at where Caro was still holding on to his hand.

She let him go with a big wince and a small blush. "Sorry. I've had a lot of coffee today."

Aubrey was vaguely aware of the small talk. Liam seemed pretty comfortable, but if she'd thought she was nervous before, she'd been a mistaken. This whole dinner had been mistake. It was as if he were meeting her *parents*. Shit. Shit. Shit. How had she not seen this? How had Sanjula and Caro not seen this? She'd brought him home to meet the folks! Clearly she'd been too focused on controlling the sex. Because whatever this was, it wasn't stepping back.

To make things worse, which seemed impossible, she was suddenly desperate for Caro and Sanjula to like him. Des-per-ate. If they didn't it would hurt her. Deeply.

"Aubrey?"

His hand was on her elbow, his head tilted slightly to the right. "You okay?"

"I'm fine. Great. Fine. I was just thinking about work."

"Anything I can help with?"

The "don't freak out" ship had sailed, but she could still pull herself together enough to avoid looking like she was having a nervous breakdown. "You could get me a bottle of wine," she said, her smile perfectly normal.

"A bottle?" He pressed his lips together for a minute, then nodded. "Just point me to the nearest liquor store, and tell me what to get."

She blinked as she played back the past few seconds. "Glass," she said. "I meant glass." Her laughter sounded mechanical and she felt like she might throw up, but instead she started toward the sink, which was the focal point of the kitchen area. "Just a glass or two of red wine. That'd be great."

At least Liam was no better at hiding his alarm than she was. That had to count for something.

"DINNER WAS FUN," Liam said, taking off his shirt. "I like your friends."

Aubrey laughed. "God, you should have seen your face when they asked you about your intentions."

"Can you blame me? They were ruthless."

"They were kidding."

"Ha, ha."

"You can put your clothes on the chair. No room for anything fancy in here like a closet or a dresser."

"Uh-huh," he said, but she doubted he'd heard her. He was staring at the art she'd put up on the only wall in her room that wasn't covered with clothes hooks. "These are good."

"Thank you." She was undressing, feeling more bashful about his laser-sharp focus on her paintings than her own nudity. There were six pieces altogether—four acrylics, two watercolors and a couple of multimedia experiments. They were different from her window designs, and each one reminded her of a certain time of her life. But they weren't all that spectacular.

"No, I mean it," he said, clearly not happy with having to look at the work from such a weird angle. "I knew you were talented, but I didn't realize—"

"What?"

He turned to her. "You're gallery good. You should have a showing. I'm just knocked out by your painting. Especially the people."

He really didn't sound like he was bullshitting. Her face grew hot. "Okay, Detective Flynn. Thanks and all, but I'm a sure thing."

The look he gave her flipped her world yet again. He'd meant it. She'd just insulted him. Over paintings she'd done at Pratt. And one from high school. "What's that about?" he asked. "Did you think I wasn't being honest?"

Oh, God. This night could not have gone worse. She loved that he thought her stuff was great, but it was strange, too, because no one she'd ever gone out with had said such things. Not without an agenda.

First she brought him here, to her home, to the closest people in her life, and now… She had to do something. Take some kind of action to avoid digging herself into an even deeper hole.

"I was teasing," she said, hoping her acting was as good as her art. "I want you looking at me. Not at the wall." She approached him slowly until she was close enough to nip his lower lip. Her hand on his fly, she prevented further discussion with her tongue. His hardening cock told her she had his full attention.

Thank God. Sex was her only hope of getting out of this without falling completely in love with him.

LIAM DROPPED HIS pants and kicked them away, grateful he'd left his shoes in the living room. Now he needed to remove his socks before she got his underwear off.

When she pulled back after his boxers had hit the floor, he noticed she was still wearing her red dress. It was short and cute, but it covered most of his favorite parts. He pulled her into his arms to search for a zipper.

She leaned her head against the bare curve of his neck. "It goes over my head. No zipper, no buttons."

"Now that's form *and* function." He started lifting the dress and found he wasn't capable of removing his socks while doing anything else. Not even kissing her. When he finally had the dress off, she looked up with a curl to her lips and eyes full of trouble. All thoughts of socks flew out the window.

"You are gorgeous," he said, and started walking her toward the bed. It wasn't a long journey. But before he let her fall, he had to check out tonight's lingerie selection.

She wore a white bra, not lacy or anything, and white underwear. Not a thong, just a regular pair of bikini panties. His mouth opened and his cock jerked, leaving a dab of pre-cum on her hip.

"Really?" she asked, looking into his eyes with disbelief.

He swallowed, then shrugged. "You're sexy. So sue me."

Aubrey blushed, and took a step back. And then, weirdly, her body stiffened and she looked at the door as if she wanted to make a break for it. When she turned back to him seconds later, she was smiling as she reached back to unhook her bra.

"Did I say something wrong? With your friends?"

"No," she said. "No. You were great."

He wanted to believe her, but something was off, and he wasn't sure this was the best time for him to have a raging hard-on. Aside from the fact that it made it difficult to think, she probably wouldn't believe him if he said he just wanted to talk.

She hadn't even dropped her bra. She held it, demurely, against her breasts. "I forgot to bring the condoms from the bathroom," she said, which would have explained her glance at the door except that she said it in her normal voice instead of the breathy, sexy way she spoke when she was eager and aching.

Confused as hell, he said, "I've got three in my wallet."

"Well, go on," she said, waving him away with her free hand. "Sanjula said they'd be back in an hour and a half, so if we're going to make any noise at all, we'd better do it fast."

"Fast," he repeated, walking across the room wearing nothing but his black socks, his erection flagging with each step. What the hell had happened? She'd been jumpy all evening. But if anyone had a right to be jumpy, it was Aubrey. Hell, the showdown with her boss was coming up and tonight she'd introduced him to her friends, which had to have been as nerve-racking for her as it was for him.

Although she'd told him more than once that sex relaxed her. Made her subconscious feel free.

Behind him, he heard her moving the covers, the squeak of the bed. So he got the condoms, draped his stuff and her red dress over the chair, then turned off the overhead light.

It didn't take long for her to flip on the little lamp that sat on a makeshift nightstand by the head of the bed. On her side, naked, head propped up on one hand, she patted the bed next to her. Her smile was all Aubrey. Inviting, sweet and wicked.

When he joined her, she pulled him into a kiss. Thankfully, it was a slow-builder. He needed a little time to get back into the swing of things. To stop thinking so much, and give the lady what she needed.

She ran her hands down his back until he relaxed a bit, and then she moved her leg over his thighs and pushed him down, his head landing on her pillow.

He got hard again quickly; how could he not with that body rubbing against him? She nipped the end of his jaw, licked the hollow between his collarbones, then moved on top of him, straddling his thighs. A moment later, he was sheathed and she was sliding down onto his cock, clenching him so tightly he couldn't control the bucking of his hips.

Too soon, the heat coiled in his groin, the beginning of the end. "Aubrey," he whispered, urgently tugging at her shoulders, not wanting to come, not yet.

But she didn't relent. When he realized her fingers were rubbing her own clit as she rode him, he shot off like a bottle rocket.

When he could see again, and breathe, she was lying next to him, her head on his chest, her leg over his. "I'm sorry," he said, his voice wrecked.

"For what?"

"I don't even know if you came."

She squeezed his side, kissed him right where she lay. "I'm fine. I'm great. Just sad that I have to go back to work."

"Seriously? Wait. What am I saying? Of course you do." Nothing to argue with there, even though it felt all wrong. "Have time for a quick backrub?" he offered. "Scalp massage?"

Her smile warmed him. "You sure?"

"I've been told I'm pretty good. So what's it going to be?"

She pulled the comforter over both of them, and stretched out on her stomach, facing away from him. "Both?" she asked, her voice muffled.

"For as long as you like."

They only exchanged a few words as he worked on her. Unfortunately, the quiet was too tempting and he started thinking again. Questioning. What she was hoping for after the window business was finished? What were tonight's nerves about? Was it all because of her deadline?

He was glad his tenure as Aubrey's muse would end soon, but then what? It was too soon to think about forever. They'd been on a roller coaster since the night they'd met. What would it be like when the ride ended?

All he knew for certain was that he wanted to find out.

CHAPTER TEN

AUBREY WAS AT Le Muse by seven the next morning, panicked beyond belief. More sure than ever that her life was completely out of control. Every time she thought about tonight's meeting with Yvonne, she went into a manic flurry of new ideas, all of which were horrible. To escape the maelstrom she'd think about Liam, and that would send her into a tailspin of sadness.

She wanted so much more from him than she could have. It was all her own doing. She understood now that she'd subconsciously set herself up to fail. The whole night at her apartment had been a farce, and she'd been the central boob in charge. As for her so-called friends, they hadn't said a word. But then they didn't get it, not really. They hadn't seen him talk about his future. His plans. They didn't know she was only a scenic byway on the road to his lifelong dreams.

That he happened to be an amazing man was some kind of perverse luck. He should have been a total prick. Gorgeous, only just bearable and great in bed. But no. Liam had to be ridiculously close to perfect.

And now it officially, unequivocally was more

than just sex. She wanted *him*. All of him. More than any other man she'd ever been with. She knew without a doubt that as a couple they would be doomed. And yet when she saw him, when she thought of him, she couldn't help dreaming of an impossible future. It was nothing short of torture.

Nothing would make the breakup easier. But there was a chance that breaking up now would help her focus on the window.

Although she hardly ever cried, she'd been weeping on and off since the moment Liam left her last night. She hadn't gone to work. She'd barely slept, either. This morning had been spent chugging down her weight in espressos and staring at a blank page in her sketchbook.

With shaking fingers, she pulled out her cell phone. She thought of sending Liam a text, but that would make her the worst person in the history of the world.

She hit speed dial four, holding her breath as tears streaked down her cheeks. She had no idea what to say to him. What if he was in the middle of a case or— It went to voice mail. Just listening to his message made her want to sob. After the beep, she sniffed a couple of times before she could say anything. "I'm sorry. I'm so sorry. You've been the best. Best muse, best friend, best lover, best...everything, but I can't do you and the window at the same time. I'm sorry." She sniffed again, balling up a wad of tissues to wipe at her nose.

"It's sooner than we planned, and I'm sorry for that, but I can't. There's no time, and I'm probably going to be fired, anyway, because I can't do this. I can't. I thought that maybe, at the last minute, when I still had time, I would be hit by a brilliant idea, but I haven't. I keep thinking about you. About us. And that's just ridiculous. I hope you don't hate me forever. Because I'll never forget you. Never. I hope all your dreams come true and you find someone perfect. I'm sorry."

She disconnected and lowered the cell to her desk. The sketch pad was ruined, just like her career. Which didn't bother her half as much as the fact that she wouldn't get to see Liam tonight. Or any night.

Her whole body twisted in a spasm of pain and she sobbed from so deep inside it felt as if her soul had shattered.

By the time her tears had dried up, she could barely see past her swollen eyelids. She'd gone through an entire box of tissues. She could forget about breathing through her nose. She could barely breathe at all.

But the clock kept on ticking, and she had one last chance to turn this nightmare into something that wouldn't humiliate Yvonne. She forced herself to throw all the garbage away, including her self-pity. She'd wept her last tear over the end of the muse experiment and now it was time to focus. To clear her mind and her heart and leave room for the magic to happen. She'd done it before. Come up with something fabulous at the last minute. She could do it again.

The desk and drawing purge turned out to be useful. She couldn't pretend she didn't ache, but putting things in order helped her calm down. The most important things now were her master lists. The first was an inventory of all the supplies she had. Both in the store and in storage.

Over the weeks of sketching she'd figured out the basics of what she'd need, no matter which idea she settled on. Artificial snow was number one, and she'd ordered plenty. The snow machine was also in storage, at the ready. Also, a sheet of Plexiglass large enough to contain the snow, but not have the flakes all over the set pieces and mannequins. Speaking of which, she had mannequins up the wazoo—males, females, two Santas and a couple of fake pets. Before the store had even opened Yvonne had stocked enough wigs to cover the heads of everyone in Manhattan.

The list of props was pretty decent, too, as long as she wanted the most boring Christmas tableau ever. Comfy chairs, a fake fireplace, a naked Christmas tree, two decorated trees, several tiny trees and a metric ton of wrapped empty boxes.

The second set of lists itemized all wardrobe selections. Naughty or nice, she had a large assortment of fantastic new items straight off the runways that she could play with through New Year's Eve.

But what did it matter when she didn't have a theme?

Or Liam.

No, no, no. She couldn't think about him. Or the message she'd left. Or…

God.

She needed coffee. And not that crap from the

break room. A trip to the coffee shop meant she would have to make herself look less like a before photo for a facelift. Screw it. She shoved on a pair of sunglasses. Just before she reached the back exit her cell rang. She dropped her purse in her haste to see if it was… "Hey, Caro."

"Don't tell me you have a cold."

"Just stuffed up."

"We're in line at the falafel place. You want anything?"

"No! I mean, don't come by. I'm really, really busy." Aubrey had meant to sound anything but hysterical. Ha.

"What's wrong?"

"Nothing. I'm meeting with Yvonne tonight."

"Oh, crap. Well, you've got to eat, right?"

"I'm not hungry. I have to work, that's all."

Caro didn't say anything for too long. "Aubrey, tell me what's wrong."

"Aside from the fact that I'll never see Liam again and that I'm going to be fired, and you'll have to find a new roommate because I'll never work in New York again, I'm fine. I'm just peachy."

"Stay put. We'll be there in ten."

Before Aubrey could say anything, the call disconnected. She hit speed dial three, determined to convince her friends to leave her alone, but when Caro answered, she only managed to say, "Bring me a big coffee please?"

Instead of heading out to the street, Aubrey got two new boxes of tissues from the restroom cabinet and holed up in her drawing room.

"I UNDERSTAND," Sanjula said, folding up her napkin after Aubrey had whined her way through the whole story, "that you're scared. And what you do when you're scared is run."

"It's not running if you've actually been fired."

"It is," Caro said, "if you're the one who's setting yourself up to be fired."

Aubrey couldn't stand looking at the stupid sketch of the scary Christmas idea another second. She got her thickest black marker and slashed an *X* over the whole damn thing. "I wouldn't cross the street for any of these," she said. "I'll have to move back to Utah. Get a job at the drugstore. Mortify my parents until they kick me out. Again."

"Shut up." Caro got off the folding chair and into Aubrey's face. "Stop it. Work with what you have. They're great ideas, and Yvonne's going to tell you what works and what doesn't. That's the easy part. What the hell were you thinking kicking Liam to the curb? Are you insane?"

"It was always a matter of time, Caro. You know that."

"No, I don't. You guys are fantastic together." She turned to Sanjula, still sitting on the edge of Aubrey's desk. "Tell her."

"I love you, Aubrey, you know I do, but you're a fool to let him go."

"Thanks. Both of you. As if it's my decision."

"Of course it's your decision." Caro rolled her eyes very expressively. "Unless you've suddenly de-cided to follow the runes or something."

"Yeah, because I'm exactly the woman he needs at his side when he runs for police commissioner."

"Why not you?"

Aubrey wanted to strangle both of them. "Are you guys purposely being dense? I never even got my degree. I'm a flake. You guys just said that. Not two seconds ago. You said I run when I'm afraid. That's not the kind of woman Liam deserves." All the air seemed to leave her body, as if she'd been popped like a balloon. "He's better than that."

"Don't you even," Caro said, taking her hand. "He's not better than you."

"Even if he weren't, I still couldn't see him anymore."

Sanjula hopped down, and grabbed Aubrey's other hand. "Why not?"

"I let him get to me. It's why I don't have the design yet. Why I'm in this mess. I got so caught up in him, I forgot to do my job. God, last night he kept looking at my college artwork…he thought my paintings were gallery worthy, and when I said I was already a sure thing, he got pissed."

"How awful," Sanjula said. "That bastard."

"Oh, shut up. You know what I mean."

Caro finally looked at her with some sympathy. "Well, then, you'd better get to work. Because once this stupid window is done, you're going to call him, and he'll come running."

Aubrey winced. "Don't say that. It's already so hard, I can't afford to set myself up like that."

"Fine. We'll talk about it another time. Now, can we do anything to help?"

She hugged each of them in turn, trying not to get tears and snot on their clothes. "No. I'm on my own."

"Don't be so sure." Sanjula hugged her back, hard. "We're with you. Yvonne's with you. There are a lot of people in your corner, and we all have faith that you'll knock this out of the park."

THE WHOLE RIDE over to Le Muse, Liam couldn't get over her voice mail. Voice mail. Who the fuck breaks up over voice mail? After all they'd been through?

Oh, he was pissed. Not just at that message, but at the fact that he'd been so shaken he'd left his meeting with the ADA.

Aubrey had sounded like hell, and utterly desperate, but lots of people were desperate around a big deadline, and Jesus, they didn't just cut out the people who cared about them.

Shit. He should never have left. It was irresponsible and he'd have to do some major damage control once he got back to the office. Just when he was really making headway with the crew, with the boss.

Damn it all to hell, what had Aubrey done to him?

Once inside the store, Liam almost barged into the back room, ready to have it out with her, but the closed door gave him a second to think. It wouldn't do either of them any good for him to be angry. She was bone-deep scared; he needed to remember that. She probably didn't even mean what she'd said. After the window went up, they'd just go back to normal. But for now, she needed him calm, so he would help her calm down.

Aubrey didn't jump when he walked in. Didn't

even look up. Of course, employees walked in and out of there all day. Which would be very inconvenient now, so he locked up. If anyone knocked, he'd deal with it.

God, she was tense. And just as miserable as she'd sounded. The steel of her spine had morphed into something brittle, bringing her shoulders forward, her dark curls tumbling over her cheeks. The grip on her pencil would break it soon. She'd slapped a few of her sketches on the whiteboard, but two of them had angry black X's from corner to corner.

"Aubrey?"

Her head jerked up, her eyes swollen and red, but wide and wild. "What are you doing here?"

"I got your message."

"And you didn't understand the part where I said I couldn't see you again?"

"I understood the words. But the explanation sucked."

She pressed her lips together before she looked down, away. "Please don't, Liam. I said I was sorry, but I can't deal with this. Not today."

"I know. You have that meeting with Yvonne." He walked to her desk. "That's also why I'm here."

"To dig my grave deeper? Gee, thanks."

"You know that's not true."

"Please, Liam. I meant what I said. I can't be with you."

Her fear was palpable, her face pale, her hands shaking. She was twisted into knots, but that wasn't news—he'd heard it in her voice mail. Looking at the misery in her swollen eyes, he wasn't feeling so hot himself. This had to be about the window, right?

She needed perspective. That's all. "I think you're expecting so much from yourself that your view of what you've already done is skewed." He looked at the whiteboard. "That one, the sleepover. That's great. It's creative and different. I've never seen the theme done that way before. And Yvonne's already said she liked it."

She stared at him for a long moment, then sniffed before she said, "I know you think I'm terrific, and that's really sweet, but I'm sorry, you're not exactly an expert. Or a blogger, or a journalist. I've got to wow this city, Liam. In pictures, on YouTube, on television and all over the internet. Nothing about a sleepover is in any way going to impress the media."

"If you'd drawn teenagers and sleeping bags, I'd agree, but that's a Manhattan penthouse, and what they're wearing is as close to X-rated as you can get on a public street. It's sophisticated and witty. Like a Norman Rockwell painting after a few martinis."

She smiled. Shook her head.

Her condescension would have pissed him off any other time. "Okay, then tell me this. Why did you keep that drawing when you've thrown out so many others?"

"I don't know. I was drunk? Distracted?"

He went around the desk and crouched next to her. It hurt when she scooted her chair back, frustrated the hell out of him, too, but he stopped her. "I think you're forgetting something pretty important."

"What would that be, Yoda?"

"Yvonne hired you because she knew you were amazing. She didn't hire you as an apprentice, or expect you to work your way up to the front window. She saw you, and knew you were the right person for the job. You've thrown away more great ideas than most of the window dressers in this town will ever come up with. Of course it's scary, but those ideas on that board? Yvonne would be thrilled with any one of them."

Aubrey sighed as she looked at him. Long enough for him to see her poor red eyes well with tears, and even though she tried hard to blink them away, a few fell. He wanted to kiss her so badly. Hold her tight, help her believe in her own talent.

"Thank you," she said, her voice as tight as a corset. "I love that you'd come here and say that. I wish it were true, but art isn't like that. Every piece stands on its own."

"No, I get that. And you're right. But remember, I was a beat cop. I walked through half a dozen pairs of shoes on the streets of Manhattan. Each one of those ideas on the board is better than anything I've seen. Even the ones you've crossed out."

He leaned in and kissed her quivering lips. "Look, we both know I'm not really a muse. The thing is, you never needed one. You've already got all the discipline, the bravery and the talent. But I don't regret a minute of pretending I made a difference."

Knees popping as he got to his feet, he tried to come up with another reason to stay, but that was just selfishness. Sure, she needed some distance until this was over, but she'd realize the time limit was just part of the game. "Once we get through this next week, things'll go back to normal. I promise. You'll feel better about everything. About us."

The change that came over her made his gut tighten and his jaw tense. The panic was gone, replaced with a sadness that was painful to look at. "Liam. I know you don't want to hear this but please listen to me. This was never meant to be anything more. I should have ended it earlier, but it was always going to end. I don't want things to go back to normal between us. I'm sorry."

All the air left the room. The dagger in his chest made it impossible to breathe. She meant it. Every broken word on that voice mail. She didn't want him. Want them. The end.

"I'll miss you," he said. "A lot."

She sniffed, nodded, couldn't meet his gaze. And she didn't ask him to stay.

CHAPTER ELEVEN

AUBREY HAD CHOSEN the thick red marker because it was the only color that felt right. Black made her spiral into darkness, purple made her throat tight, and forget about blue. Red was the answer.

Now if she only knew the right question.

So she let her arm and her hand and her fingers take over, let them make scrawls and circles and wavy lines on the biggest of her sketch pads. Unfettered, not thinking at all, just doing.

Only that wasn't true. She was thinking. Not about the window, though. Not about anything useful.

Caro telling her she'd set herself up for failure. Sanjula calling her out for running. Liam.

Her hand stopped.

Caro's voice in her head. "Work with what you have."

The marker moved, jagged shapes, no symmetry, ugly, harsh.

Caro's disappointment. In her eyes and the crease in her forehead, in the tilt of her blond fauxhawk.

Sanjula's pronouncement. "You're a moron."

It was true, but not for the reasons they suspected. Not for facing the truth. Aubrey's hand shook, but she kept on going as she thought about exactly how stupid she'd been for letting him get to her. Letting herself fall for him. She'd always known she'd end up with someone in the arts. A musician, a sculptor. God help her, an actor. Someone temperamental and selfish and as full of himself as she was. It would be stormy and dramatic and eventually tragic. Worse, it would whither into nothing when they both realized their talent was marginal, their achievements minor.

Shortly before Aubrey had left home, she'd confided in her mother that very picture of her future. It wasn't often that they shared such things. Mostly, they argued or her mother despaired. Aubrey had waited for a disagreement, a denial. Instead, her mother had looked at her with deep sadness in her dark eyes.

The marker had stopped again. She let it drop to the paper, saw the horrible red stains on her arm. Like a rash.

She tore the page off the pad and wadded the thing up until it was a tightly packed ball, all the while staring at the whiteboard.

And it hit her. The sleepover. The cocktail party. Neither one worked as singular ideas, but together? She tossed the wad behind her on the pile of other wads, and began again. This time with pencils. With purpose. It wasn't caffeine that got her blood pumping this time. It was adrenaline and magic.

LIAM SHOULD HAVE gone back to work, but he couldn't seem to get up off the couch. He hadn't even taken off his coat. A glance at his watch made him wince.

For two hours he'd been staring at that preposterous Christmas tree on the table.

Who makes a Christmas tree out of cupcake liners? He hadn't even realized those things had a proper name. They'd always just been what wrapped cupcakes and muffins. Since Aubrey had decorated his apartment, he'd learned they came in an assortment of colors and sizes. He'd ended up buying a blueberry muffin at the coffee place just because he'd been staring at it for an uncomfortably long time.

He also hadn't known that companies made novelty crime scene tape.

It had made him smile every time he looked at it. Not this time, though. Now he felt like throwing the stupid thing in the garbage, but he couldn't rally the energy to go out to the Dumpster.

Maybe as the new reality sunk in, he'd feel differently. All he wanted to do was have a drink. The Scotch in his cupboard was just a few feet away. Maybe that was good. Getting drunk wasn't his thing. He'd tried it a couple of times in college, and it hadn't ended well. In truth, the part where it was pleasant and numbing and terrific was really short, and the part where he felt like crap lasted a really long time. And hell, he already had the feeling-like-crap phase down pat.

He'd expected her to say something before he left. To stop him. It had been tempting to try to persuade her with a dose of logic and some sweet talk, but then he'd finally gotten it, finally understood that her meltdown wasn't just about her deadline. Her panic was about them. He knew there was nothing more he could've said or done.

But damn it, he liked her. Too much, obviously. When had lots and lots of sex turned into this? An incredibly complicated mess. Next to the tree sat a pair of tickets and a confirmation. The surprise weekend trip to Oyster Bay was going to be her Christmas present. He'd been trying to decide if he should have it gift-wrapped. When had he begun to think of them as a real couple?

Hell, he'd told his folks about her. His mother had been concerned that she was a window dresser. Asked him if that was a stable career. He'd stood up for Aubrey. Tried to explain that she was an artist. A real talent. There was no telling where she'd go from there.

"Fuck," he said loudly. He pushed himself off the couch and went to get the Scotch. He wished he could call a friend. Go to a bar, get cajoled into a better mood. But his whole life had been so wrapped up in his work, then in defending himself against that meme, against being typecast and dismissed. He'd skipped the part where he was supposed to make friends.

He could call Alex, his college roommate, but they hadn't spoken in too long. There was always his brother. Truth was, he didn't much care for Ted. He could go to the White House, see if anyone was there. Maybe Tony Ricci would be itching for a fight. That had some promise.

Or the Session House. Where he'd met Aubrey that first night: God, she'd been something. So bright and vibrant she'd seemed to dim the lights. Made everyone else in the bar feel like extras, props. She'd just been totally herself. Undiluted Aubrey, and it had made him drunk with want. He'd really liked that fedora. She'd worn it for him a few nights later, unencumbered by any other clothing so he could get the full effect.

Every time he'd been with her it had been like Christmas. He'd unwrap her like a present, peel away the dress or the skirt or the pants until it was Aubrey neat, like a perfect Scotch straight up.

Goddamn it, he knew what she tasted like. Smelled like. Blindfolded, he would find her in a crowd, just with his nose.

The thought of trying to forget made him crazy.

He poured himself a drink, shot it back with a jerk of his head. It burned like a slow match in the back of his throat and shook him out of his pathetic self-pity.

Fuck it, fuck this. Something had been bothering him since she'd told him goodbye. Things weren't adding up, and the hell if he wasn't going to get to the truth. He'd always had to fight for what really mattered. Why should this be any different?

He needed to be patient, though. Wait until the window debuted. Once the stress of her deadline ended, he'd get her to focus on them. He wasn't asking for forever. If she was commitment-phobic, fine. He wasn't looking to book a church. That didn't mean they couldn't stay the course, see how things shook out. For about the tenth time he listened to her voice mail, and there it was. Evidence.

She'd admitted it herself. She couldn't stop thinking about him. About them. She might be scared, but she wasn't ready to let go yet. For Chrissakes, she'd taken him home to meet her friends only yesterday. Maybe letting him get that close had set her off. It didn't matter. He wasn't giving up. It would be a bitch waiting for the damn window launch to be over with, but it would be worth it. She was worth it.

He turned to the Christmas tree on his coffee table and felt better than he had all afternoon.

"OH, AUBREY, THAT'S IT!" Yvonne turned from the sketches on the whiteboard. Her private smile, the one that was asymmetrical and a little goofy, was on full display. "The press will eat it up."

"If it all comes together. Do you think we can get enough people to participate?"

Her boss waved her concern away. "Of course. In fact, we'll have two complete showings. The first at ten, then again just before midnight. We'll have everyone change clothes at least once. That will allow us to show off more of our exclusive lingerie and provide more photo and video opportunities. But there's a lot to be done in a very short time."

Didn't Aubrey know it. "I'll need sizes, so as soon as we have people on board—"

"Yes, yes, I'll get them to you immediately. And I'll take care of the press release. I have an interview with *Time Out* tomorrow about the fundraiser, which will tie in beautifully. You just take care of the physical aspects, yes?"

"I've got it covered."

Yvonne perched lightly on Aubrey's desk. "Now,

before we move on, would you like to tell me what's wrong?"

"Pardon?"

"Makeup and eyedrops only cover so much, *ma bichette*."

Aubrey tried to make a joke but Yvonne had been so trusting throughout this process, it didn't seem fair. "I let myself get too close to someone, when I knew all along it wasn't going to go anywhere. I'm just sorry I didn't end it sooner. I might have had this idea days ago."

"I don't believe creativity works like that. Especially when there's so much pressure."

Aubrey's expression must have given away her surprise because Yvonne chuckled as she shook her head.

"I was aware of the difficulties. If you hadn't come up with this concept by tonight, I was going to insist we run with the slumber party. But this is so much better. It will highlight much more than just our inventory. The rest of New York will be sleeping, and Le Muse will be the talk of the town. It's altogether genius."

Aubrey winced at the word, never wanting to hear it again. She was lucky, that was all. "If it all works, that is."

"We'll make it work. You'll make it work. The difficult part is already done. The rest is details and timing."

"I'm sorry I made you worry."

"I hope the next time will go more smoothly."

"Next time?"

"Yes, next time. Tell me, this man. He hurt you?"

"No. I hurt him. But it was inevitable. He's a policeman. A detective with big career plans."

"And…?"

"And I think I don't want to talk about this anymore," Aubrey murmured, feeling a new threat of tears.

Yvonne smiled and rose. "Well, I have many phone calls to make. Most likely, you won't have time to think about anything else until the big event, yes?"

"Right." Aubrey walked her to the stockroom door. "Thank you so much. For believing in me."

"You have a gift. I saw that from the beginning. Now, go. Work."

Aubrey should have been over the moon. Somehow, she'd done it again. At least, on paper. Yvonne's enthusiasm was like receiving a Get Out of Hell Free card, only this time, she'd brought a piece of hell with her.

Her purse was in the bottom drawer of her desk, and she reached inside the front inside flap. How many times had she looked at Liam's trading card? She'd memorized all his answers. How he'd wanted to date, not marry. He'd taken her to the Parlor Steakhouse, although thankfully, the Mets hadn't been brought into the picture. But his Bottom Line had: "To find a woman who shares my goals and values."

Turning the card over, it seemed hard to believe that as she'd gotten to know him, he'd become better looking. She should have realized much sooner that she was in trouble. Probably should have called the deal off after the first night.

But that was her all over. Diving straight into the deep end without regard for what lay down below. She'd cajoled her way into Pratt to get her degree, only to bolt when it came time to prove herself. Every time she got involved with a man her first order of business was to figure out an escape plan.

The window designs had, up until now, felt more like a game than a job. Despite so much riding on the outcome.

And then there was Liam, who'd had a whole long-term life plan worked out before he got into college. He'd hit every goal, despite the jealousy of his fellow officers. She doubted he'd ever had a plan B, whereas she always kept plans B through Z in the back of her mind.

It wasn't even their different goals that made her the wrong woman for Liam. It was his values. The way he regarded himself as capable, as willing to do whatever it took. He wanted to make a difference in the world, make things better.

She wanted the employee discount on underpants.

Instead of throwing the card away, she found an envelope and decided to mail it back to him. The note was brief and achingly honest: "You were the best muse. The best man. Thank you for everything."

Three tears fell on the note, right on the word *muse*. She'd been so thrilled when fate had tossed him into her arms. She should have known it would end in epic sorrow.

CHAPTER TWELVE

THE COMMUNITY ROOM at the precinct had been taken over by the holiday party, crowded now with detectives, support personnel, spouses and children. Oliver Gardiner from narcotics was playing Santa and handing out gifts to the young ones.

Liam stared at the festive crowd and wondered why he'd bothered to come. He missed Aubrey, even though he knew she could never have been there with him tonight. With only a few hours until show time, he imagined she was running around frantically taking care of last-minute details.

"So, where's your girl?" Detective Lieutenant Posner asked.

"Working." It wasn't a lie, and he sure wasn't going to discuss his love life with his fellow detectives, especially not his boss. At least he could think about Aubrey calmly now that he had a plan.

Ernie Rogers nearly shoved Liam out of his way while trying to grab rugelach off a platter. "How'd she get the short straw?"

"Tonight's a big deal for her. She works at Le Muse. It's a lingerie store on Broadway and they're having a big press event featuring Aubrey's window design."

"I heard something about that," Rogers said. "Isn't it part of some big fundraiser?"

Liam nodded. "Her boss is on the board of directors of a foundation that combats the international sex trade." Sadly, he hadn't learned this from Aubrey but from watching the news while sitting in a bar missing her.

"Yeah, I saw something about that, too," Posner said. "I've been past that store. The window with the flashing women, right?"

"That was Aubrey's design." Liam smiled, and he found it didn't even hurt. No reason not to brag. No matter what happened between them, he was proud of her.

He didn't know which idea she'd chosen, probably something he'd never seen, but he had no doubt it would be a knockout. He'd gone past the store a few times. Just to check on her progress. Two days ago a curtain had been lowered, hiding most of the window. In front of the curtain were three mannequins wearing sexy nightwear, writing their Christmas lists. Above them, in thought bubbles, were video loops from different lingerie shows. Famous models with their long legs and tilted backs strutting down catwalks, showing off the merchandise.

Rogers made a crack about Posner's husband buying her Christmas present at Le Muse, proving beyond a doubt that Rogers needed to cut back on the eggnog. They were interrupted by the desk sergeant and Liam drifted away, checking out the crowd and glancing at his watch. Tonight was okay as far as work parties went, actually better than he'd expected considering he'd only come for the distraction. No sense sitting around his apartment, staring at the clock while he waited for the magic hour. He might've been too tempted to jump the gun and ruin everything.

His plan to win her back wouldn't begin until tomorrow evening, after she'd had time to recuperate. But there was no way he wasn't going to witness her triumph. All he had to do was blend into the crowd, and she'd never know.

AUBREY WAS AFRAID she wouldn't last the night. While the gallons of coffee she'd been drinking were keeping her awake after twenty straight hours without sleep, the bathroom had become her second home. Not convenient when she didn't want to take her eyes off the crew.

At least the scaffolding was securely in place, the fake snow at the ready and all the mannequins made up, if not completely dressed. The set was almost perfect, although two key pieces were still in trucks somewhere in the city.

Her most immediate worry was a seemingly simple electrical problem. The union dudes were working on it, but the whole tableau would fall apart if the machines couldn't be plugged in. Thank God the store had been closed since ten last night, and wouldn't open until after the unveiling.

She stepped out of the storeroom to check the progress on the main floor. A sizable party tent had taken over the left side of the store, and late merchandise arrivals from several designers were still being set up on the right side racks. Even though there were only three mannequin displays on the floor they still could have used more sale space. The unlucky party planners would have to tear down the tent tonight so the employees could put the store back together for the massive sale in the morning. Talk about overtime.

Yvonne's assistant, the same woman who'd put together Yvonne's charity cocktail party, stuck to her like glue, her Bluetooth constantly flashing. Her mile-long checklist seemed like another appendage.

Everything had come down to details and man-power. In addition to the regular Le Muse employees, many extra hands had been hired, including Sanjula and Caro, who were grateful for the extra money.

The only key thing missing, aside from a working plug by the window, was Liam.

"You've got that look on your face again," Sanjula said, surprising Aubrey with a jolt.

"What look?"

"The 'I miss Liam' look."

"I'm too exhausted to miss anyone. What you're seeing is sleep deprivation and terror."

"Nope. I've seen those before. This one's different. You should call him. He was your muse, after all. He played a big part in this craziness."

"Yeah, the part where it almost fell apart."

"But it didn't." Sanjula's voice went up an octave. "In fact, look how much you've accomplished in just a single week. The last one took longer and wasn't this organized."

Aubrey sighed as she looked at the ordered chaos around her. Despite her heartache, this mad idea of hers was truly taking shape. "Yeah, it has been a hell of a week. But I've had help every step of the way. And a healthy dose of luck."

"No. Luck is that Liam still wants you, even after you broke his heart over the phone. This," she said as she waved her hand at the transformation of the store, "was your hard work and brilliance."

"Oh, God, Sanjula, I appreciate you so much, but I can't talk about it now. Okay? If you had any idea what's still left to be done..."

"Fine." Her friend sighed. "I'd offer to get you coffee, but I think you might end up with caffeine poisoning. How about some water?"

"Yes, because I need to pee more often."

"Oh, so you want to faint on camera?"

"Water," Aubrey said. "Yum."

The first of their very special guests caught Aubrey's attention. They were coming through the back entrance so as not to spoil anything. Private security had taken control of the alley, checking names. Yvonne was there to meet and greet and make sure everyone understood the instructions.

More celebrities followed close behind. As the tent grew more crowded, the clueless extra help began to realize what was happening. Their excitement became a living thing, a buzz that filled the room and sent adrenaline screaming through Aubrey's body. Screw the electricians, she could probably power the whole event by herself.

A fleeting thought of Liam anchored her to the spot, and for a moment, all she could think about was the fact that he'd probably received the trading card by now. She pulled her cell phone out of her pocket. No messages. Which was as it should be. Imagine how distracted she'd be if she thought there was still a glimmer of hope for them? Yep, this was better. Now, all she had to do was stop thinking about him.

THE NIGHT HAD flown by quickly. Not only had Liam felt at ease, he'd actually enjoyed himself. But now he was getting anxious. In twenty minutes it would be time to head over to Le Muse. He just wished he knew for certain how he was going to play it. A week ago the plan had been set in stone. He'd wait until tomorrow to approach Aubrey. Now…his patience was slipping. Of course he'd wait until after the window was unveiled, but after that…

"How you doing, Ridiculous?"

The slap of a big hand on his back made him spill some of his soda. It was just Aaron, who worked white-collar crimes. They'd gone to the academy together. "I'm good. You still working on that old jalopy of yours?"

Aaron's face lit up at the topic, and he started talking about some special carburetor. All Liam could think of was how different this conversation would have been before Aubrey. He'd have gotten pissed immediately, told Aaron to fuck off and generally ruined everyone's mood, especially his own.

The nickname had lost all its power. Okay, not all, but most of it. Liam had realized yesterday that his lack of reaction had helped diffuse things. He'd even managed to speak to Tony Ricci, although the man was still an asshole.

A couple of detectives from his shift wandered over, probably because they were talking about cars. Liam really was part of the group now, even though they'd probably never let go of that damn meme.

"Well, I'm out of here," he said as soon as there was a break in the conversation.

"So early?" Aaron said. "I heard the captain's stopping by."

"He'll have to try and get by without me." Liam headed for his coat, but halfway there, he stopped and turned to his friends. "I'm going to the lingerie store to check out Aubrey's window," he said. "Because the one thing she's missing is a ridiculously good-looking cop."

AT A QUARTER to ten, the police had been called out for crowd control. The gathering of press and the public had grown so large the security team Yvonne had hired was overwhelmed.

Aubrey thought she might be sick. It didn't help that she hadn't eaten since...she had no idea when she'd last eaten. Or when she hadn't had a racing heart and an incredibly deep desire to run as fast as she could in any direction.

Sanjula and Caro hovered, but it wasn't helping. The curtain would come down in minutes. At least the electricity had been fixed. And almost all of the guests had turned up, which was something of a miracle. It seemed as if everything was going according to plan, which, frankly, was the most terrifying part.

All she could think about were the online comments, the tweets, the dislikes. It didn't matter what the subject, the majority of online comments were horrible. Given the opportunity to be anonymous, people tended to unleash the kind of meanness they rarely displayed face-to-face. She always tried to skip the nasty comments, particularly after a review of something she loved.

But this was her work, and, by extension, herself, and she knew she'd end up reading them. God, knowing her, she'd probably end up doing a Google search. *Masochist.*

If Liam were there, she could lean on him, snuggle into his arms. And when it was over, he would have distracted her, thrown away the papers, disabled the internet connection.

But he wasn't there. The window was about to become a stage, and she would win or fail in the next three…two…one.

The curtain just inside the window collapsed as if the weight had been too much. On cue, she, along with several employees of the store, frantically pantomimed panicking at the sight of the press. They moved props into place as they set the scene of a party, a very sexy party with mannequins dressed in Le Muse exclusive lingerie and intimate wear. Corsets and bodysuits and tiny bikinis. The men in their well-padded boxer briefs and thongs. Cocktails in hand, every one of the dozen plastic people seemed to be in midsentence. The decor was that of a high-end penthouse, the Christmas tree modern and sleek, all deep red ornaments and silver garlands. Music spilled out onto the street, modern versions of traditional carols, and then…

Aubrey couldn't help looking up to where Freddy, who'd volunteered for the role of clumsy oaf, tripped on the scaffolding, sending a huge amount of fake snow falling and swirling in the small space in front of the Plexiglass, driven by several well-placed wind machines, until everything inside the window was obscured.

Then it got crazy.

Despite their best efforts, some snow got loose around the madly rushing crew. Every live person in the scene grabbed at least one mannequin and rushed off stage right. From the left, models—very, very famous models—rushed in, each wearing lingerie that matched a mannequin and scurrying to take their exact positions.

Aubrey stood on the far left, guiding the models, making sure no one tripped or spilled or did some other nightmarish thing. She knew she was visible to some of the crowd outside, and she didn't want to spoil the piece, but Karmen had stepped on her kimono, and Freja dropped her martini. Aubrey would never get out in time because they only had a limited amount of snow and it was starting to settle.

Just as she called out for a replacement drink, she heard his voice.

"Aubrey."

She turned, the drink and the window forgotten. Liam was right there, inside. Not even a foot away.

"Oh, I see," he said, as he checked out how they'd created the illusion that the snow was blowing over the entire stage. "I thought it had all gone wrong. I wanted to help."

She couldn't move, couldn't even blink.

"I wasn't going to let you see me," he said, looking contrite and achingly handsome. "I'm sorry." He shook his head. "I'll go."

"Wait. I'm—" She looked at the set, at the fantastic array of famous guests who'd volunteered their time. The blinding lights shone through the window, the noise of the crowd bled inside, louder than the piped-out music.

But she had to look at Liam. "You came."

"I couldn't stay away. Not tonight." He smiled in that way of his. "The window's amazing. I wish I could hear all about it. But I know you must be insanely busy."

"No," she said, wincing as the music changed to the cue song that would set the models in motion. "Don't go. Please."

As the fake snow finally settled and the lighting from above shifted to the set itself, the crowd was finally able to see what was happening on the stage. Aubrey had to see the reaction. Had to. It was only a few steps until she was at the front door, until she stood right next to Liam. She'd done it. It truly was an extravaganza, and the people outside were going nuts with their cameras and videos. She wasn't sure what made her happier, the applause and whistles from the crowd or the man at her side.

The hand on her shoulder made her jump, but it was only a surprise for a moment. "You did it," he said, his mouth so close to her ear his breath gave her the shivers. "You knocked it out of the park."

She turned to face him. Fool that she was, she hadn't realized how desperately important it was for him to be with her. Not that it solved everything. But for now, she could be happy. More than that. Triumphant.

His smile changed as their gazes held, and then he leaned down as her eyes fluttered shut. They both jumped when someone bumped Liam's back, and nearly sent them tumbling.

An over-the-shoulder apology from an electrician didn't help much. Liam winced and stepped back. Which was not okay at all. She held out her hand. "Come with me?"

Before either of them could change their minds,

she pulled him through the maze of shelves and into the stockroom. Once the door was closed and locked, she turned to face him. She had no idea what to say.

"I lied," he said. "I came here because I had to. Because I wanted to."

"Why?" Her throat felt thick and thinking was out of the question. "I was horrible to you. I broke up with you over voice mail."

He'd never let go of her hand, and now he took the other one, as well. "That first night, I thought I'd be meeting a con artist. I had no idea that you'd be a completely different kind of artist. That you'd fall into my lap the way my card fell into your hands. I couldn't believe my luck, and then..."

Aubrey sniffled and blinked and tried to figure out if she was hallucinating. Because that made so much more sense than the real Liam being with her while outside the press was going crazy over her window and inside she was a shivery bag of caffeine and yearning with tragically red eyes and a nose reminiscent of Rudolph. The way he looked at her? It was impossible. It must be a hallucination.

"...I started to get to know you."

She frowned. If she'd gone crazy, he'd be kissing her now.

"I don't want this to be over," he said. "I barely know you. We can't be done. We're not finished."

Ah. He was real. And still not seeing the big picture. "I love that you think so, Liam. It's so tempting to believe that everything will turn out perfectly, and we'll live happily ever after. But we won't. Seriously, we're not right for each other. If we continue to see each other, it'll be tons worse when you finally realize this has all just been a moment in time, a story you'll remember years from now about the insane window dresser who wanted a muse. Can you really see me on your arm when we go to some big political fundraiser?"

He didn't answer for about twenty of her panicked heartbeats. "I have no idea. But neither do you. That's years from now. What I do know is that since I met you, I'm better at my job. I've finally gotten rid of the giant chip on my shoulder, and relaxed. Because of you. And that's not the only way you've changed me."

She sniffed and had to slip her hand from his grasp to grab some tissues.

He stroked her hair as if it wasn't also a nightmare. "You've opened the door to a world I'd turned my back on," he said. "I've been so determined to be the best cop in the city that I'd forgotten what it was like to just live. It would be a damn shame to stop now. After all, the card did fall right into your hands."

"So now you believe in destiny?" she asked.

"Yeah. I do. You know why? You're exactly the woman I've always wanted to be with. I just didn't realize it until we met."

She swallowed over the lump in her throat. "I'll end up driving you crazy."

Liam laughed. "Too late. You already do." Then he kissed her. And kissed her. To hell with the window, *this* was the single best thing she'd ever done.

* * * * *

HER VALENTINE FANTASY
Nancy Warren

For Dani Collins,
who was there from the beginning.

CHAPTER ONE

SAM BENEDICT WAS a professional voyeur. All good waiters were, he thought, as he watched the mini-drama at table 12. A waiter had to gauge the mood of a table, to be unobtrusive and efficient, so he didn't get somebody pissing all over him for interrupting a conversation or pissing all over him for not showing up in time to take orders. Most customers expected waiters to read minds. Most good waiters did.

At least, that was Sam's opinion. And probably the reason he never minded grabbing a shift if a waiter flaked. As the owner of Benedict, the hottest restaurant in Seattle, getting out front gave him a chance to interact with the foodies and have-to-be-trendies who kept him in business in the notoriously tough restaurant trade.

But the woman at table 12 would have caught his attention anywhere. She was gorgeous, in a blue slip of a dress that showed off her curves, but not in a *hey, I'm hot, do me* sort of way. More like a hint of sexiness that kept men wondering. Her hair was neither blond nor brown. It was an intriguing mix of the two. Her eyes were a clear gray with hints of blue and green that reminded him of the Pacific Northwest skies.

What was she doing with that dick? That girl and her date went together like ice cream and cod liver oil.

He figured these two for a first date. Probably met online. Ever since Benedict got voted Best Place for a Romantic Date in *Seattle Magazine* there had been more of them than ever. He'd seen plenty of dot-com first dates be wildly successful. He'd seen plenty more die on the vine. This one was dead before it started. Every time he approached their table the conversation was more stilted than the last time. The dude was completely self-involved and about as interesting as belly-button lint.

While the woman— Normally, he barely noticed the actual guests. They were numbers: seat one, table 14. If he thought of them individually it was in relation to their food order. Seat one was the halibut, two was the garlic allergy, that kind of thing. But this woman had caught his attention from the second she'd walked in, all long legs and big eyes that glanced around her with keen interest. He'd felt a buzz of energy coming from her. He'd never believed in sexual magnetism—thought it was a stupid term for horniness—but this woman truly drew him to her and he couldn't resist any more than an iron filing could resist a super-magnet.

She'd started out lively and fun but had slowly given up as the bore kept talking over her.

He'd caught her eye a time or two and he'd resisted the urge to boot the loser out of there, sit down across from her and show her how a real date acted.

Except he wasn't her date. He was her waiter for the evening and apart from singeing his eyeballs every time he looked at her, which he couldn't help, he was the perfect waiter. Although he had to wonder.

Really? What were they thinking? Valentine's

Day was a week away. If he were ever asked his advice, based on his years as a professional voyeur, he'd say never try to start a relationship in early February. Too much pressure with the fourteenth looming like the Day of Doom.

The two seemed to be done with dinner, so he waited for the bore to finish another anecdote where he was the hero of his office, but before he could offer dessert the guy was pushing back his chair.

"Where's the bathroom?" he asked Sam, who pointed the way. Guy already had his cell phone out before he'd gone three steps.

Which left Beauty alone with no bore. He stepped up to the table. *How can you stand that douche?* is what he wanted to say. What actually came out of his mouth was, "How are you enjoying your evening?" As he spoke, he picked up the bottle of wine and topped off her glass.

"The food is excellent," she said leaving out any mention of her date. And who wouldn't? "What did the chef put in the sauce over those scallops?"

He shook his head. "If he told me, he'd have to kill me."

When she laughed he felt that energy again, drawing him in. "Well, please tell him how much I enjoyed them." She glanced around. "The decor is amazing, too. Contemporary, but not cold and hard like some restaurants are. You know, all concrete and steel and glass?"

He nodded. Recalling how he'd said practically that very same thing to his designer.

"This place feels warm and relaxed while still

modern." She looked around again with an almost professional eye. "And it's a good size for functions."

He wondered if she was a restaurant critic, but he knew all the local ones. She could be from out of town, but nah, critics ordered a bunch of stuff and always tasted everything their companion ordered. No way she was a critic.

He should move on but no one in his section seemed to need him. He said, "First time here?"

"Yes."

If he caught one of his staff getting too personal with a customer, he'd have some choice words to deliver. He couldn't stop himself asking, "First date?"

Her eyes widened. "Yes. How did you know?"

Everything from body language to her guy running off to the men's room with his cell phone in hand were pretty big clues. But he only said, "You get a feel for these things."

She surveyed the room. "You mean you can tell what's between people you've never even seen before from the way they behave in a restaurant?"

"Not always, but yeah, sometimes." He glanced around himself. "Those two? At the table by the window, on your left." He indicated his head so he wasn't pointing. Waited until she had them in her sights and nodded. "They just got engaged. Watch her. See how she keeps lifting her left hand? Looks like Tourette's but really she's watching the ring on her finger. See how shiny it is? Barely worn."

"Wow." She watched for a moment and grinned. "Not Tourette's exactly, although she's doing a lot with her left hand. And I don't think she's left-handed."

"You're catching on."

And while she was busy watching other customers, he had a chance to watch her. Her pretty face, those big eyes that were studying the other diners. She turned back.

"Okay, what's the story on the older couple beside the wall of water?"

He followed her gaze. Saw a miserable-looking pair who were barely speaking to each other. Their clothes were inexpensive and it seemed as though they'd be much happier dining at home or at a family restaurant. He watched the body language for a moment.

"Wedding anniversary. Probably twenty-fifth or thirtieth. My guess is that somebody gave them a gift certificate here as an anniversary present when they'd have preferred a new set of towels. They don't like fancy food, think fine dining is a waste of hard-earned money and, after all these years being married, don't have much left to say to each other."

"Depressing. But believable."

"I'm only telling you what I guess. I could be wrong. Maybe normally they're the happiest couple in town, but they just buried Grandma."

"Your first story seems more real." She looked around some more. "Okay, what about the four-some in the middle of the room. Older couple and a younger couple?"

He barely glanced at the table in question. "Easy. He's a rich business guy, very successful. He and the wife spend six weeks a year golfing in Palm Springs. That's their only daughter. The young guy is the boyfriend the parents don't think is good enough."

"Who are you, Sherlock Holmes?"

He grinned at her. "Nope. They're regulars."

She laughed, enjoying his teasing.

He said, "You're not the only one not having the greatest evening."

She ran a finger around the stem of her wine-glass, which he found ridiculously sexy. "I should have made it a coffee. Dinner's too much of a commitment for a first date."

"I agree. I always go with the coffee."

She looked up. "Oh, are you—" Then she stopped herself.

"Single?" He finished her question for her in the direction he hoped it had been headed. "Yeah. I am."

He wanted to say something more. Ask her out?

And then the douche returned. Since Sam was hanging around the table, he said, "Allow me to tempt you with Chef's special dessert tonight. He's calling it Valentine Fantasy. It's made with Valrhona chocolate and fresh cream and a hint of raspberry. He says it tastes like sex." Because he couldn't help himself—it was that iron filing thing again—he caught her eye when he said that and experienced a sudden, hot surge of lust.

She held his gaze and he instinctively knew she was feeling the sizzle, too. Her voice was low and sexy. "I've always thought that if sex had a flavor it would be chocolate."

And in that second a vision of her, naked and

wet while he teased her with chocolate, took him so strongly he stopped breathing.

He wasn't supposed to crush on the customers, he reminded himself as he took their orders, the Fantasy for her, and an overpriced crème brûlée that they kept on the menu for dickheads like her date.

OH, NO, SAM thought when he next swung out of the kitchen, the guy at table 12 was pulling out his smartphone again. Seriously?

Dude, no.

Not the fake text thing, he begged silently. Don't do this to that sweet, sexy woman. But sure enough, bad first-date guy made a pantomime of shock, then distress. Sam could see his lips moving, saying something like, "Emergency, gotta go." He practically leaped from his seat, putting his hand up to his ear, thumb and baby finger extended in an *I'll call you* gesture. And then he charged out of the restaurant like his ass was on fire.

Sam would have bet his life savings that bad first date had set up the fake emergency when he was in the john. Classy.

As much he was glad to see the back of the guy, Sam saw two problems with his fast exit. First, he'd left a gorgeous, hot chick sitting by herself in a busy restaurant on a Friday night before she'd got to dessert. Second, he'd ditched her with the bill.

Sam hoped he was as nice as the next guy, but he was running a business. He turned tail and grabbed a server's assistant. "Get the bill prepared for table 12 right away. But don't put the desserts on it." He finished delivering meals to table 3 and then grabbed the bill, already slipped into one of the black folders with the stylized B logo on the front and immediately walked to table 12.

"Will he be back?" he asked the lone woman at the table.

"God, I hope not." She acted as if her date running out on her hadn't bothered her at all, but he swore he could detect a hint of hurt in the depths of her clear gray eyes.

"Still want your dessert?"

She shook her head. Then she glanced at where her date had been sitting and Sam saw the moment she registered that he'd stiffed her for dinner. With a small sigh, she said, "I'll just take the bill."

He dropped the folder on the table, then, because it was his restaurant and what the hell, said, "We keep a car and driver. Some of our regulars like the service. He'd be happy to drive you home."

She smiled her gratitude and again he had that odd feeling, as though there was more between them than a few hot glances and a little chitchat while he'd waited her table. "Thanks. But I'm staying locally."

"No problem. Take your time." He wanted to touch her, maybe brush his fingers over her shoulder to let her know she was awesome and amazing and deserved better. In fact, he wanted a lot more. Toyed with the idea of asking if he could see her, then figured he'd come across as a bigger knob than the one who'd left five minutes ago.

He did the smart thing. He went back to the kitchen where the usual organized chaos prevailed.

When he returned, the woman at table 12 was gone. He picked up the folder and flipped it open, assuming there'd be cash inside.

There wasn't.

Nor was there a credit card.

In the space where a credit card should have been was a hotel room keycard.

She didn't seem like the dine-and-dash type. And, while she wouldn't be the first female customer who ever propositioned him, he doubted the room card was anything but the slipup of a distressed woman who got dumped on her first date. More likely, she'd meant to put a credit card down and, well, who knew what she'd been thinking?

All he knew was, he needed to get paid, and she needed to get into her hotel room.

He gazed toward the front door but she'd already left. He stood for a moment, thinking, then ran into the back and told Barney, the most efficient waiter he had, to take over his few remaining tables.

Eloise, one of the sous chefs, was adding the spun-sugar flourish onto the forgotten Valentine Fantasy. She drizzled the heart-shaped chocolate with raspberry reduction. On impulse, Sam said, "Box that up, will you? She's taking dessert to go."

Seconds later, he headed for the door out onto the street.

"Hey, Sam, you coming back?" Chef yelled.

He turned. Thought of that sweet sexy woman currently heading back to her hotel without a keycard or a date. He had no idea what was going to happen. Maybe nothing. Probably nothing.

But he recalled the instant connection they'd felt. Said, "If I'm not back, close up, will you?"

"Sure thing."

And he jogged out onto the street.

He knew from the keycard that table 12 was staying at a trendy boutique hotel in the next block and he headed in that direction. The evening was cold and he hadn't bothered to grab a coat, so he walked swiftly, the wet streets and dripping trees telling him that it had only recently stopped raining.

He saw a woman he thought was table 12, seat two head into the hotel and took off running. He pushed through the glass doors, jogged through the lobby and caught up with her as she pushed the elevator button.

"Hi," he said.

She glanced around. Took a second to place him and then said with surprise, "Hi."

He produced the folder and opened it to show her the keycard. "You gave me your keycard instead of your credit card."

A quick blush suffused her cheeks and her hand flew to her mouth. "Oh, my God. I'm so sorry. I just—I wasn't thinking. I'm so sorry. Oh, I already said that." She opened her small clutch as the elevator doors opened. Then she looked at him, embarrassment still warming her cheeks. "I've got cash upstairs. I hate to take you more out of your way, but I don't want to make the walk of shame back to the restaurant with my credit card. I was— No man's ever dumped me in the middle of a date before."

He liked her. There was honesty and humor in her gaze. "Sure," he said. "No problem." They stepped inside the elevator and the doors closed. They were the only two riding up. He could smell her light fragrance, feel the energy between them. He said, "Not that it's any of my business, but that guy was a total dick."

She snorted with sudden laughter. "I know! I had no idea he'd be so full of himself. But it's February and—"

"Valentine's Day is coming," he finished for her. "I know."

They rode up fourteen floors. She said, "I hope this hasn't inconvenienced you too much."

"Not really." He could see she felt bad enough. "I got somebody else to cover my tables."

The elevator stopped and the doors opened. She preceded him into the hall. He followed her to her room and then handed her the keycard.

"Thanks."

Then he produced the small, square bakery box.

"What's in there? Handcuffs so you can take me in?"

She gazed at him over the box and he felt again that strong, sizzling sense of connection. He wished she hadn't put the idea of handcuffs into his head. Now he pictured her cuffed to the bed while he pleasured her to the edge of madness.

Her lips tilted in a smile so sensual it melted him. He was almost overwhelmed by the urge to kiss her.

He stepped closer. "I've brought you your Valentine Fantasy."

CHAPTER TWO

JESSICA LAFAYETTE OPENED her door with the keycard the hot waiter handed her, his last words still echoing between them. Her Valentine Fantasy? Could this horrible night be about to turn around?

"Thanks," she said, holding the door open so he could enter. "I'll get your cash." Which left her with the dilemma of wanting to give him a very generous tip for causing him so much trouble and not wanting to embarrass either of them.

"Don't worry about it now," he said. "Enjoy your dessert." Which meant he was planning to stay for a while.

Perfect.

She realized she didn't even know his name. Benedict wasn't one of those *Hi, my name is Darrell and I'll be your server tonight* kind of places. It was much too upscale for that. Which meant she didn't know the name of the guy she was inviting into her hotel room.

Slut! a voice in her head screamed.

Hell, yeah! her inner rebel cried.

Because clearly, following the rules hadn't worked for her sex life. She'd been following rules so long she'd forgotten the thrill of bending them, even snapping a few now and then. She'd been serious, smart and hardworking all her life. She was the type of friend who never blabbed secrets or forgot birthdays. Which meant that she had a good degree, a great career, was beloved of her friends. But, while she'd been working her ass off in her job as an event planner and listening to her friends bitch about guys, she'd dated men who were too much like her. They put most of their energies into their careers, their sports and their buddies.

She'd ended up with a completely shitty love life.

Which is why, when another dateless New Year's Eve came around, and her BFF Morgan asked her about her New Year's resolution, she hastily revised her answer from the planned "increase ab workout to three times a week and lose an inch around my hips" to a slightly tipsy "have some seriously hot sex with a gorgeous guy."

"It's going to take you all year to get a decent shag?" Morgan demanded so loud everyone in the vicinity turned. Put vodka inside Morgan and the effect was the same as putting a megaphone in front of her mouth.

"No," she whispered back, hoping her friend would take the hint. "I'll do it by—" her mind searched for an obvious have-great-sex-by date "—by Valentine's Day."

"Way to put it out to the universe! Hot sex by V. Day. You go!" Morgan bellowed.

And, being the follow-the-rules-type of girl, once the hangover had passed, she signed up on two internet dating sites plus tried to spend fewer nights at the office and get out more socially. In the five weeks since she'd begun, her tally of great sex was exactly zero.

Tonight's date was pretty typical of her luck so far—a guy on the rise in banking. She'd realized within three minutes that the only way he'd get her naked was if he bored the pants off her.

The waiter, however, was a different story. Everything about him, from the dark brown of his eyes to the wave in his slightly too long hair, to the way he moved, with smooth confidence, got her girl parts humming.

There were moments, when he was describing the chef's special creations for the evening, that his deep, sexy voice might have been saying, "The first fresh asparagus of the season is lightly steamed and drizzled in basil-infused olive oil," but what she heard was, *I want to take you up against that wall and rub basil-infused olive oil over your body and then lick it all off.*

And right then she decided that her problem was that she kept dating workaholic bores. She should totally be dating waiters and ski instructors and golf pros, guys who worked to live rather than lived to work.

It was as if fate, the universe, her fairy godmother or some combination of the three, had offered her a guy who had so much sexual confidence that it was making her light-headed. And who obviously wasn't too concerned about work, since he'd blown off the rest of his night's work so easily.

Perfecter and perfecter.

"Would you like your Valentine Fantasy now?"

he asked in that low, sexy voice that made her inner thighs quiver.

She didn't even know his name.

Sex with a stranger. Was that her fantasy?

Maybe. She thought everything about this man and this night was a fantasy. And the thing with fantasies was, they only worked if you totally let yourself fall into them.

She nodded.

The door shut behind them with a click. He stepped closer, close enough that she could feel his heat, see that his eyelashes were thick and curled. He was tall, his shoulders broad, the black shirt and pants that she supposed were his uniform made him look like an outlaw.

He smelled like chocolate. She remembered that foolish remark she'd made about thinking if sex had a flavor it would be chocolate. She'd been half-joking at the time, but he really did smell like the best, darkest, richest, most decadent chocolate.

She opened her lips, moistened them with her tongue and watched him stare at her mouth as though mesmerized.

Then he flipped open the box and she realized it wasn't him who smelled like chocolate. It was the dessert. The glorious over-the-top, heart-shaped, raspberry-drizzled, sparkly fantasy of a dessert.

"That is probably the prettiest dessert I've ever seen."

"I'll tell our pastry chef," he said, sounding proud. She thought it was cool that a waiter took such pride in his place of work.

There was a tiny pause. She could grab a wad of cash and get rid of him, or she could work on that New Year's resolution with a gorgeous stranger.

"Would you like to share it with me?" she asked.

"I'd like to share a lot of things with you," he said, confirming her suspicion that he was as into her as she was into him. Excitement fluttered in her belly. She was so glad she'd packed a few condoms in her makeup bag just in case.

"Please, have a seat," she said, realizing he'd been on his feet for hours. She indicated the sofa that sat in front of the window.

The suite contained a convenience kitchen and she opened the fridge and removed the bottle of champagne the client had given her today as a small thank-you at the end of the trade show and conference she'd organized. Seemed like the perfect time to open the bubbly.

She grabbed a couple of wineglasses from the glass-fronted cabinet above the sink and a couple of forks from the small cutlery drawer. She passed him the bottle. "Would you?"

"Absolutely."

She scooted down beside him and he opened the bottle with the most professional of slight pops, no cork banging into the ceiling and champagne foaming on the carpet. He poured wine into two glasses and handed her one.

The wine was pale gold and bubbles chased each other in the depths. Raising his glass in a toast, he said, "To unexpected pleasures."

His words were casual enough that he could be

referring to the wine, but the way he looked at her suggested he was taking pleasure in being there. With her.

The word *pleasures* had her blood acting like champagne in her veins. She felt light, effervescent. They both sipped and then she reached for the dessert box.

There were four white plates in the cupboard but she was pretty sure she'd make a mess of that pretty dessert if she tried to divide it and put it on plates. She wasn't the handiest woman in the kitchen. Besides, there was something incredibly intimate about sharing. She left it in the box.

She put her fork into the soft chocolate, taking the very bottom tip of the heart. He watched as she tasted it. "Oh," she moaned as the flavors burst in her mouth, the smoothest, most sinful chocolate, the sweet tartness of raspberry and hints of almond and something else she couldn't name.

"Try it," she said, aware that he was watching her the way she'd been eyeing the chocolate creation.

"Okay," he said, and leaned forward. He lifted a hand and gently wiped a speck of chocolate from her lower lip. Just the graze of his finger pad on her sensitive skin made her shiver. Holding her gaze, he put his finger into his mouth and sucked off the chocolate.

A funny sound came out of her mouth, like a strangled moan and, correctly interpreting the sound to mean she wanted more, much, much more, he leaned right over the box and kissed her.

The feel of his mouth on hers was electric. His

lips were warm and firm and commanding in the way he simply took over her mouth.

Which was absolutely fine with her. Her lips opened and his tongue slipped in, tasting her, teasing her, overwhelming her with the flavors of chocolate, champagne and hot, sexy man. She pressed closer, wrapping her free hand around his neck so she could play in the unruly, thick hair that fascinated her.

They kissed for a long time, tongues tangling, breath mingling, hearts thumping. At least hers was. She felt excitement build inside her, strong and fast. And yet there was no hurry. She loved that he seemed content to kiss her until the end of time, not use a kiss as a quick signal that he was about to rip her clothes off and get right to the sex part as her last boyfriend had done.

He pulled back at last and she saw that his eyes had a stunned expression in them, which she was fairly certain would be matched in her own eyes.

"Wow," she said shakily. "You are a great kisser." Best kisser in the world, actually. Best kisser since the mouth had been invented.

His grin was intimate, secret. "The kiss tells everything, don't you think?"

She nodded even though she wasn't entirely sure what he was getting at.

He reached out and took the fork from her hand, pushed a generous bite of Fantasy onto it and raised the fork to her lips. Oh, God, he was feeding her, and making it seem like foreplay, which she supposed it was. As her mouth opened to accept the rich dessert, he said, "I think if the kiss strikes sparks, you know the sex will be amazing."

Again that sound came out of her throat, not a purr, not a growl, not a moan—well, maybe a moan—but it all lumped together in an incoherent cave-person sound. He must have correctly interpreted the sound as a "yes, please, I wantwantwant, needneedneed, some completely amazing sex."

And she wanted it, needed it, now.

Gently, she took the fork out of his hand and put the Fantasy-in-a-box on the table. Then she closed the distance between them. This time, she did the kissing. She brushed her lips gently over his, then pressed against him, taking the kiss deep, deeper.

At the same time, her hands were busy, exploring the contours of a seriously buff chest, abs that felt rock hard. He wrapped strong arms around her and began doing some exploring of his own. She could hear traffic sounds from way, way down below where, amazingly, the real world still carried on. But up here there was no sound but their breathing, growing more heated by the minute.

The next sound she heard was her zipper sliding stealthily down her back. How glad she was that she'd chosen to wear her sexiest lingerie tonight, hoping her date would rock her world. Wearing something delectable against her skin made her feel sexy.

The irony was not lost on her that she'd dressed for a man who'd blown her off on their first date and she was clearly about to sleep with this man who hadn't even asked her for a date.

She considered asking him his name, but one of

her dark, secret fantasies had always been to make love with a stranger. No one but her battery-powered rabbit knew how many times she'd fantasized about having sex with a man who showed up one day, dark and sexy and perhaps a little dangerous, who drenched her in passion, took her to places she'd never imagined possible. He wasn't part of her past, and there was no future beyond her orgasm—he was only here in this present moment to give her pleasure.

In her wildest dreams she'd never imagined living out her fantasy.

It seemed she was about to do exactly that.

She did know a bit about who he was, of course. He was an excellent waiter at one of the top restaurants in Seattle. Sure, he could still turn out to moonlight as a serial killer, but all her instincts about people—and they were pretty good—told her she could trust him.

She leaned forward so the blue fabric slipped off her shoulders and slid to her waist.

The sound he made was satisfyingly incoherent. He reached out and traced the outline of her breasts through the ecru lace of her bra. Her nipples ached for his touch and she could feel them acting as pushy as they knew how, thrusting forward, begging for attention.

But he didn't rush there. Not yet. He continued his slow exploration of her body while she began struggling with the buttons of his black dress shirt, fumbling in her need to see him, touch him, taste him.

When at last she had his shirt open she understood her own haste. The man was gorgeous. Tanned

skin that suggested he loved the outdoors, muscles
that confirmed he was athletic. He helped her pull
the shirt all the way off and she wondered if carrying heavy trays of food and drink had built up his
arms like that. She suspected other, more vigorous
pursuits.

Other than the perfect thatch of chest hair that
continued in a coy line to disappear into his pants,
he had no distinguishing marks. No scars, no tattoos, no piercings.

She placed her open mouth on the hot skin of his
chest and felt the strong pound of his heart against
her lips. While she was over there, she tackled his
belt buckle. He kicked off his shoes and dealt with
his socks while she worked his zipper carefully over
an impressive package.

He cupped his hands over hers for a moment and
held her in place for a moment. His dark eyes held
her gaze. "Are you sure about this?"

She squeezed gently. "I've never been so sure
about anything," she whispered.

CHAPTER THREE

SAM DIDN'T DO casual sex anymore. He couldn't remember the last time he'd had a hookup. But he hadn't had a girlfriend in a while, either. He and Chantale, the temperamental chef he'd worked with at his last restaurant, before he went out on his own, had ended when she threw a chef's knife at him. She claimed she'd aimed to sink her deboning knife into the side of beef hanging in the walk-in fridge, but the homicidal look in her eye had suggested to him that backing slowly out of that relationship might be a healthy choice.

Luckily, she'd soon fallen for a baker at Pike Place Market and the two were now settled happily, and distantly, in her native Toulouse.

As his hands touched silky warm skin and he heard the sighs of an aroused woman, he realized he hadn't had sex in almost three months. He'd been crazy busy with the restaurant, and to clear his head and stay in shape, he liked backcountry skiing in the winter and biking the rest of the year. Which hadn't left him a lot of time for women.

Maybe it was a buildup of being horny, but he never remembered wanting a woman as much as he wanted this one. She was funny and serious at the same time, sweet and sexy in one package. Gorgeous and a little insecure, an absolutely packed pantry of opposites.

And no one knew better than a restaurateur how amazing a dish turned out when filled with complementary opposites. So, he let this sweet and spicy woman take her bold and timid hold of him. She finished with the zipper, reached in and gripped him.

They both gasped. If she'd been only bold, he might have been turned off. No man liked having his meat handled the way a butcher handled sausage. And if she'd been too timid he'd have felt that maybe she was too far out of her comfort zone and he'd feel bad, maybe slow things down. But she was both bold and timid, which was so arousing that he couldn't have stopped. Not on his own. If she pulled her hand out of his pants and said she'd changed her mind, then okay. No harm, no foul.

But if she wanted to keep exploring, to slide her sweet, sexy hand up and down like that, he wasn't the man to stop her.

Except that if he didn't, this was all going to be over way too fast.

So he took her wrist in a gentle grip, pulled her slowly away and kissed her palm. When she looked at him in inquiry he had to be honest. "You're doing me in," he whispered. "I want to last a long time for you."

Bold and timid danced back and forth in her gaze and finally bold won. She said, "Who says there's only going to be one time?"

He grinned at her. "Oh, you are my kind of woman."

Then he looked at her fully. "You know what the problem with us is?"

"There's a problem? Already?" She looked as though she didn't know whether to laugh or panic.

"Oh, yeah. A big problem." He shook his head. "There are way too many clothes between us."

She nodded as though giving this problem deep consideration. "You're right. There are. What do you suggest we do about it?"

He hiked his hand slowly up the skirt of her blue dress, bunching the fabric with him as he went. He felt her skin tremble beneath his palm. The skin grew warmer as he traveled slowly north. "I think we should take some of these things off."

"That's a very sensible idea."

As strange as it was, he wanted to see her, and he also wanted to drag out the waiting, tease each other a little more. She put a foot up on his lap and ran her foot slowly up and down his thigh, moving a little closer to his cock every time. He felt as if he was going to explode right there.

He reached over, took a sip of champagne. Offered her his glass and she sipped, watching him over the rim of the glass with big, sexy eyes so she made it part of their foreplay. So much for slowing things down.

He was going to have to move things along and take charge or she was going to have him embarrassing himself like a callow teenager.

He put the glass down with a decided click. Took her foot off his lap and placed it on the coffee table beside the wine.

This of course spread her legs.

Her breath caught but she didn't stop him, simply

opened herself to him in a way that made him feel her trust. Want to take such good care of her, give her all the pleasure that he suspected she hadn't always had in the past.

He had no idea where the thought had sprung from, but something about the way she looked at him made him wonder.

Oh, he was going to make it up to her for every bad lover she'd ever had, for every guy who'd ever taken his own pleasure selfishly and then rolled over and gone to sleep without satisfying her, for every guy who plunged into her sweet body without preparing her properly, for every guy who ever walked out on her on a date.

He was determined to wipe all those memories away and give her pleasure like she'd never known. At least for tonight.

He said, as politely as he knew how, "Could I ask you to lift up your hips for a second?" He could almost have added *ma'am,* so polite did he sound.

"Of course," she answered, just as polite, then he had the pleasure of watching her lift her hips, and he caught the dress and slipped it down, over her butt, down her thighs. She had to put her feet closer together for a second so he could finish getting the dress all the way off.

Then he tossed the blue fabric to one of the armchairs, where it pooled like a fabric lake.

He turned his attention back to long, golden thighs, slender feet still clad in strappy shoes that he very much liked. Her panties were barely there— some color that wasn't beige or cream but somewhere in the middle. The panties matched the bra. Three triangles that teased rather than hid her secrets.

Her body was a glory. Curvy, toned, soft where a woman should be soft, with enough muscle that he knew she wasn't a couch potato. Her breasts weren't particularly large, but her nipples were exquisite. Made even more so by the almost-covering of lacy fabric.

The panties teased him with a triangle of curls that he was pretty sure were already damp with arousal.

She hadn't moved so, while he had her in that position, he said, "I'm going to have to ask you to lift your hips again."

"You're very demanding," she said, not moving an inch.

He considered the statement. "I want to slip your panties off, but if you prefer, I could rip them off?"

Her intake of breath was quick and sharp. He saw the muscles of her belly clench. She gazed up under her lashes. "Are you strong enough?"

He held back his grin. She was so much fun. He'd had no idea. His hands had held his entire body weight when a line had broken while he was ice climbing on Mount Rainier. He'd scaled rock faces all over the world. He did not think a wisp of silk was going to be too much of a challenge. But he pretended to consider.

"I could try."

Again that quick in and out of breath. The ripple through the belly. He was rock hard and aching for her.

"Good. Because I really don't feel like lifting my hips again."

He moved closer, close enough that he could smell her arousal, see the pink of her nipples darkening. He said, "Then you'll have to open your legs again."

She made a sound he'd never heard before. Like a sigh, a cat's meow, and a giggle all mixed up in the blender. Naturally, he didn't make her do all the work herself. He circled his hand around her ankle and lifted her foot and put it back on the table beside the dark green champagne bottle.

He took the other foot and rested it on the back of the couch.

Then he settled himself between her thighs.

She was spread wide for him. "Are you comfortable?" he asked, as if he was a flight attendant and she was settling into her aisle seat.

"Uh-huh," she answered, so breathless he could barely hear her.

"Good. Now let's see about getting rid of these panties."

He wanted to rip them right off her but he didn't. He took one finger and slipped it beneath the fabric. As he'd guessed, she was already wet and ready. Good. Excellent. He let his finger slide, right over her, brushing her clit so she shifted and moaned.

Enough already. A man could only take so much.

He took his two hands, started at her knees, trailed them up her thighs to where they hit fabric. He grabbed the scrap of nothing that drifted over her hip in both hands, pulled once, heard a satisfying ripping sound. Her hips jerked.

He smiled.

Did the same thing on the other hip. And the panties were no more.

He peeled the layer of lace away and there she was before him. Open, hot, wet.

He dipped down. Tasted her. And knew no pastry chef on earth could ever make anything taste more like sex than her salt-honey.

"Oh," she cried. For a second he felt her thighs close against him, but he continued lapping, and her legs fell slack.

Her moans and cries were the sexiest sounds he'd ever heard. He continued pleasuring her with his mouth. She tried to stop him once, putting her hands on his head. "Wait, I want you in me," she cried.

He took her hands in a firm grip. Glanced up at her. "We're only starting," he promised, and went back to loving her with his mouth.

He could taste her arousal, knew she was close. When her hips began to dance, he followed her lead as she thrust mindlessly against him. He pushed a finger inside her and she cried out. He stayed with her until her cry exploded and he felt wetness flood his tongue.

CHAPTER FOUR

JESSICA FELT AS though she were a pleasure surfer riding wave after wave. But still she felt empty. She could barely form words but she tried. "Want. You. Inside."

Best she could do. She had condoms, too. Where the hell were they?

He was looking at her in near panic and she realized he hadn't brought protection, either. "Condoms, purse," she managed to say. It had to be there somewhere. But she sure as hell couldn't move.

"I'm on it," he said. As he stood she realized he was still wearing his pants, and the massive erection he was sporting was pretty much all that was holding them up.

He grabbed her purse, handed it to her, while he finished stripping off his clothes.

She fumbled, found a stack and shoved the whole thing toward him. She couldn't have ripped a perforated line. Not in a million years. She didn't think any of her muscles or tendons or nerves or brain cells were currently working on anything but staring at this beautiful naked man in front of her.

He was so gorgeous.

The tanned skin, the muscles, the long legs, the lean hips. The cock!

Her insides were still quivering post-orgasm. She felt both deeply satisfied and needy. As she watched him sheath himself with quick efficiency her inner trembling only increased. Then their eyes connected and she forgot to breathe.

He settled once more between her legs. He fitted himself to her and then, holding her hips in his hands and gazing deep into her eyes, he pushed himself gently inside her.

"Oh." The word spilled out of her. He was stretching her, filling her, thrilling her. Mindlessly, she lifted her hips to take in more of him, deeper. She gripped his hips and pulled. She felt so needy. She couldn't even explain it, only knew that on some basic level she had to have him.

He seemed to understand or maybe he shared her sense of desperation for he pushed all the way into her. Then, taking her face in his hands, he kissed her deeply.

She could taste herself, taste him, and suddenly the pair of them went crazy. He thrust hard and deep inside her and she wanted more. She grabbed his hips, pulling him into her even as she thrust up, pushing against him until she could feel herself building again.

His breathing was ragged, and she could feel heat building; when she ran her hands up his back, ridged with muscle, she felt his sweat.

Words clogged her throat, she could only feel. She reached up, kissed him, pushing her tongue into his mouth. They were out of control, both of them, moaning and thrusting and grabbing at each other. The tempo increased, and she was panting as though in the last leg of a marathon. Every cell in her body was buzzing with electricity.

And then, she felt the pressure rise, unbearably, so it had to blow.

Her moans turned to cries, and she exploded again.

He thrust once more, again, and she heard his groan, felt him shudder inside her. Then, all those rigid muscles seemed to relax at once and he slumped, moving her body so there was room for both of them on the couch. Side by side. Touching from chest to feet.

When they had their breath back, he rolled away and headed for the bathroom to deal with the condom. She padded naked to the kitchen and poured herself a glass of water.

As she moved, she felt the little post-climax pulses still. She didn't think she'd ever felt so relaxed.

She heard the toilet flush. He emerged, as naked as she, and for a moment they looked at each other.

"That was—" She tried to find words. Couldn't. So the "that was" echoed around them for a long moment.

Then he stepped closer. "Yeah," he said. "It was." And he kissed her.

She wouldn't have believed she could become aroused again. Not for a few days anyway but, amazingly, she felt excitement build again as he kissed her.

And she felt him grow hard as their bodies rubbed together.

He moved and she moved with him and, suddenly, they were at the edge of the king-size bed and he stopped kissing her long enough to flip back the duvet. Then she was falling back, back onto soft cotton sheets that felt cool against her overheated skin. He followed her and she felt the rough hairiness of his legs as they brushed against hers, the strength in the arms that held her.

She'd left the curtains open but all the lights off, so between the little bit of moonlight and the reflected light from all the high-rises it wasn't completely dark, and she could make out shapes and shades.

He was both a shape, long and solid beside her, and a shade, a sepia tone, maybe. She'd been as intimate as a woman can be with a man and she didn't even know his name.

Ha, she thought.

He'd brought the other condoms and placed them on the side table. She reached for one. Sheathed him with her two hands, making a caress of it, and then she straddled him.

He was her nameless boy toy, and she was going to play.

When they'd worn each other out and she was lying with her head on his damp chest, her hair a tangle and her body boneless with a combination of pleasure and exhaustion, she said, "Do you think we should introduce ourselves?"

The rumble of his chest suggested he was laughing silently. He put out a hand, the same hand that had recently thrust inside her most private places. "I'm Sam."

She put out her hand, the one that had held his cock and grasped his butt in passion, urging him to thrust harder. "Hi. I'm Jessica."

They shook hands. "Nice to meet you, Jessica."

"Nice to meet you, Sam."

A minute ticked by. "So, are you in Seattle on business?"

Of course, he thought she lived somewhere else. How was he to know she lived in Belltown? She'd stayed in the hotel to be right on-site for the trade show and convention and then she'd stayed on an extra night so that she wouldn't have to rush home and change and drive back into town for her date.

She could tell Sam that she lived locally, but she kind of liked this little fantasy she had going. Two nameless strangers, a hotel room, an affair that only lasts a night.

Maybe she'd feel differently in the morning, but right now she loved the way this made her feel. So she said, "Yes. I'm here for a conference." Which was perfectly true. "I'm an event planner."

He nodded. "Where's home?"

"I'm from Chicago." Again, perfectly true. She was from Chicago. She simply didn't live there anymore. She'd moved to Seattle a year ago to take her current job.

"Long way from here."

"It is. Though there are plenty of direct flights." Shut up! Why had she said anything so stupid?

He only nodded.

"How long have you been a waiter?" she asked, to get off the subject of her supposed home in Chicago and how easy it was to get there.

He shifted and looked at the ceiling as though his résumé might be pasted there. "On and off, since I was in college."

"On and off?"

He shrugged his impressive shoulders, which made her head ride up and down. "It's a job with a lot of flexibility. I've traveled, done some trekking, lived a few different places."

Oh, how she envied him in a strange way. She'd been so career focused the most she'd ever managed to travel at one time was two weeks. And, overachiever that she was, she'd crammed so many cities, from London to Moscow, into fourteen days that they all sort of ran together in her head like a European mash-up.

How many times had she thought how nice it would be to sit in that café where nobody famous ever wrote a novel or hatched a plot, or got murdered? Simply sat to enjoy a lingering cup of coffee and to watch the world go by?

"I envy you. Do you have any more big trips planned?"

He drew in a breath, then seemed to change his mind about what he was going to say. "I'm pretty settled into my routine right now," he said simply. She didn't think it was what he'd originally planned to say.

She placed her hand on his naked belly, knowing he'd be gone soon. This was weird and awkward having a get-to-know-you chitchat while they were naked. He'd heard her cries of ecstasy and didn't even know her last name.

Not that she particularly wanted to know his last name. But she wanted the intimacy of their talking to match the closeness of their physical interaction.

Here they were, lying in her bed in a tangle of sheets getting their breath back. What went on behind those dark eyes? What were the memories and experiences she'd never know, never share? She wanted to talk about something personal. She said, "Tell me a secret. Something you've never told anyone."

CHAPTER FIVE

SOMETHING HE'D NEVER told anyone? Sam understood, or thought he did, that she needed some kind of emotional intimacy to match the incredible power of what had just happened between them physically.

He wanted to oblige, but he didn't have a lot of secrets that weren't boring shit like PIN codes.

He hadn't told her that he owned Benedict. He'd let her go on thinking he was a waiter. Why had he done that? He had no idea. Except that he kind of liked the freedom. For some reason he couldn't fathom, people took him a lot more seriously now that he owned a restaurant than they had when he served food. And tonight he really didn't want to be taken seriously.

Besides, there was nothing secret about the fact that he owned a restaurant. It wasn't a cover for money laundering or working in the CIA or anything. If she searched online for Benedict she'd see his picture. No. Something more confidential seemed required.

"A secret, huh?" He gazed up at the ceiling again, thinking. He could hear her soft breath slowing down as her heart rate returned to normal, feel her warm skin against his, her curious eyes on him as she waited.

One thing popped to mind, but he felt foolish mentioning it. But, when she looked at him with those eyes that still had a dreamy edge to them, he knew he'd tell her anything. "Okay," he said, "I can't believe I'm telling you this, but a couple of months ago, I faked an orgasm."

She laughed, a delighted sound with an edge of sexiness that had things stirring again down south. "I'm not falling for that. Come on, give me a real secret."

"Honestly. You are the only person I've told. And I'm seriously threatening my manhood and my rep by telling you. I'm not proud of it, but I faked it."

She rolled over so she was facing him, and as the sheet shifted he was treated to a tantalizing drape of cotton that wrapped under her breasts, making her look like a Greek goddess. "You can't be serious."

"It's not only women who fake it."

"And how exactly would you go about faking a male orgasm?" she asked, still disbelieving but willing to play along. "What about the, um, emission?"

Well, he'd opened up the subject, he supposed he was going to have to spill. "The secret to the successfully faked male orgasm is in the acting." He cocked an eyebrow at her. "Something you women know all about."

"I don't know what you mean," she said, but there was a little smile on her lips as she said it. "How would you act something like that?"

She seemed so fascinated that he indulged her. "A little extra thrusting, a few loud moans, a deep, wet kiss. That's the acting part. And then, a quick whip-off of the supposedly full condom, a speedy trip to the bathroom and you can flush the evidence. No one's the wiser."

"But who was she? I mean, what were you doing having sex if you weren't that into it?"

"It was my last girlfriend. She was kind of crazy. Hot, but crazy. I think I knew it was already over." And then she'd thrown the knife and definitely severed the connection.

Her eyes widened. "You're serious, aren't you?"

"As serious as global warming."

"This is like finding out that the earth revolves around the moon. Or that Santa Claus beats up old ladies when he's not delivering presents."

He chuckled. "Life's full of surprises."

She shifted again and he couldn't resist the urge to lean over and run his tongue over her berry-pink nipples. "So," she said, clearly thinking, "are you the only guy out there doing this?"

He glanced up. "We don't boast about it, or talk about faking orgasm over martinis like you girls do, but no, I don't think I'm the only one."

"But why?"

He shrugged. "Probably for the same reason you do. We're tired, don't want to hurt a woman's feelings or make her feel bad. Maybe we've had a drink or two too many."

The curiosity in her expression turned to alarm. "So, do you do it a lot?"

"It was the first time for me." He thought back on the incident. "Honestly, I never should have gone out with her. She was hot and absolutely amazingly gifted in the kitchen—she was a chef—but..." He pointed to his head. "Nothing upstairs."

"Does that matter to you? If a woman's not very brainy? If it's just a hookup?"

He thought about it. "Back when I was twenty-two I wouldn't have cared. Now?" He reached out and stroked a finger around the globe of her breast. "I think a woman's brain is the sexiest thing about her." He circled a finger around the other breast. "And I don't really do hookups."

The puzzled look was back on her face. "If you don't do hookups, what's this?"

He reached over and cupped her chin, moved closer until he was a whisper away from her passion-swollen lips. "This," he said, "is a miracle."

She sighed, kissed him back with enthusiasm. But he wasn't twenty-two anymore in a lot of ways. He wasn't quite ready to go again.

"So," he said, pulling back slightly. "Your turn."

"My turn what?"

"Oh, come on. Your turn to tell me a secret. I told you one."

A wrinkle appeared on her forehead as she thought deeply.

"And I don't want some boring crap about how your uncle Fred was adopted."

Her mouth fell open. "How did you know my uncle Fred is adopted?"

He tweaked her nipple between his fingers. "Funny girl, huh?"

"Okay. A sex secret." She pushed a hand through her hair, messing up the already mussed strands adorably.

"And don't even bother telling me you once faked an orgasm. That's no secret from anybody."

She glanced at him under her lashes. "I had sex listening to the Rolling Stones."

He burst out laughing. "Everybody's had sex listening to the Stones."

"No. I mean, at an actual concert." She blushed and started fussing with the sheet, straightening it as if she was a chambermaid.

"With Jagger?" He had to ask.

She snorted with laughter. "No! With a guy I was seeing. I was eighteen or nineteen, I forget. We were at this concert in Chicago. Huge. Thousands of people. Of course, we couldn't afford the best seats, we were up in the cheap seats and 'Satisfaction' came on. He grabbed my hand and pulled me out into the aisle. You know how it is, people are dancing in the aisles, but he pulled me up higher, to the back, and—" She sucked in a breath. "I can't believe I'm telling you this." He was enjoying her telling of the story more than the story itself. He loved watching the play of emotions over her face. A little embarrassment, remembered excitement.

"I was wearing a jean skirt. He stood behind me. I think he was wearing a big raincoat. Probably he'd planned the whole thing in advance for all I know. Anyhow, the coat sort of fit around both of us and, well, he slipped my panties off and then, you know, standing there, with the bass thumping, he took me from behind." She gulped. He could feel her skin quiver against him.

But he didn't interrupt. On some level, she was reliving that moment. He wished that had been him, taking her while the music bounced around them and thousands of fans added to the energy.

"That was the best sex I ever had," she said softly. "Until—"

"Until?" he prompted softly.

She brought her focus back to the present. Gazed into his eyes. "Until tonight."

He felt a rush of pure ego. He'd rocked her world. Oh, yeah. Then, as quickly as it came, the emotion fled. And a kind of anger took its place. She was way past eighteen now. "You haven't had great sex in—what?—ten years?"

"Pathetic, isn't it?"

"You are so responsive, so exciting." He reached over and kissed her. "I'm not going to say this is the best sex I've had in a decade," he teased her with his grin, "because I'm not as pathetic as you."

"Oh." She smacked his biceps with her closed fist in a punch so girlie he barely felt it.

He grabbed her still-closed fist and brought it to his lips. "But tonight is right up there for me, as well."

Again she seemed shy, almost embarrassed. Her look was sweet and honest. "Really?"

"Really."

And then suddenly he was twenty-two again. Full head of steam and ready to go. And so, he discovered, was she.

"WANT TO KNOW another secret?" Jessica felt free, weightless, so filled with amazement that this was happening to her that she wanted to tell him, this man who'd made her New Year's resolution a reality.

He seemed less excited to hear her story than she was to share it. "I don't know," he said slowly. "Will I have to tell you one?"

She scratched her fingertips down his already stubbled cheek—he was so adorable. "No. Only if you want to."

"Okay then. You can tell me."

She was having so much fun running her fingertips down his face that she kept going, softly over his jawline, down his neck, hitting his chest. She could sense that he was enjoying the attention. "On New Year's Eve my friend Morgan challenged me to make a New Year's resolution that wasn't about work or personal improvement." She laughed at the memory, realized she'd had more to drink than she'd thought. "So I told her I was going to have amazing sex before Valentine's Day."

He pretended to glance at his watch. "You've only got a week," he said. "You'd better get going."

She reached over, nipped his shoulder with her teeth. "I've accomplished my New Year's resolution already," she said, soothing the nip with her tongue. "With a week to spare."

He turned to her, his eyes so big and dark she thought she could get lost in them. "I don't think I've ever fulfilled anyone's New Year's resolution before." He shook his head. "I've sure heard enough, though. Big holidays are hell on wheels when you're in the food industry. You always have to work, and on New Year's, if you don't get some drunk chick sticking her tongue down your throat, you get to hear all the ways people you don't even know are going to change their lives. Starting, of course, tomorrow."

She gazed at him in shock. "Women you don't know kiss you?"

"You'd be surprised."

"Not really. You are very kissable."

"So are you."

She yawned.

"You going to kick me out?"

"What?"

"It's four in the morning. If I stay much longer I'll fall asleep."

"Oh." She looked at him, not sure of the right thing to say. The men she slept with were usually guys she'd been dating for a while. It was understood they'd stay at her place, or she at theirs. Usually, an overnight bag was involved. It was all so preplanned and, she realized, unexciting. So, what was the protocol when you hooked up with a waiter? She had no idea. Decided simply to ask him. "Do you want to go?"

"No." Okay, that seemed clear.

She heaved a sigh of relief. "I want you to stay."

"Okay, then." He sounded kind of relieved, too, she thought.

He tucked his body around hers and she turned onto her side, the only way she could ever get to sleep. His body settled behind her, spooning her. His palm settled over her breast as though it belonged there. She liked the feeling of being cocooned in his warmth.

"Good night," she said softly.

He kissed the nape of her neck. "Night."

CHAPTER SIX

JESSICA WOKE WITH an unfamiliar feeling of warmth and the happiness of a woman who's just had the best dream. As she surfaced to reality she realized that last night hadn't been a dream and the warmth was coming from the man still snuggled, naked against her body.

As memories flooded back, hot and furious, she felt warmth stir deep within her, even though her body was tired, her muscles well used.

When she stretched, the man at her back woke suddenly. She watched him blink and then turn to her. He looked like a scruffy pirate with his dark-stubbled cheeks and black hair. She watched him go through the same memory process she had only seconds ago. "Good morning," he said, giving her a sudden grin.

She squinted at the clock. It was ten. She'd slept so solidly for the past six hours that she felt wonderfully refreshed.

Now what?

There was a moment that wasn't awkward so much as... *Breathless,* she supposed, best described the feeling she had as she stared across the pillow at a man she hadn't even known twenty-four hours ago and with whom she'd just spent the night.

"Morning."

He stretched, yawned and rolled out of bed, totally unselfconscious. His body was so good she couldn't help but watch him as he headed to the bathroom. Those long, muscular legs had wrapped around her, the hard butt and lean hips, the muscles of his long back fascinated her. When he disappeared into the washroom she missed the view.

Not feeling as confident that she wanted him to see her totally naked in daylight, she hopped out of bed and donned the thick cotton hotel robe hanging in the closet. When he emerged, she was already putting on coffee.

He came up behind her, put one arm around her waist and with the other lifted the mass of her hair and kissed the nape of her neck.

"Is that your way of begging for coffee?" she teased.

"Nope. It's my way of saying last night was amazing."

She was glad he couldn't see her smile. It was a combination of Mona Lisa and the Cheshire cat.

She knew he was leaving; of course, he was leaving. It's what you did after hooking up with a woman you'd only met the night before. One you believed lived in a different city.

She busied herself taking a couple of white mugs out of the cupboard, finding sugar and the single servings of long-life milk supplied by the hotel. The coffee bubbled and hissed but she could still hear him behind her, the unmistakable sounds of a man dressing.

She turned at last, found him on his hands and knees searching out something—socks? Shoes? He made a sound and reached under the couch. Pulled out a single black sock.

He sat on the floor to pull the sock on, and then he was rising, as smooth as the athlete she knew he was.

"You staying for coffee?" she said, trying to sound cool.

He hesitated and all at once she remembered she hadn't yet paid him for the dinner last night. As he said "Sure," she blurted, "I'll get my purse. I owe you for last night."

The grin he gave her was so devilish she felt herself blushing. "Normally, I don't charge."

"No," she said, laughing. "Not for the sex. For the dinner."

He stepped forward, kissed her swiftly, then said, "I bought you dinner last night. We'll call it our first date."

"But—but I was with another man."

He shrugged, still with that teasing light in his eyes. "I'm a pretty liberal guy."

She poured coffee. "You make it sound like we had a threesome."

"I'm not that liberal."

She passed him coffee and he shook his head when she offered him milk and sugar. He drank it black.

And he drank it fast. She supposed it was from working in restaurants. He probably gulped all his meals and drinks between waiting on tables. By the time she'd finished with her milk and sugar, he was already putting down his mug.

And she wasn't ready for him to go.

He pushed his feet into his shoes, then turned back. "What time's your flight?"

"My flight?"

Then she realized he thought she was flying out today and decided she wasn't going to lie. As she opened her mouth, he said, "I was wondering if you've got time for Sam's Special Seattle Tour."

Oh. He was offering to spend the day with her.

"That sounds—"

"I mean, depending on when you have to leave. I need to get to the restaurant by around three."

"That works for me. If you can drop me off back here on your way to the restaurant?"

"Perfect. I'll run back to my place and change. Pick you up in forty minutes?"

"I'll wait downstairs."

He eyed the strappy shoes she'd worn last night that were tumbled on the floor beside the couch. "You have walking shoes?"

"Uh-huh." Sounded like they were going on a walking date.

"Okay. Downstairs. Forty minutes."

She was showered and dressed in twenty.

The nice thing about being in a hotel with only one suitcase was she didn't have a lot of time to stand in front of her wardrobe and dither. She had limited choices. She wore the jeans she'd paid way too much for because Morgan insisted they made her ass look great and they'd get her laid. Which might have been true if she was a woman of no discrimination. A pair of flat-heeded ankle boots, a black cami, a casual jacket and a multicolored scarf. Big earrings were her only jewelry.

She brushed her hair until it fell in shiny waves, kept her makeup minimal—her SPF moisturizer, a slick of mascara and a swipe of lip gloss. When she checked herself in the mirror she liked what she saw. There was a sparkle in her eyes and color in her cheeks that had nothing to do with cosmetics. A night of great sex was better than a day at the spa complete with makeover.

Maybe she'd rushed a little so she'd have time to share her big news.

She texted:

Mission accomplished.

She waited for a return text but instead her phone rang.

Morgan. Too impatient to text.

"Are you kidding me?" Morgan said the second she answered, all pumped as if she'd just finished a killer workout and chugged a couple of Red Bulls. Which was probably exactly the situation. "You had great sex with the banker?"

"Not exactly."

"Lousy sex," Morgan said in an I-told-you-so tone. "I warned you, didn't I? Right from his pro-file you could tell he'd be terrible in bed."

"I did have great sex," she almost purred. She was always the good girl to Morgan's wild woman, so it was nice for a change to be the one with the surprises.

She heard Morgan slug liquid from a can. Maybe not Red Bull. Maybe Diet Coke. "Make up your mind, girl. Which is it? Are you still drunk or something?"

She giggled, delighted with herself. "No. I am not drunk. I did have great sex and I did not have sex with the banker. Who, you were right, was a complete dud from the second I met him."

Morgan was not going to be so easily distracted. "Holy crap, you had sex with somebody else?"

The nice thing about always being the good girl, the reliable friend, was that when she stepped out of that role the reaction was outstanding.

"Yep." She zipped up her overnight case, ready to wheel it down to her car.

"Who? Who was it? I mean, you head out for dinner with a guy whose profile was so boring Match.com should have put a warning label on it, and next thing I know you've had sex with somebody else? How could you do that? How could you go clubbing without texting me? I'd have come with."

"Of course I didn't go clubbing without you. As if."

"Okay, what am I missing? Who did you sleep with? The cab driver?"

"The waiter."

There was a moment of stunned silence.

"You mean the guy who was serving you during your lame date?"

"Yep."

Morgan laughed, one of those laughs so infectious that Jessica couldn't help but join in. "That's some cojones. He came onto you while he was waiting on you and the banker?"

"No. Not really." Then she thought back and supposed Sam had been sending her subtle signals even before her date ended. "I mean, there was definitely chemistry between us, right away. You should see him. You'd understand. And my date being awful, and going off to the bathroom for ages, gave us time to talk. He's amazing."

"Look, I was going to do laundry, but I'm thinking brunch. Now." Morgan was one of the first people Jessica had met when she moved to Seattle. An operating room nurse, Morgan worked long hours under high pressure and could get a little wild when she was off shift. She was also the kind of person who went out of their way to help a friend and never made a big deal about it. The two women were different in lots of ways, but deep down they shared basic values. Morgan was also a person she could be completely honest with and vice versa. She could say, "Do these pants make my hips look big?" and get a real answer, not make-you-feel-good fake flattery. So, she didn't hesitate.

"Can't. He's coming back for me. We're spending the day together."

"Oh, wow. Congratulations. You did it." She laughed again. "Have the best day. Drinks, then. Tonight."

"Done." Because, of course, she needed to share every delicious detail with her best friend.

She wheeled her case down to the front desk to check out, and found herself instead asking for a late checkout.

"How late?" the desk clerk asked, scanning her computer screen.

"Four?"

She knew she was pushing it, but she also knew that it was probably pretty quiet now that the conference attendees had left the hotel.

"Sure." The woman nodded. "No problem, Ms. Lafayette."

"Thank you so much." She dashed back up to return her suitcase to her room and returned to the lobby with a couple of minutes to spare. She stepped out onto the sidewalk in front of the hotel glad the rain was still holding off. The gray skies were lightening and she thought there might even be a glimpse or two of sunshine if they were lucky.

An already familiar figure turned the corner and headed her way. She took a moment to study Sam as he strode toward her on long legs. He was a head-turner that was for sure, as she discovered when a woman gaped at him even as she was holding another guy's hand.

He didn't even notice. He glanced up, saw her and waved.

She felt like the luckiest woman in Washington State. No, make that the world.

Like her, he wore jeans and boots. On top he wore a dark blue shirt and a beaten-up leather jacket. His hair was still damp so he must have raced through a shower. In fact, she realized, he must live really close to here to get home, shower and change and return to the hotel on foot.

He smiled, a slow, sexy smile when he drew closer to her. She felt every cell in her body respond. "You ready for Sam's Special Seattle Tour?"

"Yes. I am."

"Excellent." He held out his hand and she put hers into it. So easily, as though they were a holding-hands couple instead of two people who had just met.

There wasn't any awkwardness, either, where he walked too fast or swung his arm in some strange tribal rhythm that she couldn't catch onto. They fell into step as easily as if they'd been taking Saturday-morning walks together for years.

He headed her down the hill in the direction of the water. "First stop," he said, "will be for a cup of real coffee. At the world's first, and original, Starbucks."

It'll be full of tourists, she thought, but then of course that's what he assumed she was.

She joined the other tourists, pulled out her smartphone and took a photo. Then, knowing Morgan would want to see him, and knowing she wanted to show him off, she got Sam to pose in front of the Starbucks.

They went in. Stood in the inevitable line and she ordered the same tall skinny latte she always ordered in coffee shops and he had a grande dark roast coffee.

"Now, we walk over to Pike Place Market," he said, sounding very much like a tour guide. "This market opened in 1907 and is one of the oldest con-tinually operating markets in the country. It takes up more than nine acres."

"Wow. I didn't know it was so old."

"Neither did I." At her questioning look he said, "I looked it up on Google when I got home. Didn't have a lot of time, so don't ask me anything. If I don't tell you, I don't know."

He was so adorable. "Okay. No questions…1907. Wow. That's old."

As they walked, he said, "And that body of water, as I'm sure you know, is Elliott Bay."

"And how old is that?"

He pushed her with his hip. "Smart-ass."

She couldn't believe how much fun she was having. And the truth was, even though she lived here, she rarely came to the market. She always seemed to be so busy and it was easier to stop at a big grocer than to brave crowds and find parking and go from stall to stall. But all she had to do was breathe in to realize how much she was missing.

The veggies were so fresh, the cheeses so varied, there was every kind of fish and bakery product and soup and spice you could imagine. And every item added its own note to the complex aroma.

Naturally, the place was packed to bursting with shoppers, browsers, tourists and a few lost-looking souls she suspected were homeless.

"I'd love to take you out for brunch, but we only have a few hours. I suggest big sandwiches. We can eat them outside."

She realized she was starving and readily agreed.

As they walked past a cheese display, a voice called out, "Sam, my man."

Sam walked over and shook hands with the guy

behind the cheese counter. They had a short, animated discussion and next thing she knew, he was coming back with two chunks of cheese on squares of waxed paper. "It's new in," he explained when he rejoined her. "Locally made. A soft goat cheese."

She popped the portion in her mouth and moaned with pleasure. "That is good."

He chewed slowly, seeming to take the entire cheese tasting a lot more seriously than she did. Finally, he nodded slowly. "You're right," he said. "It is good."

"You know the cheese guy?"

"Sure. The food business is a small world."

Turned out he also knew a few of the other merchants and exchanged greetings or a quick wave with several of them.

"Do you want to pick a sandwich or do you want the sandwich of the day? Which is usually spectacular."

"Sandwich of the day."

He nodded. "Want a soda or something?"

She held up her half-finished latte. He'd tossed his empty cup almost as soon as they'd reached the market.

"Let me buy the sandwiches," she said, moving forward, but he waved her away.

"My city, my treat."

He seemed to get through the throng of people at the deli mighty quick, she would almost have guessed there was some favoritism involved. Soon, he had a brown paper sack and once more took her free hand and led her out.

It seemed almost quiet once they were back on

the street. They found a bench and she was glad of her jacket as they sat, soon joined by a seagull who paced up and down three feet in front of them, never taking its black beady eyes off that bag.

The sandwich was, of course, spectacular. With prosciutto and blackened red peppers and some kind of delicious cheese and tomatoes and what she guessed was aioli all on dense Italian bread. Each sandwich was also enough for four people.

She munched happily, watching as Sam demolished his sandwich with strong, white teeth. He managed to eat neatly but so fast that she had barely managed one bite by the time he was halfway through his sandwich.

The seagull looked concerned.

She gazed across the gray waters and said, "Tell me your story."

CHAPTER SEVEN

JESSICA LOVED THE fantasy of sex with a stranger, was secretly thrilled that she'd actually fulfilled her secret dream, but now they were two real people out together in the daylight. She liked him, not only as a hot, exciting man in her bed, but she enjoyed being with him. She didn't want him to be a stranger anymore. She found herself wanting to know all about him.

Well, she knew he was good with people, an excellent waiter, could interpret body language and was great in bed. Oh, and that he'd once faked an orgasm and didn't like stupid women. She wanted the rest of his background to wrap around those few facts.

"My story," he said in a soft voice as though trying to decide where to begin. "Let's see. My dad worked for Boeing as an airline mechanic. My mom stayed home with my sister and me. Annie was older and bossed me around. She grew up to be a lawyer, no surprise. She was the brainy one. I was the athlete."

She could picture him, too. She bet he'd been the star quarterback, with all the girls after him. The kind of boy who never would have looked at her twice back in high school. Then he burst her stereotype by saying something that surprised her.

"My grandmother lived with us. She was Polish—loved to cook. I'd hang around in the kitchen with her while she told stories. She taught me to cook and to love food."

"That's pretty unusual. Here I was thinking of you as the star quarterback."

He half grinned. "I was that, too." He thought for a moment. "I went to college, mostly to please my folks, but I'd been waiting tables since high school. I liked the freedom it gave me. But I already told you that."

"Will you always be a waiter, do you think?" She hoped she didn't sound judgmental and already wished she could swallow the words along with the blackened red pepper and aioli.

"I think that whatever you choose to do you should be the best at it. Who cares if it's menial work or brain surgery? The secret of happiness is making the most of every minute." Then he scrunched up the bag loudly. "Sorry, that was my rant. It pisses me off when people look down on people who serve them."

"I wasn't—"

"I know." But it seemed that he didn't want to share anything more.

He turned to her. "How about you? Your life story?"

She was still scrambling from feeling as though she'd inadvertently insulted him. She, who always tipped twenty percent because she appreciated how hard servers worked.

"My life story. Let's see." She put down the half of the sandwich she'd barely made a dent in and offered him the other half, which he took and bit into with as much relish as he had the first time. Incredible.

"My dad's an engineer. Mom's a nurse. There are three of us kids and we grew up in a pretty happy family. The folks split when I was in college. They were both so careful only to say nice things about the other, which they must have got from counseling or some self-help book, that none of us ever figured out what happened. Anyhow, I majored in marketing and ended up as an event planner. I love what I do. But it's pretty demanding, as you can imagine. You have to be organized, persuasive, creative and able to handle a lot of stress."

"And do you want to be an event planner forever?"

Was he being snarky because she'd asked him that question or did he really want to know? She decided to assume he really wanted to know. "I think so. But someday, I'd like to have my own firm. I've always thought that when I have kids, it would be nice to work part-time. Maybe have an office at home."

He nodded, not seeming to think she was a fifties throwback or anything. "I always liked having my mom and my grandma at home. If you can do it, why wouldn't you?"

"Exactly. It's kind of a five-year plan for me."

His lips twitched.

Oh, God. He'd known her for a day and already he was laughing at her and her five-year plans. "Are you laughing at me?"

"No. Maybe a little. I think plans are great. But it's amazing how life always gets in the way of them."

She leaned forward until her nose was an inch from his. "I made a plan at New Year's Eve and I'd say that worked out pretty well."

For a moment their gazes locked. "Point taken."

She leaned forward a little closer until their lips brushed. Then backed away. "Okay, then." She took the last sip of her coffee to hide her smile.

"No visit to Seattle is complete without a trip up our famous Space Needle," he said, when they'd finished lunch.

"Sounds like fun." Sure, she'd been up to the observation deck once, but she hadn't been with Sam. She suspected this time would be a whole lot more fun.

They walked to 5th and Pine and waited for the monorail. It was fun riding on the train, looking at downtown Seattle whizz by. In less than five minutes they were at the Needle.

This time, she got pushy and made sure she bought the tickets, including entrance to Chihuly Garden and Glass. While they were waiting for their "launch time" they wandered the Chihuly Garden, not too colorful at this time of year except for the astonishing glass sculptures that bloomed all year-round. They entered the glass house, a domed conservatory and looked up at the red and yellow and orange bursts of color, created by artist Dale Chihuly. She couldn't help but smile. He said, "I always feel like I'm under water and those are some kind of underwater anemone, or maybe really colorful jellyfish."

"Me, I see umbrellas. Crowded together, all keeping the rain off." She loved the artist's colorful glass sculptures, so brilliant against the gray light, as iconic as anything else in this wonderful city.

"It's time for us to ride up," she said, checking her watch.

"We have ten minutes," he said.

"Sorry, it's my job. Being an event planner I get pretty stressed about meeting schedules."

He chuckled. "Okay. I'd rather stand around than have you stressed on your day off." He took her hand once more.

Soon they were whisked up the Needle to the observation deck.

He put his arm around her as they strolled, enjoying the 360-degree views. "We're lucky it's clear today," he said. "What a great view of Rainier."

"You talk about that snowcapped mountain like you two are buddies."

He smiled. "We are in a way, though I respect that peak a helluva lot. But you climb Rainier and you've done something."

"You've climbed Mount Rainier?" She'd known he was Mr. Fit Outdoors guy but—wow.

"Sure. I love the challenge."

"I prefer that mode of travel." She pointed to a ferry chugging its way across Elliott Bay. In the distance she could see the Cascade Mountains and she was reminded once more how much she loved her adopted city.

"That's Chicago, that way," he said, pointing generally southeast. He sighed, pulling her closer. "Sure seems like a long way from here."

"I do quite a lot of business here in Seattle," she said.

"Good."

She wondered if he was serious. Did he really wish she were closer? Or did he like the idea of a weekend fling and then she'd be gone and he could get back to his own life? She really wished she knew.

When they walked back to her hotel, she noticed that their hands were gripping tighter, as though they didn't want to let go.

She thought about telling him that she lived right here in town, but she knew she'd first of all feel stupid that she hadn't told him before and, second, she had just enjoyed the most perfect, blissful relationship of her entire romantic life.

Did she really want to screw it up?

They stood outside the brass-and-glass doors of the hotel. They turned to each other. He put his hands on her shoulders. "Well—"

"Would you like to come up?" she asked.

"You still have your room?"

She edged closer to him. "I got a late checkout."

She heard him breathe in, almost as though he'd won a reprieve. As if he didn't want this day to end any more than she did. "I only have an hour, but I would love to come up."

"Then let's not waste a second of that hour," she said.

They held hands all the way up in the elevator, not saying a word, simply holding on. Her skin felt feverish with the persistent thrum of arousal.

They held hands down the corridor, and only left off when they reached her room and she had to get her keycard out of her bag.

She looked at it and thought she'd hang on to it

forever as a souvenir of the most amazing night of her life. If she hadn't made that foolish mistake and slipped her hotel card instead of her credit card.

IT WAS DIFFERENT this time. So different from the fun and purely carnal night they'd shared. It felt as though the day they'd spent together, even the limited amount of their lives that they'd shared, had made a difference. They weren't one-night lovers anymore.

They were something more.

He undressed her slowly, the soft afternoon light coming in from the window. Every touch was a caress. When she looked into his eyes she wondered how she'd fallen so hard, so fast.

She wanted to ask him if he was feeling it, too, this strong connection, but she didn't have the words. And even if she could have found them, she didn't want to risk spoiling something so special by finding out that she was the only one feeling as though something monumental had happened.

Instead, she did what she always did. She decided to sift her thoughts, analyze the situation, think things through. She was glad he didn't know she lived here. She had time, space, she could mull over her feelings, talk them over with Morgan, who was so much more experienced with casual sex than she was.

And then he kissed her and her brain switched off.

She couldn't think anymore. She could only feel. His lips, when he kissed his way down her throat, to the dip in her collarbone, flicking his tongue there. Moving on to her breasts. He kissed her breasts as though they were delicious. Strangely, for a man who ate food and drank coffee so fast, he really took his time in the bedroom. Here, he must realize, he didn't need to rush.

Her jeans were so tight she had to help him, wiggling her hips as he pulled. She said, "My friend Morgan told me if I bought these jeans I'd get laid."

"Your friend Morgan was right." He tossed the jeans to the floor and then climbed on the bed to go after her panties. "But then you could wear potato sacks and I'd want to do you."

Between kissing and playing, she managed to help him out of his clothes until they were both naked. Her skin seemed so pale next to his, her bones so much smaller.

The way he touched her, he seemed to feel it, too, as though she were breakable. Fragile.

She wasn't though. She felt more powerful than she'd ever felt in her life. She felt as though she could ride him, subdue him, dominate him if she chose. He was hers. Maybe only for another hour, but he was hers absolutely.

And to prove it, she took him.

Rolled on top of him, took his rock-hard cock into her body, where already it felt familiar. Then she reached for his hands, those big, brown, mountain-climbing hands and gripped them. Those hands had scaled tough mountains and also scaled her defenses. As she rode him, setting the pace, starting slowly, she thought how much they'd held hands today, and how much she was going to miss the feel of his palm warm against hers.

She rode and rocked, kissing him deeply, letting her hair fall like a curtain around them until their breathing was labored and she could see his eyes go dark. She knew he was holding back for her, holding on, and she drove herself faster, feeling the pressure build and build until she couldn't stop the grip of pleasure and the cries that escaped her mouth as her head fell back. Even as her body gripped his, she felt him quake beneath her, plunging up and deep, so deeply inside of her, and then his own cry of completion.

She slumped down onto him, a half smile pasted to her face.

"I think we were both wrong," she panted.

He made an inarticulate sound, like "hunhj?"

"I saw fireworks behind my eyeballs when I came. It looked like the Dale Chihuly exhibit, all those bursts of color. Maybe it's not about flowers or umbrellas or sea life. Maybe it's about sex."

"From now on, whenever I see a Chihuly I will think of you. And this moment."

He smelled so good. His skin, his hair, everything about him appealed.

After a few minutes, when neither of them spoke, just let their breathing return to normal, touched each other and held on, he groaned. Checked his watch.

"Jess, I've got to get going. I'm already late."

She nodded, feeling she missed him already and he hadn't even gone yet.

"Mind if I have a quick shower? Don't want to go to work smelling of sex."

She wanted to say something smart and funny, but

she found she didn't have smart or funny in stock. She said, "Sure."

"I'd ask you to join me, but then I'd miss the dinner shift."

"I know."

He rolled out of bed and soon she heard him in the shower. Seemed he showered as fast and efficiently as he ate.

He was back out again in ten minutes. He dressed swiftly, walked over to where she was still lying naked on the bed, and said, "Could I get your email or something?"

A spurt of pure joy went through her. He wanted her email.

Yes!

"Of course you can."

He pulled out his phone and she gave him her email address. She was going to ask for his but decided to wait and let him contact her first. He didn't ask for her phone number, she noticed, but hey, email was something. Even if he never contacted her, at least he'd asked.

He kissed her, slow and sweet. "It's been amazing," he said.

Oh, he had no idea. *Amazing* was too easy a word for what she'd experienced. She called a good cup of coffee amazing. When her skin was glowing from a power yoga workout she said she felt amazing.

This? Sex with Sam?

She needed a whole other vocabulary.

CHAPTER EIGHT

"TELL ME, TELL ME, tell me!" Morgan said the second she walked into their favorite hangout four hours later. Morgan had managed to snag a table and already had a vodka martini on the go.

She jumped down from her seat and pulled Jessica in for an impulsive hug, squealing as she did so. "You look fantastic, by the way. Your skin is glowing and you've got that heavy look in your eyes that says *I just got laid and it was fantastic.*"

"Well, I did. And it was."

Morgan waited impatiently while she ordered a glass of red wine, then, the second the waitress had moved away, she said, "Tell. Me. Everything. Now!"

So she did. From the very beginning.

Morgan nodded and repeated "told ya so" through the beginning of her date. She was suitably pissed on Jessica's behalf that the banker not only ditched her but ditched her with the bill.

"Oh, but that's the best part," she said, leaning in. "He did me such a favor."

Morgan did not look convinced, her short-bobbed hair bouncing as she shook her head. "What, you're on some reality show where you have to burn through your paycheck?"

She leaned closer and told Morgan about putting her room key in the folder instead of her credit card.

"Oh, that is smooth! And the best part is you would never even think of doing something like that on purpose."

"Of course not." She shook her head. "It was a total accident. I was so embarrassed. I mean, the poor guy didn't even catch up with me until I was already at the hotel." She shrugged helplessly. "And then, what could I do but invite him up to my room so I could give him cash?"

"What could you do?" Morgan echoed, making her eyes so wide with fake innocence that her eyeballs nearly rolled out of their sockets.

They both snorted with laughter. And then, of course, she had to share every glorious moment. Even the telling made her feel hot all over again. The only thing she left out was when they'd swapped secrets in the dark because, well, they were secrets. But she did pull out her phone and show off Sam's picture, the one she'd snapped outside Starbucks.

Morgan looked at the photo, back at Jessica and nodded. "Oh, yeah. This one? He wouldn't even need a profile. That photo says it all. He's gorgeous."

"I know."

"So? When are you seeing him again?"

"I don't know," she wailed.

"What? Are you telling me he's the kind of guy who—"

"No. It's not him. It's me." She sighed and kicked her foot up and down under the table, a habit she had when she was fretting. Since Arcade Fire was playing, it was easy to pretend she was air-tapping to the music.

All around them, men and women were interacting, in couples, in groups, or strangers meeting for the first time. There was laughter and soft conversations, some guys at a stag night already getting out of control.

Morgan knew her pretty well. She sipped her drink and waited.

"It's like I finally figured out how to have a casual fling. A night of wild sex with a virtual stranger. I seriously did not even know his name until we introduced ourselves. That was after we'd already had sex."

Morgan gave an earthy chuckle and raised her glass in a toast.

"So I figure, all right. I've finally cracked this casual hooking-up thing that everyone else seems to do easily and that I never figured out before."

Morgan nodded. This was not news.

"I thought if I don't tell him that I live right here in Seattle, then I don't have to screw up the most perfect, incredible night of sex I've ever had."

She took a sip of her wine. "Well, technically, I guess I already screwed that up because we had sex again this afternoon."

"Still amazing?"

"There aren't words."

Morgan considered. "Then, technically, it doesn't count as a screwup."

"Good."

"Why didn't you tell him you live here? 'Cause I am not getting it."

"Because I'll wreck it. I'll get serious and want

more out of the relationship. I'll try and get him on a five-year plan. I'll send him application forms for MBA programs and try to make him into somebody he's not." She took a deep breath. "I'll fall in love with him!"

There was a long silence. She glanced up at Morgan, who was looking at her with understanding and maybe a hint of pity. "Oh, honey. You didn't."

She figured it was safest not to answer.

"EARTH TO SAM."

Sam jumped at the sound of Pete's voice. He was standing in the kitchen of Benedict. He got the feeling the chef had called him before and he hadn't heard him. Truth was, he'd seen a tray of Valentine Fantasy desserts and slid right off into his own fantasy. Except it wasn't fantasy.

It was memory.

"Yeah, sorry. What's up?"

"Table 5. They're in from New York—loved the meal—wanted to compliment you personally."

"Good. Be right there. Thanks." He pulled his head out of his ass with an effort. Mingling with the customers was part of his job and he usually enjoyed it. He loved hearing how great his place was, who wouldn't?

He got himself out front and met the New Yorkers, accepted their praise and posed for a photo with them. Then he made the rounds. "How was dinner? How'd you like that wine? Our sommelier had it brought in specially, you know. Isn't that dessert wicked? Chef says it tastes like sex." That got a laugh, as it always did. And he tried not to think about Jessica.

At least, not until the place had cleared and he'd closed up.

He sat in his tiny office behind the kitchen and made the schedule for the following week. Valentine's Day was next Friday, a big day and it fell on a weekend. He scheduled full staff, pulled in extra kitchen help.

That done, he wrote an email.

Dear Jessica,

What was he doing? Writing to his long lost great auntie? He crossed out *Dear Jessica.* Tried again.

Hey, Jess,

Maybe she hated *Jess.* Maybe it was the name kids used to tease her with in grade school.

Hey, Jessica,

Not great, but he could always come back and fix it. He'd be here all night if he didn't move past the salutation. He rocked back on his chair. Thought about the woman he'd said goodbye to only a few hours ago.

I miss you.

Oh, jeez. Why don't you write her a love song

while you're at it? Or a poem? Get her name tat-
tooed on your ass?

He deleted I miss you.

Now he was back to:

Hey, Jessica,

The curser blinked, like it was tapping its feet
with impatience, saying, *Come on already, I don't
have all day here.* He began typing once more.

I was looking at a Valentine Fantasy dessert and all I
could think of was you. You look good in chocolate.
And you were wrong. Sex doesn't taste like chocolate, it tastes like you.

Was that gross? Too personal?

He crossed out the last two sentences. He liked
the reference to the dessert, though. He thought she
would too.

Oh, what the hell. She lived in Chicago. It wasn't
like he was embarrassing himself with someone he
could run into in the street.

I feel stupid even saying this, but I miss you.

If you feel stupid even saying it, dumbass, then
don't. He crossed that out. Thought for a second.

If you were still here, I would invite you to my place
and I would cook you dinner. I boasted about what
a good cook I am, I would like to prove it.

I'd invite you for dinner, but I'd get in eggs and
things for breakfast. Because I'd be hoping.

He had no idea what to put as a sign off. *Love*
was too personal. *XO* was too cute. *Sincerely* was
for business letters. He ended with nothing but Sam.

Then, before he could delete the whole thing and
start over, he pushed Send.

And then he headed home wondering how he
could feel lonely for someone he'd only known for
a single day.

CHAPTER NINE

JESSICA WOKE UP on Sunday with a full to-do list. Work out, get groceries, call her mom for their weekly check-in. It was a pretty unofficial ritual, but Sunday was a day that usually worked for them both to catch up and exchange advice.

She brewed coffee and checked her email. There wouldn't be anything from Sam, she told herself. He was way too cool. She'd probably hear from him Monday or Tuesday—if she heard from him at all.

So when she saw SamIAm she clicked on it right away, her coffee forgotten.

Hey, Jessica,

Okay, casual, but he'd emailed her one day after they'd seen each other, so that was good.

I was looking at a Valentine Fantasy dessert and all I could think of was you. You look good in chocolate.

She felt warmth begin to cover her body. If she closed her eyes she could relive that night, almost smell the chocolate.

She read on.

If you were still here, I would invite you to my place and I would cook you dinner. I boasted about what a good cook I am, I would like to prove it.

I'd invite you for dinner, but I'd get in eggs and things for breakfast. Because I'd be hoping.

Oh, wow. He hadn't exactly said he missed her, but it was implied in his wishing she were still around. Right? Or was he merely saying he wanted to have sex with her again?

He'd signed it simply, Sam. No *love*. Not even an *XO*.

But he'd emailed and she figured that was pretty damned good.

She took a sip of her coffee and the flavor exploded on her tongue. Dark, rich, sensual.

A cool woman would wait. Morgan would tell her not to be too eager. She read Sam's message again and went all gooey inside. Maybe she'd type an email now, because she had time and she felt like it.

Then she'd send it later.

Hi Sam,
It's so good to hear from you.

What was he, a client she was hoping to land? She deleted that.

The curser blinked at her like a wagging finger that seemed to be saying, *Everybody else can manage casual sex. What's wrong with you? You can't even send a sexy email!*

She was hopeless. She abandoned the email. Texted Morgan.

U going 2 power yoga?

Got back: Yep, CU there.

There was no time to talk before their class. They'd met at power yoga when she first moved to Seattle and both took it seriously. They'd bonded over green tea next door at the coffee shop and their friendship had grown from there. They spread their mats side by side in the crowded studio. She liked the vibe, even if it was practically a Lululemon fashion parade. All those flatteringly stretchy black pants with the bands of color, the sexy yoga tops and the toned bodies. It was a mixed-age range, lots of young working yogis like her and Morgan, some middle-aged people, a few old ones. "You're as old as your spine," the instructor reminded them as they went into a back bend and she felt like the oldest person in the room.

There were a few men, maybe ten or so. But, she reminded herself, her practice was about her and the mat. So, she tried to concentrate and stretched and strained and sweated in harmony of a sort with a roomful of people.

After it was over they headed to the coffee shop next door for herbal tea. Morgan flopped down on the black faux-leather comfy chairs they'd managed to snag. "What is it about men and yoga? They're always married, gay or repulsive. I'm thinking of taking up cycling."

"I hate cycling. I'm always afraid I'll fall off my bike and get run over."

Morgan yawned. "I almost fell asleep in Shavasana," she said. "I need to get more sleep."

Shavasana, or corpse pose, was her favorite time, right at the end when she lay still and was supposed to meditate for a few minutes. Instead she'd been distracted.

"I was trying to compose a sexy email."

"You know, if yoga was a credit course, we'd both fail."

"I know. I feel a lot more relaxed, though."

"I like what it's doing for my arms." Morgan flexed her biceps, which did indeed look buff. Then she dropped the pose. "Sexy emails to whom?" She emphasized the *whom* like a grammar teacher.

Jessica felt herself fall into fluttery-girl mode. "Sam." She said it as though there were two syllables in *Sam*. What on earth was wrong with her?

"I'm guessing he got in touch."

She nodded. "I tried to email him back, but I was so worried about coming on too strong that I considered recounting a work anecdote."

Her friend shook her head and took a fortifying sip of green tea. "How are you going to get anywhere if you're too scared to send an email?"

"I don't know."

"Okay, get out your phone. I will dictate."

Jessica got out her phone, hoping for the best but knowing she could always delete if Morgan didn't come through.

"Dear Sam," Morgan dictated.

So far so good, and interesting that Morgan didn't find *Dear* too personal.

"I live right here in Seattle. Surprise! Give me your address and I will come right over and jump on your hot, gorgeous bod." She glanced up. "What? You stopped typing."

"I am not sending that."

"You want to know how to send a sexy message? That's how. You want more sex? Tell the guy you live here."

Jessica deleted what little she had typed.

Morgan said, "You want unconditional love? Get a dog."

That was the trouble, of course—she did want love. She felt she'd fallen halfway there when all she'd been trying to do was have one night of earth-displacing sex. How had she screwed it up? Already?

Morgan pushed her hands through her short, copper bob. Checked out a couple of guys who walked into the coffee shop wearing biking clothes and carrying helmets. Two women, similarly clad, came in right behind them and she lost interest.

"What's the worst that could happen if you took a chance and told him you live here?"

It didn't take her long to answer because she'd already thought through the consequences of telling Sam that she lived in town. "I could make a fool of myself. He could have a girlfriend, be a commitment-phobe, pick up female diners on a nightly schedule." He'd told her he didn't do hookups anymore, but it didn't mean he was telling her the truth. He thought she was only passing through town—he could have told her anything.

Except that, somehow, she'd felt his honesty. You couldn't fake the look he'd had in his eyes. At least, she hoped it couldn't be faked.

"I hope you get a discount when you get your insecurities bundled like that," Morgan said.

Jessica sipped tea. "This is all your fault. You were the one who encouraged me to set that stupid New Year's resolution."

"You're right. It is my fault, and I feel terrible." She grabbed up Jessica's phone from where she'd placed it on the small table between them, on top of a newspaper where someone had half finished a Sudoku and abandoned it.

"What are you doing?" she asked, feeling deeply suspicious.

Her tone caused the young guy beside them, an intense bearded guy who was reading James Joyce's *Ulysses* to glance up from his book. He had graduate student written all over him, but for now he seemed more interested in the human drama playing out beside him in the coffee shop than he was in twentieth century Irish lit.

Morgan punched her thumbs rapidly over Jessica's phone. Why didn't she use her own phone? Then suddenly Morgan passed the phone to Jessica, who was so stunned she held it to her ear.

"Benedict," a young, female voice said. "How can I help you?"

She could hear the bustle of a busy Sunday brunch at the restaurant. The sounds pulled her back to thinking of Sam and the incredible night they'd had.

"Ask for him," Morgan said in a loud whisper.

She gaped at her friend, who was nodding reassuringly. She was right. What did Jessica have to lose? "Is Sam there? The waiter?"

"We don't have any waiters named Sam. Do you mean Sam Benedict? The owner?"

"Um. I'm not sure. I'll call back."

She ended the call.

"What?" Morgan asked. "You look stunned. He left? He died? His wife is at the hospital giving birth?"

She laid the phone back down on the newspaper. "The woman who answered said the only Sam who works there is the owner. Sam Benedict."

Morgan chortled. "You made out with one of the top young entrepreneurs in the city?" She slapped her black, stretchy yoga-panted thigh with her open palm. "Oh, that's funny."

"No. It's not. I thought he was a waiter. I was so proud of myself for falling for somebody for once who isn't driven to succeed."

"Did he ever actually say he was a waiter?"

She recalled their talks about life and career—which had been very brief. She remembered that he'd taken her to task when she'd asked if he aspired to something other than waiter, but by doing that he'd also avoided telling her that he wasn't one. "No. He didn't say he was the owner, either."

"Like you never said you weren't from out of town. You both assumed stuff and neither of you made corrections. That's interesting, don't you think?"

But Jessica didn't answer. She was too busy searching online for Sam Benedict on her smartphone. And yep, there he was. Even on the tiny screen, the sight of him made her heart bump. He was pictured in the *Post-Intelligencer* in an article about the best new restaurants in town. And there was another photo with him and some foodie that had been published in *Gourmet*.

She held the phone out for Morgan, who oohed. "Yep. That's the same guy who posed for you outside Starbucks. No wonder you're pining. You can see by looking at him that he burns up the sheets without even trying."

"I must be losing my touch," Jessica said. "How did I not recognize him? I know all the hot, trendy places in town. I stay abreast. It's my job!"

"Don't beat yourself up. You've been doing all those boring conferences and corporate openings lately."

"It's true. And I did suggest that restaurant because I knew it was the hottest new place. But still. I am losing my edge."

"Oh, I think Sam Benedict sharpened your edge for you just fine."

"Morgan!" Jessica darted her eyes in the direction of the grad student who hadn't turned a page in *Ulysses* for quite some time. His coffee cup was long empty.

Morgan was sublimely uninterested. She always took people eavesdropping on her conversations as a compliment.

"You know what you should do?"

"Yes." She was already thinking. She had a high-end charity fashion show she'd been asked to organize. She'd been thinking of interesting venues. The people who supported events like this got sick of the same hotel ballrooms. She was thinking that if they upped the ticket price and made the event seem even more exclusive, Benedict would be the perfect spot. The restaurant could open during a time it was normally closed or slow, a Monday lunch, perhaps. "I could organize a special event there."

"So not what I was thinking."

"Don't even share with me what you were thinking, because I can tell from the wild look in your eye I'm not doing it."

Morgan turned to the grad student. "Excuse me," she said, as though he hadn't been listening to every word. "You're a man. If a woman was hot for you, would you rather she throw some business your way or would you rather she show up in a trench coat and heels with nothing on underneath."

When he pushed back his glasses and grinned, he looked like an intellectual Seth Rogen. "Those two options aren't even in the same league."

"Not doing it," Jessica said, rising.

"I could lend you a trench coat."

"Rather die."

"Too bad," both Morgan and the Seth look-alike echoed, like an embarrassment duet.

"I've got to go and get groceries. I'll see you later." When she headed out the door, she glanced back and found Morgan and her new friend in conversation.

She didn't need Sam's expertise in body language to know what they were talking about.

CHAPTER TEN

WHEN JESSICA GOT home, she put away her groceries, showered, combed out her hair, climbed into comfy jeans and a sweater and settled herself in front of the computer.

How hard could it be?

Hi Sam,

She noticed one of her nails was chipped and went for a nail file.

She scraped the nail until it was smooth and, as she did so, she stared at the two tiny words on the screen, then deleted them.

Then she picked up the phone and called her mother. Her mother wasn't home. She was probably on a date—because her mother was a good communicator.

Back to the email. She did a few neck rolls but she was already loose from the yoga. Okay. She pictured Sam, not so very far away, busy serving customers. Actually, he probably didn't serve customers all that often. He probably oversaw the entire care and feeding of the first dates, the bad dates, the too-long marrieds and the out-of-towners. Hopefully, there were some lovers there, too. The kind who made you believe in forever.

Dear Sam,
I thought about you today.

Was Morgan right? Should she let him know she lived closer than he'd believed?

She pushed her hair around, helping it dry faster while she thought about the idea of putting herself out there, turning fantasy into reality and facing the possibility that some fantasies are meant to be left as exactly that.

Further internet research revealed absolutely zero about Sam Benedict's private life, though she did see a couple more photos of him at a media event she'd have attended herself if she'd been in town. And there he was on the website for the restaurant, though he only appeared in a group photo with the key staff. She liked that he didn't splash his big ego all over the website. He made it clear he was part of a team. She supposed that's why he'd been waiting tables the other night. He probably chopped veggies when they were short of kitchen help, too. He was that kind of guy.

I went to yoga this morning and while we were lying in corpse pose at the end, instead of emptying my mind and meditating, I thought of you.
And our time together.
Thanks for turning one of the worst nights of my life into one of the best.

I would love for you to cook for me. What are your specialties of the house?
Jessica

THE AIR WAS cold and crisp and Sam's lungs ached from the workout. The skins on his backcountry skis gripped the fresh snow as he and his three buddies hiked their way up a remote slope in the Cascades.

It was Wednesday, the day Sam usually took off, but they were close enough to town that he'd be back in time to help out with the dinner shift. Carson, a medical resident, also had the entire day off; Mitch, a heavy crane operator, was currently happily laid off for a couple of months; and Lars, a guy he'd met when he'd been traveling in Sweden, was doing his own round-the-world adventure.

The four were all fit, compatible and experienced in the backcountry. Avalanche risk was low and the sun was not something a person ever took for granted when living in the Pacific Northwest.

As he sweated and toiled his way up the slope, hearing the hush of fresh snow as he packed it down, the odd squeak of equipment and his own heavy breathing, Sam wondered what Jessica was doing at this moment. It was a thought that bounced into his mind too often. But it was strange. Now that they were emailing each other several times a day, he felt he was closer to her than anyone in his life. He told her things. Dumb, unimportant things. Important, deeply personal things.

Because she always got him. If he made a joke, even on email, she didn't misunderstand. If he told her a story, she offered one back. It was like their relationship was deepening.

With one huge drawback.

No sex.

No contact of any kind.

How could he fall for someone he'd barely spent any time with?

He'd heard about people falling in love online and, even stranger, falling in love with avatars at Second Life, so he guessed he wasn't that crazy falling deeper for someone he'd spent less than twenty-four hours with. At least he'd met the woman.

Sam was so busy with his thoughts he didn't realize he'd powered ahead until he found himself alone at the top of the hill. Virgin snow surrounded him. Evergreens hunched, weighed down with layers of snow like frosting, and sun sparkled off the pure white surfaces. He could see the crisscrossing tracks of a rabbit, feel the sun on his face. He waited until his companions caught up.

They pulled the skins off their skis, stuffed them in backpacks. This was the moment they'd toiled uphill for.

With his skis pointed into the virgin powder headed down a slope few knew about, he let out a rebel yell and took off. The three others fanned out, all of them finding their own routes, carving their own signatures into the new snow.

For a two-hour uphill hike they maybe got a twenty-minute run down. They didn't care. Every turn was a rush, it was like sex, he thought, the pump and glide, the feeling of blood pumping and excitement coursing through his veins.

And of course, the thought of sex brought Jessica to mind. He'd love to bring her up here. He wondered if she skied. He'd ask her tonight.

He looked forward to their emails far too much.

He was seriously thinking of taking a few days off and flying down to Chicago. Why not? He'd worked hard for months with barely a day off. There were restaurants in Chicago he wanted to try, and he couldn't think of anyone he'd rather have sitting across a dinner table than the sweet woman who had rocked his world.

After their ski down, all wind-reddened and pumped, the four decided to head to a local brewpub for a late lunch. Sam could only spare an hour, but he wanted to hang out with his buddies a little longer. They were all so busy it wasn't easy to find time for all four of them to get together. They piled onto a green leatherette bench and all ordered burger platters. The other three had beer but, knowing he had to work later, he stuck with iced tea.

They spent a few minutes congratulating themselves and each other on their great timing—getting out on a day when not only was there fresh snow but sunshine, too, and on their great run down the hill.

When their food came, they chomped into it with big appetites well earned.

"Who's up for doing this again sometime this week?" Mitch asked. He had the most time of all of them. But it was sure tempting to try and carve out another half a day.

"I am not certain," Lars said, then announced that he was thinking about heading back home to Sweden earlier than he'd planned.

"Why?" Mitch asked the question, but it was obvious all three of them were wondering.

Lars looked a little sheepish. "It's a woman," he said, in his accent that American girls seemed to think was pretty damned adorable. With his blond hair, bright blue eyes and the physique of a Nordic prince, he never lacked for female company. He'd mentioned a girl back home a time or two, but Sam had never thought it was serious. But then, as he'd admitted to Jessica during their late-night secret sharing, guys weren't big into blabbing intimate stuff.

For a second he considered asking his three companions if they'd ever faked an orgasm and had to gulp iced tea to hide his grin. As if.

But Lars wasn't talking about faking it—he was talking about cutting his world tour short. For a woman.

A week ago, Sam would have called him crazy and tried to talk him out of such an insane idea. He'd have reasoned that he had the whole rest of his life to settle down but limited years for travel and adventure. Now, he had a lot more sympathy for the romantic Swede.

"You're crazy, man," Mitch said into the stunned silence. "You're like a babe magnet. Sow your wild oats. Sow them all over the place. Then you can go home with a full bank of memories stored up for the days when you've been married for a few decades and you're old and wrinkled and can't get it up anymore."

Lars grinned, showing toothpaste-commercial-white teeth, and said, "I miss her. I knew I loved her, but I thought I could put it all on hold for a year, you know, meet some other women. Make sure."

"Sounds like a good plan to me," Carson said through a mouthful of fries.

Sam kept quiet, feeling oddly cheered. Maybe he wasn't the only romantic fool on the planet.

Lars glanced around at each of them. "She phoned me. She thinks I don't care enough. There's a guy who keeps asking her out. She was thinking of going with him." Lars shrugged his shoulders, but there was a gleam of fury in his eyes. Sam was uncomfortably reminded that he was from a land of Vikings famous for plunder and violence. Lars might be modern and civilized but, deep down, nobody was going to mess with his woman.

Carson didn't see it that way. He snorted. "She's playing you, dude."

Lars shook his head. "Astrid's not like that. She wanted to be honest with me. It's one of the things I like best about her. Her honesty." He dipped a fry into ketchup and stared at it for a moment. "It means giving up South America," he said.

"There's a woman who's better than South America?" Mitch sounded shocked.

"To me, she is." He ate his fry. "You all think I'm crazy?"

"Yes," Mitch said.

"Totally," Carson agreed.

"No," Sam said. He reached out with his glass and toasted Lars. "Not at all. South America's not going anywhere. You could go for your honeymoon. But love? That doesn't come along every day."

If he'd announced he was going to be twerking in Miley Cyrus's next music video his buddies couldn't have looked more surprised.

Mitch found his voice first. "You're saying you agree with him?"

"I do. Yeah."

"What happened to you?"

"I met a woman, too."

"The kind you give up South America for?"

"I think so. Maybe." He nodded. "Yeah."

"Who is she?" Lars asked, sounding happy to have a fellow lovesick fool to hang out with.

"You're not banging another crazy cook, are you?" Carson demanded. "I am not stitching your hide back together if this one has better aim with the knives."

"No. I don't think she's the violent type. She's not in the restaurant business."

"You only meet women in the food trade. We barely see you. When did you meet a girl?"

No way he was going to share the details with this crew. They were his closest friends, but still, some things a man didn't tell. "She's an event planner," he said. Which was true. "She came into the restaurant and we hit it off." Also true.

"And it's serious?"

"I think it might be."

"How long have you known her?" Damn, the question he'd have rather avoided.

"Let's see, today is Wednesday." He counted back. "Six days."

Now the three of them were staring at him. Even Lars no longer looked like they were fellow travelers on the road of love.

"Are you crazy?"

"I think so. Yeah."

"So, you've spent six days, that's—" Carson calculated swiftly "—a hundred and forty-four hours, minus the time you work and—" he gestured around the table "—the hours you've spent with us. Even if you are spending every second of every day together, there's no way you're in love."

"Haven't you ever heard of love at first sight?"

Mitch looked vaguely nauseous. "You've been hanging around the Valentine's Day card section in Walgreens again, haven't you?"

"So, how are you going to wine her and dine her on the fourteenth when you own a restaurant?"

He blew out a breath. "She lives in Chicago."

Mitch hit his own forehead with his fist. "Dude," he said.

CHAPTER ELEVEN

"DOES YOUR CLOWN do dogs?" Walt Miller asked Jessica. Mr. Miller was the CEO of a medium-sized tech company that was hosting its first public open house. They'd nailed down the displays, the caterer, the media, the promo giveaways, and now he was talking about some special events for children. The clown had been her idea. Uninspired, but usually popular.

Does your clown do dogs?

Jessica blinked. Who knew these days? "I don't think so," she said carefully.

"Giraffes? Elephants?" The man twisted his two hands as though he were wringing out an imaginary towel.

"Oh, you mean does my clown make balloon animals?"

"Yeah. That's right."

She really needed to get her head back in the game. "I can absolutely find a clown who does balloon animals. I wonder if we should have a second person doing a craft of some sort. Some kids are frightened of clowns."

"Sure. Good idea."

She made some notes, and they talked about some ideas for computer-related games that might appeal to the tiny Jobses and Gateses who would show up at the open house, dragged there by their parents and relatives who worked at the company.

Fifteen minutes later, she was back in her car and on her way to a meeting with the charity putting on the fashion show she was hoping to organize at Benedict.

An hour later, she walked out of the meeting feeling that this event was going to be something out of the ordinary. She hadn't mentioned Benedict specifically, only the idea of something more intimate that would take over a restaurant. She'd make sure she could get the venue first, then wow the committee.

As she headed back to her car, she passed a lingerie store display window decked out, naturally, in red hearts and featuring some of the most exquisitely sexy underwear she'd ever seen.

She stood there on the sidewalk for a moment, imagining.

SAM STOWED HIS skis in the front hall closet where he kept his exercise stuff. He stripped his outerwear off and walked into his apartment. He should head straight for the shower, but he knew he was going to check his email first.

He downloaded his new messages. Felt his already good mood lift. She'd sent him a message.

If you were here was the heading.

He clicked it open, ignoring messages from a supplier and from a big-time politician wanting to take over the restaurant for a fund-raiser.

If you were here, I would put on a private fashion show for you. I went shopping today on my lunch hour. I don't know why I did it. I was coming back from a meeting with a client, and I saw a window display. Of course, it was a Valentine's display. There was this one outfit that I fell for. I walked on, told myself it was ridiculously expensive and impractical.

I got maybe half a block and then I turned around and went in.

I thought, if I don't love it when I get it on, then that's it. I'm not trying on anything else.

I put it on. Honestly, the change room in that place is like a movie star's boudoir. There was an extra chair in there. I imagined you were sitting in it. I slipped into the outfit and I didn't see my body the critical way I usually see it. I imagined it through your eyes. And you know what?

He shook his head as though answering her rhetorical question. What he knew was, he was hard from sitting there reading a stupid email and imagining he was sitting in a plush chair in a lingerie boutique, probably somewhere on Chicago's Magnificent Mile, and watching Jessica parade in front of him in something sinfully sexy and barely there.

I hope you bought it, he thought to himself.

I loved the way you were looking at me in my imagination. I bought it.
Thinking of you,
Jessica.

Sam sat there at his desk in front of his computer, wearing nothing but his boxer shorts, now tented, thanks to Jessica's email. No woman should own lingerie like that and keep it in her drawer. Or, and here he thought of Lars's Astrid, even think about dating some other guy who happened to be geographically closer. Wasn't going to happen.

He didn't think he had any Viking blood in him, but he absolutely understood the surge of bloodlust he'd seen in Lars's usually mild blue eyes when he'd said Astrid was contemplating dating another man.

Jessica's lingerie-shopping story was obviously meant to arouse him, which it had. For all he knew, she'd invented the whole story for fun. He kind of doubted it though.

He felt that he needed to see this for himself.

When he got to the restaurant he dealt with a minor tantrum in the kitchen. Maurice, one of the sous chefs had been hitting on a young and gorgeous server's assistant. Sam had been keeping an eye on things and was thinking of taking the sous chef aside, except that Francine seemed to be handling him fine.

He had no idea what Maurice, whom they called Mo, had said, but when he walked into the kitchen Francine was tearing a thick and bloody strip off the man, half in English, half in French and some of it in Italian, he thought. But it was so rapid it could have been Spanish. Mo was going four shades of red in the face and backing up until he was pressed against the kitchen counter, while the SA ripped him a new one.

When she saw him standing there, she finally stopped. And glared.

"You got something to say?" she challenged him.

He glanced at Mo, who looked as though he wished he could bolt into the walk-in refrigerator and lock himself in. Possibly forever. Sam caught the gaze of every man in the kitchen, including Patrick, who raised one eyebrow as if saying, *Go ahead and handle this.*

Then Sam turned back to Francine. "Not a thing," he said.

She'd taken care of the situation in her own way and pretty thoroughly at that. "Now, let's get to work."

Everybody scrambled to their stations and Francine headed back out front with the salt she'd come into the kitchen to fetch.

He waited until he got into his office to let the grin out. He'd learned some expressions he'd never heard before. In any language.

He couldn't wait to tell Jessica all about it.

And he realized he was starting to do that. To view incidents that happened to him and think about how he'd word it when he wrote to Jessica.

And damn, he needed to see that lingerie.

If she had made the whole story up, no problem.

He'd drag her into that lingerie boutique and pick out one of everything in her size. Then he'd sit in that big chair and watch as she tried on everything. He might not only look, either.

He might have to touch.

When the food prep was mostly done, Patrick brought in two plates of tonight's special. Fresh, local lamb, early asparagus, and potatoes Dauphinoise. He'd put his own spin on everything. Sam tasted, as he was meant to, approved of all of it, as he was also meant to and nearly always did. They used the time to talk about suppliers, what was fresh, ideas for coming menus, staffing issues. Patrick was his right hand and fast becoming a bit of a local celebrity chef. Sam suspected other restaurants had tried to steal him. He worked very hard to make sure his chef was far too happy to think of leaving.

He was also a close friend.

"You spend the day at the beach?" Chef asked.

He shook his head. "I was skiing." He felt the tiredness in his muscles, the relaxation and contentment that a day in the backcountry brought him. "It was amazing." Knowing Chef didn't share his passion for getting outside and sweating, he left it at that.

Patrick shook his head. "Me, I slept in. Made breakfast for Martha and we read the papers until noon." He grinned. "Then we went back to bed."

Martha was a TV reporter for the evening news. Their relationship worked partly because she also worked nights.

"We all relax in our own ways."

Sam said, "I guess. Listen, when things calm down later in the month I'm thinking of going away for a few days. Can you handle things when I'm gone?"

"Maybe you should put Francine in charge."

They shared a moment of quiet amusement, then he said, "Yeah. Of course. Be good for you to get away. You've been working too hard."

"I love what I do. It doesn't feel like work."

"But—?"

"There's a woman."

"Cherchez la femme."

"Exactly." Oh, he'd be searching out the woman all right. And he hoped, when he found her, that she'd be wearing the exquisite lingerie he now couldn't get out of his mind.

"I've never been the kind of man who goes goofy over a woman."

"You never had the right woman before."

"Exactly."

"Where does she live?"

"Chicago."

Patrick tilted his head one way and then the other. "Could be closer, but could be farther."

He thought of Lars and Astrid and thought that at least Jessica didn't live in Sweden. That clearly belonged in the plus column.

A lot of things belonged in the plus column, he thought as he composed an email to her much later, after he'd closed the restaurant and gone home.

His apartment seemed quiet; he was still wired from work as he often was, so this was a nice time to settle in bed with his laptop and talk to Jessica.

If I were there...
I have a million ideas of what I'd do if I were there with you. I want to see you in your new lingerie, and take it off you slowly. I was thinking how much I want to be with you. And then I thought, why the hell not?

Okay, he was going out on a limb here, he realized. Maybe it was the combination of Lars worrying about losing Astrid to another guy, and the relentless hearts-and-flowers mood of most of his customers as they crammed in before-the-big-day dates with spouses, lovers and dates.

Didn't matter. He needed to know if she was as into him as he was into her.

I am desperate to spend more time with you.

Nothing like putting it all on the line.
But desperate?
He deleted that.

I long to spend more time with you.

Better.

I wish I could spend February 14 with you, but obviously it's impossible since it's one of the busiest days and nights at Benedict.
But I am thinking of taking a few days off later in the month and coming to see you in Chicago.
What do you think?
Sam.

He read over what he'd written, realized he was pushing her a little bit, but then if she didn't want to see him again, he'd be better to know now than to keep getting deeper and deeper into an online love affair.

Besides, in his opinion, love affairs should always be conducted in the flesh.

CHAPTER TWELVE

JESSICA WALKED INTO the bar where she was meeting the girls for an after-work drink followed by sushi. It was a regular date and whoever could make it, made it. There were usually four or six women, and sometimes a couple of guys tagged along.

Morgan spotted her the second she walked in and rushed up to her. She started to say, "I have a surpri—" And then stopped. Stared closer. "What have you been doing to yourself? You look like you just got back from a week at the spa and I know you've been at work all day because we texted."

She felt the excitement that had been bubbling inside her start to spill over. She hadn't even told Morgan, because she'd wanted to share the email in person. "Look," she squealed, pulling Sam's latest message up onto her screen.

"Read it!"

Morgan raised an eyebrow. "Will it make me blush?"

"Do you even know how to blush?"

"Good point." Morgan began to read. At the end, she yelled, "Yes!" and grabbed Jessica in a quick hug. "Omigod, he is so into you. He's coming to Chicago. And you don't even live in Chicago."

"I know. I was worried I'd been too personal telling him about the sexy lingerie I bought, but it was exactly the right thing to do. Now he wants to fly down to see me."

"So, what are you going to do now? Move back home?"

"No. Definitely not." She shrugged. "I'll think of something. It's not like I lied or anything. I didn't correct his mistaken belief, which is different."

"And not really something he can call you on since he let you continue thinking he was a mere waiter and not the Benedict who owns Benedict."

"Exactly."

"So, you'll email him the truth?"

"I'm working on it."

"Well, work on it fast, before the poor guy ends up in the Windy City all alone."

She shook her hair back, feeling in love with the world and every single person in it. "Who's all here tonight?"

"The regulars. Plus a couple of plus-ones."

"Oh, yeah? Anybody interesting?" Something about Morgan's too casual tone suggested she might have come tonight with her own surprise.

And had she ever.

When they got to the round table around which half-a-dozen of her girlfriends sat were two men. The first, Josh, she knew was on and off with Diane their stockbroker friend. Looked like they were on again. And the other guy was familiar but she couldn't place him. He sort of looked like somebody famous. When he saw her he gave her a half wave, as if he sort of knew her, too. Then it hit her. He was the Seth Rogen look-alike from the coffee shop. He'd obviously abandoned *Ulysses* for Morgan.

"I don't think you were introduced the other day," Morgan said, looking pretty pleased with herself, "but this is Phil. Phil, this is Jessica."

"Hi, Phil."

"Hi, Jessica."

When a waitress arrived with a huge plate of nachos, she ordered a beer and then, under cover of the flurry of napkins and general chatter, said to Morgan, "I can't believe you picked up the guy from the coffee shop."

"Please. He did the asking."

"Does he know how old you are?"

"Shut up! He's only a couple of years younger."

"I thought he was a grad student."

"Nope. He's teaching. Already has his PhD." She sighed. "He's so intellectual and yet kind of adorably clumsy, you know?"

"Not your usual type."

"Exactly. Which has to be a good thing, right?"

"Oh, yeah."

"He reads me poetry," she said in a low voice.

"Really?"

"Yes. I can't believe how sexy poetry can be."

Everybody was in a good mood, it seemed. By unspoken agreement they never complained about men when there were guys in the group, so the conversation stayed on work, bands, new movies and what everybody was doing for the weekend. With Valentine's Day being Friday night it was a slightly touchy subject, but then Diane announced she was having a party Friday and everybody was invited.

She glanced under her lashes at Josh as she said it, so Jessica figured it meant he was still on probation but if he showed up at her place Friday it signaled he was interested, and if she let him stay, it meant they were back on. At least, that's what she thought was going on.

Phil and Morgan were flirty and adorable.

And Jessica had a man who wanted to fly hundreds of miles just to see her.

Life was good.

SHE WASN'T TOO late home, so she waited until she was curled up in bed to pull out her laptop.

If you were here...

Jessica reread Sam's email for about the fortieth time and felt almost as warm a glow as she'd experienced the first time she read it.

She replied,

I long to see you again, too.

It was so true. She ached with wanting.

Get your big day out of the way and we can talk about travel plans next week.

She hoped that didn't sound too casual, but she didn't want him booking anything, obviously.

She typed:

When I see you, I will be wearing my brand-new lingerie.
   Love, Jessica

She pushed Send.
He must have been checking email at that moment for an almost instant response came back.

Not for long.

A wave of intense arousal hit her. She got out of bed, went to her closet and pulled the lingerie bag off the top shelf. The lilac tissue, imprinted with the boutique's name, rustled like the sound of birthday and Christmas mornings. She eased out the gorgeous, sexy silk and satin. It was the palest of pinks, with hints of lace. And there wasn't much of it. She'd never owned a garter belt before, but the clerk had assured her that with her long legs the French stockings would be fabulous.

She gave in and tried the whole outfit on and had loved how she looked. The best part was that she could wear a perfectly respectable dress on top and when he unwrapped her—well, hopefully he'd feel like he got his birthday and Christmas mornings all rolled into one.

Knowing that he wanted to see her again, enough to take time off from a busy restaurant and fly hundreds of miles made her brave. Brave enough to accept her own insecurities and face the truth. This was more than a fun one-night fantasy.

How much more she had no idea, but she was certain of one thing. There was no way she wanted to go through the rest of her life wondering how much more there could have been if she hadn't been too chicken to take the plunge. To put herself out there.

By Thursday night she hadn't heard anything from Morgan but one quick text earlier in the day that said simply: *Love poetry.* This was followed by three smiley faces.

That was good, of course, but really, Phil must be all the way through *Leaves of Grass* and working his way through Wordsworth, Keats, Shelley and the rest of the romantic poets by now. He'd be hoarse from reading!

Or more likely, knowing Morgan, worn-out from sex.

Morgan should give the man a break and call her friend, who could use her advice right about now.

Maybe not advice. What she really needed was a bit of Go Girl! Get your man! Jump his bones! And a whole bunch more slogans ending in exclamation points, which Morgan was so good at giving her.

Jessica had to accept that she could really use a little nudging in the man-hunting, "go bold or go home" department.

But her prime nudger seemed to be otherwise engaged. Or, at least, what Morgan was nudging was an intellectual, poetry-reciting cutie pie.

Jessica was on her own.

Okay, she thought, I can do this.

She reminded herself that she was a professional event planner.

She was very good at planning ahead.

When she got nervous, she reread the emails she and Sam had exchanged during the past week. She loved how they flowed from the I-miss-your-hot-body-type messages at the start of the week to really opening up and getting to know each other as the week progressed. Maybe it was the fact that she was alone with her keyboard that she felt so free to tell him things.

And, of course, his honesty and openness coming back to her only increased the intimacy.

She had a couple of calls to make, a few things to organize.

She picked up her phone, started to chicken out, then she stormed to her bathroom, put the lights on full and stared at her reflection in the mirror. She tried to put Morgan's cocky expression on her face and she yelled at herself.

"You can do this!"

"What have you got to lose?"

"You go, girl!"

Then, still glaring at her own reflection, she punched numbers into her cell phone.

CHAPTER THIRTEEN

SAM WOKE TO the sound of a dog barking like crazy somewhere outside. Or maybe inside his building. Hard to tell. All he knew was that he hadn't had nearly enough sleep. He'd worked long past closing last night, making sure everything they could possibly do ahead for Valentine's Day, one of the biggest days in the restaurant calendar, was done.

By rearranging the seating they'd squeezed two extra tables in. He didn't like doing it, but now two very happy couples were off the waiting list. One was a guy who'd almost cried, he was so happy. He planned to propose to his girlfriend during dinner. In a busy restaurant. On Valentine's Day.

"Good luck to you," Sam said, agreeing to have a bottle of chilled champagne ready, assuming the poor woman actually wanted to marry a man who got teary over a restaurant reservation.

He'd finally fallen into bed around three. Now it was what? Eight? He groaned, shoved a pillow over his head, wanting one more hour. But the dog started up again. Another dog? A squirrel? Who knew, but the barking grew shriller and more hysterical until Sam gave up and rolled out of bed.

The steady tapping of rain on the skylight in his

apartment only added to his less-than-stellar mood. Valentine's Day. And the sky was pissing all over him. And his own personal valentine was miles and miles away.

Perfect.

He put on a pot of coffee, adding extra grounds because he could already tell he was going to need the turbo punch of caffeine.

He waited until he had his first mug in hand and then fired up his computer. Foolish to feel hopeful.

But he felt a rush of relief when he saw an email from Jessica. It had an attachment. A goofy, silly ecard with huge animated hearts and a computer-generated version of an old love song. He smiled, appreciating that she'd put in the effort. What had he expected? A bouquet of roses?

But then he hadn't sent her anything. Well, he didn't have her address for a start. Or her phone number.

He emailed her back.

Happy V. Day.
I liked the card. Thanks. I'm not good at cards and flowers. But I do have something for you. I'll be giving it to you in person. I can't wait to see you!

He thought for a moment and continued.

Valentine's Day is both the best of days and the worst of days in the restaurant trade. The tips are good, the business is booming, and most of the customers are out to be pleased, but it's crazy busy.

And the expectations are ridiculous. How can you prove you love someone in a single night?

Shouldn't we be proving to the people closest to us that they matter every single day?

Does that make me sound like a fool? Probably. I admit, I'm in a mood. A barking dog woke me up too early. Instead of working solidly from ten this morning until the last lovesick romantic wanders out the door tonight, I wish I was spending the whole day with you.

He wondered what she was doing tonight and then didn't want to ask. If she was going out on the town, he did not want to know. His day already seemed dark and dreary enough.

Then he mentally smacked himself upside the head. He should be beside himself with excitement. His restaurant, the massive risk he'd taken, had paid off. Benedict was full most nights. Today was going to be their busiest day on record and there was a huge waiting list of disappointed diners hoping to squeeze in thanks to last-minute cancellations.

He and his team had made a success in one of the toughest businesses around. A man who took that kind of achievement lightly was a dick.

He decided he wasn't going to be a dick.

Not today.

He ended his message saying, I'll email you when I get home. I'll tell you a secret. Got a guy hoping to get engaged tonight. Keep your fingers crossed the gal says yes.

Sam.

He went to the closet, pulled down a small gift bag from the top shelf. He'd bought the thing on impulse, walking past a gift store a few days ago. A small glass—he didn't know what it was. A paperweight? Something about the colors had reminded him of Jessica. He thought about the colors in her eyes, the blue-and-green lights against the clear gray. And he recalled how enthralled she'd been by the Dale Chihuly exhibit. Of course, this one wasn't a Chihuly. He'd have needed a few thousand for that. And it wasn't a knock off, either. This artist had her own style. He'd stepped into the store on impulse. When he picked up the piece it had felt smooth in his hand and the colors and shapes swirling inside made him think again of Jessica's eyes, especially when they were sparking with passion.

And passion, he reminded himself, as he looked at the small piece for a few minutes before restoring it to the top of his closet, was what the love of food and serving foodies was about.

He found himself reminding himself of his own pep talk as he sloshed through puddles to get to the restaurant.

He felt the energy in the staff as they arrived. Some were pumped about being so busy, knowing they'd be worked off their feet but also knowing that the customers would be happy, the tips exceptional. Some seemed as if they had better things to do.

When all the prep was done and they had a few minutes to spare, he called everybody together.

He looked around at his crew. The chefs and kitchen help, the servers, the assistant servers, the hostesses, the bussers, the sommelier, the bartend-ers. He found himself grinning. "Happy Valentine's Day!"

He received a chorus of "Back at ya" and some weak grins.

"This is going to be a record day for us. Our first Valentine's Day. I rely on you guys every day to make Benedict work, and you never let me down. I am proud of what we've accomplished. You should be, too. I personally would never go near a restau-rant on Valentine's Day." General laughter and agree-ment. "But most regular people haven't figured that out yet. They are coming to us today to celebrate. Maybe it's the beginning of a relationship, maybe it's an old married couple. Maybe, like Dave at table 4, somebody's going to propose. Whatever brings them here, they are trying to show that special person they care. I want us to remind every single customer, no matter how busy it gets out there, that we care too. Let's show Seattle that we know love!"

Maybe it completely sucked as a pep talk, but he felt good for sharing his thoughts and he felt the energy shift. There was more joking around, more smiles. When the doors opened and the chaos began, he felt the team shift into gear smoothly and effi-ciently.

He did the rounds, made sure everyone was hav-ing a good time. Helped out as needed, coaxed Francine out of the storeroom when she became overwhelmed with missing her boyfriend in Geneva.

They barely had time to reset the tables and grab a quick staff meal and then the dinner rush began.

He kept an eye on table 4, delivered the champagne personally when a relieved Dave gave the signal that she'd said yes. After Dave slipped the ring on her finger and she ran around the table to throw her arms around him, they both cried, so he figured Dave had found the right woman.

Naturally, with that kind of performance, the couple was greeted with hearty congratulations from nearby diners, and as word quickly spread, the room erupted into spontaneous applause.

It was a good night, Sam began to realize as he gazed around at his patrons, some of whom were regulars and some brand-new to Benedict.

He slipped out a couple of Valentine Fantasy desserts to the newly engaged couple compliments of the house and then turned his attention to helping behind the busy bar.

It was closing in on midnight when the last diners were gone, the last dishes done and he realized the night had been a huge success.

He high-fived Chef.

He thought about suggesting a nightcap, then he noticed a bright pink envelope sitting prominently on the counter with his name on it.

"What's this?" Had the staff gone in for a Valentine card?

He glanced at the few remaining staff, but nobody seemed to be too interested.

He ripped open the flap.

Inside was a Valentine card all right.

It said, "Tonight is for You," on the front. There was a sketch of the outline of a pair of sexy legs and a pair of lips. Okay, then, not from the staff. Intrigued, he opened the card.

Inside was a keycard. A very familiar card. He knew which hotel and he was pretty sure he'd find himself going to the same room where he'd spent one of the most amazing nights of his life.

Along with the keycard was a handwritten message.

I'm waiting for you.

He laughed out loud.

"What?" Chef asked.

"Turns out I have a hot date for the evening," he said, unable to keep the smile off his face.

There were a couple of Valentine Fantasy desserts left. "Box me up one of those desserts, will you? And take the other one home to your wife."

He grabbed a chilled bottle of his best champagne, collected the dessert and headed out into the night.

It was still raining, but what did he care?

He stopped briefly at his apartment to pick up the gift he hadn't imagined being able to give to Jessica so soon.

He had a million questions about how and why, but he knew they could wait. Until morning.

For now, he had a very important woman to see. And a very important Valentine Fantasy to deliver.

He grabbed an extra ten minutes to shower and brush his teeth, stuff some condoms in a reusable shopping bag with the gift and the wine. Then he picked up the pastry box and headed to her hotel, every inch of his skin beginning to burn as he thought about having that sweet, hot woman all to himself. All night long.

He was so aroused just thinking of all the ways he was going to make love to her that he had to hold the bag in front of him as he rode up the elevator, thankfully alone.

He walked along the corridor, feeling her draw him closer. He knocked on the door. Waited.

The door slowly opened for him and there she stood, wearing lingerie so silky and erotic that even his vivid imagination hadn't been up to the job.

She smiled, shy and sexy—and his.

He stood there stupidly, the bakery box in one hand, his bag in the other. The moment stretched. She put her hand up and pushed her hair back, hooking it over her ear. She glanced at the box and said, "You brought me my Valentine Fantasy."

"No," he said, finally finding his voice and crossing the threshold into her room. "You brought me mine."

He had his arms wrapped around her and was kissing her deeply as the door swung slowly shut behind them.

* * * * *

Jina Bacarr wrote the award-winning *The Blonde Geisha* and *The Japanese Art of Sex*. She worked as the Japan consultant on KCBS-TV, MSNBC, TechTV's *Wired for Sex*, Canada's *Pleasure Zone*, British Sky Broadcasting's *Saucy TV*, Venice's La Biennale, *Men's Health Guide to the Best Sex in the World*, *Passport to Pleasure*, The Vision Board and Playboy TV. She is author of *Naughty Paris*; *Spies, Lies & Naked Thighs*; *Cleopatra's Perfume* (an RT Reviewers' Choice Award nominee); and *The Blonde Samurai*, an *RT Book Reviews* Top Pick.

NAKED SUSHI
Jina Bacarr

To Roberta Brown,
who has always been there for me.

CHAPTER ONE

NAKED AND AS helpless as a beached mermaid, I held my breath. I was about to get eaten by the sexiest man alive.

I knew taking off my clothes was not a smart career move. But did I listen?

Did I?

Out of work and desperate, I had no choice but to take this gig if I wanted to survive. So here I was, lying on a table nude except for a shiny pink thong, banana leaf and yellow pom-pom chrysanthemums, which covered my breasts.

A live sushi plate.

Rose petals lay scattered around me, and was that pickled ginger I smelled?

What if I sneezed?

It got worse when I saw the gorgeous man who got me fired from my computer job grabbing a sliver of red tuna off my belly, pinching me.

Ouch, that hurt.

He gave me the "sorry, babe" look that got me into trouble in the first place. Those smoldering dark eyes of his had led me into temptation. Self-assured and no doubt used to getting his own way, he oozed danger from every pore. I would have followed him to hell if he'd asked me.

He didn't. Instead, he seduced me on top of the copy machine at midnight. His tall, athletic body crushing mine against the glass, his hands everywhere. And every dark fantasy I ever had came true. An orgasm that kept coming. And coming...

I groaned.

God, look at that grin. He knew what I was thinking. He knew I wanted him even if I was majorly pissed at him.

Then he had the nerve to wipe his chopsticks across my midriff, leaving a trail of sticky white rice. His tongue flickered out as if he intended to lick the gummy rice off my bare skin.

Oh, yes, please!

I dared not move a muscle.

I couldn't believe I was lying here naked, belly up, with raw fish spread out all over my body, even around my pubic area. Waiting for this guy to make his move. He appeared unconcerned by the fact I was at his mercy. I would have died if his sexy lips nibbled on me, lips that I imagined were both soft and rough, tender yet insistent in finding out what was underneath that crisp, brown banana leaf glued to my mound.

As if I was going to let *that* happen.

Phew. I smelled like raw fish, tasted like raw fish, and I had raw fish, cold and slimy, sliding down between my thighs, much to the delight of the salivating man breathing on me. I felt so vulnerable lying here, unable to move, as I watched him licking his chops.

I stifled a groan in the back of my throat, imagining him pushing his probing finger into me, testing the moistness inside me, his touch arousing me before his mouth found the pleasure of my pinkness. Sucking on me, giving my swollen clit so much attention I could hardly stand it.

In my mind, he stroked me faster and harder, delicious sensations building inside me and the ache turning into an unrelenting agony when he went down on me and—

Dream on. I'll never let my defenses down again. How can I?

It was because of *him* I got fired from my job. I allowed my overripe female hormones to be seduced by this man with a slow, irresistible smile.

And a great butt.

He looked amused, which annoyed the hell out of me. Because of my indiscretion, I wasn't getting unemployment checks, my savings were almost gone, and my rent was due.

Naked sushi, indeed.

I wasn't just pissed. I was going to get even.

IT ALL STARTED weeks ago when I was working late, preparing to copy the cue sheets for a commercial spot due in the morning. No big deal. Five minutes of slaving over a hot copy machine, and I'd be heading home to my studio apartment with Chinese takeout.

A single girl's best friend, next to her rabbit vibrator.

The office manager had gone home, so I decided to do the job myself, though I wasn't familiar with how the new machine worked. I was a computer research analyst programmer for a video game company, better known in the world of corporate acronyms as CRAP.

It was a private joke among programmers. No corporation could run without our snappy codes and erratic symbols splashed across pages of files that looked like Jackson Pollock got stuck inside a computer.

I liked my job.

I analyzed and edited clips of our company's ads and video games and then recoded the video and audio files and converted them for various media. I also did postproduction, including sweetening the videos with music. When I got bored, I'd get creative and do fun things, like embed hidden erotic poems into corporate microdots in PowerPoint presentations. Easy as texting if you knew how.

All you had to do was create a new text box on a slide and type in sexy stuff like, "Did your last date speak French without an interpreter?" Then change the font color to the background color to make it invisible before shrinking it down to a small, dot-sized box. Add a grid, note the box's location, and then send that to all the programmers. The clued-in ones without computer anxiety knew how to read the sexy message. Made Tuesday morning meetings a lot more fun.

I also added sexy French words to the background tracks on test video games. I was good at picking up languages. And I loved messing around with spy stuff, which was why I'd applied to the CIA, FBI, DEA and ATF.

I never got past the written exams.

I found out sporting anchor-girl glasses didn't place me high on their list of qualified applicants. I was saving up to get Lasik surgery before I got canned, but I could never get the cash together.

Then there was the matter of my questionable background. I was a security risk because I didn't know who my parents were. How could I? Officer O'Malley found me when someone dumped me at the 16th Street Mission BART Station while I was still in diapers. He gave me his surname and called me Mary Dolores after the mission nearby, but the guys knew me as "Pepper." I started calling myself that in the eighth grade to rev up my sex quotient.

Since it was doubtful I'd make it as a covert operative, I was determined to be the best at my job. I was really comfy at my last place of employment. You *could* call me an arty techie, which was why things like outdated office furniture and dirty bathrooms, leaky ceilings and vermin of the four-legged kind bugged me.

I found out you can't escape the two-legged ones no matter how cool the decor was. I worked at one company with a gang of programmers who thought using soap was for girly men. Worse yet, I could hear rats scurrying above me. When a ceiling tile came loose and I saw a tail and two little feet dangling over my head, I bailed.

At my last job we had airy working spaces, bathrooms with cut flowers and a lunchroom with a junk

food menu to die for. Unlike a lot of software companies who dip their sticks in Silicon Valley, my
ex-boss took over a restored Victorian house in San
Francisco and turned it into a first-class company
facility.

I loved discovering the secrets of the old house,
including hidden cabinets, desks with locked draw-
ers, even a concealed entrance.

And I had my own office. No backseat surfers
peering over my shoulder and trying to tell me how
to write code. Add to that a steaming-hot mocha latte
on my desk every morning and I was stylin'.

Damn, I wanted my job back. That place was *cool*.
It was the *why* I got fired that had me pissed.

I had sex in the copy machine room. My cheap
surrender over the copier, buttocks thumping, my
rear end overexposed.

I admit it took two to fandango, but it wasn't *all*
my fault. I was hungry—and not just for Chinese
takeout. I spent way too much time alone. It wasn't
easy keeping a man interested when you get excited
by new software programs and he had a hard-on.
My last boyfriend dumped me because I worked late
nights stressing over things like audio warping.

I noticed guys didn't dig chicks who knew more
about their computers than they did. Consequently,
my dating life consisted of hanging out at a virtual
world website and having an orgasm while I watched
my flashy avatar have all the fun.

So who could blame me for taking advantage of the situation when I cornered a stud in the
copy room?

Not just any stud, but my dream guy.

For years, I'd pined over the bad-boy type. Bare chest ripped to please and tease. Cute butt. And a lazy swirl of black hair that covered one eye at just the right angle. Daring a girl to go further into the dark with him...

And *not* look back.

Maybe it was because I was tired of Chinese take-out or because I forgot to buy new batteries for my bunny vibe. Or maybe my new underwear was too tight in the crotch. Whatever the reason, I was feeling extra horny that night.

It all seemed surreal.

Midnight. Quiet offices. Dark shadows everywhere. Beckoning me like black holes you could fall through and land in an alternative universe.

I could almost hear the creepy *Rocky Horror Picture Show* music guiding my every step as I tramped down the empty hallway.

Then I noticed a light coming from under the copy room door.

I stopped. I wasn't alone. Who else was here, then?

I should have minded my own business, gone home and copied the damn thing in the morning. But the snoopy part of my personality that was convinced I had the makings of a spy wasn't about to walk away.

As soon as I opened the door, I discovered a guy I'd never seen before, making copies. I didn't think it totally strange since Mr. Briggs, the owner of the company, recently hired an up-and-coming video game designer to boost sales in new media. I figured he was copying the Playmate of the Month to hang up in his locker. All the guys did that.

It never occurred to me to slam the door and run for help. I was too involved in eyeing his hard butt.

And those shoulders. Yum.

He was wearing a black baseball cap and black sweats, which should have alerted me that something was wrong, but it added to my fantasy of getting locked in here with him after hours.

I burst out with a cocky, "Copying corporate secrets?"

He spun around and my breath quickened. My eyes fixed on the bulge in his sweatpants with both apprehension and desire. Spiky black hair covered his dark eyes like the mane of a wild animal; his mouth curled into a snarl that relaxed when he saw me.

"Who are you?" he asked, with a teasing smile. The dark shadow of a two-day beard heightened the cut of his angular jaw. "Security?"

His hand edged toward his pocket, a movement that didn't escape my eye. What was he reaching for? His smartphone?

I laughed in a casual manner, trying to keep the conversation light. "Who needs security with *you* around?"

He grinned and then took his hand away from his pocket and cupped my chin. When he stared into my eyes, my knees turned to honey, all warm and melty. A shiver went through me.

"What's your name?" he asked.

"Pepper."

"Are you as hot as your name?" he wanted to know, bumping his hip into mine, his hot breath steaming up my glasses. His tough, sexy talk took me to a place I'd only dreamed of going. His voice gripped me, making me squeeze my pubic muscles in a delicious manner and then release them.

"How'd you like to find out?" I said, tossing him a wicked grin.

I loved saying that, figuring he'd laugh like the other programmers and then slap me on the back and ask me to go have a beer.

Imagine my surprise when he didn't.

His MOUTH CLAIMED mine, his lips moist and hot rubbing on my dry, cracked skin. He extended his curious journey to my bottom lip, nibbling on it until I surrendered to him like a hungry guppy. As if I had any choice. Before I could take a breath, his tongue darted into my mouth, sucking the air from me. That delicious moment stirred the fires in me left unattended for too long.

I couldn't get enough of him.

Tasting, probing, exploring me in a long, uninterrupted kiss. I was acutely aware of his intentions, that he was demanding something I wasn't ready to give. Sex with an improper stranger. Something new for me, seeing how I'd always skated through life on the sidelines.

Not tonight.

We were alone in here. Kissing like two teenagers, making loud noises and tearing at each other's clothes. Nothing but the sound of our ragged breathing and the steady hum of the copy machine to keep us company. Drumming through my head like a vibrator on cruise control. I purred like a kitten, listening to my inner rhythm and loving it. I gave in willingly, my hormones flowing in harmony with his need, my need.

"Silly, dumb, stupid" were adjectives I'd use to describe my actions, but what girl stopped to think when a kiss was *this* good? I didn't. My body became the prey of this corporate raider Casanova. His hands were all over me, toying with my heavy red-plaid flannel shirt, yanking at the buttons hanging on for dear life. With one small tug, he popped off the top two.

Oh, Lord, what next?

I did nothing to stop him when he cupped my breasts, wondering how far he'd go. He trailed his fingers along the flimsy black lace edging of my bra.

"Mmm…" he moaned. Was he enjoying the kiss? Or surprised that a geek like me was into sexy underwear?

Just wait until you see my new French-cut black satin panties, I wanted tell him. But I was so conscious of his devouring mouth on mine, my entire being trembling with suppressed emotion, I didn't dare break the lip-lock.

Besides, I wasn't going to let him get that far.

Was I?

Pressed up against the copy machine, I began to have my doubts. I couldn't move, as surely as if I were tied down, my legs spread wide apart, his groin pressed into my mound. His hands wandered. Oh, boy, did they wander, searching up and down my body, his fingers pulling apart my shirt and letting it flap in the cool breeze blowing through the over-head AC vent.

"Oh, yes," I barely breathed when he broke the kiss and then placed his hands on each side of my waist and squeezed it. I couldn't stop the shiver that ran through me when he touched my bare skin. I wanted him to go back to eyeing the cute black lace edging of my bra with a front hook.

A front hook, I wanted to shout.

No fancy maneuvering needed to prove to me how much of a stud he was by reaching around and un-doing my bra with one hand.

My nipples ached for his touch, but he seemed fix-ated on stroking and then pressing the flesh on my hips. His hands roamed over my buttocks and then up and down my legs, gripping and squeezing them with a cavalier vigor that did me in. I arched my back toward him to give him greater access to me.

He grabbed my crotch.

I moaned. Damn, did it get any better than this?

Who would have thought I'd get caught in the copy room with a sexy guy when I had to work late? Not me. Had the geek fairy godmother heard my prayers and brought me a man of my own?

A little voice crept into my head, telling me to grow up and quit believing in fairy tales like my best friend, Cindy, but I couldn't turn back now. I pre-tended I was a bucking bronco and this cowboy was taking me for a long, sexy ride. I writhed, humped and nearly assaulted him. I grabbed his black T-shirt and raked my nails up and down his chest. Wanting to touch him, feel him.

I breathed desire in his ear, not wanting to let him go. Still, I walked a delicate tightrope with this man. My ego was on the line. On one hand, I yearned to break boldly out of my shell. To act upon this chance encounter without guilt, no regret. Let him touch me, fondle me.

On the other, I was scared shitless.

What if I disappointed him?

This was a common problem with me. Analyzing the hell out of everything I did, even sex. I was no sleek avenger with all the right moves. I was more like the sassy-mouthed brainiac in the spy flicks who sat at her computer, tapping out answers on her fancy keyboard. Not that I'm bad looking, but I came off as an easy mark when I tried to flirt. I was too eager to please without thinking about the consequences.

Not tonight.

Sexually charged up, incredibly intense, I decided to go for it. I stepped out of my ordinary world and relished this escape from reality. My blue-rimmed spectacles slid all the way down my perspiration-slick nose. I didn't push them back up.

How could I?

I was completely helpless in his arms when his hand dropped down between my legs, his fingers pressing against me. I wiggled my ass. I wished my jeans were off and he was pushing through my pubic hair until he found my throbbing clit.

Just thinking about it made me moan again; the steady pressure of his fingers rubbing against the rough denim stressed me out. I sensed this man possessed an enjoyment of sex that went way beyond a casual cop-a-feel.

A buzzing excitement slithered through me when I rubbed up against him, primal-like, daring him to tame me. I imagined him pulling down my jeans and panties and then probing me with his tongue, massaging all around my clitoris with his mouth. I growled, the low sound coming from the back of my throat.

That aroused him more.

I wiggled my hips, hoping he'd get the message. Something about the methodical yet sensual way he touched me set off a slow burn between my legs I couldn't ignore.

"Don't stop," I whispered, pulling on the drawstring of his sweats, but I couldn't untie the knot. "It feels so good."

"You tempt me, babe," he said, kissing the nape of my neck. "Are there cameras in here?"

I shake my head. "Mr. Briggs is too cheap for that."

"Then what are we waiting for?" He kissed me again, deeper this time, his hands holding me tighter. Pulling at my jeans and searching for the zipper hidden beneath the button-down flap in front.

"Allow me." I unbuttoned the flap, nearly ripping it off.

"I'm curious," he said, drawing down the zipper on my jeans with an alacrity that set me on edge. "How did you know I was in here?"

"I didn't. I thought everyone had gone home."

"You're *sure* no one's around?" He nibbled on my earlobe and then licked all around my ear until I shivered with pleasure.

"Yes. It's Super Tuesday."

"What's that?" he asked.

"Poker night. The guys meet at Sam's Bar after work and memorize cards." A lightbulb moment flickered in my brain, making me ask, "How come they didn't invite you?"

"I prefer strip poker." He ran his fingers over my bare midriff, digging them down into the elastic waistband of my panties. I moaned and instinctively pushed against him. From the grin on his face, I could see he was turned-on.

"How about a game of Five-Card Stud?" I mumbled no louder than a whisper. Could he smell my need, moistening my panties with droplets of desire? *I* could, which meant I couldn't wait much longer.

"I've got a winning hand right here," he said, grabbing my ass.

What would happen next, I could only guess. Anticipation, I found out, could be as good as or better than the sex.

I didn't have long to wait to find out.

He turned me around and faced me toward the copier and then slid my jeans down below my thighs. Next, he pulled down my black silky panties and then ran his finger up and down the crack in my rear, eliciting a moan from me. I wiggled my butt as his fingers moved up and down in an intimate manner so close to my anal hole I couldn't stop panting.

The naughty girl in me was overly excited by what

was happening to me in the chilly copy room. I felt daring with my pants down in this high-tech room in an old Victorian mansion, once the seat of respectability.

And, boy, was I turned-on.

In spite of the air-cooled temp, I seethed with heated anticipation when he positioned himself behind me and then eased forward to push the bulge in his pants against my bare butt. I heard the snap of a condom.

"Is that a new one?" I asked him, hopeful.

That surprised him. "Don't worry," he said, laughing. "The expiration date is years away."

I sighed, relieved. If I were thinking straight, that would have alerted me that something was wrong. Most programmers I knew carry subprime, expired condoms. But I wasn't thinking straight. Instead, I twisted my head around and saw him pull out his dick and slip a raincoat over it.

Jeez.

"Big" didn't begin to describe him.

I licked my lips.

I arched my back in total surrender when I felt his erect cock push against the cheeks of my backside. He found me wet and ready for him when he inserted one finger and then two inside me. Without a word, he slid into me with ease. I rode him without fear, his cock moving in and out of me, my passion building, his breathing becoming more erratic with each thrust. I squeezed my eyes, and I swear tears escaped onto my cheeks. My feelings became so intense I couldn't help myself.

I moaned and moaned and moaned.

I didn't care about anything else then. All I could do was let go. I couldn't believe my luck. This was *me*, Pepper, desired by a sexy man. Instead of always being on the outside looking at the cool people, I was having a booty call at midnight, and it was sublime.

His hips smacked into my butt, pushing his cock into me, his breathing coming loud and fast. I could barely utter a word. My throat was hoarse from letting go of my emotions and the pent-up feelings buried so deep inside me. I couldn't *wait* for release. I swear he sensed my desperation. He nuzzled his face in my hair, muttering sexy endearments in my ear, his musky, intoxicating smell overwhelming me. Then he fucked me harder, his thrusts stronger, his rhythm unchanging as his cock filled me until it was almost painful. I didn't care.

"Harder," I yelled.

The stirrings of a powerful orgasm built inside me. That delicious spiral of something intangible swirling around inside you. Promising you a taste of pleasure beyond what you've experienced; pleasure you will do *anything* for.

I couldn't hold back much longer.

I leaned forward over the copy machine, pushing my buttocks up against him, urging him on. His body stiffened against me and he yelled out, his voice ragged, vibrating off the walls.

The room swayed in front of my eyes, the steady rhythm of *sex, sex, sex* beating in my brain like frenetic drummers with ceaseless energy. A surge much like an electrical charge gripped us both, racing through his body and into mine.

Then he came.

His explosive climax set off an out-of-control response in me. I went wild, crying out, thrashing about and slamming my hands down on the platen glass of the copy machine. Crazed, frantic, lost in whirling abandon, I slid my sweaty palms all over the machine. Wild, pawing, and scratching like a wolf in heat.

Oh, my God, it was good.

It didn't last.

In a wild moment, I pushed the copy button by mistake. A powerful white light flooded into my face as the light bar moved back and forth, blinding me.

I hit another button and a blaring alarm went off.

Oh, shit.

I was a goner.

CHAPTER TWO

Damn. I couldn't see.

Groping helplessly, I fumbled around, trying to turn off the alarm, my panic mounting. Screeching, raw sounds grated on my ears, sending my passion into a nosedive.

No. No.

I pushed the button again, but the noise wouldn't stop. I pushed another button, then *another*, but the damn thing kept shrieking like a video game villain gone berserk.

"What the fuck—" yelled the stud in black sweats, slipping out of me and then pulling up his pants.

"I can't turn it off," I cried out, frantic.

He pulled his baseball cap down lower. "Sorry I can't help you, babe. Gotta go."

Before I could pull up my jeans, he grabbed the file along with the copies from the exit tray and started for the door.

"*Wait!*" I yelled. "I didn't come yet."

"I owe you one," he said, kissing me on the cheek. Tender-like. That surprised me. Then he saluted me with the tip of his cock—I mean, *cap*—before he raced out the door. I noticed then his hair looked weird, askew. It didn't hit me until later he was wearing a dark wig under that cap.

"You can't leave me like this," I moaned, sinking down to my knees with my jeans squashed around my ankles. "You can't."

I squeezed my pubes together, but the unbearable ache in my groin wouldn't go away. And that noise. I couldn't stand it. I hit the machine with my fist, expecting it to blow up in my face. I didn't care if it did.

To my surprise, the noise stopped.

The room went deadly quiet. Like a tomb.

I let out my breath and wiped off the sweat running down my cheeks, my neck. The silence was worse. My passion refusing to die, my ego suffering, my mind telling me I must withdraw, retreat. Forget him.

I couldn't.

I wanted to cry.

I was caught up in a web of fantasy that had crossed over into my real world, and I didn't want to escape its spell. I wanted to remain in this sexual wonderland like I was Alice.

Still groggy, frustrated, I noticed the stud had dropped the original file on his way out but taken the copies with him. Curious, I reached over to grab the sheets of paper spread out on the floor.

No sooner did I wrap my fingers around the official-looking documents than Ms. Sims, Mr. Briggs's office manager, burst through the door, yelling, "What the hell are you doing in here?"

The Wicked Witch of the West.

In person.

She glared at me through her glued-on lashes. You'd think she'd never seen nude buttocks before when she saw me scrambling to pick up the papers scattered everywhere. My bare ass was up in the air, my thighs still wet with excitement.

I didn't get along with the tall, skinny woman with the perennial *Vogue* smirk on her lips. Ms. Sims— no one knew her first name—always wore black, including jet black earrings that dangled to her shoulders. I swore under the gaudy fluorescents her skin had a green-gray tinge. She'd never liked me from the day I was hired. I was the only programmer the agency had in their job bank who could write the code they needed, so she was stuck with me. And she knew it.

"I was working late on that commercial spot—" I began, pulling up my jeans.

She ignored my explanation. "How long have you been using the copy room for your trysts?"

"Pardon me?" I asked.

"I wouldn't be surprised if you were sleeping with the whole department," she said, twitching her nose at me like a squirrel. "On *company* time."

"That is so not true, Ms. Sims," I protested, waving the papers around in a circle. "The guy flirted with me and then kissed me. It went downhill from there." I didn't tell her that *I* came on to *him*, never dreaming where it would lead: straight to paradise until the machine went wonky.

"I warned Mr. Briggs this would happen if he hired a female programmer."

"That has nothing to do with it, Ms. Sims," I said.

"I'm a good employee. I'm always here on time, and I work late. I even put the toilet paper on the spool in the girls' bathroom the way you like it." Over, not under. Ms. Sims liked to be in control of everything, even where you took a pee.

She pushed her dangly earrings off her shoulders and then motioned for me to hand her the documents. "Let me see what you were working on."

"These papers aren't mine—" I insisted, handing her the wrinkled sheets of paper.

"Then whose are they?" She grabbed them out of my hand, nearly tearing them in half.

"The new video game designer," I insisted. "I found him in here making copies."

"You're lying. He doesn't start until next week." She held the papers flush against her flat chest so I couldn't see them.

"What?" I blurted out, disbelieving. My thighs quivered and *not* in a good way. I'd been played, but by whom?

"No more excuses, Pepper. I want answers. *Now!*" she screeched.

"I—I…" Nothing came out. I swallowed hard and squeezed my butt cheeks together until they burned. Of all the low-down, dirty tricks, this was the worst. The geeky types I work with must have sent the stud here to punk me. Oh, my God, what if they'd set up a hidden camera in here? What if my big moment had already gone viral on the internet? Oh, shit, I was had.

"Admit it," Ms. Sims said, prodding me. "You

sneaked a man in here and had sex with him while you copied confidential documents."

"I did *not* copy any docs," I said, trying to convince myself it was just a practical joke. It couldn't be anything else, could it?

"Then what were you doing with Mr. Briggs's—" she cleared her throat "—tax returns. They're not for your eyes or anyone else's."

I shook my head, not getting it. Why would this prankster make copies of my boss's classified information? Unless—

Red and blue lights flashed on and off in my brain like a squad car was chasing me. It all made sense. How the stud was surprised to see me, asking me if I was security, and reaching in his sweats for what I bet was a gun. Then sweet-talking me into letting him kiss me while he felt me up. Checking me for a weapon, I bet. And I unbuttoned my jeans flap to help him. Talk about dumb chick moves. *That* was the dumbest.

"That guy was a thief," I said under my breath. That statement knocked the wind out of me.

That was only the beginning of my downfall.

I leaned against the copier and tried to zip up my jeans but couldn't. Wetness greeted my fingers along with a pungent smell both sweet and musky. Panic filled me.

What if the condom had broken?

With that disturbing thought racing through my brain, I vaguely heard Ms. Sims babbling on about how she'd come back to the office to get her cell phone. When she heard the alarm go off, she ran to the copy room. A tall man wearing a baseball cap and black sweats knocked her down and rushed past her. When she opened the door and found me with my jeans down, she assumed I had invited him in.

I tried to explain to her what happened, but she wouldn't listen to me. That didn't surprise me. She had this thing against hiring girls who wrote code.

That was just the excuse she needed.

She fired me.

The bitch.

FBI SPECIAL AGENT Steve Raines had a plan for this evening's mission—pick the old-fashioned lock on the back door of the Victorian mansion with the skills he'd learned as a kid from his older brother and then sneak upstairs and copy the documents he'd been angling to get his hands on for months.

After he got what he came for, he'd scram out of there before the spiders knew he'd disturbed their sticky webs.

It should have been routine.

It wasn't.

He never expected to meet up with a sexy redhead who had a come-hither look about her that steamed up her glasses and made him hard. At first, he wasn't bothered by her intrusion. If anything, he was turned-on by her unexpected appearance. In his line of business he spent many lonely nights camped out in the wet and the cold, doing surveillance. Strip-searching her was an entirely pleasant experience and one he'd enjoy doing again.

He doubted he'd ever have the chance.

Things got sticky when she came on to him like gangbusters. She'd given him no choice but to have sex with her or blow his cover.

The question was, how was he going to explain his indiscretion to his boss?

"Did you get the docs from Briggs's office?" Jordan asked him, her fingers tapping on the phone at the other end. Patience was not her virtue. Never had been, though she knew how to hold 'em when the target was in sight but not close enough for a sure kill.

This was not one of those times.

She wanted answers. *Now.*

Steve had stopped at the drive-through for coffee and then pulled into a dark alley and parked his old Buick behind a large trash Dumpster. For several long minutes, he studied the copies he'd made with a pen flashlight before dialing her on his cell. Special Agent in Charge Jordan Parks played hardball with her agents the same way other women picked out shoes: she liked the ones that dazzled her eye.

Still, she was tough and ran her operations lean and mean. She got the job done or she never would have lasted in this business. He admired her for that, but he wouldn't let her tell him how to run his mission. As long as he came through with the intel, he knew she'd let him play ball *his* way.

Except that tonight he'd scored in one way and fouled out in another.

"Well, Steven, I'm waiting," she purred. Or was it more of a growl? "Did you get the documents?"

"Not exactly—"

"Exactly what *do* you mean?"

"I had them in my hand, when *she* showed up."

"Who?"

"This redhead. She works there and caught me copying the docs."

"Night crew?"

"You could say that," Steve said evasively. He wasn't sure *who* she was, but he'd sure as hell find out.

"You're losing your touch, old boy." He heard her smirk. "What happened? Did she suck you up with her vacuum cleaner?"

She emphasized *suck*. Steve said nothing. He was used to her bad jokes.

"No. She's funny and very pretty—"

She cut him off. "Did you get rid of her?"

"I…well, you see…" He stalled, remembering how surprised he was to find black lace covering her bra when the buttons popped off her shirt. His hands ached to unhook her bra and cup her big breasts, but he was a man in a hurry. He'd frisked her to make sure she wasn't private security packing heat. "I made love to her."

"I imagine she couldn't resist your charm," she snarled.

"It works on you every time."

"Can it, Steven. You're the best-looking field agent I have, but the FBI didn't hire you for your looks."

He let that pass.

"Believe me, Jordan, you haven't seen this girl." He whistled under his breath. "She's sensational."

He'd never forget how she'd ground her butt into

his groin, teasing him, making him crazy. Dry humping him until he couldn't take it any longer. To knock him off balance? He had to find out. He'd slid her jeans down over her smooth skin and grabbed her ass. A more perfect ass he'd never seen. And one that gave a guy all kinds of sinful thoughts. Damn, he was going ballistic over this chick.

Why? Because she'd touched a nerve in him.

For all her brave talk, he swore she wasn't as easy a lay as she made out.

Maybe it was the glasses, which he found sexy, that gave her the innocent air. In the end it was his job to make sure she wasn't a threat to him.

"Listen up, Steven," Jordan was saying, "we've been trying to bring in this corporate sleazeball for months and get him to talk." She paused, no doubt to gulp down her coffee. Black. Always. "And now you're telling me when you get the chance to get the goods on him, you let your dick do the talking."

"You'll have my full report in the morning, Jordan," Steve promised, knowing he faced another sleepless night. He hadn't copied the whole file, but what he *had* seen didn't advance the investigation. Frustrated, he downed the last of his coffee. This case was keeping them both up late. Briggs had drawn the attention of the FBI when his bank reported that he split up large financial transactions into smaller ones and then tried unsuccessfully to take his name off them. They needed evidence to prove he was structuring the transfers to evade reporting them. It didn't stop there. It was the *why* that had them baffled. According to their sources, Briggs had made several unexplained overseas trips. Not to mention extravagant dinners at posh hotels, yet Pepper said her boss was cheap.

Steve's gut told him something bigger was at stake than tax evasion. He'd put out feelers on the street and had a few nibbles. What he'd learned so far wasn't pretty. He suspected Briggs was involved in money laundering. All he needed was proof.

"I want to see you in my office first thing in the morning," Jordan finished with a yawn. "Is that clear?"

"Anything you say, ma'am," Steve said, signing off, knowing she hated him calling her *ma'am*.

"Seven o'clock *sharp*," she insisted. *"Before* breakfast."

"I'll bring the beer," he said, grinning. "You bring the doughnuts."

Then he hung up.

He pulled the baseball cap down low over his eyes to take a quick snooze, planning his next move. His balls tightened. *Damn*, he couldn't concentrate. How could he even think? He couldn't forget his encounter in the copy room with the redhead. There was something about that girl that got under his skin.

He intended to find out more about this Pepper. Who she was, where she came from. And why she was working late. That made her suspect in his eyes. She knew something, but what?

He intended to get a full report on her.

Pepper. Smooth, round ass. Sweet, sexy bod.

A perfect fit for his dick.

Are you as hot as your name? he'd asked her.

You bet she was.

This case just got a whole lot more interesting.

THIS WAS ONE goddamn screwed-up night.

I'd barely zipped up my jeans when the Wicked Witch of the West made me pack up my things and give her back the key to the girls' daisy-wallpapered bathroom. We were the only two who used it since the company wasn't big on hiring females unless forced to do so. All the other employees were guys. No receptionist up front. Nobody answered the phone when customers needed tech support since all the calls were routed overseas.

Just rooms filled with programmers and graphic art designers. A geek junkie's heaven on earth.

Then Ms. Sims recited the employee policy to me like it was the Miranda Rights.

"You are hereby ordered not to contact *anyone* at the company after your termination," she said, stuffing the documents she'd taken from me into a folder. I grabbed my coffee cup and closed up my backpack. I assumed she would report the break-in to the protection services Mr. Briggs hired to keep out interlopers.

Which made me wonder—

Where was the security guy who walked the perimeter? This wasn't the first time he'd messed up. The only reason he kept his job was because he was Ms. Sims's nephew.

"Why not?" I asked, confused. I often traded programming shortcuts with the guys.

"If you dare to initiate conversation with our employees," she said, hands on her hips, "I will contact the authorities and have you arrested as an accomplice."

"Accomplice to what?" I wanted to know. "You got your file back. Nothing was taken."

Except my pride.

I didn't mention the copies. Why make things worse? Mr. Briggs's tax records couldn't be that important unless he had an ex-wife no one knew about. Besides, I'd never live it down if anyone found out about this, especially Cindy. We've traded secrets and diaries since high school. She'd think it was romantic and want all the juicy details.

"True, but you *did* allow that man in here." She fumbled around for the right words. "He could have seen our new video game design."

"I doubt it." I threw the words back at her. "He was too busy eyeing my ass."

That did it. The wrath of the Emerald City flying monkeys rained down upon me.

"You little slut," Ms. Sims screamed. "Get out, *now!*"

I swore I saw smoke coming out of her ears. I shouldn't have said that, but I couldn't help it. She'd had it in for me since Mr. Briggs hired me. She was the Queen Bee until I arrived. She was jealous since I got all the attention from the guys. Was it my fault she didn't know WTF code from the acronym for the expletive?

That was the end of my career at the video game company. The office manager threw me out on my butt with no references, no severance package.

Nada. I got screwed and the thief got away.

All because I forgot to buy batteries for my vibrator.

I FIGURED I wouldn't have a problem finding work since video game programmers were a hot commodity. Yeah, right. Nobody told me the job market had gone cold. Or so it seemed to me. Over the next week, I sent out fifty résumés a day online and went on interviews only to have them tell me they've stopped interviewing for that position. Which was a nice way of saying "not interested."

Worse yet, I discovered no one would hire me because I'd been fired for "misconduct of a nonbusiness nature." That piece of information was leaked to me by a kind soul at the unemployment office. I was persona non grata there, as well. No checks from the state hit my mailbox. Even those online personality tests had it in for me with their trick questions.

You're fucked. You'll never work in this town again.

I shouldn't have mouthed off to the office manager, but my offbeat personality had its roots in my traumatic childhood. Shuffled from one foster home to another, I pulled off numerous crazy stunts to get attention. When I was in junior high, the other kids wouldn't stop bullying me, saying I was different and didn't have a real family. So I hacked into the school computer to find out what was in my file. Much to my disappointment, I didn't find out anything I didn't already know.

When I was in high school, I wrote a software

program to help me learn fact-driven data at a faster pace. Instead of praise for my efforts, I got stung for my antics. You'd think I'd done something wrong, like designing a T-shirt with a logo that was really a cheat sheet. Since then, I learned to shy away from people to keep from getting hurt.

When I went away to college to get my degree in computer science thanks to a scholarship, I found the only way to be accepted as an equal by the über-geeks was to play down my looks with jeans and red plaid flannel shirts.

And glasses.

I shied away from getting contacts. I had to admit I used the specs as a shield against the world. Recent life-changing moments showed me I couldn't hide anymore. The naked truth was, I was desperate. Past-due rent and an empty fridge were a real incentive for me to rev up my computer skills.

Time for me to do a little snooping to set the record straight.

DAWN.

There was something about my old company at this time of day that got to me. Like it wasn't real, only imagined.

A gothic gingerbread house.

Fog sat lazy and white over the trolley wires, while the winding streets gave off a mood of non-chalance before dealing with the seething passion of the morning sun. Birds flitted from tree to tree, flapping their wings to keep warm.

I pulled my flannel shirt closer around me to keep

out the wet chill as I traipsed in my clunky leather boots through the pink and white azaleas around the back of the house. I was amazed how the delicate flowers tugged at their roots in their attempt to grow tall and strong like the wisteria vines hugging the worn brown sandstone. They provided great cover for my private entrance, allowing me to enter unseen through a hidden door leading into a basement room used for storage.

It was a jib door that looked like a window. When lifted and opened, it led into the rear of the house. Most likely it had provided a discreet means of entry for the Victorian gentleman or lady wishing to return home unobserved.

For me, it was the perfect way to sneak inside and put my plan into action.

I treaded carefully so as not to disturb the plump cat snoozing outside the secret door. A habit of hers recently. I'd arrived at the office before anyone else and then waited for the security guard to make his rounds before gaining entrance. No worry. I knew his habits. He did his job in slo-mo. By the time he came this way again, I'd be long gone. I knew what I was looking for. We all left our digital footprints. You just had to know where to look.

Two days ago I installed a device to track the keystrokes the office manager made on her keyboard. Yesterday I recovered it, uploaded it to my computer and then retrieved her password. I was well aware I was guilty of hacking, but I firmly believed I'd been fired unjustly. I felt warranted in righting that wrong. I just wanted my life back.

I sat down at her computer and, after a few clicks, I was in.

Yes.

I drew in my breath, nervous and excited as files popped up on the screen. It didn't take me long to find what I was looking for: a list of former employees. I knew that Ms. Sims used an off-site human resources company to answer job inquiries about their ex-staff. She must have given them the off-putting information about my termination. All I had to do was change that info in my file.

I scrolled through the names, looking for my moniker. Once I found it, I'd change the reason for my dismissal to "termination without cause." Then I'd add that I was part of a company layoff.

Next, I'd write a letter on the video company letterhead documenting that my efforts were of value to the company, but "because of the weak economy and a slowdown in the technology field," they'd had no choice but to terminate my employment.

With luck, no one would notice the change in my file, and I could email it to the various job banks to clear my record.

It didn't work out like I planned.

My file was gone. Disappeared. Like I never existed.

I stared at the computer screen as if I were reading another language, one beyond my comprehension. I felt dumb, foolish. I traced my steps again, tried another file, opened it. Nothing. Another file, still nothing.

I sat back, thinking. How did Mr. Briggs intend to

explain my disappearance to the IRS? It occurred to me that might not be a bad thing. Still, I kept searching through the files, scrolling up and down, doing a name search.

I came up with zip.

What happened?

Where was my file?

I didn't even blink, as if by sheer mental force I could will the pixels to form my name. Zilch. I rubbed my eyes. Nothing changed. Finally, I had to admit no computer trick or maneuver was going to bring back my file. I couldn't fix what wasn't there.

That left me no choice. I had to see Mr. Briggs in person and demand an explanation.

That presented a new problem. How was I going to get close enough to confront him? No doubt Ms. Sims would have security haul my ass out before I could talk to him. I would have to corner him somewhere off the premises, but where?

I had bounced forward, my feet flat on the floor, opening various files while looking for his calendar, when something strange on the screen caught my eye.

What was this?

Mr. Briggs was doing business with companies I didn't recognize. Offshore companies, by the locales of their bank transactions. Weird. I shrugged it off, since outsourcing work in this business was common.

I closed the file and kept looking until I located his calendar. Scrolling through it, I could see he was out of town for the remainder of the week. Then he had meetings across the Bay at snooty banks with security so tight even I couldn't hack into their system. Later, a haircut at an exclusive salon. I *could* go all scissor hands and scare the hell out of him until he gave me my job back. Not a good career move.

Wait. Next Thursday he had a luncheon appointment at a place called The Mermaid's Tale.

A sushi restaurant.

Cool.

I knew just the person who could help me snag a gig there.

Cindy Ball.

Former prom queen. Do-gooder. And all-round girl-gone-wild.

Better yet, she owed me one.

CHAPTER THREE

"I CAN'T DO IT, Pepper," Cindy said, glossing her lips so red she looked like a fire hydrant eager for a hot firefighter to push her buttons. "I could get fired."

"You've *got* to help me, Cindy," I pleaded, "my life depends on it."

"That's what you said when Mr. Ambrose found out you were doing my French homework and he threatened to fail us both." She kept glancing down at her phone. She was waiting for a text from her agent about an important audition.

"He didn't, did he?"

"No, because you discovered he was sleeping with the girls' tennis coach." She raised a finely drawn brow. "You always were a snoop, Pepper."

Thanks, Cindy.

Still, it was Cindy who came to my rescue when the foster family I was living with tossed me out after I checked their computer and found out they were bilking the system. Her parents were squeamish about having a high school tech whiz with a questionable past under their roof until I showed her dad how to use his new computer software to maximize his tax deductions. Without their support, I would have fallen through the cracks and ended up on the streets. Instead, I went to college and dragged Cindy along with me, much to her family's relief. We were best pals, though we had different goals. I wanted to be a spy, which made Cindy roll her eyes. She wanted to be a reality TV star. I put up with her dreams and she put up with mine. No questions asked. It was an unbreakable bond between us.

"You wouldn't have passed his class without me, would you?" I shot back.

"No, but—"

"I *so* need this favor, Cindy," I said, poking around her cramped bedroom. Her Barbie doll collection with their sparkly gowns and tiaras grinned at me from every corner. As if they knew my ass was on the line.

"The restaurant owner has strict rules about any-one taking my place at the table," she insisted. She bit down on her lip anxious-like when she heard a text come in.

"Just this once," I begged. As long as I didn't spill sake all over Mr. Briggs, I didn't see what the big deal was. "I'll give you the tips, too."

Cindy looked at me funny, which I didn't under-stand. Last I heard she was a waitress at The Mer-maid's Tale in between acting gigs. If you could call being a pair of dancing legs in a commercial an act-ing job.

"I'm not allowed to accept tips," she said, read-ing the text.

"Why not? The Mermaid's Tale is a hot spot for business luncheons. Are these guys that tight with their money?" I asked. When the one-percenters stopped tipping the pretty waitresses, you knew the economy was bad.

She blushed. "I got promoted at the restaurant."

"Are you a cook?" I asked, imagining myself chopping up raw fish and cutting off a finger.

"I'm a sushi model."

"A what?"

"Men eat raw sushi off my naked body."

"Jesus fricking Christ." I flipped out at the thought of having to take off my clothes to get my job back.

"You may be in luck after all, Pepper," Cindy said, tapping a message on her phone. "I just got word the hair show audition is next Thursday."

"So?" Why did I ever come up with this dumb idea?

"The manager is cool about letting me go on auditions since he's an actor, too. He won't say anything." Her face lit up. "I'll do it."

"Hold on, Cindy, I wouldn't want you to lose your job," I said, stalling. Suddenly my bright idea didn't seem so bright. This was *so* not in my line of work. I was a programmer, not a supermodel.

"Where's your James Bond spirit, Pepper?"

"You don't wear *anything?*" I had to ask. The idea of my body as the sushi blue-plate special of the day made me cringe. I got goose bumps thinking about the icy cold fish wiggling between my thighs, even if they were *dead* fish.

"A banana leaf covers me *here*." She pointed to her crotch. "And big chrysanthemums cover my breasts."

"*How* big?"

"Big enough. Since I got my implants, we're about the same size."

I still wasn't convinced. I'd been hiding my body under red flannel tent city so long, I wasn't sure I'd pass the hot bod test. Sure, I was thin because I often forgot to eat when I was working, but I didn't have a tan. Cindy assured me I could wear body makeup. It was like having a thin sheet over your bare skin, she said.

A sheet over my face was a better idea.

I'd die of embarrassment if anyone I knew saw me lying spread-eagled with raw fish all over me.

Then I recalled Ms. Sims snarling at me to pack up and leave, waving her broomstick if she'd had one. A surge of daring rose up in me. This was my only chance to confront Mr. Briggs and find out why I was terminated and wiped off the face of the employment roll like an outdated floppy disk drive.

The question was: How bad did I want my old job back?

Enough to take off my clothes?

I looked down at my own Barbie cleavage peeking through my flannel shirt missing two buttons. The idea of taking down that superstud who had me bare-assed over the copier was also a big incentive. Once I got his attention, I'd fill Mr. Briggs in on the burglary and give him a detailed description of the thief, though I'd leave out his dick size.

There were some things they didn't show you in a police lineup.

Besides, he came and I didn't.

It was payback time.

MARY DOLORES O'MALLEY, Steve read, peering at the data from the secure site popping up on his computer screen. *Date of birth unknown. Place of birth unknown. Parents unknown.*

He tossed his empty foam cup into the trash can next to his desk. That was a heavy load to carry. No trace of who you were or where you came from. His problem was just the opposite. He knew all too well where he came from.

His mother was a decent sort, but she'd gotten knocked up by the local bad boy and had then produced Steve's older brother. Tom knew his way in and out of trouble better than any comic book hero. When Steve was a kid, Tom *was* his hero after his old man took off. He looked up to him. Tom taught him how to hot-wire cars and jimmy open locks and every other ruse in a thief's bag of tricks. He could con a con man. Steve wanted to be just like him.

Until a bullet stopped Tom cold.

A bullet meant for Steve.

Tom had tried to go straight, but it didn't work. He fell in with a bad crowd and pulled his kid brother in with him. He died in the dirty street surrounded by a rival gang, kicking and beating his broken body.

No hero's death for him.

Before he died, he begged Steve to get out of the old neighborhood and not to end up like him. Only through the intervention of the local priest did Steve escape the streets *and* his past. The clergyman helped him sign up for the army. Afterward, he went to college and then joined the Bureau. There, while taking down the bad guys, Steve could use the special "talents" he'd learned from his brother.

He was about to close the file, when—

Hey, what's this?

He couldn't believe what he was seeing. Pepper had applied to various government agencies, including the CIA and ATF.

And the FBI?

She'd filled out the paperwork, taken the Phase I entrance exam and scored quite high. She'd been invited to take Phase II, but she never followed through. She got cold feet.

Why? he'd like to know.

As if he ever would. No reason to keep her on his radar. Mary Dolores—Pepper—was clean. He was convinced her playacting with him in the copy room was harmless. Thank God, she hadn't done his case much damage. He'd found another way to get to Briggs and he intended to put that plan into action right away.

Meanwhile, Pepper had no idea who he was. He had to keep it that way.

Steve grinned. He wondered how she had explained their rendezvous and the out-of-control copy machine to the woman he'd brushed by in the dark hallway. He imagined her embellishing the story and turning it into a wild tale. Most likely, she made him out to be her boyfriend needing a little late night nooky.

He sighed deeply. Too bad it wasn't true.

Steve looked at his watch. It was almost twelve. He had a meeting with Briggs and he couldn't be late.

He clicked off his computer and watched her file disappear into a cyber never-never land. He had to get Pepper O'Malley off his mind. The last thing he needed was a sexy computer geek with a great bod tangled up in his life.

HE'S HERE. COMING closer to the table filled with sushi where I lay spread out like a topless mermaid on a giant half shell. I recognized his gruff voice.

Seymour T. Briggs.

My ex-boss.

I drew in my breath and squinted through my fake eyelashes, twisting my head and moving my shoulders, nearly shaking loose the yellow pom-poms glued to my breasts. Petals flew through the air, landing on my nose. I blew them off to get a better view.

Damn, who was he talking to?

Tall, dark-haired, well dressed. Moving through the restaurant with the assurance of a man who knew women wanted him. He kept his eyes straight ahead; his shoulders were broad and powerful, propelling him forward like a sleek jet fighter ripping through the skies. A trip to the moon and back.

And he'd taken me with him.

Damn. It was *him*.

The stud from the copy room.

What the hell was he doing here?

He sat down at the table with Mr. Briggs and barely glanced at me.

But I recognized *him*, even without my specs. My throat was dry, my heartbeat went wild, and I swore my honey juices drizzled down between my legs.

Talk about embarrassing, since I already had a customer sitting at my table. The man sniffed, smiled and then picked up a piece of fish on my leg with his chopsticks and popped it into his mouth.

I hardly noticed. I couldn't keep my eyes off Mr. Stud.

My, he cleaned up nicely.

Gone was the rugged biker look. He was a *GQ* ad in the flesh. He looked smokin' hot in a pinstriped dark suit with a cool-blue shirt and midnight-blue tie. Professional, but I knew that an air of wildness existed under that polished exterior. His dark hair was cut sleek on the sides with just enough length on the top to give him that bad-boy look I loved.

That didn't explain his covert activities copying Mr. Briggs's file.

Who was he?

A sudden rush of fear made me shiver, and cool perspiration dripped down the sides of my face, my nerves attacking my courage. A sudden twitch in my leg made me jerk wildly as if I were a puppet and someone yanked on my string. My gyrations made the sushi rolls sitting on my thighs bounce up and down, giving the customer sitting within striking distance the opportunity to grab one with his chopsticks. He pinched me, but I felt no pain. I was distanced from what was happening to me, as if I existed in a parallel dimension.

I closed my eyes, trying to calm my racing heart. It wasn't like I could get up and leave. I *had* to stay. Or Cindy would lose her job. And I wouldn't get my job back.

Yet all I could think about was—

The stud wouldn't recognize me without my glasses and my clothes, would he?

Only a foolish girl would think that.

It wasn't as if our shoulders merely touched when we bumped into each other in the copy room.

We had sex. Him thrusting, me pushing.

I breathed him in, filled with the warm, evocative memory of that night. Heady musk mixed with the rich smell of office leather, cool AC blowing in my face. I loved it. Sexy encounters like that rarely happened to me. It wasn't like I had this prejudice against intimacy. I was afraid of where it would lead me. Someplace I didn't want to go, where I would have to face who I was, where I came from. So I went for the cheap thrill, the quickie sex.

This was the first time it had backfired on me.

Or had it?

What was I afraid of? *He* was the thief, not me.

I licked my lips, a new plan orchestrating itself in my analytical brain.

All I had to do was convince Mr. Briggs this man was a burglar. A denizen of the night with criminal intentions that went way beyond seducing an innocent victim. Me, of course. Then I'd have my old job back in spite of his office manager firing me during one of her Queen Bee moments.

I wiggled my pink-tipped pedicure with the red rose petals stuck between my toes and smiled. I was all set to show my ex-boss he couldn't mess with Pepper O'Malley—*and* get even with Mr. Stud. You know what they say.

Revenge was sweet.
Even when it tasted like sushi.

"MR. BRIGGS...*MR. BRIGGS,*" I whispered, trying to get his attention. He couldn't hear me. The creepy customer at the end of the table was making slurping noises. I motioned for him to back off, but he was intent on scoring another sushi roll off my thigh.

"I've been trying to crack the Japanese market for two years with no luck," I heard Mr. Briggs say to the stud from the copy room. "What guarantee can you give me your company can do better?"

"We have experience in the Asian market, Mr. Briggs," he said, choosing his words *and* his sushi with care as he plucked a sliver of *toro* off my leg.

I winced and my mouth dropped open. Experience? He had experience all right. He knew how to fuck. So what was he doing here with Mr. Briggs?

"A Japanese manager won't research new software on his own," he continued, "but ask a colleague for a recommendation."

"And your company can provide me with such recommendations?" Mr. Briggs asked, curious.

"Yes. Our strategy is to partner with Japanese insiders familiar with what we call 'the hidden market.' My company prides itself on having a strong network of well-informed personal contacts familiar with Japanese business strategies."

Listen to that bullshit he was feeding Mr. Briggs. Where did he get off acting like a big shot?

I'd grant him one thing, though. Up close and personal fit him. The burning in my belly reminded me *how* personal.

"It will take more than lunch in a Japanese restaurant to convince me you've got these contacts," Mr. Briggs said, picking up his chopsticks and grabbing a wiggly piece of octopus off my stomach. Yuk. "Though I admit using the body of a beautiful woman to please the eye is innovative."

"*Very* beautiful," the stud said, surprising me.

Beautiful? Me?

Nah. He didn't mean it. He was cozying up to Mr. Briggs. That was all.

They chattered on for endless minutes. Another businessman sat down at our table and ordered a beer. I paid him no mind. I was waiting for the right moment to get Mr. Briggs's attention. My sixty-minute gig was almost over. Another model would be here soon to replace me.

Finally, the moment came when I saw the stud from the copy room turn around to order drinks from the kimono-clad waitress.

"Hey, Mr. Briggs," I whispered out of the side of my mouth. "It's me."

"Who?" he asked, choking on the octopus.

"Pepper O'Malley. I used to work for you." I rushed my words. "I'm a software programmer. Video games, commercials. I'm the whiz kid who rewrote all the codes for the *Dragon Beware* game after the last guy screwed them up."

"I—I have no idea what you're talking about, young lady." My ex-boss looked flustered, pulling at his collar, his walruslike double chin tripling in size. "I don't know you."

"Yes, you do. Your office manager fired me after this bozo sitting next to you cornered me in the copy room—"

Mr. Briggs glared at the customer dribbling soy sauce on my thigh.

"No, not *him*," I sputtered, giving the jerk a dirty look when he smeared the salty mixture on my leg. "The guy ordering drinks."

"How did you know I was here?" Mr. Briggs whispered, the angry look in his eyes telling me he *did* recognize me.

"That's not important. I want my job back—" I clammed up when the stud turned back around and handed Mr. Briggs an Echigo beer.

"Imported from Japan," the stud said.

I rolled my eyes. Mr. Briggs was not a Miller-time kind of guy. Expensive champagne was more his style, according to the accounts I saw on his computer. *Very* expensive. And here I thought he was a cheapskate. The company was doing better than I imagined.

Not Mr. Briggs. He looked like he was about to throw up. I wasn't sure if he looked sick because of what I'd said to him or the ice-cold beer staring him in the face.

"How come the model can flirt with you and not with me?" said the jealous customer, sticking his chopsticks straight up in his rice bowl. Bad manners in a Japanese restaurant.

"She's *not* flirting with me." Mr. Briggs put down

the beer and wiped the sweat off his face with his monogrammed napkin. "She—she used to work for me."

I cringed.

This was getting dicey. The stud was giving me the eyeball, his eyes questioning, his heated glance moving over my heaving breasts and then down to my crotch. I should have kept my mouth shut.

Mr. Briggs turned to him. His voice shook as he said, "I think we should finish our business elsewhere." He threw down his napkin and then got up from the table and left.

"I'll be with you in a minute, Mr. Briggs," said the stud, nodding toward the quiet customer about to grab a slice of avocado off my shoulder. Without changing his deadpan expression, the man put down his chopsticks, got up and followed Mr. Briggs.

I couldn't believe it. They were working together.

My back stiffened. So what happened now? They roughed up Mr. Briggs in a dark alley? Stole his credit cards? Drove him to the ATM and mugged for the security cameras?

I wasn't prepared for the stud's next move.

"Well, if it isn't the sassy redhead from the copy room," he said with a smirk. He grabbed a spicy tuna roll off my thigh and ate it in a sensual manner, smacking his lips and rolling his tongue.

"Surprised to see me?" I quipped.

"I didn't recognize you without your glasses." His dark eyes roamed up and down my nearly nude body. The look in his eyes was hot enough to burn the flower petals to cinders. In a low, sexy voice he said, "What the hell are you doing here?"

"Trying to get my job back," I shot back at him. "Until you screwed it up."

I'd rather die than let him know how seeing him again affected me.

He slid his chopsticks under the flowers covering my breasts in the pretext of grabbing a slice of fish, rubbing my bare skin and sending tiny sparks through me. I clamped my legs together.

Damn, why did he have to do that?

"You shouldn't interfere in matters that don't concern you," he said.

"I wouldn't be here if you hadn't seduced me."

"*I* seduced *you?*" He laughed. "You're the one who tried to convince me you're as hot as your name." He leaned over and dangled a chopstick dipped in hot wasabi over my quivering tummy. "Pepper, isn't it?"

"I'm surprised you remember."

"That's not *all* I remember," he insisted, pulling yellow flower petals off my breasts with his chopsticks, one by one.

"Hey, sister, talk to me, too," yelled the disgruntled customer at the end of the table, grabbing his chopsticks out of the rice bowl.

"The lady isn't talking to anyone." The stud jabbed me in the buttock. I winced. "*Anyone*, is that clear?" he said. "Or she'll find herself swimming with the fishes instead of lying with them."

"You can't threaten me," I said in a clear voice, though I was shaking inside. "If anything happens to Mr. Briggs, I'll go straight to the police and tell them what happened in the copy room."

"Everything?" he said, egging me on.

"*Everything.*"

"You want your job back that bad?"

"Yes. I—I need the money to pay my rent. And to eat. I don't get to take home the leftovers."

He looked surprised. "You're not kidding me, are you?"

I shook my head.

For a moment, a look of tenderness came over his face and I almost trusted him. Almost.

Then he retrieved a wad of bills that made my eyes bug out, peeled off several and stuffed them into my hand. "Now we're even. Keep your mouth shut or Mr. Briggs won't be walking so good."

I could feel the crinkly bills filling my palm, tempting me, but that wasn't my style. I tossed the hundred-dollar bills down on the black velvet table. "I don't take bribes."

"Consider it a tip."

"I'm not allowed to take tips," I said, echoing Cindy's words.

The unhappy customer tried to pinch a hundred with his chopsticks, but the stud was faster. He grabbed the wad and stuffed the bills back into his pocket.

Snickering, he turned and said to me, "I'll see you around…*Pepper.*" Then he grabbed another tuna roll off my thigh and jammed out of the restaurant before I could say sayonara.

I KEPT PRESSING the on button on my cell phone, but nothing happened. It was dead. Damn, they shut off my service. I told them I'd pay them soon. A lot of good *that* did me. How was I going to call for help? There was no pay phone in the dressing room or anywhere in the restaurant.

I grabbed the short pink kimono Cindy had left hanging on the door and put it on and then peeled off the yellow flower petals sticking to my breasts. The thick adhesive tape smarted when I pulled it off. I let the kimono hang loose as I walked around the dressing room, pressing the button and then sliding and tapping my fingers all over the screen, trying to make it work—

"I wouldn't do that if I were you."

I spun around. It was him.

Looking angry but gorgeous. I let out a deep sigh. Why did this guy have to be so damned good-looking? I almost wished we were back in the copy room. Me with my butt up in the air and him behind me, sliding down my jeans.

That was before I knew he was a thief. I couldn't drop my guard around him.

Not this time.

"Did you forget something?" I said, cocky.

"Yes. *You*."

"What?" I asked, not understanding.

"I had a feeling you wouldn't follow my orders." He came closer; I stepped back. "Put down that phone."

"What if I don't?" I said, stalling. I pretended to

text a message on a screen that was darker than my roots. Lucky for me he couldn't see that.

"I'll have to take you with me."

Oh, my God, he was going to kidnap me.

"Like hell you are."

In spite of my wild attraction to this hottie, I had no desire to become a missing person statistic.

I ran for the tiny bathroom, hoping to lock myself in, when he did some fancy martial arts move on me and knocked the cell phone out of my hand. When I leaned over to pick it up, he grabbed me around the waist and then reached inside my short pink kimono and pinched my nipples.

"I've been wanting to do that since I saw you lying on that table looking as sexy as hell," he said with a big smile.

"Why don't you take your hot chopsticks and go play somewhere else," I said, shooting him a cool "I'm not interested" look. I refused to let him turn me on.

Instead, I tried to kick him in the balls.

He anticipated my maneuver and backed away with a hip-hop move any rapper would envy and sidestepped my foot.

"You vixen," he said, growling. Then he grabbed me around the ankle and knocked me off balance. I slid down to the floor, landing on my butt.

"Ye—ow!" I cried out.

"Ready to give up?" he asked, staring at me.

"No way, José."

Winded, I started kicking wildly with my bare feet, my kimono open and spread around me. I pushed out my chest, my nipples pointing straight up, begging for him to bite them. Hoping he'd take the bait so I could try out the karate chop I learned in a self-defense class. I had no time to lose. My ex-boss could already be hogtied and quartered in a dark alley like a bluefin tuna ready for market.

"You leave me no choice, Pepper," he said in a husky voice. Before I could take a breath, he sat on me, grabbing my wrists and slapping handcuffs on me with the finesse of a man used to tying women up.

"*Let go of me!*" I yelled.

"Not until you calm down, you little hellcat."

"Then what are you going to do?" I asked. "Make raw sushi out of me?"

"You almost ruined six months of work with your sex games."

"Sex games?" I said. "*You're* the one stalking Mr. Briggs. Breaking into the company offices and seducing a helpless employee—"

"You? Helpless?" He laughed. "I've never seen a woman with so much fire in her."

That gave me an idea. A smart girl would use her sex appeal to talk her way out of this situation.

I slowed my breathing and changed my tactics. "You're not going to leave without satisfying me…." I licked my lips, nice and easy, my tongue making a wet circle around my open mouth. "Are you?"

He crossed his brows, and I swore I saw a flicker of interest in his eyes. It quickly disappeared. "You can't blame a guy for wanting to make love to a beautiful woman, Pepper. But I'd never leave her hanging, unless my ass was on the line."

"You mean *my* ass."

"Don't be so squeamish," he said, making light of my misery. "You know the drill. I saw an opportunity and I took it. Nothing more."

Inside I was hurting from his remark, but I kept my game-face on. I refused to let him see how much his words stung me. "I don't believe you. A man doesn't come like you did if it's only a quickie."

"It's a perk in my line of work," he said with a snicker.

"Oh, yeah? Who do you work for?" I dared to ask him. "A syndicate? A rival software company? Or are you just an ordinary thief?"

I saw his mouth set in a firm line, his breath coming faster. I'd hit a nerve.

"There's nothing ordinary about me." He gripped my wrists tighter, the sheer power of being helpless stimulating me, though in this situation my primal urges were better left suppressed.

"Oh?" I teased him. "I don't remember. Show me."

"I didn't come back here to make love to you—"

"C'mon, fuck me. I dare you." I wiggled, making my breasts bounce up and down, giving him an eyeful. I refused to panic. Keep him talking. "I bet you can't get it up again."

"Your game won't work, Pepper. I have a job to do and you're in the way."

Uh-oh. I didn't like the way he said that. Like I was about to get tossed out of a speeding car in the middle of the night. I would have wet my panties if

I was wearing any. I wasn't. In my mind, a thong didn't count.

I saw him reach into his jacket pocket. I tried to scream, but he clamped his hand over my mouth, shutting off my air. I struggled while he ripped the pink silk belt off my thin kimono and gagged me with it.

"This will keep you quiet," he said. I kicked him in the shin, making him yelp. "*Damn*, I've never had so much trouble with a woman. Why didn't you mind your own business?"

I twisted and turned my body, going wild. What did I have to lose? He was going to plug me with a bullet between the eyes anyway.

I couldn't believe my luck when Cindy burst through the door.

"Pepper, I got the job—" She screamed when she saw him sitting on me, my hands cuffed and pulled up over my head, my mouth gagged. "Don't anybody move," she cried out as if she were auditioning for a cop drama. "I'm calling the police."

"Stay right where you are, miss," the stud ordered her, pulling a gold badge and ID out of his coat pocket and shoving them into her face. "Special Agent Steve Raines, FBI."

"*Oh, my God*, Pepper," Cindy gasped, her hand going to her mouth. "What have you done now?"

No, no, no. I twisted my head back and forth, trying to get the gag off, tell her the badge was a fake. Had to be. He would have told me that night in the copy room if he was working for the FBI, right?

I kept struggling, anything to get him off me. I knew he was going to kill me as soon as she left.

"Tell my partner standing guard outside to come in," he said. "I'm going to need a hand here."

"Yeah, sure." Cindy gave me a look of pity. "Don't worry, Pepper. I'll get you out. *Promise*." Then she ran out, slamming the door and leaving me alone with this guy.

Come back, Cindy. He's going to kill me.

It was too late. She was gone.

But I wouldn't give up without a fight.

I learned how to take care of bullies growing up. Kids calling me names, knocking my glasses off, trying to take me down. I fought back, used my brains to get through school and secure a good job.

No phony secret agent man was going to take it away from me.

I couldn't describe the survival-like spasms jolting through me, energizing me. No sooner had he turned his back to me than I brought my cuffed hands down and slammed them on the back of his neck, stunning him.

He slumped to the floor, moaning, his badge and ID card landing on the carpet.

I grabbed them and stared at the gold badge for a long moment. I couldn't believe what I saw. The government creds looked oh so real.

A sick feeling hit me.

Jesus.

I'd just clocked a G-man.

CHAPTER FOUR

I SPENT THE next two hours sitting half-nude in a gray room with no AC and no windows, taking a polygraph test. Back and forth went the convo like a volleyball on steroids. Two guys and a woman in plainclothes grilling me.

No one cracked a smile.

Them asking and then *me* answering questions about my ex-boss, his office manager, the other programmers, even the cleaning staff.

I was surprised they didn't ask me what birth control I used.

"Did Mr. Briggs make overseas trips?" they wanted to know. "Ask you to make bank deposits for him? Pay you in cash?"

"I write code," I said, trying to keep my cool. It wasn't easy. Sweat dripped down between my breasts. I didn't dare wipe it away. They'd probably book me for lewd conduct. "I spend my workday up to my eyeballs in funny symbols. Believe me, not *one* of them is a dollar sign."

"What about the other programmers?" they asked. "Did any of them boast about making extra cash? Give you the idea they may be in on the operation?"

"No."

"Any strangers hanging around who looked suspicious?"

I rolled my eyes and then shot a glance over to Agent Steve Raines, trying to keep a straight face. I could rat him out, make him squirm, but I had a better idea.

"There was this delivery guy who came on to me in the copy room…." I added the "delivery" bit to make it sound good. It wasn't a big lie, so I hoped the machine wouldn't notice.

"Yes?"

I adjusted my glasses and said in a bored voice, "But he didn't make much of an impression on me."

He coughed.

Gotcha.

"Any unusual emails? Computer files compromised? Strange deliveries to the office?" someone asked me.

My inner geek bell went off. Now things were getting too close to home. If they found out I hacked into my ex-boss's computer, I'd be headed off to the gray bar hotel pronto.

I had to throw them off course.

"Yeah," I said in a husky, dramatic voice that would make Cindy proud. "We had some weird stuff going on last week."

A hush fell over the room.

"Tell us, Miss O'Malley." They leaned in, waiting to hear what I had to say.

I grinned big. "Some jerk at the deli sent over a goat-cheese-and-broccoli pizza instead of our usual double cheese, double pepperoni. The guys were pissed."

Faces crunched, teeth clenched. My attempt at humor didn't go over well. The lie detector machine screeched to a halt. The operator shook his head and the feds whispered among themselves, giving me dirty looks.

I waited for them to decide my fate.

Tick-tock. Tick-tock. My heart pounded in my chest like a bad ringtone.

Finally—

"You attacked a federal agent, Miss O'Malley," said the interrogator with a stiff shirt collar and a stiffer dick, by the bulge in his pants. He kept eye-balling my sweaty cleavage spilling out of my kimono. "That's a crime and a punishable offense."

"*He* pounced on *me*," I said, pointing to the man who fucked me in the copy room. I refused to admit to anything. I knew my rights.

"What Miss O'Malley means," interrupted Agent Steve Raines, clearing his throat, "is that she believed I was a threat to her. She had no idea of my identity."

I blinked, disbelieving. He was lying. He'd clearly identified himself. Then I caught my G-man hottie giving them a look that said to go easy on me. My eyes widened. What was up?

"She broke the law, Steven," another agent chimed in. Female. Pretty in a classy way. Perfect hair. High heels. Higher IQ. I'd get no reprieve from her. "No excuses."

"Haven't you ever walked on the wild side, Jordan?"

"No."

"You should try it sometime." Then he grabbed my arm and pulled me out of the room. My teeth chattered. I'd never been so freaking scared in my life. I imagined the agents chasing after us, but I heard nothing but my ragged breaths in my ears.

"Who is she?" I asked.

"My boss. Special Agent in Charge, Jordan Parks."

"Oh," I whispered.

Steve laughed. "Pay no attention to her. Jordan keeps her rep squeaky clean and wrapped up tight, like she's wearing pantyhose."

I nodded. Even an FBI agent had problems with a diva boss. Who knew?

I wasn't off the hook, he said, but he wanted to speak to me alone. Without the suits coming down on me like vultures feeding on a dead horse. He took off his jacket and put it around my shoulders and then led me down the hall to another room. Empty, except for the two-way mirror. I prayed no one was on the other side.

"Sorry I had to cuff you, Pepper, but I couldn't let you blow my cover with Briggs."

"Why didn't you tell me that night in the copy room you were with the FBI?" I had to ask. No one could see or hear us in here. Despite my stiff neck and aching shoulders from being the fresh catch of the day, I wanted to find out more about Steve Raines.

"I couldn't. I wasn't there on official business,"

he said, shutting the door, "but on a hunch based on information I picked up from a federal wiretap."

He explained how he lured the security guy away with a phony emergency, making it easy for him to sneak inside the building. I didn't want to dent his ego by telling him that wasn't hard to do. The guard welcomed any excuse to take a smoke break.

"I had to make you believe I was a thief to cover my tracks," he said.

"Then why did you tell them I didn't know who you were when I slammed you on the back of the head?" I asked.

"Orange isn't your color," he said, looking me over with a you-are-so-hot smile. "Besides, I like you."

"I don't believe you," I shot back.

"Why not?"

"Lying is part of your job." I pushed his jacket off my shoulders. A heated flash of anger raced through me. I wasn't going to fall for his sexy, smoldering look, trying to make me believe he was into me. I wasn't fooled. We were on his turf now. "You're good at it, too."

"So I've been told." He looked away from me, staring at the two-way mirror as if he could see his own past. Funny, he didn't look smug, which surprised me.

"By who?" I asked, more curious than I had a right to be.

"A terrorist."

"You're kidding me, aren't you?"

"No, the bastard was threatening to shoot his hostage. A teenage kid he held by the throat." The federal agent wiped his mouth with the back of his hand, as if the memory left a bitter taste on his tongue.

I looked at him. I saw something disturbing in his eyes when he turned back toward me. I met his stare. "What happened?"

"I shot him."

Jesus.

"What if you'd missed?" I asked, a sick feeling creeping over me like wet, slimy worms crawling down my cleavage.

"I had to take that chance." He put his hand on my shoulder. "Like I took a chance on you, Pepper."

"I don't get it."

"In my business, you get a sixth sense about people," Steve said, making me crazy when he began rubbing the back of my neck. "The way you came on to me all sexy and flirty, eager to prove to me you were more than a hot programmer made me wonder if you really *were* the wild and crazy girl you pretended to be."

"So what did you find out?" I said, loving his hands on me.

Oh, please, yes, keep going. It felt so good.

"You have a raw hunger in you that cries out to be nourished," he said, his lips brushing my skin, his mouth possessing me. "But you're afraid to let yourself go, so you come on strong."

"You're no pushover yourself, Steve," I told him, daring to call him by his first name. If he was going to get personal, so was I.

He relaxed his expression and then his face turned

serious again. He held me close to him, his strong arms tight around me, as if he had something to say and wouldn't let me leave until he said it. "It comes with the job, Pepper. What the public doesn't see is the anguish you face every time you can't get a conviction or a hostage situation goes wrong. It eats you up inside, but you go on."

"What keeps you going?" I asked. I never expected to hear this stuff from him.

"A promise I made to my brother before he died."

"Yeah?" I pulled away, intrigued. I never had any family except for Cindy. She was like a sister to me. I'd die if anything happened to her. Why was he telling me this? I couldn't believe I was getting all touchy-feeling with a guy who could have had me fitted for an orange jumpsuit. Only then did I see a pain in his eyes I'd never seen before, a determined resolution in the set of his jaw.

"I joined the Bureau after I got out of the army," he said.

"You were in Iraq?"

He shook his head. "I served with my unit in Afghanistan after I lost my older brother."

"You want to talk about it?" I picked up his jacket, slipped it over my shoulders and listened.

"Tom was a two-bit hoodlum. He never had a chance after our old man took off. He started cutting school, using drugs." Steve paused and then scraped peeling gray paint off the table with his finger. I could see the furniture was repainted over and over with the same iconic shade of gray. As if to dull the pain suffered here. "He taught me everything he knew, but in the end he admitted he was wrong and didn't want me to follow in his footsteps."

"What happened?"

"He tried to go straight," Steve said, clenching his fists, "but he was murdered in a gang attack in our old neighborhood."

My hand flew to my mouth. "Oh, I'm sorry."

"Homegrown terrorism is a real threat we can't ignore, Pepper."

"So you joined the FBI."

He acknowledged my comment with a nod. "I hit the streets every day to take down the bad guys so people can go on with their lives, never knowing how close they came to losing that freedom." He looked at me and I saw the fierceness raging in his eyes, like a primitive animal ready to pounce. I shivered. "I do it for my brother, and for everyone like him who paid the ultimate price."

"Why are you telling me this?" I wanted to know. This was serious business. Way beyond a little tax-payer like me getting fired. What was his game?

"Because I believe you feel like I do." He leaned down, so close to my lips, I swore he was going to kiss me. He didn't. Instead, he shocked the hell out of me when he said, "We need people like you willing to put themselves on the line."

My mouth dropped open. "You did a background check on me, didn't you?"

He gave me that half smile of his that made me melt. "I had to make sure you were clean."

"Then you know I applied to the FBI when I got out of college," I said, smoothing a strand of loose hair away from my face in a nervous gesture. "I didn't make it."

I didn't clue him in that I lost my nerve and didn't finish taking the tests after my background came into question. I was afraid they'd find out things about me I decided I no longer wanted to know. It was safer that way. It allowed me to live in a dream world with no responsibility to my past.

I looked again into his face and saw the puzzled expression etched on his features, as if he were waiting for me to explain further. I didn't. To my relief, he returned to the present situation.

"Now do you understand why I had to get out of the copy room without you knowing who I was?" he said, emphasizing his words. "I was looking for the intel that would explain how Briggs transferred funds to hide his dirty little secret."

"What secret?"

"High-class call girls," Steve said. "In Thailand, Hong Kong, Japan."

I let out a low whistle. "So that's why he's so determined to get into the Japanese market." I paused, thinking, "His office manager said the documents you copied were Mr. Briggs's tax returns. She was lying."

He nodded. "I found company bank transactions from years ago, but they weren't much help. Not surprising. Briggs is a new player in the game. No doubt the woman is privy to his dirty dealings, making me suspect Briggs keeps what I'm looking for hidden in encrypted computer files."

"Can't you get a search warrant and seize his financial records?" I asked.

He shook his head, frowning. "It's not that easy."

"Really?" I couldn't imagine the FBI having to ask for permission to do anything.

"Not since a federal judge handed down a decision against keeping NSLs secret—"

"What's that?" I asked, curious to find an acronym I didn't know in this world of OMG, LOL and RAT. Remote Access Tools. A bored programmer's fave pastime. Watching unsuspecting computer users doing weird things on their webcam, often sexual in nature. Not me. I preferred my fantasies in the flesh.

Like now.

I reveled in all this spy talk. Wishing we were two agents talking shop.

"NSLs are national security letters," Steve said, "where the Bureau collects private information on a target, like financial and phone records." He explained the Bureau found its hands tied with the recent crackdown on issuing such letters. "This operation will be put on ice for years if we can't gather the evidence we need to build a case against him."

I wiggled my fanny, knowing I had a secret.

"Not if I can help you get it."

A DARK, MOONLESS night hid us as we sneaked around the back of the old Victorian house, better known as my former place of employment. I got a cheap thrill up my backside when I showed Steve how to slip through the secret door and his groin nudged my butt cheeks. Even through my sturdy jeans I could feel his rock-hard erection.

Dream on.

Hey, a girl has to take what she can get. All through college, I spent my nights reading a handbook on string-searching algorithms instead of sporting a G-string. I never regretted it until now. I knew nothing about hotness, how to figure into that sexual equation of boy-beds-girl and thereby discover my self-worth. I always thought working hard and using your brain were all you needed to succeed in the corporate world.

Look where it got me.

No doubt I was now on the FBI's watch list, though Steve assured me no charges would be filed against me if I cooperated with the investigation. *That* part was cool. What sent my sex-o-meter into a nosedive was that after our heart-to-heart, my new BF was all business. No head rubbing, no shoulder touching.

Nothing.

I kept my hands to myself. Had to. I was on a mission to clear my name and if hacking—I mean looking for a security hole in the company's computer, Steve's words, not mine—got the job done, then I was up for it.

Lucky for us, the guard was on foot patrol on the other side of the building. Most likely smoking his favorite blend by the smell of it.

Giving us time to get inside.

"Be careful," I warned Steve, bending low. "We might not be alone." I was fearful he might trample a plump, happy cat, snoozing near the door, with his heavy black boots. To my surprise, the kitty was nowhere to be seen except for a series of paw prints tracked inside the house. My heart skipped a beat, hoping nothing had happened to her. The tawny feline was the only one I could trust at my old job.

Steve cut through the narrow passage opposite from the phony window where we'd entered. "Where does that lead?" he asked.

"To the main reception area."

"Then what? I need to get into Briggs's computer."

"Not his computer. His office manager's." I told him about the companies I'd spotted in a file on her computer and the offshore locations of the bank transactions associated with them.

"How did you secure the password?" he wanted to know.

"CTI," I said without missing a beat. "Creative techno intervention."

"You mean hacking."

"I call it saving my butt."

He shook his head, grinning. "You wait here, Pepper, out of danger. You could get hurt if Briggs and the men he's working for show up."

"What could be more dangerous than being cornered in a room with you with my pants down?" I asked, following him. I caught a brief glimpse of the copy room with its big machine and cold platen glass. My pubes sent out a text alert. I squeezed my thighs, remembering Steve's hands on my waist, his hot breath on the back of my neck.

"You never fail to amaze me, Pepper," he said,

making me wonder if that was a good thing or a bad thing. After all, what did I know about the art of seduction? I was new at this. I worked two jobs in college and missed spring break when all the girls went au naturel and let the guys lick tequila body shots off their breasts and crotch.

I just smiled and went all computer geek, creeping into Ms. Sims's office like I was following the yellow brick road. Sitting down at her desk, I slid my fingers over the mouse, squeamish about leaving fingerprints, and turned on her computer. I entered the password and double-clicked on a file, then another. And another.

"Holy shit."

"What is it, Pepper?"

"There's not just one file, but two more listing companies I don't recognize, along with their shipping schedules and banking info. PacWest Comix, Tech-More Digital, Blue Seahorse Software." I read more names off the computer screen, digging my fingers deep into the pocket of my red plaid flannel shirt.

"So?" Steve asked, leaning over my shoulder. I wished he would cup my breasts, but my FBI hottie wanted answers more than he wanted to cop a feel.

"When I first spotted them, I figured the company was outsourcing work. Now I have my doubts." I kept digging through the files. "We'd have to write a new video game every week to keep up with the work demand from this many companies. Even I'm not that good."

Steve chuckled. "Don't underestimate yourself, Pepper."

I smiled to myself, secretly pleased at his remark. "I doubt if they're new customers, either. All our clients are informed on a regular basis about next year's video games and upcoming marketing strategies." I opened another file outlining the latest advertising campaign. "I was right. None of these companies are listed here."

"Most likely they're shell companies used to transfer funds back and forth." Steve stood behind me, his hot breath hitting the back of my neck and sending a shiver up and down my spine as he shined his flashlight on the computer screen.

I sat up straighter, enjoying the closeness between us. Pushing my breasts out, hoping he'd get the message. He didn't. Damn.

"I can't believe my ex-boss is a crime lord."

"Most likely he fell in with a syndicate who promised him bigger profits if he played ball with them. Like using his company as a front for illegal money laundering. I've no doubt Briggs got in over his head when he started using call girls to transport dirty money to offshore accounts." He snickered. "Not to mention getting some action on the side."

I wrinkled my nose. Somehow I couldn't picture Mr. Briggs getting it on with a cardboard-face bimbo.

"Why would he do it?" I asked, leaning in closer. Steve pretended not to notice. "The company is doing well, our sales figures are up—"

"When a CO starts thinking with his dick instead of his brain," he said, "chaos follows."

I couldn't resist adding, "Do you always think with your brain?"

"I wouldn't be here if I did." He rubbed the back of my neck and the cool night air seeped through my flannel shirt. "Transfer these files for me, Pepper," he said, leaning over me, his face so close to mine the stubble on his chin scraped my skin in a pleasant, sexy way. "I don't want to get caught in here when the sun comes up."

"You mean we're not going to finish what we started over the copier?"

"And have you set off the alarm again?" he said, pinching my butt. "Don't tempt me."

"I'm curious," I asked, trying to change the subject to cover my disappointment. "What do spies do when they finish a job?" I inserted a thumb drive into the computer. "Go to Disneyland?"

He laughed. "Sorry, Pepper, you'll have to play Sleeping Beauty and lay low while I wrap up the case against Briggs."

"Any suggestions where I can…lay low?" I burned the files onto the thumb drives and then safely removed them from the computer. I was about to stuff them into my pocket when Steve grabbed them, but not before his hand brushed against my breasts, making me moan.

Thank you, God.

He said, "We'll discuss that *after* we get these files into the right hands."

"Speaking of hands…" I rubbed up against him and ran my hand up and down his thigh. His hard muscle flexed under my fingers, telling me my superman was human after all.

"Do all computer programmers think about sex 24/7?" He kissed the nape of my neck, nuzzling my ear, and then ran his fingers up and down my shoulders. I wanted to fall into his arms with joy when he wrapped his hands around my breasts. My nipples peaked like two peas under a hard mattress. I closed my eyes and then let go with a sigh of unbearable pleasure. I tingled when he unbuttoned my shirt, sliding the flannel off my shoulder and caressing my bare skin.

"I can't help it," I whispered, closing my eyes, my whole being alive to the sensation of his lips trailing kisses on the back of my neck. "I work with hard drives all day."

"Lucky for me," he said, digging his fingers under my soft, foamy bra cups and working his way up toward my hard nipples. Pinching and twisting my buds and then pulling on them like they were knotted rubber bands. I groaned.

God, I couldn't stand it. I wanted his fingers in me. Not one, two. Yes, two.

Steve slid his hand down my jeans, making me shiver with delicious anticipation. Yes, closer... closer...oh, yes.

I was floating in a la-la land of happy contractions when I heard angry voices coming from downstairs. I pushed away from him, every nerve in my body alert.

Who the hell was that?

Steve flipped off his flashlight and gestured for me to stay put, but I followed him anyway. I was so not letting him out of my sight. Not with those fingers.

Racing on tiptoe across the corridor, we peeked over the railing and looked down the winding stairway. There below I saw Mr. Briggs and his office manager, Ms. Sims, arguing in the foyer. Then he pushed the button on the creaky, old elevator.

Jesus fricking Christ. We didn't have much time.

Steve grabbed my hand and pulled me back into the office. Without a word, I turned off the computer. Steve wiped it clean along with the mouse and then we headed for the stairway.

We were too late. The elevator was slow, but not slow enough. The door was opening.

They'd see us.

I freaked.

CHAPTER FIVE

"WE HAVE TO HIDE," I whispered, instinctively taking his arm.

"Where?" he asked. "I can't blow my cover with Briggs."

I saw the supply room door open halfway. "In here."

We barely had time to squeeze inside the dark room and close the door when Mr. Briggs and Ms. Sims swept past our hiding place. A whiff of her tart perfume sent a wave of nausea through me. Yuk. I cracked open the door and heard my ex-boss ordering her to check her computer files. The overhead light went on, and a familiar whir filled the silence. The cascade of blue windows coming up on the monitor cast an eerie glow on their faces.

Zombies best described them.

I cringed. What if they saw us?

Could Mr. Briggs fire me twice?

I pulled back out of sight, the sound of my breathing loud in my ears. Or was that Steve breathing down my neck? Nice. I couldn't stop a shiver wiggling down my spine. Damn, this was no time to rev up my libido. We had to bail out of here and slip through the hidden entrance unseen.

Still, I wasn't complaining about the delay in our getaway. What girl would? Crushed up against his hard body in the small dark room, I couldn't get enough of him pressed up against me, his hands caressing my back. Up and down. Slowly. His lips brushing the bare skin on my neck. Every nerve alert.

I rubbed that special spot between my legs where my jeans cut into me. Damn, it burned. I wouldn't be able to control my pent-up passion much longer. Not when it felt this good. A slow fire simmered in my belly, evoking a pleasant ache that set me on edge.

Until I heard Mr. Briggs say, "I thought you erased that girl from your computer."

"I'm *sure* I deleted her," said Ms. Sims, tapping her long black nails on her keyboard like a freak show organist. "Yes, her files are gone."

"I still can't figure out how she knew I was going to be at that sushi restaurant."

The office manager stopped typing on her keyboard. The silence was so acute it made me want to grind my teeth to assure myself time hadn't stopped. "I can," she said.

"What do you mean?" Mr. Briggs asked, clearing his throat.

"She's been poking around in here."

"*What?*"

"See for yourself. I entered the luncheon information on your calendar. She must have hacked in here and found it." She raked her nails across the wooden desk, straining my nerves even further. "I *told* you she was too smart for her jeans."

I let out my breath, pleasantly surprised. A compliment from this woman was akin to scoring a date with a *Cosmo* hottie.

Mr. Briggs snorted loudly. "Then she had access to all my files, the little bitch."

Ouch! *That hurt, Mr. Briggs*, I wanted to shout. I saved this company from going into the toilet when a rival software firm tried to steal our code. I stayed up two days straight patching up the holes. And *this* was the thanks I got?

I exhaled. Loudly. I was ready to bust outta there and tell him to go fuck himself when Steve pulled me back. His hands gripped my butt. Hard.

"Cool it, Pepper."

"I'm not going to let him get away with calling me names," I whispered, squirming. I opened the door wider and saw my ex-boss pacing up and down and wiping his sweaty face with a paper towel.

"This isn't the time to get personal." Steve held me in a tight grip. I couldn't move. "There's more at stake here than your pride. A good agent wouldn't let that bother her."

"What are you saying?" I asked.

"Think about it, Pepper" was all he said.

I let it go, seeing how Mr. Briggs was fit to be tied. Smacking his palms on the desk like a hungry walrus. "I want you to back up everything on that computer," he told his office manager, "and then erase it."

Ms. Sims lifted her crooked brow. "That could take hours."

"I don't care. *Do it.*"

"This wouldn't have happened if you hadn't in-

sisted on hiring her," she mumbled, rubbing it in.
Mr. Briggs ignored her and left.

His footsteps faded away and then the elevator
bell dinged as the door closed. The upstairs was quiet
again except for the office manager tapping away
like the Mad Hatter on speed.

"What are we going to do?" I whispered to Steve,
leaning my head back against his shoulder. The air
in the small room was stuffy and made me sweat.
"We can't leave without her seeing us."

"Looks like we're stuck in here for the rest of the
night," he said in a low, dreamy voice that turned my
legs into warm, gooey caramel.

"You don't sound disappointed."

"Are you?"

I heard an excited murmur from him as he pushed
his groin into my ass, asserting his maleness with an
undeniable show of power. I couldn't deny I loved
it. His unrelenting bulge pushing into my butt crack
made me hover on the verge of a climax. Feeling all
hot and sticky, I contracted my pubes just a little.
Okay, more than a little. I enjoyed the surge of pleasure racing through me.

Yes, yes.

"I'm sure that's hard on you," I said, reaching behind me and grabbing the bulge in his pants to demonstrate my point.

He stifled a groan. "I know how to fix that."

"Yeah?"

"Yeah," he said in a low, sexy voice.

My nipples tightened and a flutter of anticipation settled low in my belly. He lifted up my T-shirt

and unhooked my bra. I nudged up against him and closed my eyes. I was just settling into the heat of the moment when—

"*Me-ow.*"

"What the hell is that?" Steve asked in a loud whisper.

"It sounded like a cat." I felt something furry crawl up my jeans leg, tickling me. A shudder went through me.

What if it wasn't a cat—

Gathering up my courage, I bent down and wrapped my hands around a wiggling creature, then a second one. I held the tiny bundles of fur up to the light peeking through the door.

I smiled.

"Kittens. So that's why the cat was fat and sassy," I said, hugging the little creatures with the Hello Kitty cuteness. "She must have followed me inside the house and then sneaked in here to have her babies."

"They'll be safe here," Steve said, opening the door wider. "But we have to make a run for it."

"We *can't* leave the mother and her kittens," I protested, holding two in my hand and putting a third one into my shirt pocket.

"We have to, Pepper. It's against Bureau policy to put witnesses in the line of fire," Steve said, wearing his FBI hat, "including furry ones."

"So was making love to me," I reminded him, both of us keeping our voices to a whisper. "But that didn't stop you."

His eyes focused on me for a minute and then he grabbed the mother cat. "Let's go."

Hugging the wall, we slipped out of the room without the office manager spotting us and made our way down the hallway. I swore my shoes squeaked. We were nearly at the stairway when a milk-hungry kitten scratched my hand.

"Ye-ow!" I cried out and bumped my hip against the railing. I lost my balance and—

"Oh, shit!" I said under my breath. The room whirled around me and I saw the marble entryway looming in my face. I was dizzy, but all I could think about were the kittens. I'd never forgive myself if—

"Steve, the kittens!" I called out in a harsh whisper.

"It's *you* I'm worried about, Pepper," Steve said, hauling my ass up by my jeans waistband before I went over the railing. "The kittens have nine lives. You don't."

I fell into his arms, still hugging the tiny felines. I couldn't help but stifle a cry. No one ever worried about me before.

God, it felt good.

I didn't have time to enjoy the moment. Ms. Sims was acting like a diva behaving badly.

"Who's there?" yelled the office manager.

She rushed out of the office and scanned the hallway but didn't see us. She looked disheveled and bleary-eyed, every hair out of place. Catching my breath, I could see her black pencil-slim pants and high-heeled pointy shoes, her skinny butt swaying back and forth like two pomegranates.

"Be ready to move out," Steve said, holding the wriggling mother cat. He let her go and, with a loud *me-ow*, she scampered across the polished floor, sending the office manager into a tirade of expletives. Who knew the woman had such a sexist vocabulary? She slammed the office door shut and went back to erasing the files from her computer.

"*Go!*" Steve whispered, grabbing the feline. We left the same way we came in. No guard in sight. Ms. Sims must have sent him on an errand to keep him out of her way. She didn't trust anybody, even her own nephew. It wasn't until we were speeding away in Steve's old Buick, the mother cat and her kittens snuggled in my lap, that I could breathe again.

"Thanks for not abandoning them," I told him, hugging the little furry angels close to my heart and cuddling them. Their tiny tongues licked my fingers. I closed my eyes and leaned back against the seat. I couldn't believe my maternal instinct was so strong. And this from a girl who never knew her own mother. That thought tugged at my heart.

"All in the line of duty." Steve squeezed my knee. "Don't worry, Pepper," he said, grinning. "They'll be put into witness protection with plenty of milk and cat food."

I put my hand on top of his and squeezed back. Nothing more needed to be said. I knew he'd find them a good home. Though Steve tried to play hardball with me, I saw the look in his eyes when he spied the defenseless cat and her brood. Tender, caring. Here was a man who'd never turn his back on the underdog.

I never doubted he'd save the mother cat and her kittens.

Not once.

What surprised me more was that he'd let it slip that he was worried about me. This coming from a street-tough, straight-talking G-man.

Oh, my.

Be still, my heart.

He didn't mean it.

Really.

Did he?

"You AND YOUR damn doughnuts are ruining my fig-ure, Steven." Jordan grabbed a glazed special out of the box on his desk and bit into it.

Nice and slow.

Teasing him. A trait of hers with her male agents when they were on her "naughty boy" list. Steve had worked with her long enough to know she had some-thing on her mind and it wasn't doughnuts.

Or sex.

"What do you want, Jordan?" he asked, putting down his cell. He had a man keeping the eyeball on Pepper. He'd been so tied down with the Briggs case, he couldn't do the job himself. He was worried about her. The field agent had just called in to tell him she was headed out this morning in a hurry. What she was up to now, he could only guess. She jumped into situations faster than a bunny banging on his drum. Steve ordered him not to lose her.

"Nothing except a sugar high," she said between bites.

"Don't tell me you're PMS-ing," he said, knowing she hated that. She'd been on him for days to file his report on Briggs. He couldn't. The file was still wide-open, like a pole dancer's legs doing a split. "This has to do with Pepper, doesn't it?"

She paced up and down, her smart, metal-gray stilettos tapping on the warped wooden floor. Gray slacks. Black turtleneck. She maintained a professional image at all times. At least, on the surface. Underneath she simmered with a slow burn and, man, could she kick ass.

"I see you're on a first-name basis with the mark," Jordan said. "How'd you manage that?"

"Tradecraft."

"Don't lie to me, Steven. I didn't need to see her polygraph exam to know the girl was lying to us." She slam-dunked the half-eaten doughnut into the trash can by his desk. "You made quite an impression on her, didn't you? Enough for her to jeopardize her freedom by hacking into her ex-company's computer."

"I insisted."

"*That* I don't doubt."

"You have to admit, Jordan, the girl is a whiz kid with computers. She can decode *anything* and get into the most sophisticated software." Steve explained how she'd cracked the password on the office manager's computer. "I've never seen anyone with such a knack for bypassing antivirus software and finding the holes in the system."

"Isn't finding holes *your* job?" Jordan smirked.

She poured herself a cup of coffee. Into *his* cup. Black.

He ignored her barb. "Pepper knows her way around a hard drive better than the most seasoned spymaster. I've never seen anything like it."

"You wouldn't be trying to recruit her, Steven, would you?"

"Why not?" Steve said. "The Bureau could use her talents. We're dragging our asses when it comes to corporate security. You know as well as I do, Jordan, the hackers are beating us."

"Same old Steven. Always thinking of the Bureau first."

She squeezed his balls through his jeans. He gritted his teeth, but he didn't flinch. Pepper would be a good fit for the FBI if she could just get past her fears. Not let them cripple her mind. He'd seen that happen to his brother. Never felt good about himself, always had to prove something. Tom fell into a rabbit hole and never climbed out.

He didn't want to see Pepper take her smart skills down the wrong road and end up lost and abandoned.

"You succeeded in a man's world, Jordan," Steve said, complimenting her. The Princeton grad had overcome a childhood with an alcoholic parent and a house with little to eat but stale cereal.

She exhaled. "It's not easy being a female in this business. You have to work ten times harder than the men, and when you do, they call you a troublemaking bitch." She leaned back against the doorjamb and licked her lips. "But I wouldn't trade it for anything.

Where else would I find myself surrounded by hand-some men like you?"

"So why not add a little sugar to your coffee?" Steve said, sliding his chair across the floor and taking his cup back.

"I admit Pepper O'Malley fits the profile of a good agent. She's smart, creative, adventurous. But that's not everything, Steven. Under pressure, even the best candidate can crack." Jordan shoved the metal trash can across the floor with the heel of her stiletto. "What makes you think she's got what it takes?"

"Pepper is that good, Jordan. Let me prove it to you."

"No can do. You compromised yourself by fucking her. You're off the case." She leaned over him so he could get an eyeful of her full breasts, her nipples pointing through her tight sweater. Her way of keeping her power secure in her empire. "Agent Barker will take over."

He cocked a brow. "I've never seen you this jealous before, Jordan."

"I've never seen you take such an interest in a material witness before." She crossed her arms over her chest in a show of authority. "The higher-ups are on my ass to wrap up this case before someone blows the whistle and the media get wind of it. I've got a team sitting on Briggs day and night. He's bound to slip up."

His cell chimed—a text. His Japanese contact. Briggs wanted to take a meeting. That gave him an idea.

"What if I promise you I can get a taped confession from Briggs that will stand up in court?" Steve said. "Will you put me back on the case?"

Jordan smirked. "Does it involve you getting into that girl's pants?"

Steve grinned and then stuck his middle finger through the hole of a crispy, glazed, sugary, doughy delight. "Care for another doughnut?"

"YOU WANT ME to do *what?*" I asked, adrenaline racing through me like popcorn popping outta control. I turned down a rainbow-painted path and headed toward Bongo's Pizza Playland.

"Wear a wire," Steve said, not missing a beat. "It's the only way we can nail Briggs." He was hot on my tail. I wasn't a happy camper. I hadn't heard from him since our *Breakfast at Tiffany's* rendezvous, complete with the rescue of the cat, like in the film.

And now this?

"You've got to be crazy." I didn't care how good-looking Special Agent Steve Raines was. I was *not* going to jeopardize what little future I had left by letting the FBI hot-wire my bod so they could listen to everything I said. What if I said something stupid? Like how I hacked into the company computer?

Or, worse yet, admitted I'd gone all Bruce Lee and zonked a federal agent? I'd be sent to a planet far, far away faster than you could send R2-D2 to a recycling bin. "Now, if you'll excuse me, I have a job interview and I'm late."

I rushed through the bright red double doors into the pizza parlor and put on my best cheesy-clown smile. I prayed Steve wouldn't follow me. Why bother? He knew my routine. He'd had a tail on my ass all week. I wasn't so dumb that I didn't notice a guy with tattoos following me. Guys with tattoos *never* followed me.

So I wasn't surprised when Steve showed up with his scary request. It wasn't enough the FBI had seen me half-naked and put me through an interrogation like I'd tried to get past airport security with a double latte. Now he wanted me to play Mata Hari. I *knew* what happened to her, and it wasn't pretty.

"Hi, I'm Pepper O'Malley," I choked out, handing the balding manager my résumé. He smelled like garlic and had pepperoni stuck in his teeth. I held my breath. "I'm here for the ball-pit job."

"You got any experience?" he asked, and then sneezed on my résumé.

"Yeah, sure," I said, unnerved. "I play with balls all the time."

He snickered. Too late I realized what I'd said. Then he explained to me that all I had to do was keep the kids' ball pond filled with red, blue, yellow and green hollow plastic balls. Hey, a job is a job. And you get free pizza, a programmer's main food staple. So what if being trapped with a bunch of screaming kids in a padded cage wasn't my dream job? A girl had to eat.

The manager stuffed my résumé into his jeans waistband and then looked me up and down while he picked his teeth. With a penknife. "Do you have good people skills, Pepper?" His eyes lingered on my breasts.

"I love kids," I blurted out.

"She hates kids," said a deep male voice behind me. It made my nipples hard.

Steve.

He didn't stop there.

"She eats them for breakfast."

"Who's your boyfriend?" The pizza parlor manager wanted to know, staring at Steve like he wanted to put him through a sausage grinder.

"He's *not* my boyfriend," I said, my spirits sinking.

"I'm her pimp," Steve said, and then he grabbed my arm and pulled me out of the pizza parlor. Holding me by the elbow, he steered me toward his unmarked car parked in an alley. Nobody around. Perfect for a kidnapping.

"Why did you do that?" I asked, jumping into the passenger seat rather than make a scene. I didn't want to go downtown to the federal building a second time. "I answered a hundred online ads, and this was the only job that would talk to me."

"Cool it, Pepper, I've got a better offer for you."

"Since when did wearing a wire for the FBI pay the big bucks?"

"You're going to be a companion girl," he said, checking his messages on his cell.

"A *what?*"

"Your job is to entertain Japanese businessmen."

My eyes bugged out. "I'm *not* taking off my clothes again."

"You don't have to. You'll wear a recording device here." He slipped his hand under my baby tee and cupped my breast. Okay, so he had my attention. Next, he flicked his finger under my bra strap.

Oh, that wasn't fair. He knew I was dying for him to pinch my nipple.

"What if he gives me a bear hug and finds the wire stuck to my tits with duct tape?" I asked, trying my best not to get turned-on. I didn't want to go down that road only to be disappointed again. I liked Steve too much to play games.

"It's not like the old days, Pepper, when you had to wear a clunky, battery-operated recorder. Everything's digital. The recorder is implanted in a jeweled pin." He smiled that devil grin of his. "No one is going give you a New Jersey pat-down but me."

He leaned over and ran his hands expertly up and down my rib cage, then between my thighs, taking time to dig his finger into my crotch. He rubbed his thumb into the tight denim cutting into me.

Pushing, probing, stroking, delicious sensations filled me up. I squirmed. So much for me not getting turned-on. It was pure hell for me not to unzip my jeans and slide them down my thighs so he could finger me.

I decided to play along. Let him try to convince me.

What did I have to lose?

I had no intention of wearing a wire.

"How do you know Mr. Briggs will be at this fancy party?" I leaned in and ran my finger along the sexy stubble on his chin. I loved the way he touched me, made me feel good.

But I wanted more.

I didn't want to press my luck, but I couldn't help wishing he'd kiss me.

"He's eager to meet my Asian contacts," Steve said, grabbing my fingers and entwining them with his. It was a romantic gesture and one that made my bachelorette meter soar even if he *was* trying to con me. "There will be several pretty models at the hotel. All you have to do is follow the script I give you. There will be a surveillance team in place. We'll move in quietly and take Briggs into custody after we get what we want."

I pulled away. I wanted to see my ex-boss pay for what he did to me, but those old feelings of doubt lingered in my mind. Like smelly gym socks left in your tote bag. You didn't want to open it.

"I can't do it."

"Pepper—"

"Mr. Briggs may be a crook, but you're asking *me* to be a snitch."

"You want to be a spy, don't you?"

"Yes."

"Then be one."

He had a point. For years, I'd watched every cop and spy show on TV. Learning the lingo, imitating their moves when they kicked down doors, practicing my two-handed gun pose.

Still—

"What if I screw up?" I had to ask.

"You won't, Pepper. I'd stake my badge on it."

"You would?" I asked, disbelieving.

"I would."

He tilted my head back and claimed my mouth

with the most intoxicating pair of lips a girl ever knew. Burning with need, melting into me, pressing harder when I reached around his neck and held him tight. I parted my lips and he entwined his tongue with mine, leaving me breathless.

If this was a bribe, bring it on.

I pressed my breasts against his muscular chest and moaned so loud I shocked myself. "Don't stop, Steve, please don't stop."

He gave it to me hot and long, sweetening the moment with trails of kisses up and down my neck and then sticking his tongue into my cleavage. Tickling me, unhooking my bra. He circled my breasts, but he didn't play with my nipples.

What the—

"Suck on my nipples, *please*," I said, jiggling my breasts like a wound-up Kewpie doll.

"No."

"You know you want to," I teased, biting down on my lower lip. Was that *me* talking?

"Not until you promise to help me take down a corporate thief. A man who is a liar and a cheat."

"Steve, I—I—"

"You can do it, Pepper." He cupped my breasts and squeezed them.

Oh, the frustration. Whoever thought he'd resort to such torture?

Jesus, I thought I was going to die.

I begged him to bite my nipples. Twist them. Wet them with his tongue. Blow on them. Do *something*.

No, he said. Not until I promised to do what he asked.

I writhed about in the bucket seat of his old Buick, the split leather cracking under my butt. I was in an emotional pickle. I wanted to be a spy and when the opportunity was handed to me on a silver platter, I froze. I knew this was my defining moment. No more daydreaming about being a spy girl.

Do it or forget it.

That meant I had to let go, get over my fears, and if it took wild, passionate sex to put me over the top, then so be it. I couldn't stand the burning in my belly another minute.

I gave in.

"Okay, Steve, I'll *wear* the damn wire."

He grinned wide. "I thought you'd see things my way."

"Do I have a choice?" I asked, panting hard.

"No, but I do." He bit my nipple hard, then the other, and I fell headfirst into exquisite pleasure.

CHAPTER SIX

"JEEZ, MR. BRIGGS," I muttered in a flat voice, "what a surprise seeing you here."

"*No, no, no*, Pepper," Cindy said, exhaling with a loud *whoosh*. "You're too stiff. Try it again."

I pulled in my gut and clenched my pubes. "*Jeez, Mr. Briggs—*"

"You sound like a robocall," Cindy said, exasperated. "Now say it with feeling. Give it *oomph*." She cleared her throat. "Jeez, Mr. Briggs, what a big surprise seeing little ol' you here." She batted her Dolly Partons.

Her lashes, not her boobs.

"I'm not trying to seduce him, Cindy. I'm trying to get a confession."

"Whatever. You have to be *in the moment*. Think of something way more important than Mr. Briggs."

"Like Steve's dick?" I teased.

She sighed. "You'll never be an actress, Pepper, if you don't give it your all."

"I'm a tech-head, not a drama queen."

She shot me a dirty look and fluffed her hair at the same time. That was a joke between us ever since high school when she was cast as the Good Witch of the North in a spoof of *Wicked* and I worked the special effects "wizard" board.

"So? Didn't I let you sprinkle techie dust on me so I could learn how to use that image-fixing software you bought?" she reminded me.

"Yeah," I said. It was a matter of survival. Cindy was determined to zap her freckles from her headshot.

"Then *you* can learn how to pronounce your vowels and how to breathe properly."

"I don't *want* to breathe, I want to die." I tossed down the script Steve had given me and sank into the big easy chair in her parents' living room. She couldn't afford her own apartment. Acting wasn't exactly a high-paying job, though she was determined to convince me otherwise.

She tried the I-did-it-and-so-can-you approach.

"You know that hair show I did?" she said, bubbling over like fizzing soda pop.

"Did they cast you or your dark roots?"

Cindy ignored my sarcasm as she always did. She was my best friend. She put up with me.

"I've been dying to tell you, Pepper. A TV producer saw me and wants to cast me in his new reality show about four single girls who can't live without their phones."

"What's it called?" I asked with a smirk. "*Confessions of a Cell-Phone Princess?*"

She rolled her eyes. "All I have to do is live in a store window with three other girls with no communication to the outside world except our smartphones. The girl who gets the most votes from the viewers wins fifty thousand dollars." She sighed. "Just think, Pepper, I could move out on my own."

With that Barbie collection?

She'd never find a one-bedroom apartment that big.

"What about your intimate moments?" I asked.

"I don't know all the details," she admitted, furrowing her pencil-thin brows.

"Like bathroom breaks and lonely nights with your vibrator." I wasn't surprised at Cindy's news since recent stats suggested more people in the world had a cell phone than a bathroom.

"Oh, I never thought about that." She perked up. "Well, anyway, I'm sure they'll work the kinks out. What's more important now is getting you your job back."

"I wouldn't do this if Steve hadn't kissed me."

"He's that good?"

"Better," I said, my whole bod humming, the memory of his kiss and the promise that went with it stirring my desires. I rubbed my thighs together and moaned.

"*That's it, Pepper!*" she said, her lips parting in a big O. She was so excited she jumped up and clapped her hands together. "You're *in the moment*. Now, try it again…."

And so it went for hours with Cindy directing me like we were doing a *Star Wars* sequel and I was Princess Leia. Too bad I didn't have her lightsaber. All I had was a measly recorder between me and exile to a doomed planet for fired programmers. God help me.

Finally, we had it down to where she thought I just might pull it off.

I thought about how what had started out as a job fixer-upper had turned into something far different. Because of Steve. This sexy FBI agent had flipped my world into a new orbit. Melted my resistance. Forced me to face my fears. No matter what happened, there was no turning back.

I jumped when the holy grail of polyphonic rings ripped through the air and my cell phone lit up with a now familiar caller ID.

Steve.

"The eagle…that is, the walrus," he said, referring to my oft-used description of my ex-boss, "has landed."

I gulped.

Lights. Camera. Action.

This was it.

The big takedown.

Oh, my God, I just wet my pants.

MY ASSIGNMENT: GET Mr. Briggs to hire me back. Not as a programmer, but as a courier. Board a private jet. Deliver documents to his contacts in Asia. Then return with cash or drugs hidden in my—

No, I couldn't even think it. It was too gross.

Hopefully, I'd never get that far. Once he made me the offer, I was off the hook. That is, wire.

I blinked through my star-crossed, false eyelashes and checked out the private lounge in the hotel filled with happy partygoers. Japanese and American businessmen drinking expensive whiskey and gulping down cubes of Kobe beef and truffles. Pretty young models wearing thigh-high, slinky dresses and spike heels. Their long earrings dangled over their bare shoulders when they laughed, provocative and jazzy.

Was I the only one not having a good time?

I glanced briefly into a dark corner and spied a couple making out on the couch. Two men drinking and laughing pointed to them. One of them must have told a dirty joke. I moved on before they zeroed in on me. I had never felt so vulnerable. My skin prickled like I was a chicken with its feathers plucked. Yet I knew Steve and his team were here somewhere.

Watching me.

"Do you copy, Pepper?" I heard him say in my earpiece. The microbud was the latest in surveillance technology, giving me the freedom to move about and receive information.

"I'm here, Steve," I whispered, grabbing a martini off a tray. My third. I scanned a trio of businessmen watching a pretty girl balance a champagne glass on her forehead while they trickled the bubbly down her cleavage. "But Mr. Briggs isn't."

"Keep looking. You'll find him. And when you do, *be sexy*. Make him forget you were ever a programmer."

Easier said than done.

I was afraid to jiggle my boobs. Steve had fastened a faux diamond pin with the tiny digital recorder onto my low-cut dress. What if it came loose?

At least I could see where I was going. The Bureau had staked me with soft contacts for the job, or so Steve said. I was sure the money came out of his own pocket. I considered it a personal loan, and I intended to pay him back as soon as I found work.

I sipped my martini. Sea salt and orange mixed on my tongue as I peeked over the rim of my glass. I shook, not stirred, my courage. Revved it up all the way. Swaying my hips so the sparkly pin caught the light. Swinging my silver-sequined purse with the long chain over my shoulder. I had this fantasy I *was* a spy. Especially in this setup. An intimate lounge with cut crystal and glass, blue velvet couches and purple walls that reminded me of a scene in a Bond flick.

The villain's lair.

How juicy.

I scoped out the men drinking at the long mahogany bar.

There he was. I saw Mr. Briggs raising his glass in a toast with an Asian businessman, his other hand grabbing the man's business card. Perfect timing. I knew his game: Get a foot in the Japanese video game market and he was set.

Not tonight, Mr. Briggs.

My job was to convince him that he "owed" me a job, and I would blow the whistle on him if he didn't hire me.

Remembering what Cindy said about being in the moment, I thought about sex as I sashayed over to my ex-boss.

Steve's big dick. And his hands all over me.

No wonder I had a big smile on my face when I came up behind him. "Jeez, Mr. Briggs," I said, tapping him on the shoulder, "what a surprise seeing you here."

Flustered, he spit out his drink and then turned to see me grinning at him. "You show up in the strangest places, Miss O'Malley."

"I'm a whiz kid, remember?" I said, leaning in closer. "Your calendar is an open book to me."

"I don't know what you're talking about," he said. "Leave me alone."

"Not until you give me a job."

"I just hired a new programmer to take your place."

"That's *not* the job I want." I cozied up to him, licking my lips. The Asian businessman next to him smiled, bowed and left. "You could send me to Japan to work on your *other* business."

Mr. Briggs wiped his sweaty brow with his cocktail napkin. "I don't know what you're talking about."

"I think you do." I sipped my martini, flirting with him and batting my thick eyelashes like a pop music queen. "All that lovely, dirty money flowing into your hands, and all you have to do is wash it clean."

"Are you trying to blackmail me, Miss O'Malley?"

"All I want is what you owe me, Mr. Briggs. Back salary and my key to the exec girls' washroom."

That last part was off script, but I couldn't help it.

"What?" he asked, not getting it.

I took a deep breath and got back into character fast. "I hear there's *beaucoup* bucks in moving overseas money through phony shell companies—"

An irritated female voice butted in. "Excuse me,

honey, but Mr. Briggs isn't interested in balling you, so lay off."

Holy shit. It was Ms. Sims looking glam, if you could make a witch glam. Her perfume reeked, as usual. Where did she get that stuff? It smelled like hair dye.

"Did you fly in on your broomstick?" I asked, feeling smug.

It took her a moment to recognize me.

"Pepper O'Malley," she screeched, "what the hell are you doing here?"

"Mr. Briggs and I are discussing business," I said, standing up to her. "Now if you'll excuse us."

"I'm calling security."

"Don't be so hasty, Genevieve," Mr. Briggs said, nervous.

Genevieve?

"Miss O'Malley is going to be our new business associate."

Did you get that, Steve?

"Make him offer you a job outright," I heard in my earpiece.

Damn, this wasn't going according to plan. I needed more courage. I downed the martini in one gulp.

"Mr. Briggs wants me to be a courier for the company," I said in a clear voice.

He acknowledged what I said with a brief nod and a weak grin.

"Make him *say* he wants you to move money for him, Pepper," Steve whispered in my ear. "We need his voice on the tape."

"You want me to be your new courier to Japan and pick up phony documents *and* cash. Right, Mr. Briggs?" I said, the vodka cruising to my brain in a slow, easy fashion. I will not get dizzy. "Who would ever suspect me? I'm perfect for the job. After all, I wrote the damn video game program."

I burped. Loud.

Mr. Briggs didn't notice. He was too busy freaking out, praying no one had heard me. I don't know where my sassiness came from. Either Cindy was a damned good acting teacher or three martinis was a damned good incentive.

"She's *crazy*, Seymour," Ms. Sims said, pulling on his arm. "Don't agree to anything."

"Are you going to let *her* run *your* business, Mr. Briggs?" I said, not letting up. I was enjoying this. Big-time.

"No," he began, "but Ms. Sims is in charge of the overseas accounts."

I was sweating pink. Hot and heavy. I still didn't have his confession.

I made one more try.

"I *need* this job, Mr. Briggs. Say you'll hire me to move cash for you, *please!*" I begged him. Jeez, that was dumb. Overkill. I broke the spy rules. I couldn't help it. My pulse kicked up its heels higher than I wanted to go. My desperation showed.

Something popped in Ms. Sims's brain.

She looked me up and down. I swear she was onto me and knew the fake diamond pin stuck in my cleavage was a recorder. "Something smells fishy here, Seymour. Who let her in here?"

"*Who cares?*" he said, going postal. "I'm hiring her to be a courier for us. If I don't, she'll go to the feds and tell them everything she found on your computer. The phony companies, the overseas dirty money, *everything.*"

"Keep your mouth *shut!*" Ms. Sims swiveled her head from left to right. She gasped loudly when she saw Steve and two men in plainclothes closing in on her. "*You fool! You damned fool.* Look what you've done."

She pushed me hard, knocking the glass out of my hand, then bolted. She left poor Mr. Briggs wiping his forehead and demanding he be allowed to talk to his lawyer. I ignored him. Steve could take care of him. Ms. Sims was right. Something *did* smell. Her exotic dill weed perfume lingered in the air.

I jammed after her.

This was one takedown I was going to enjoy.

Ms. Sims had the advantage. No one knew why she was running. She could be headed to the bathroom to toss up the fried squid kebabs. Or reapply her demon-red lipstick. She also hadn't downed three dirty martinis *and* she was used to maneuvering the corporate world in sky-high heels. I wasn't. That didn't stop me. I sprinted through the devil's lair like a regular speed freak, my arms flailing about like I was a roller derby queen.

Nothing could stop me.

Until—

A trio of businessmen blocked my way. They were

trying to look up a model's skirt when she bent over to pick up her earring.

"*Excuse me, excuse me,*" I busted out, knocking off a Japanese businessman's glasses when I zinged past him. Then I slammed into a waiter carrying a tray of empty plastic champagne flutes. Down we went like dominos. I heard the loud *crunch* of plastic under my butt as I landed.

Ouch.

Huffing and puffing, pulse racing, I yanked off my silver-heeled kicks and then got to my feet and took off. I ran out into the hallway and looked up and down, but Ms. Sims had disappeared.

Damn.

I figured she was hiding in the bathroom, when—

There she was. Heading toward the exit. Two purple potted palms stood on either side of the private elevator.

I took off, my bare feet gliding over the plush plum carpeting so fast I was almost airborne. I was determined to grab her before she got into the elevator.

"*Stop, FBI!*" I shouted out. I have no idea where my courage came from to falsely identify myself as a fed, but it seemed like a good idea. I opened my purse and pulled out an expired department store credit card and flashed it under the overhead light.

Gold, it wasn't.

Tarnished pewter, maybe.

Like my ass, if I didn't make the collar. Talk about being in the moment, as Cindy would say. Anyway, Ms. Sims turned around and saw my feeble attempt at pulling this off.

She threw back her head and laughed. "You gotta be kidding me."

"No joke, Ms. Sims," I said, so close to her I could smell her revolting perfume. "I—I'm with the FBI."

Technically, I wasn't lying. I was *with* the feds, but I wasn't one of them. Yet I had sense of belonging, knowing I'd helped them get the dirt on these two. I knew now Ms. Sims was the instigator and poor Mr. Briggs was her patsy. His kingdom for a lay. Why did men always fall for that stunt?

What mattered most to me was that I didn't give up. Didn't let my fears sidetrack me. I could do this. I got a funny chill then. A strange sense this was what Steve wanted me to feel, that I had the moxie to make it as a federal agent.

I soon discovered it wasn't all about flashing a badge and giving a shout out.

The doors opened and Ms. Sims raced into the elevator all smiles and then pushed over a potted plant to block me from following her. Dirt flew everywhere.

"I always said you were dirt under my feet." She jabbed the elevator buttons to make the doors close.

"You won't sweep me away that easily," I shot back, and then I shoved my bod through the doors seconds before they closed on my boobs.

Ms. Sims was one angry conspirator.

She smashed her palm into my face and then pulled my hair. I refused to let her petty chick move throw me off balance. I kicked her in the shin. She yelped, but that didn't stop her. She ripped off the pin attached to the front of my low-cut dress with her claws, scratching my shoulder and making me wince.

Oh, yeah? No one takes my decoder pin.

I grabbed her wrist and squeezed hard until she dropped it. She yanked on my exposed bra strap. It broke and my breast fell out of my C-cup.

What the hell?

I wasn't going to let a bare tit stop me.

I'd shown more skin at the sushi restaurant.

I dove at her while she tried to get the doors open; she sidestepped me. I pushed her; she shoved me back. She punched the buttons, the doors opened, she tried to get out. I tripped her. She went down like a long-legged giraffe with an angry lioness hot on its tail, her butt up in the air. I jumped on her back and straddled her before she had a chance to kick me, and then I pulled her arms back toward me and did what any good FBI agent would do if they didn't have a plastic zip-tie.

I cuffed her with the long chain on my silver-sequined purse.

"I COULDN'T HAVE hogtied her better myself, Pepper," Steve said, wrapping a black velvet tablecloth around my shoulders. I shivered when his hand slipped to my bare breast. Thank God, no one could see him.

"Too bad you missed the foxy catfight," I said, loving his touch. He was giving me what I wanted and needed, and I would take down the inglorious Ms. Sims all over again if he promised not to stop.

"Thank God, you weren't hurt," he said. He nuzzled his face in my hair, his breath hot on the back of my neck. I got all warm and fuzzy inside, hearing his words.

He hustled me through the chaos, taking control, answering the questions thrown at us. Even in the dim light, I could see his eyes were on fire, his whole body moving in exact precision. As if he were in the heat of battle. Orchestrating the takedown of Mr. Briggs and Ms. Sims smoothly and with the expertise and know-how of a trained field agent.

That was when it hit me.

This was how an FBI agent operated in the real world, not the virtual fantasy sandbox where I played. Fool. I'd been so caught up in "being in the moment," I'd turned that moment into a sideshow. I imagined the two federal agents muttering to each other that I overreacted, backed up with comments about me being a typical female, even if I did take down the target.

I dropped my chin to my chest. I was ashamed of my bravado, my tasteless theatrics. I was no closer to joining the FBI now than I'd been before tonight. The truth was, my dream seemed further away than ever.

I didn't tell Steve how I felt. He had high hopes for me and I'd let him down. Yet I couldn't believe how he kept me close to him, protecting me, while he barked orders to the hotel staff to serve drinks and keep the party going. The situation was intense, edgy, and the sooner they cleaned up the scene and got their prisoners out of here, the sooner everyone would forget the FBI had shown up as an uninvited guest.

Everyone except Mr. Briggs.

He couldn't resist a parting shot at me before they took him away in handcuffs. He pulled hard to get away from the agent gripping his arm to have his say.

"You never would have caught on to me without Miss Smarty-Pants here," he sputtered, glaring at me. If looks could kill, I was among the walking dead. "I should have fired her months ago."

"Then why didn't you?" I looked right back at him and didn't blink a phony lash.

"Because you were the best programmer I ever had." He shook his head. "Who would have thought the FBI hired agents *that* smart."

I beamed. Damn, that felt good. My ex-boss thinking I was an agent *and* giving me the credit for his takedown.

"Briggs is right, Pepper," Steve whispered in my ear. "It's *your* collar."

I nodded, loving hearing him say that. But this was no cop show. I had stepped through the fourth wall tonight and become part of the real world. I could no longer hide behind my glasses. Nor did I want to.

"That doesn't mean the next time I want you running around cuffing suspects half-naked," Steve continued, his voice stern. We headed toward the parking garage, the party chatter and clinking glasses behind us, the plush gold-and-red carpeting under my bare feet masking our footsteps. "The Bureau has rules about that."

"The next time?" I asked, my pulse racing.

"Fighting white-collar crime is important business, Pepper," he said, "and you've got the talents the Bureau is looking for."

"What about my employment record? Ms. Sims deleted everything." I kept pace with him, stretching my neck to keep my head level with his chin, emphasizing my height sans heels as if to prove to him I was no slouch. That I could fight cybercrime and keep the workplace safe for all of us who sit down at a computer every morning and log on with a cup of java and a Twitter addiction.

"A few phone calls to the right sources and we'll have your job record cleared," he said. "*And* your back-unemployment checks."

"You forgot one thing," I said, hating to bring it up. "I've got a record with the FBI."

Steve grinned. "After what you did for the investigation tonight, I can convince Jordan to make sure there's no account of you slamming me on the back of the neck. And I wouldn't be surprised if she pushed your paperwork through pronto."

I smiled. Jordan. His sexy boss. Cool.

"We'll get you set up for the second phase of testing," he continued, "and when you pass—"

I loved hearing that. His words gave me the confidence I would need to get through the process.

"—I don't see why you can't start your training at the academy with the next class." Steve paused in the dark stairway and kissed me. Not sexy. Deeper than that. Soulful. Caring. Something I always wanted but never had. "On *one* condition, Miss O'Malley."

"What's that?" I breathed, knowing I'd agree to anything with his lips so close to mine, his hand playing with my bare breast under the black velvet.

"You have to follow the rules of the game."

"Like you do?" I asked.

He smiled, but he didn't answer me.

"Do you agree?" he said, leading me to his un-marked car. Double-parked.

"Yes."

Keep it simple. No wordy explanations, no beg-ging.

"And you're sure you have what it takes to be a special agent?" he asked, unlocking the passenger door.

"Yes."

"There's no stopping you, no matter what they throw at you?"

"No." My heart was racing, drawing all my re-serve together to keep focused, make my dream crys-tallize.

He jumped into the car. I followed. "Then be at my place tomorrow night at eight o'clock sharp." He gunned the engine and sexy vibrations zapped through me like I was hot-wired. My libido went from zero to ninety in a heartbeat. "I'll show you the ropes."

He gave me the address in his clipped, agentlike manner, not repeating it, expecting me to set each word in my mind and not forget it.

"I'll be there," I told him. He smiled and then jammed his old Buick out of the underground park-ing garage like Batman on a mission. I held on tight.

Boy, will I.

CHAPTER SEVEN

EIGHT O'CLOCK COULDN'T come soon enough.

Steve laid out the tools of his trade in a precise manner, taking care to make certain the sake was cooled to room temperature, the linen ropes smooth and pliable, the roses' effusive scent intoxicating.

And his dick hard.

He didn't have to worry about that. His groin tightened, his breath quickened. He remembered how his agent-in-training moved when he was in her, her back dipping instinctively to meet him as he drove her home. Him yearning to finger her in her most secret place. Her knowing only that the burn between her legs intensified with each stroke. Moaning like a slave begging her master to take her. To fuck her. Her pleasure mixed with her curiosity, like sipping fine wine from a king's silver goblet. The taste was made sweeter by the experience.

Steve tied the rope into an intricate knot, winding it this way and that. Precise, its artistry appealing to the eye. Cool to the skin. Such a knot would make Pepper squirm when he wrapped it around her breasts and then pulled on it. Gently, then harder... making it tighter. Making her moan. He couldn't wait to see her breasts standing up, her nipples erect.

He looked at the clock. Ten minutes before eight.

Would she be on time?

Or would she run from the challenge?

He imagined she was filled with apprehension, her emotions over the top, her heart pounding.

Her juices flowing.

He was betting on her avid curiosity to break down any resistance. Especially after she'd had a taste of what she could do when she'd taken down Sims. *And* Briggs. Using the computer files and taped confession secured "from a reliable source" as evidence, he'd had no trouble getting a search warrant to raid the offices of Seymour T. Briggs for paper documents and additional computer files relevant to the ongoing investigation.

All that was left to wrap things up was to bring Pepper into the Bureau.

Steve knew what he was getting into. He was putting himself on the line, something he'd never done before. But she'd changed his mind about training a woman with the techie mind of a computer programmer. She was soft and curvy and all female. She'd impressed him with her raw talent and sex-on-top-of-the-copier routine. She was a natural. He couldn't wait to begin her training. Not every woman would consent to enjoy the erotic evening he had planned.

He had no doubt Pepper would.

Her big green eyes staring at him, her full, pink lips parted in wonder, her high cheekbones finely sculpted. Innocent, but as sexy as all get-out. His mind flipped through his mental notes again as he'd done every night since he met her.

Tall. Big breasts. Great legs.

Long, flyaway hair that shimmered red-gold like a never-ending sunset.

But there was more to her than her gorgeous bod.

Her curiosity amazed him. Her smarts challenged him. And her brazenness charmed him. In a world of spies and counterspies, secrets and lies that often left him frustrated and disillusioned, Pepper was the one real thing he could count on. A woman who said what she meant and looked damned sexy saying it. No regrets, no teasing a man until he couldn't walk straight and then dropping him like a hot poker. She played it straight. Shot from the hip. And fit into his arms perfectly, her head snuggled against his chest, his arms snaked around her beautiful curves.

He couldn't tell her how he felt. Not yet. First, he had to get her into the spy game.

And then?

It was up to her.

He was convinced Pepper had a bright future at the Bureau. *If* she could learn to trust her instincts and believe in herself. Years of self-doubt had wound themselves around her ego like a tight rope. Taut and unbreakable in her mind. Choking her ambition. That was where *he* came in.

Steve had planned this special evening to give her that confidence.

He had concealed his feelings well, giving small hints of his intentions toward her. Why not? She fit the profile of a good special agent. Reading body language. Going on the offensive when confronted with a difficult situation. Not backing down.

He'd never forget how she yelled out "*Stop, FBI!*" in a loud, convincing voice. He had to smile. He could imagine her racing after the elusive Ms. Sims, Pepper's big breasts bouncing up and down. Christ, he couldn't contain himself when he'd caught up to her and saw her beautiful tit exposed, her pointed nipple tempting him. His first instinct was to take her hard bud into his mouth and suck on it.

He would have if they'd been alone.

They weren't.

His two backup agents couldn't take their eyes off her. Steve had ripped a black velvet cloth off a table and wrapped it around her. He still remembered her soft mewling, her head against his shoulder. Then they did a fist bump. It was a moment he'd never forget. He'd ignored his cell phone ringing. Jordan. His only thought: protect Pepper at all costs. For the first time in his career, he let his heart rule his head. He knew that wasn't how an undercover agent acted, that getting too close to the witness often led to guilt feelings if there was any screwup.

The only guilt he felt was putting her in danger without the proper training.

He'd soon fix that. He'd run her through the drill. Give her the opportunity to learn how to deal with any situation. Meanwhile, his team had Briggs in custody. And Pepper had Ms. Sims tied up like a prize pig ready for market.

He grinned. Tied up.

Yes, that was the idea.

Steve let the rose petals drift through his fingers onto the bed covered with satin sheets as shiny as black cod. The cedar fragrance of the *hinoki* wood headboard blended with the floral essence, while the velvety softness of the petals reminded him of that delightful spot between her legs. That special place where he could let himself go—something he never did, even when fucking a woman. He didn't dare. Always on the alert, always ready for trouble, Steve never dreamed *anyone* could make him let down his guard.

Pepper did. She made him laugh. Something he hadn't done in years.

He held his breath in anticipation of the moment when he'd again pull her jeans down to her knees. Then slip his hand between her thighs and press one, then two fingers inside her. Stroke her clit, explore her. Then make her his.

Christ.

His mouth went dry. To quench his thirst, he grabbed the bottle of sake and tilted his head back, the cool drink sliding down his throat. *Smooth. Rich.* Its lingering sweetness left a pleasant, fruity taste in his mouth. *Perfect.* The rice wine was the nectar of the gods. And she was his goddess.

What if she didn't show?

He wouldn't believe that. *Couldn't.*

Tension filled him as he held the glass bottle in his hand, running his fingers up and down its slender neck. Its rounded bottom was curvy, like a woman's. Like Pepper. But she was more than a wildly tempting invitation to sex. She was special to him. No one in his life was like her. Sure, he'd had women. Sexy, beautiful women. But none could compare to Pepper O'Malley.

The doorbell rang.

It was five minutes *before* eight. Steve smiled.

For tonight, he had one mission.

Make her cry out with pleasure.

Over and over again.

THE ROPE PRESSED into me and hit my clit spot on.

I clenched my muscles tight. God, that burned. But wonderfully so. I did it again, shocked by my own brashness. I was right about Steve acting like a man used to tying women up. Did I hit the mark. I didn't pride myself on having insight into how men's brains worked except when it came to computers, but I tapped into the intimate desires of this man bound by strong beliefs that bordered on kink.

But oh, what kink.

I was nude, lying on my back. Red rose petals scattered on my breasts, belly, and thighs, a thick white rug hugging my body like a sensuous cloud. I breathed in a fragrant mist delivered from a bubbling fountain scenting the air around me. Whatever fears I had when I stepped into his world were gone. I was bathed in muted backlighting and—

Tied up.

Naked sushi *à la bondage*.

When I arrived, my FBI hottie had wasted no time ordering me to strip while he watched. When I asked him why, he told me a special agent should be prepared for physical inspection at any time.

I blushed. His request had an intimacy about it that surprised me. Turned me on. As if he were seeing me naked for the first time.

I nodded and obeyed.

First my tee came off, then my bra and best jeans with the rhinestone buttons. When I stood nude in front of him, he said nothing. Instead, he pressed his palm against my pubic area, cupping then squeezing me. Not hard. Just enough to set off tiny tremors in me.

His gesture took my breath away. I couldn't move.

Then his cool hands stroked my thighs, sending a chill through me before he moved upward and caressed my breasts. His fingertips lingered on my pert nipples before pinching them so hard I couldn't help but cry out, the painful pleasure startling but pleasing.

I was already wet when his hand dropped to my buttocks, kneading my soft flesh before moving to my thighs, parting them and slipping his finger inside me. I began to move against him, but he insisted I wasn't ready yet and removed his finger without giving me the satisfaction of having him stroke my clit.

Wanting, needing, crazed with desire, I fell into his arms without resisting when he picked me up and carried me into a spa with a sunken tub. I held him tight around the neck. He liked that and smiled at me. Then he bathed me with unscented soap, taking a soft white cloth and rubbing me from head to toe. Warm water seeped into my pores when he drizzled the soapy suds down the crack of my butt and the backs of my legs.

"You're beautiful, Pepper," he said, pulling the cloth between my legs and hitting the nerve-rich area around my perineum. I arched my back, a pleasurable moan escaping from my lips. "And so sexy."

"Nobody ever called me sexy," I said, spreading my legs and shuddering with pleasure when he ran the rough texture of the cloth over my vaginal lips and then parted them with his fingers. He rubbed the cloth back and forth across my clit, making it burn. "Mmm…I like that."

"You'll like this more." He moved up my belly, then my rib cage, washing my breasts, swirling the

cotton ringlets of the cloth around them until they
glowed pink. I pushed out my chest. He didn't dis-
appoint me. He pulled on my nipples, making them
pointy and erect, then let them go. "Your nipples are
perfect for—"

"Nibbling on?" I asked, hoping, waiting.

"Soaping up." He reached under my breasts and
cupped them in his strong hands, my nipples pointing
straight ahead. Begging for him to put his mouth on
the hard buds, one then the other, sucking. I couldn't
stop looking at him, watching his hands holding my
breasts, massaging my flesh. I could see behind his
dark eyes how aware he was of my response to him.
And that aroused him.

Teasing, he lathered up his hands and then capped
my erect nipples with translucent soapsuds, pinching
them between his thumbs and forefingers long and
hard until I could stand it no more. Still, he didn't
suck on them. He called it the "Spartan touch." In-
dulging in foreplay but denying me pleasure until
the right moment. Expending his energy on making
me want more but giving me only enough to keep
me in a limbo of anticipation.

The game took on new meaning when he cooled
me down with a tepid shower so my body temperature was ready for—

"Sushi," he said, explaining this was one meal
I'd never forget.

Then he began tying me up.

Stroking me with the long, white rope. Slapping
it on my butt with a pleasant sting and then sliding
it down between my thighs in a slow crawl before
bringing it upward and twisting it around my breasts.

Pulling on my nipples until they peaked. Long, lustful minutes passed as my mind worked overtime, wondering when, *when* he would speak.

Not a word.

I lay stretched out on the white rug, waiting. Watching as he secured my wrists together and then executed intricate knots around my waist, breasts and thighs. The taut pressure made me aware of my body and heightened my senses. Every time I tugged on the rope, it squeezed my breasts, making me moan.

I'd never felt so vulnerable, lying here, my bod bound with soft rope. Yet I also sensed an aura of security, as if Steve was protecting me by tying me up. I didn't understand why I felt this way and that bugged me. But the delicious sensations filling me up pushed any doubt from my mind.

"Not too tight?" he asked, pulling on the linen rope encircling my waist, under my breasts and around my thighs.

"No," I mumbled, dreamlike. I relished the subtle strength of his power when he tugged on the end of the rope, pulling me toward him but not to him.

A show of dominance, reminding me *he* controlled my movements.

I wiggled, or tried to, but nothing moved except my breasts. His skillful rope-tying around my orbs forced my breasts to stand up and not flatten out, my nipples waving at attention, hard and taut. Glancing down, the sight of my body squirming but powerless added to my growing feeling of arousal.

"I can't move," I said, grunting and straining at the ropes.

"Good."

"Does that turn you on?"

A sly smile eased the tension on his face. "That's not the objective."

"Then what is?"

"You'll find out." Steve brushed my cheek with his lips, but nothing more, keeping me wanting. It was most definitely a nipple hardener.

A cool, new sensation wiggled through me when Steve arranged the sushi on my body. No food porn, he said; no oysters that looked like vaginas or raw salmon with the taste and texture of my nether lips.

Instead, on my belly he arranged buttery yellow-fin that would dissolve on his tongue. Crimson tuna crowning my nipples, and purple-hued octopus tendrils swirling around my breasts.

According to Steve, raw freshness was key to good sushi.

Better yet, he said, was a live woman. How experiencing the fish eaten off the bare skin of a female heightened the taste of the food.

Next, it was show-and-tell time.

He pinched my nipples and then smeared spicy wasabi on my skin, his tongue gliding over my belly, licking it off. Next, he plucked tuna off my hard bud with his teeth, biting it as he did so.

I arched my back, gasping with delight, wanting more, flowing with his rhythm. Him eating, sucking, licking, biting. Me moaning and writhing in pleasure. I felt no fear, no danger in being tied up and defenseless, something I'd never experienced with anyone.

Little did I know what was coming next.

When I thought I couldn't stand the deep burning in me another second, Steve unloosened the knots around my thighs and spread my legs.

"Ever heard of *wakame sake?*" he asked.

I shook my head. "I didn't see it on the menu at The Mermaid's Tale."

"You could call it a Japanese body shot. It means drinking sake." He pointed to my pubic area, all naked and pink and wanting, not to mention wet. "From *here*."

My eyes widened. Was he kidding? I hoped not. I was filled with rising feelings of desire, approaching something new and, like I said, kinky. I was finding out this man knew no limits.

He burned like incense. Slow and intoxicating. Knew no fatigue.

Oh, yeah.

"I hope you're thirsty," I said, daring to push up my hips and expose my lower swollen lips for his approval. I swore I could see them glistening with my juices.

He smiled. "*Very* thirsty."

Pouring sake into a small cup and setting it aside, Steve told me it was vital to stimulate me first to create the flow of my juices and mix it with the flavors of the sake.

Stimulate me? How?

I had no idea how aphrodisiac a pair of lips could be.

To demonstrate his prowess in the traditional sake art, he kissed the soft spot between my legs. Lightly at first, lapping up the moisture beading between my lower lips. Then, more demanding, opening me up to his insistent probing and making me twitch uncontrollably against his mouth.

Not letting up, he pushed inside me with his tongue,

flicking and rolling it over my hard clit. Exploring me, tasting me, teasing me without mercy, his tongue thrusting in and out. Deeper and deeper.

I thrashed about wildly, pleading with him not to stop. Reveling in the rising, burning ache weaving a serpentine dance of pleasure in my lower body, making my need for his cock more intense—

He stopped.

Was he mad?

I struggled against the ropes binding me, frustrated. I wanted to grab his dick, sit on it, let it carry me to the brink of orgasm, ride it long and hard, but I couldn't move. Exasperated, I let my head fall back and the room spun around me. Everything seemed to blur. I heard him breathe hard and then let out a low groan.

I forced myself to focus my eyes on him. I watched in unbearable anticipation as he trailed a finger over his lips and inhaled my aroma, and then he leaned down and licked my inner thighs, his tongue traveling over my bare skin.

He was avoiding my sweet spot, damn him.

Why, why?

Knowing I was watching him, he lay on his stomach, opting for a better view while he blew his hot, moist breath on my mound. Coaxing my lazy pubic hairs to flutter like daisy petals bowing to an insistent breeze as he brushed up the curly hair with his fingers.

Next, he put a black silk pillow under my head and shoulders, putting my body at a slight angle, and then he poured light and fragrant sake into my navel until it overflowed. Though the sake was room temperature, I let go with a slight shiver. The sake tickled me as the liquor flowed from my navel downward and through my pubic hair, making it sway to and fro like seaweed.

Lubricating me.

I wiggled my hips, waiting for his tongue to slither inside me and soothe my aching clit.

I didn't have long to wait.

Steve put his head between my legs and lapped up the sake. Filling his mouth with the tepid rice wine mixing with my juices. His tongue left a trail of fire up and down my inner thighs, then along my nether lips, while a myriad of blissful spasms ripped through me. Bending toward him, I couldn't help but expel a long, low moan of sublime pleasure.

He wasn't finished.

I heard the flick of a condom wrapper and then saw him slipping it on his erection.

"I owe you one, remember?" he said, waiting for my reaction.

"How could I forget?"

What more could I say? The lovely fire in me hadn't cooled, only intensified.

I sparked and tingled as my approaching orgasm escalated, though I lay here tied up with delicious knots and rope inhibiting my every movement. A rolling ball of fire coming at me with all the force of a creature out of the darkness, invading yet electrifying. The tension of not being able to move made me reach for it even harder, forcing me to arouse my own strength to grab on to it.

I realized then that was what Steve wanted to teach me. To become a special agent for the FBI required straining against the mental bonds that in the past had sabotaged my efforts. How I found excuses that kept me from going after my dream job because I was afraid of being rejected. How I blamed instead what I believed was the bum rap life threw at me. In reality, my own lack of self-confidence prevented me from achieving my goal.

I arched with desire, my breathing heavy, expectant, my legs spread, my buttocks quivering. This was no fantasy video game we were playing, though I was embarrassed to admit I'd found them arousing in the past. Spreading the thighs of my buxom avatar wide and allowing an equally sexy male avatar to slide into her three-dimensional image.

Not anymore.

I didn't hold back when Steve came in me, sensing this was a magic moment, that pulse of excitement I'd longed for but never experienced. We were breathing as one, wrapped up in raw emotion that exposed my soul as well as my body.

Hot damn.

This was one orgasm I owned.

And *so* much better than any video game.

EPILOGUE

PEPPER HERE.

That is, Special Agent Pepper O'Malley.

Smarter, with new insights into myself, some painful. My libido is satisfied and every inch of me is primed to be the best special agent I can be.

No more running through hotel lobbies, waving an expired credit card in the air and yelling, "*Stop, FBI!*" I graduated from the academy, and I got my own gold badge and creds.

And I got my guy, too.

Steve said he has to marry me to keep me out of trouble.

Me, in trouble?

Only when he's around…

God, I love that man.

* * * * *